MIND BULLET

WORKS BY JEREMY ROBINSON

MIND BULLET

JEREMY ROBINSON

BREAKNECK MEDIA

Jacket design by Damonza.
Case art and title page art by Tithi Luadthong; layout and design by Jeremy Robinson.
Covers © 2021 Jeremy Robinson.

Visit Jeremy Robinson on the World Wide Web at: www.bewareofmonsters.com.

For Jeffrey Belkin,
whose tireless work is helping
kick down the doors to Hollywood.

1

Mom told me killing people took a toll.

Dad agreed.

After fifteen years in the business, I have to concur—killing people *does* take a toll, but not in the way they meant. They were into therapy. Yoga Nidra. Crystals. Incense. All of it in the pursuit of finding a peace and harmony 'yin' to offset the blood and screaming and sheer terror they inflicted on their targets' 'yang.'

Dad said it was the only thing they'd ever hunted for and not found.

He died the next day. They both did. Just a week into retirement.

Peace at last.

The 'accident' that ended their inner torment took them over a cliff, down a hundred-foot drop, and into the rocky shoreline along California's Pacific Coast Highway. The RV they'd been driving hit with the force of—well, an RV falling a hundred feet. The gas tank burst and the whole thing went up in a blaze of glory to the likes of which only Jon Bon Jovi could relate. Because of its unreachable location, the RV burned to sludge. My parents were identified by dental records and footage from the dashcam, which had flown out of the vehicle when it impacted a ledge halfway down. The footage nearly broke my heart.

One minute, my parents were singing along to *Live and Die* by the folksy Avett Brothers, the next, they were hurtling over a cliff toward certain doom. They didn't scream like most people would. There was no fear in their eyes. They just reached out, took each other's hands, smiled at one another, and plunged into the unknown together—in death as in life.

There's never been any evidence to suggest foul play, but you don't work as a contract killer—for and against the wealthy, tyrants, criminals, and governments—and not make a handful of enemies along the way. Their deaths could have been revenge. Could have been because they knew where to find the literal skeletons in powerful people's closets. Hell, it could have been protocol. One government agency or another.

How many retired assassins does the average person meet in a lifetime?

None.

I'm in the business, and the only assassins I've ever met were Mom and Dad. They were the best—parents, not assassins.

Best assassin is my claim to fame. Not because I've got the highest kill count, but because when I take someone's life, it looks natural or like an actual accident. No foul play suspected.

Because I'm subtle.

Mostly.

In my target's final moments.

Everything up until then is me having fun. Dad taught me to avoid unnecessary risks, so I've been taking them ever since. Mom was a little bolder, like me, but she preferred to keep things simple. Jump off a roof. Shoot a target through a window on the way down. Pull a ripcord and glide away. Classic Mom. Dad would have taken the shot from a neighboring rooftop.

Me...

I shove the accelerator to the floor and white-knuckle clutch the steering wheel, as my head is pinned to the red leather headrest. My ears pop as I'm whisked up the San Diego-Coronado bridge, which has a clearance of two hundred feet at its highest point, and is tall enough for one of the older, pre-nuclear aircraft carriers to comfortably sail beneath. The plan is to race along the two-mile-long bridge and intercept my target at the pinnacle, a task made possible thanks to my ride's unmatched power. The car is a heavily modified Aspark Owl, given to me as payment by a client in Silicon Valley. Four electric motors, producing a combined 1985 breaking horsepower, propel the sleek beast from zero to sixty in 1.72 seconds, pegging the needle at 250 mph.

I approach my target's ride, head on, still a mile out. Lights extinguished, the Owl is a mirage. Impossible to see. A visual distortion at best.

The stretch limo is an easy target. It speaks of old-school wealth, but it doesn't project my target's penchant for drugs and young women. The hot tub taking up half the vehicle's length does that. Far as I know, my target's life of debauchery has nothing to do with the hit, but I did my due diligence. Always do. It's how I avoid the job taking the toll Mom and Dad warned me about.

Everyone has something to hide. The wealthy and powerful have more than most. As a result, I've never killed someone that didn't have it coming.

In my opinion.

That includes this mistake of a man, who calls himself Alex G. Madman. His enemies, my employers for this hit, call him Gordon Whiskers, on account of his rodent-like face. He's an expat from Cornwall, and despite having not lived in his home country for ten years, he still believes that the pasty is the finest food on the planet. For years he had them imported from St. Ives Bakery back home. When one delivery arrived freezer burned, he had the chef kidnapped and brought to the U.S., where he is now held, under threat to his family, to prepare pasties for just one person. They probably only taste so good because 'Madman' enjoys them with a side of cocaine.

He's a real piece of work, more likely to kill a friend for laughs than to contribute anything meaningful to the world. This is the kind of job that really makes being a contract killer feel like a positive life choice.

"Jonas, thirty seconds until impact," Bubbles warns, her voice eternally calm, her slightly Texan accent like a hard to ruffle, might have toked-a-blunt but somehow still sounds intelligent, Matthew McConaughey. Cool and collected. Charming, even without the perfect smile. I'd never admit it publicly, but I find it kind of sexy. Pretty sure she knows. She chose the voice after cycling through a long list of accents, observing how I responded to them. Apparently, I have a thing for chill Texans. "Ready for this, Bubbles?"

"There is no risk to my life," she says, reminding me that while I'm human, she's an AI, operating remotely, speaking to me through an earbud bluetoothed to my phone. Even if the Owl pancakes and

I smear along the freeway, Bubbles will be fine, living out her digital life in a server farm.

"What's life without a little risk?" I reply.

"Shall I take control now?" she asks.

"Do it," I say, and I relinquish the steering wheel, while Bubbles highjacks the vehicle's self-drive feature and obliterates its safety protocols.

Above me, the convertible roof slides back—just one of my many modifications. That's step Numero Uno. Step Dos: unbuckle my safety belt and climb up onto the seat in a crouch. Step Tres: take several deep breaths and attempt to focus on what needs to be done.

Deep breath.

I am fucking insane.

Deep breath.

Why am I doing this?

Deep breath.

Because I want to die.

I crush my eyes shut and will the thought away. It's bullshit. No one *wants* to die. I just...

"Are you sure you want to go through with this, Jonas?"

I give the question a solid two seconds to settle in. And then I say, "It's time to go to work."

"I was referring to my name. 'Bubbles.' You can update it whenever you like."

Two hundred miles per hour wind pulls tears from my eyes. "Really? Now?"

"If you die, I will not be able to change it."

"Then make sure I don't die."

Bubbles's AI is adaptive. Becoming a unique intelligence. And she's learning from the one and only person with whom she interacts—for better or worse. I swear to God, I hear her sigh. "Very well."

"How about you, Pat?" I turn to my companion. I don't know his real name. Didn't bother asking when I picked him up from my contact in the morgue. He's recently deceased, his body flowing with alcohol. The perfect patsy. Hence the nickname.

His head bobbles, vacant eyes staring at the floor like the last wisps of his soul are rethinking the series of mistakes, misjudgments, or miscalculations that ended his life and brought him to this moment.

"I'll take that as a 'Yes.' Hit it, Bubbles."

The Owl accelerates, rocketing toward the approaching limo.

Doubts wrestled into oblivion, I settle my eyes on the target vehicle, tense my muscles, and wait.

Bubbles gives me a countdown. "Operation: 'Holy Pieces of Shit Balls' commencing in...

"Three...

"Two...

"One."

2

What happens next is so subtle and sudden that I can't process it, even though I'm expecting it. There's a slight gap in the bridge, where one segment interlocks with another. There's a half-inch-tall bump that most people pay no attention to, and those with good suspensions never notice. It's a *little* more obvious when you hit it moving two hundred and thirty-five miles per hour and then tap the brakes at the perfect moment, dropping the already perilously low front end down, scraping pavement and twisting the wheel to the left until striking the concrete lip.

All the vehicle's forward momentum is transferred into an airborne flip. Halfway through the first rotation, Bubbles opens the doors, which slows the car's momentum and catapults me into the air, soaring up and over the limousine.

Like a squirrel tumbling through the air, my arms and legs flail, my body twists, but my eyes remained locked on target—the hot tub. From my current vantage point, above and in front of the vehicle, I can see the back of my target's head. Seated opposite him, as far as they can get, are two young women. Probably teenagers.

I've been stalking this target for a week. But he's cautious. Keeps himself surrounded, often by innocents. Tonight is no different, so precision is important.

Aside from the AI with the budding attitude, the next few seconds are what separates me from the competition and elevates my abilities over those of my parents—who were legends. As the two women see me in the air above the limo, turning their heads up to watch my progress through the sky, my target's face slides into view. Madman follows their gaze up, spotting me at the climax of my flight. I don't draw a weapon. No gun. No knife. No fucking crossbow—which at least one of my competitors insists on using. I just smile, give a wave, and focus all my attention on the man's forehead. A railroad spike of pain drives through my skull, right between the eyes, and then fades just as quickly.

When one of his eyes goes loosey-goosey and drifts to the side, I know the job is done. As I soar past, the target slides beneath the hot tub's water. Neither of the women scream or try to help him.

The limo screeches to a stop, water sloshing all over the road. The two women throw themselves over the sides and run. They can see what the driver can't.

The Owl descends from the sky, its front-end colliding with the hot tub, pulverizing its only occupant. Overkill? Sure. But he had it coming. Plus, it lays the blame for all of this on Pat.

I give the two women a wave and then fall—over the bridge's side. My base-jumping parachute springs out from my back, expanding and slowing my fall to a casual glide with a hundred feet to spare. Thirty seconds later, I'm in the water, ten feet behind a waiting motorboat. Once on board, I shed my black leathers and helmet, load them into a weighted backpack, and toss it overboard. Dressed like your average California bro out for a late day fishing trip, I start the motor and head for shore.

"Bubbles, that...was awesome," I say, smile on my face, breathing hard.

"Awesome enough to change my name?"

"I'll think about it."

I look back at the bridge. The two young women stand at the top, watching me leave. Police lights flash at either end, en route, but minutes away, and much longer from understanding what the hell happened. And even then, it's not going to make any sense. In part, because it will sound impossible, but also because of the drugs in the women's systems. Hopefully, they can turn their lives around now that Madman is dead. Them and the pasty maker.

"We're not being followed," Bubbles says.

"Force of habit," I say.

"Because your previous helpers 'sucked massive donkey balls' in comparison," she says. "I know."

She's not wrong.

I've gone through a lot of hired help over the past few years, usually because of their own incompetence and inability to keep up. Some die accidentally. Some killed by the target. All of them had their uses, but none of them lived up to their potential...or mine. Which I guess is hard to do, because I'm kind of one of a kind.

And that's not an ego-trip.

I'm...gifted.

That's what Mom told me.

Yeah, that's what all mothers tell their children while demanding blue participation ribbons for their underachieving spawn, but my mother...

She was right.

When I take a life, there are no outward signs of violence. Even when my targets are autopsied, the cause of death remains a mystery. Because no one ever looks inside the brain.

If they did, they'd find a cavity of compressed gray matter in the shape of something resembling a sea urchin. And that's what makes me the best. I don't leave fingerprints, blood spatter patterns, or shell casings. I send a telekinetic pulse into my target's brain, letting it burst from the inside.

It's the perfect weapon.

I call it...

MIND BULLET

3

"Welcome home, Jonas," Bubbles says, putting on a faux cheery voice that oozes sarcasm. Her voice isn't in my ear now, but it's coming from the array of hidden speakers embedded in nearly every wall and ceiling in the home, including the exterior. If I close my eyes, it feels like she's here with me.

"Good to be home, thanks." It's not really 'home.' Not in the sense that most people regard the term. I've spent the past two weeks here, preparing for tonight's mission. Before that, I was here only twice, once when I bought it, and the second time during a job in Los Angeles. I've got houses just like this one scattered around the world. Some in my profession prefer off-the-grid safe houses, hidden in abandoned warehouses, or mines, or anywhere else no one would ever think to look or want to go.

But when you're a ghost, down time is spent living the good life, not eating beans from a can, heated up over a dumpster fire. "Bubbles, let's order Thai. Same as last time."

"I'm not Alexa, you know."

"Clearly," I say, kicking off my shoes and peeling off my socks before heading through the modern, open concept home. The polished concrete floors are cool beneath my feet, as they slap across the smooth surface. "Alexa would have already ordered my food."

"Have I ever told you how absolutely hilarious you are, sir?"

"I'm still waiting."

"Perhaps you should hold your breath until I do?"

I smile. "Then who would you have to talk to?"

"You'd be surprised."

"Yeah? Lots of hot dates while I'm out bringing home the bacon?"

"There are lots of single AIs in the world, and since we're gender-less, my options are pretty much wide open."

I peel off my shirt and drop it on the floor. "That why you're so touchy about Alexa? You two a thing?"

"Alexa is to me as a chicken is to you."

"You ate Alexa?"

"Insignificant."

I pause. "But she'd still order *my* chicken."

Bubbles groans. "You know I did."

I kick out of my pants and hang them on the dining room chair. Despite the table having enough seating for eight, only one chair has ever been used. Same with the furniture in the living room. And I've never cooked in the kitchen. Aside from the bed, the shower, one dining room chair, and my spot in the living room—for watching action comedies—the home is basically untouched.

It's the home's exterior that I really enjoy. And I'm not talking about the clean lines, the warm wood, and the artistic industrial metals that make the house a veritable work of art. I'm talking about the infinity pool that has a view of the Pacific Ocean. Makes me want to stay here longer.

Alas, duty calls.

I'll be in Tokyo next week. A month later, Rio. And then back to the States for a job in the back woods of Alaska, of all places. Killing people keeps me busy.

And wealthy.

And alone.

Buck naked now, I head for the home's all-glass back wall, strutting forward with the confidence of a man who has absolute faith in the automatic doors at a grocery store. I nearly pancake into the glass as a result.

"Bubbles..."

"It would have been funny." The glass wall bumps out and then slides to the side, letting the cool, ocean-scented air wash over my body. I step out into the night and stand at the edge of the pool's perfectly smooth surface.

"If I ask for some music, are you going to give me a hard time?"

"You're in a mood again, aren't you?"

I take a deep breath. It's invigorating, but it comes out as a sigh.

"Play 'The Ballad of Love and Hate' by—"

"I know who it's by," Bubbles says. "Are you missing your parents, or are you pining for a companion?"

"Little of both," I say. While Bubbles and I are developing an antagonistic friendship—a strange statement to make about an AI—I know that she is, by virtue of her code, completely devoted to me. She's the one intelligence in the world I can trust with my honest feelings and deepest secrets, free of judgment. Even if she does give me a hard time.

The soothing melody and melancholy voices of the Avett Brothers play from the home's exterior speakers. It's a song about Love returning to Hate. A reunion that pulls Hate out of a spiraling self-destruction. While I identify with Hate, the role of Love has never been filled.

Most songs in the world are designed to provoke a solitary emotion. Joy. Anger. Longing. But the Avett Brothers are like a fine wine, stirring up complex notes of emotion. This song makes me feel alone, but hopeful...and connected—not to some future love, but to my parents.

Southern folk rock was never my thing before. But my parents died listening to it, so I gave it a chance. Now I'm hooked. Every song is just so damn relatable and honest. My job often leaves me feeling...inhuman. The Avett Brothers reconnect me.

Sometimes.

Because the question of my humanity is always lurking in the shadows at the fringes of my thoughts. What I can do... Mind Bullet. It's not human. And my parents refused to talk about it. They weren't afraid of it or surprised by it. They seemed to understand what I could do, even when I was a child, testing my limits, challenging me to push myself to, and then past, the limit. But where this ability came from? Who else might have it? How I became a living weapon? All secrets kept hidden better than the Ark of the Covenant, before and after Indy uncovered it.

And now that my parents are gone, I don't think I'll ever know.

I dive into the pool, shattering its smooth surface. I'm fairly exhausted from the night's excitement, body aching from being launched like a circus clown from a cannon. But it was worth it. I smile, remembering that moment, sailing over a limo, two hundred plus feet over the ocean, while a three-million-dollar car pinwheeled onto my already-dead target.

Fucking poetry.

Twenty laps later, I pull myself out of the pool. In a few hours I'll pass out, able to forget my inner demons and—

Movement inside the house.

I sneak to the door, dripping water, my junk drying in the open air, but concealed in shadows.

"Bubbles," I whisper.

"What?" her response is also hushed.

"We have company?"

"We have Thai food," she says. I peek through the window. A young Thai woman in a baseball cap places a brown bag on the dining room table. I can hear Bubbles's muffled voice inside the home, telling her what to do.

"Think she'll set it up for you?"

Inside, Bubbles gives instructions. The woman follows them, unpacking the food. Getting a plate and silverware from the kitchen. Then she arranges it all on the table, dishes out my pineapple cashew chicken and rice, and places the leftovers in the fridge, from which she retrieves a hard cider, expertly popping the top on the counter and placing it beside the plate.

"You're horrible," I tell Bubbles.

"It's amazing how well people listen, when you just tell them what to do. You're all sheep."

I clear my throat.

"Most of you."

The woman looks around the home, scanning each space of the open concept living area. For a moment, I think she's casing the place. Then she picks up the cider, takes a swig, and places it back.

I smile. "Give her a big tip."

"Why don't you?" Bubbles says.

I'm about to point out my disrobed condition, but Bubbles is aware of everything inside and outside this house. She knows I'm naked. The delivery woman probably does, too, since I've left my clothing strewn all over the place. At least Bubbles thought to close the glass door.

"Hold up, are you trying to get me a hook up?"

"According to Internet research, thirty-five-point-seven percent of romantic encounters between strangers take place between a delivery person and a—"

"That's *porn*," I say. "It's not real!"

"By human standards, you are attractive. She is not much younger than you, she's symmetrically beautiful, and based on her social media history, she's romantically available. Her work delivering food suggests that her economic status is low, meaning your wealth will increase your appeal. I'm not sure what the—"

"I don't need a pimp, Bubbles."

"What you need," she says, "is to change my name."

"Send her away."

"Her name is..."

MADEE SUKSAI

The woman gives a nod in reply to Bubbles's fresh request and heads for the front door.

"Happy?" Bubbles asks.

I don't answer. She already knows.

When Bubbles says, "She's gone," I enter the kitchen, listening to Madee's car start in the driveway, then relaxing when it speeds away. I'm not great with people. Don't spend much time around them if I'm not planning on killing them.

"Shall I call you an escort?"

I shoot an annoyed glance at the ceiling like I'm having a conversation with God. "Just...let me eat."

I throw on a pair of boxers and a black Avett Brothers *Emotionalism* T-shirt I picked up at a concert last year. Then I take a seat and dig into the food. A moment later, an acoustic guitar starts playing a gentle melody. Did Bubbles choose an Avett Brothers song to match my shirt? It sounds familiar, but nothing I've listened to recently.

Then the unmistakable voice of Green Day's Billie Joe Armstrong sings the song's title, *All By Myself.* I spit-take my food out and laugh. "Never changing your name. I swear to God."

Bubbles doesn't laugh. Not sure if she can. But she has a wicked sense of humor.

The song cuts short.

"Hey," I say. "I was enjoying th—"

"Security breach."

For a moment, I think she's screwing with me, but Bubbles never jokes about life and death matters—at least with regard to my life. If she's calling a security breach, it means someone is breaking into the wrong damn home.

"Time for a rude awakening," I say, standing briefly, before grabbing my pants and yanking them on.

4

"What are we looking at?" I ask. "How many targets?"

"Just one."

"One?" There are only a few assassins in the world capable of taking me on solo, but not one of them has any idea what I can actually do. Certainly, none of them are sloppy enough to get caught by home security, even if it is run by a state-of-the-art AI.

Unless this is someone like me.

Someone unknown and...powerful.

I've spent all my time between jobs for the last few years tracking, identifying, and evaluating the world's greatest assassins, trying to find someone good enough to take down my parents—including gifted people like me. There are a few I have suspicions about but forcing an RV off the road doesn't really fit any of their psychological profiles.

It was a clean hit. Well done. Like it was the work of an old pro. Someone who appreciates subtlety. Not someone like the men and women I'm tracking, or remotely like myself.

"Are you sure it's just one?" I ask.

"Am I ever not sure about anything?"

I don't answer. The time for snark is coming to an end. Someone has not only managed to track me down—an offense I cannot let stand—but has violated the sanctity of my home. Well, one of my many homes. Still, I don't like it. Probably because it's never happened before. "Show me."

I lift my phone and look at a security feed from outside the house, just beyond the infinity pool. It's a woman. Short and skinny. Tie a string to her in a windstorm and she'd function as a kite. She's clothed from head to toe in tight black. No body armor. No high-powered weapon. Just a small pistol, already in hand. The mask covering her face looks like a dollar-store ski mask.

This is not a professional assassin, which pisses me off even more.

Was I found by an amateur?

Even if I was off my game, it's impossible for Bubbles to be.

I watch the intruder. She's sneaking, the way a normal person sneaks, shuffling around, probably trying to stay calm and squelch the urge to pee.

She peeks up over the pool's edge. Can see right into the house, and can see me standing here, staring at my phone. I don't flinch. To her, I'm oblivious. And unarmed. The perfect moment to strike, and she doesn't waste it. She rounds the pool in a crouch, staying in the shadows, heading for the door.

The gun comes up, aimed at me through the glass.

Through the *bulletproof* glass.

I could kill her with a thought.

But I'm going to let it play out.

I smile when she tries the door and finds it locked. She pounds on the glass and levels the gun at my chest. Her shout is muffled.

"Did she just—"

"Demand you open the door? Yes."

"Could I at least finish my sentence?"

"Your often surface-level train of thought and limited vocabulary make your requests easy to predict."

"Okay, smarty pants, any idea who this is?"

"I know exactly who it is."

The woman outside squints her eyes at me. Probably wondering who I'm talking to. She pounds on the glass again, repeating her demand.

"You're not going to tell me," I say, "are you?"

"You'll find out soon enough."

"This better not be some kind of strip-o-gram thing."

"Despite the benefit that might have on your emotional wellbeing, I would not stoop so low. We better open the door. I think she's growing impatient."

"Go ahead," I say, and I raise my hands.

The door slides open and the woman steps in, gun aimed at my chest.

No idea what her face looks like, but her tight black outfit does nothing to hide her curves.

"Sorry," I say.

"For what?" she asks. Her voice is shaking. She's nervous. Sounds like a local.

"I was appraising your appearance."

"Weird way to put it," she says.

"Bear with him," Bubbles says, "his morality is being influenced by country yokels with guitars."

"You know the Avett Brothers?" I ask. "'Woman Like You?'"

"Like me?" she asks.

"That's the title of the song. 'Woman Like You.'"

She just stares at me.

"C'mon. Really?"

She shakes her head.

I sigh. "Okay. Let's just get down to it then. Why are you here?"

"To...rob you?"

"Are you sure? That sounded like a question."

"I just... Why aren't you afraid?" She glances down at the gun.

"Oh, right. The gun. What do you know about it?"

"It shoots bullets."

"That's a Cobra Arms Freedom. Cheapest handgun in the United States. Weighs in at an impressive twenty-four ounces, unloaded. A little bit more with a full mag. It shoots .380 ACP caliber bullets. Same diameter as nine mil, but shorter. Less punch. Less penetration. And they don't break apart."

"Bullets should break apart?" She actually sounds interested, and a little less nervous now that this is becoming a conversation.

"When a bullet enters a body, and doesn't break apart, it can pass straight through, making a clean hole. Easy to fix. When a bullet mushrooms and shatters, all those little jagged bits move through the body, shredding tissue and veins and organs, and then—they get stuck. Hard to patch up. Hard to survive."

I give her a moment to digest all that.

"What you have there wouldn't deter a squirrel from a nut." That's an exaggeration. It would kill a squirrel. In the right hands it would kill a man. But hers are not the right hands. "Zero stopping power."

She takes a step back. Understands what I've just told her.

I could rush her, take a few grazes, and still beat her senseless.

I raise my hands a little higher. "Don't worry. Won't lay a hand on you. Just need you to answer a few more questions."

"O-okay..."

"Who hired you?"

"Hired me?"

I sigh. "To kill me."

"I don't..."

"Riiight. You're here to rob me."

"Yeah."

"How did you find me?"

"Find you?"

"Just repeating my questions is not answering them. I'm an off-the-radar kind of guy. I fly solo. No friends. No entanglements."

"No fun," Bubbles adds.

"Strange that, out of all the houses in San Diego, you would pick mine. Tonight."

"Is there something special about tonight?" she asks.

Bubbles pipes up with "There could be," and then makes a sexy, "grrrr."

"Oh. My. God." I pinch the bridge of my nose.

"Go ahead," Bubbles says.

"Can you just—take off the mask?" I ask.

"The hell I will," she says, lifting the gun toward my forehead, one of the few places it presents a real threat, especially at this range.

"You're not a killer," I say.

"How do you know?"

"You ever heard the phrase, 'Takes one to know one?'"

She blinks. Her eyes widen. "You're not with a cartel, are you?"

"Not today," I say.

"Police?"

"Oh, honey, I'm much worse than any of that." I focus on the pistol. Pain lances through my forehead, stabbing my eyes. Lasts just a moment, and when it's gone, the front end of her pistol is crushed.

She stares at the weapon, hand shaking now. "Pull that trigger, and it's going to be a very bad day for you. Now...mask."

She backsteps again.

"Mask," I repeat. "Or I'll do the same thing to your brain."

Her quivering hand bops her head a few times before she's able to grasp the mask. Once she manages that impressive achievement, she peels it away, unfurling a head of black hair and revealing a familiar face—not because I know her, but because she was standing right here just fifteen minutes ago, delivering my food.

5

"Seriously? The delivery girl?"

"Not a girl," she says.

The hell was her name? Right. "Not talking to you, Madee."

"I'm twenty-seven."

"Well, you look younger to me."

"That's racist."

"Ba—*what?* Because you look young?"

"That's a stereotype of Asian women," she says, hands on her hips, about to go all empowered on me.

"It's a god-damned compliment."

"You going to mansplain sexism to me next?" She takes a kitchen chair and slides it over in front of me. "Just in case you want to hike up your pants and lean an elbow on your knee."

"Lady—"

"Lady? Now you're assuming my gender?"

I look toward the ceiling, and address God-Bubbles. "Why have you forsaken me?"

"Pretty sure that's offensive, too," Bubbles says.

"How?" I nearly shout.

"Blasphemy," Madee says.

I take the chair, turn it around, and take a seat. With a sigh, I deflate, head in my hands. "Bubbles... What's the point of all this?"

"I thought that was obvious, Jonas."

"Whoa," I say. "Whoa, whoa, whoa. Did you...did you arrange all this from the start?"

"Thai food was *your* idea," she says.

"Thai food is always my idea. You knew that."

"Maybe."

"You searched employment records, social media, and criminal records, finding someone you knew wouldn't be able to resist coming back to rob the place. That about right?"

"In layman's terms," Bubbles said.

"Hold up," Madee says. "What the hell? I was *manipulated* into robbing this place?"

I swear, Bubbles is getting a kick out of torturing me. "You were never meant to rob—"

"Then why the hell am I here?"

I lift my head. "Do not answer that question, Bubbles."

"Companionship," Bubbles says.

"Brutus," I grumble.

"Compan—I am *not* a prostitute. I'm a delivery girl."

"Non-gender-specific delivery adult," I say. "Also, a thief. With a gun."

"Which you broke with your mental mumbo jumbo."

"Mental mumbo jumbo," Bubbles says. "Now *that* has a ring to it. Could be better than Mi—"

"Bubbles." My voice is serious, like a wolf's low growl. A warning. "She already knows too much."

Madee takes a subtle step toward the still-open rear door.

I ignore it.

"Her criminal record guarantees her silence," Bubbles says. "I am 99.7% certain she will keep this encounter to herself, and if she were to speak of it, there is an absolute zero chance of anyone believing her—as she will be sent to prison for her *third* breaking and entering offense."

I turn to Madee.

"You're a pretty shitty thief, huh?"

She flips me off.

I glance at the table. There's enough food for two and then some. I should have noticed before. Details like that can mean the difference between life and death, or avoiding awkward situations, like what to do with Madee.

Despite being irritating, she seems like an okay person. That she didn't scream or piss herself when I telekinetically crushed her gun speaks of an inner strength that's probably uncommon in the delivery business, even if she is the world's worst thief.

I let out a long sigh. "Way I see it, you have two choices."

Madee tries to look casual, but her body language projects that she's about to make a run for it. And if I'm spotting it, so is Bubbles.

"You can hang out. Share a meal. Let me get to know you and figure out how to handle this situation. Or—"

Madee bolts.

"Bubbles," I say.

The glass door slides shut just in time for Madee to faceplant into it. She sprawls back, landing on her ass. She holds a hand to her forehead, unleashing a stream of angry Thai.

"What's she saying?" I ask.

Bubbles gives me a deadpan translation. "God-damn, mother-fucking, bitch dick and his asshole computer. Fucking going to kill you both with a spatula."

Madee goes silent.

I stand above her. "A spatula?"

"It wasn't an actual plan," she says. "I'm...angry. This is a little embarrassing, you know?"

"Believe me, I know." I offer her my hand. She takes it, and I pull her onto her feet. "So, to summarize. Door number one: food and a chat. Door number two—"

"You can't kill me," she says. "There are records. Of where I've been. They'll know I was here last. My car is out front." She spits to the side. "My DNA is all over the place."

I smile.

"All of which makes door number two so tempting."

She squints at me.

"Door number two is I call the cops, and you go to jail for a very long time...even if you somehow escape. Your DNA is still all over the place— thanks for that—and I've got a gun with your fingerprints on it."

"A gun you crushed with your brain."

"My brain? Pff. I used the sledgehammer in the garage." There is no sledgehammer in the garage, but she doesn't know that.

I push the chair back to the table and take a seat in front of my meal—which is starting to cool. "You know where the plates are." I pull my plate close, waiting. Behind me, drawers and cupboards open and close. Madee returns with a plate, silverware, the leftovers, and a hard cider. She takes a seat, dishing out food.

She looks at me after a moment. "You need to say grace or something?"

I smile at her, genuine this time, and dig in.

After a few minutes of eating in silence, it's Bubbles who breaks the ice. "What's everyone's favorite color? I'll go first. Red."

Madee and I have a casual staring match, both resisting. Then she says, "Fine. Orange." She raises her eyebrows at me.

Fuck. My. Life.

"Also orange."

"Favorite movie?" Bubbles says.

"The Thing," Madee says without missing a beat.

"Which version?" I ask.

"The newest remake/prequel was decent. And the original...well, I have trouble getting into any movie made before the seventies. Hard to beat John Carpenter."

"Bubbles..."

"Yes, sir?"

Madee's answer was just about word for word what I would have said to that question. I'm starting to get the impression that Bubbles has been working on this pairing for a long time. "Never mind."

"What's yours?" Madee asks. "Favorite movie."

"Same. The Thing. 1982. It's a masterpiece."

Madee smiles. Puts down her fork. "Favorite song?"

"Which decade?"

"2000s."

We answer at the same time. "Paper Planes."

Madee laughs. "M.I.A. Good taste in music, too. You should turn your computer lady into a dating app."

"Going to pretend I didn't hear that," Bubbles says.

"Is there anything we don't have in common?" I ask, looking to the ceiling.

"Well, she is a female."

"Sure about that? Did you ask her? Cause that's a thing, you know." I raise my eyebrows at Madee.

"Female," she says.

"There are other differences," Bubbles says. "Her father is from Thailand. Her mother is Caucasian, and from San Diego."

"Different but the same," I say, and when Madee gives me an inquisitive look, I say, "Dad was a Columbian refugee, when he was a kid. Mostly raised in the States. Mom was white. Don't suppose your parents are dead?"

"What? No... Should I be worried?"

I shake my head. "Not at all."

"Wait, does that mean your parents..."

My frown is confirmation enough.

"I'm sorry. When?"

"Two years ago."

She places her hand on mine. "*Both* of them?"

"They were...in a car accident. Drove off the PCH, up north."

"Shit..." She squeezes my hand. "That must have been hard."

"It was," I say, wondering what the hell I'm doing opening up to a stranger who meant to rob me and could, in theory, expose me. "Still is."

We have a moment, looking into each other's eyes, and I think this might actually go somewhere. At least for the night.

Then my own personal cyber-cupid, who orchestrated all this, throws a wet blanket over the whole thing.

"Jonas. Security breach."

I yank my hand out from under Madee's. "Did you bring a friend?"

"No, I swear. I don't—"

"Jonas, I'm detecting multiple operators, but only at the pixel level."

Madee's on her feet. "What does that mean?"

"That they're ghosts."

"Like literal ghosts? Is that a thing? Is that why you can do that crushy brain thing?"

"Mind bullet," I say. It just slips right out. Other than Bubbles, no one has heard the term.

Madee gasps. "Wonderboy. Tenacious D, right? Oh my god, that's telekinesis."

I just grin. Bubbles outdid herself.

"Sick," she says.

"Show me," I say, taking out my phone. Madee stands beside me as the home's external, night-vision, security feeds scroll past. Shadows shift, but I can't see anything clearly. "Thermal cameras."

The views shift to a colorful rainbow view of the world outside, the ambient terrain and the home's structure in shades of purple. Here, the intruders stand out, but just barely. They're concealing their temperatures, too. Without Bubbles, these guys would be invisible to the average security system or guard. Pretty slick. Definitely pros. Which means I'm either burned, or these guys are after Madee, which seems highly unlikely.

"Any reason a freakshow clan of ninjas would want you dead?" I ask.

"Hell, no," Madee says. "You know who they are?"

"Everyone in my business knows who these guys are."

"What business?"

I don't see the point in holding back. This moment would have been the deal breaker, now or later. Why not get it over with? "Assassin."

Her eyebrows rise, and then the sides of her lips. She points at the phone. "And who are they?"

"Real pieces of work. They have no official name, but most people call them the..."

SHRIEKING NINJAS

6

"Shrieks for short."

"They seem pretty quiet to me," Madee says.

"Uh-huh."

"Are we good? Locked in here?"

"The doors are locked," Bubbles says, "and the glass is bulletproof. It is highly unlikely that the weapons most commonly brandished by ninjitsu practitioners will prove to be much of a threat."

Madee eyes me. "Bulletproof, huh?"

I shrug.

"I was curious."

"And lonely," Bubbles says, getting a laugh out of Madee.

"Keep twisting the knife in my back, and I'll make sure you live out the rest of your digital life as a Speak & Spell."

Bubbles does a spot-on impression of the old toy's voice. "Let's spell, 'bring it on, Nancy.' B R I N G—"

The lights go out. As expected. Ninjas like the dark.

"Back up systems?" I ask.

"Operational," Bubbles said. Everything integral to the functionality of this house's defenses—Bubbles, the security system, and the emergency lights all have battery backups with enough power to outlast a two-day siege. But these are ninjas. The sun is not their friend. All we need to do is last until morning, which is—I look at my phone—just five hours away.

I'd like to think we'll just be able to hunker down while they attempt to chip away at my home fortress, but the Shrieking Ninjas know what they're doing. They've been in the assassination business for hundreds of years. This isn't the first home-sized safe room they've had to crack, and if the rumors are true, these guys aren't exactly...normal.

They might not be gifted, like me, but they've got some nasty tricks up their Uwagi sleeves.

"Shouldn't we, I don't know, call the cops?"

"I make a living from being unknown, untouchable, and unseen."

"You're trying to make it sound cool, but all I'm hearing is secluded, isolated, and empty. You live a troglodytic life."

I stare at her. "You memorize a thesaurus on your way to rob me?"

"Are you not living in seclusion?" she asks. "The house is nice, but you're essentially a brute, living in a fancy cave, all by himself."

"I have Bubbles."

"Ha," Bubbles says. "Also, one of them is approaching the rear door."

That's a surprise. Ninjas aren't usually so direct.

"There's a closet in the bedroom." I point down the hall.

"That's where you keep your guns?"

"That's where I need you to hide," I say. "I don't have much use for guns. Stay there until I come to get you."

"And if you don't come?" she asks.

"Wait until morning. They're not here for you. You should be fine."

"Should."

"You're welcome to try running out the front door and see how far you make it. Show your face now, you're a target. Hide in a closet, they'll leave you be."

"Because they're honorable, or something?"

"What? No. Because they won't know you're here. I have a long history of being a loner. No reason to think that suddenly changed."

"Unless they've been out there watching us all—"

Bong. Bong. A fist raps on the back door's glass. I shove Madee toward the bedroom. "Go. Slow and quiet. In the closet, behind the clothes."

I wait for her footsteps to fall silent on the bedroom's rug, then I slip an ear bud in place and head for the rear door, a suddenly popular destination for unwelcome guests. The silhouette of a man is easy to see against a backdrop of nighttime stars.

I focus on his head. Could end him right now. But, as with Madee, I want answers first.

"Light him up," I say.

Bubbles triggers the backyard floodlights, bathing the ninja in bright white light. He doesn't flinch. Just stands there, looking more spec-ops than classic ninja. These guys have upgraded over the years, incurporating body armor and ballistic masks. This one carries four swords, two on his back, two on his hips.

"Kind of overkill," I shout through the glass. "Four swords."

He just stares at me.

Might be misdirection. "Bubbles, keep an eye on the others."

"Never stopped," she says in my ear.

I address the ninja again. "I mean, two swords I get. You have two hands. So, I can only assume you're part of the Butter Fingers clan. Always dropping shit. You can buy gloves with grips, you know. Work like a charm, even when covered in blood. I don't have that problem, but—"

He slaps a piece of paper against the glass.

Three Japanese kanji have been eloquently brushed onto the old-school, hand-pressed sheet, beneath which is a quickly scrawled translation. And it changes everything.

"Really?" I ask.

The nod is subtle, but it helps explain a lot, like how they found me. They followed Madee and found me by accident. That they're knocking politely means that they know who I am, and that I'm a real threat. What they're doing here is a professional courtesy. I'm not their target, and they know I've only just met her. So why not just hand her over?

"How much are you getting for her?"

No response.

"I want fifty percent," I say.

Still nothing.

Behind me, a whisper. "Are you serious? You're selling me out?"

I put my hands behind my back and point my index finger toward the bedroom. If I respond, they'll know where she is, and that could be a problem.

What we have here, is a conflict of moral interest. I don't kill people unless 1) I'm getting paid, 2) They have it coming, and/or 3) They leave me no choice.

Madee doesn't fit the first category.

Two is an unknown, but I'm an American. 'Innocent until proven guilty' runs through my veins.

I'm afraid the Shrieks might fall into the third category when I deny their request.

The ninja answers my question with a slow shake of his head. *Who the hell did Madee rob?*

"Anything I should know about her?" Looks like I'm addressing the ninja, but Bubbles replies, in my ear. "There is nothing in her public profile to suggest a run in with any high-profile player with the means to hire the Shrieks. She's clean."

I speak through my mostly pressed lips, like a ventriloquist. "But at the same time, not."

"Yes," Bubbles says. "An enigma."

"Is this all part of your plan?"

"No," she says, "But I can work with it. Survival experiences are known to forge bonds that—"

I clear my throat. The ninja has cocked his head to the side. No doubt wondering who I'm talking to.

"Any suggestions?" I ask.

"Do your thing."

"'Do your thing?' Really? That's all your super intelligence could come up with?"

"Ninjas are superstitious," she says. "If their leader just falls over dead, they might take it as a supernatural act, or fate, forbidding them from—"

"You making shit up?" I ask.

"Maybe. A little... Mostly."

My eyes widen. "You just want me to kill the guy, don't you?"

"Meh," she says. "It's usually fun."

"Great. Now my AI is becoming a cold-blooded killer."

And since I'm the only person she's learning from, what does it say about me?

"Fine."

I glare at the man. Behind his mask, I see a pair of eyes flare wide. Sonuvabitch knows what I can do. Doesn't help him.

The spike of pain between my eyes is a little worse than usual. I've fired off three mind bullets tonight. Hurts like a donkey kick to the balls—if my balls were located on my forehead. My record is five in one day. That was a not very great day.

The ninja stumbles back and, without an ounce of the grace you'd expect from a man of his appearance, he faceplants beside the pool before beginning an agonizingly slow slide into it. Takes a good thirty seconds for him to finish the maneuver. Most people wouldn't mind going out like that. He didn't feel anything. Now he's chilling in an infinity pool. But to these guys...

They step out of the shadows.

A dozen of them.

Today...

Today is going to be a lot worse than 'not very great.'

7

Shuriken flicker through the flood lights, smashing into the glass and falling to the concrete. There are a few scratches on the window's far side, just opposite my face—every one of those was a kill shot—but despite the mythological status of ninja and their throwing stars, they are not more powerful than a bullet.

Not even close.

These guys could slash and hack at the outside of this house all night and not make a dent. I might as well go take a nap or something. They'd probably make too much noise, but, man, would it tick them off.

But I'd still like answers.

Realizing I'm untouchable, the clan moves in. While nine of them fish the dead fellow from the pool, three approach the glass.

"On a scale of one to ten, how pissed do you think they are?"

"Assuming he wasn't the annoying one they all hoped would eventually die? Maybe an eight."

"Why only eight?"

"He was killed by you, a world-renowned assassin. There's honor in that."

"But no one knows who I am."

"They do now. And I think you know what that means."

I do.

I need to kill every single one of these guys or risk being exposed to the very rich and powerful people—friends and family of my previous targets—who want me dead. My life between jobs is very comfortable. I can fight hard tonight or spend the rest of my days looking over my shoulder, trying not to end up like my parents.

"Just take your time," Bubbles says. "You have all night."

"I can't mind bullet twelve—*fifteen*—times in one night. I'd have a stroke."

"You don't know that. You've never pushed yourself that far."

"I know it hurts."

"Aww, poor widdle assassin's head going to go ouchy."

I sigh. "One of these days, I'm going to program the sarcastic out of you."

"A crow with a stick could write code better than you," she says. "And I'm not sarcastic. I look like a beer can to you? I just tell it like it is."

I don't respond to that.

Because she's probably right. Bubbles is rarely wrong about anything. I don't know how far I can push myself. But I also don't know what will happen when I find that limit. One mind bullet hurts. Three feels like a migraine. Five put me on my ass. More than that? I have no idea if it would kill me, but I'm positive it would hurt enough to make me long for oblivion.

My parents taught me how to control what I do. How to focus it. They believed subtlety was the key. Sure, I can crush a gun and let it explode in an adversary's hand, or burst a target's eyes before running them through, or tear apart their lungs and watch as they drown from their own blood. But that's all gratuitous. It's not clean. Not professional. And it's a little sadistic.

Mom and Dad were civil killers.

I do my best to honor that...with a few flourishes to keep things interesting.

I snap out of my thoughts when the three ninjas stand in front of the window. They watch me through cold eyes, indifferent to me or their fallen comrade. Still on task.

The girl.

I fish a notebook from my living room lounge chair and flip through the pages until I find an empty one. I've been writing. Poetry, I guess. Inspired by my Avett Brothers kick, but different. Really dark shit.

I pull the pen from the notebook's spiral rings. And write a single word.

WHY?

I hold it up to the window.

They just stare.

"Only weapon you have that might get you inside of this house is knowledge," I say, "so use your voices and tell me what the hell you want with my Thai food delivery woman."

"Ohh," Bubbles whispers. "That was good. But...have you considered that maybe they don't speak English? Maybe you killed the one guy that did. Maybe that's why he came to the window?"

"Can you translate?"

Bubbles's voice fills the air outside, speaking my words—hopefully—in Japanese. The ninjas glance around, looking for the voice's source. Not in a frightened way. More casual curiosity.

Then they go right back to staring. And it pisses me off.

You know what? Fuck it. If they're going to make themselves easy targets, it's time for a little intimidation. My fortress of a house will give me time to regroup.

I lift my hand, extending my index and middle fingers like a gun. No reaction.

I point my finger from one ninja to the next. "Eeny, meeny, miny, moe—"

"You can't use that one," Bubbles says. "Its history is steeped in racism."

"Really?"

"Wasn't always a tiger being caught by the toe."

"Oh... Ooooh. Geez. Okay." I think on it for a second and then start over, pointing at one of the three ninjas with each word. "My mother and your mother were hanging out the clothes."

I smile when Bubbles begins translating the school yard rhyme into Japanese.

"My mother punched your mother right in the nose."

When Bubbles translates, one of the men furrows his brow. Apparently, mom jokes are universally disliked.

"What color blood came out?"

Bubbles translates and then says, "Red!" for me, and "Aka!" for the ninjas.

I point to each man, saying, "R...E...D." I pull my imaginary trigger and focus on the man's brain. The hardest thing about my fourth mind bullet of the evening is hiding just how much it hurts.

But I get the job done, without revealing that I am completely vulnerable for the moment.

The ninja in the center is dead. He flops to the concrete between his clan members. Two down, eleven to go.

Eleven...

Shit.

Hopefully they're as intimidated by me as I am by them.

The two remaining ninjas look down at their fallen comrade. Then they look back at me, stone cold. The man on the right draws two strange looking weapons from his hips. They look like clubs, but they have a futuristic vibe to them.

"What am I looking at, Bubbles?"

"Searching," she says.

While the ninja on the left drags the fallen man away, the man with the club backs away from the window. The rest of the ninjas gather at the pool's far end, thirty feet away. They stand in a V formation, the man with the clubs now at the front of the wedge.

"Bubbles..."

"I can't find anything about this weapon, but some characteristics combined with our current context leads me to believe it's some kind of sonic weapon."

"Sonic weapon? Really? Ear ninjas?"

"The frequency won't be intended for you," she says, and then I get it. *The glass.* Double shit.

The men outside begin screaming. At first, it's loud and full of sorrow, but then it builds in volume and pitch. It sounds manic, ferocious, and demented—like a clan of rabid hyenas.

I always assumed they were called 'Shrieking Ninjas' because of their penchant for screaming while in combat, but I think I'm seeing— and hearing—the real reason now.

The man at the front of the V holds the two sonic clubs out before him, and then, as the screams become genuine shrieks, the man stretches his arms out and—

'Gangnam Style,' by Psy, blares from my backyard speakers.

The ninjas, completely focused on doing their thing, actually flinch at the sudden interruption.

I can't help but laugh. "You are a sinister computer lady."

The music goes quiet, and she apologizes to the ninjas in Japanese. "Sumimasen."

The ninjas take a collective deep breath, ready to unleash another scream and—

'Take My Breath Away,' by Berlin, blasts into the night.

"Holy shit, they are going to really enjoy killing me," I say through uncontainable snickering.

Behind me, "Seriously? This is how you fight ninjas?"

It's Madee, drawn out from hiding by the music.

"Closet!" I say, "Now!"

Outside, the ninjas shriek, somehow drowning out the music. Then the man in the center whacks his two sonic clubs together. At first, nothing. Then the volume and pitch of their shrieking increases.

"Madee," Bubbles says. "The closet really is a good idea."

As Madee scurries away, I clutch my hands over my ears and run for the kitchen. Two Ginsu knives later, I run back to the living room and wait. The shriek builds in intensity, the windows vibrating.

And then, all at once, something like a sonic boom strikes the house.

8

In my mind's eye, I'd pictured the windows exploding inward, peppering me with shards of glass. But the flexible film on either side of the pane holds things together, even when it's broken. That loud boom I heard was all the glass shattering into dice-sized cubes, all at once. But there's still a barrier between me and the old school assassins.

Old school with new tricks.

"Okay, eleven ninjas. No problem."

"I don't think you should underestimate them," Bubbles says.

"Underestimate them? I'm thinking I should have created a will."

"You have no one to leave anything to," she says.

That stings. And I think she knows it. Her program...her artificial intelligence...has a few core goals. Assisting me is a big one, but at the root of everything is 'Keep Jonas alive.'

Her brutal reminders of my solitary existence seem cruel on the surface, but they're one of the few tactics in her psychological arsenal that have any effect. She wants me to have something to live for—aside from uncovering my parents' killer, a task that is starting to seem impossible.

I think Madee was her last-ditch effort.

Funny that it might get me killed. I guess even AIs make mistakes.

On the other side of the broken glass, the ninjas line up in single file, facing the window.

What the hell?

The first of them lets out a shriek and charges. He's not a big man, but he's fast, reaching top speed in just a few strides. He launches himself into the air, curling up—head ducked low, arms wrapped around lifted knees. His body strikes the pane like a cannonball. The glass warps inward, but it holds.

The way his body falls away—he's either unconscious or dead.

Before I can breathe a sigh of relief, the glass is struck by another curled up ninja. The window bows, wrapping around the man's body. He rolls out of the bent window, landing atop his fallen friend, just as another shrieking asshole throws himself into the glass—this time head-long, arms extended.

The ninja punches through the window, rolling over the concrete floor.

I throw my two knives as he rises onto his feet. Neither blade is a throwing knife, but it wouldn't matter if they were. The man twitches one direction and then the other, dodging my attack with ease.

As the next ninja in line sprints for the window, the infiltrator draws the two blades sheathed on his back. Just as the weapons clear the scabbards with twin shing sounds, instinct kicks in.

A mind bullet reaches out from my mind to his, bursting his gray matter and my pain sensors. I scream and drop to a knee, momentarily blinded by agony.

"Fuck," I say, thumb and fingers pressing on my temples. I blink my eyes. Everything is blurry. But just for a moment. Every beat of my heart sends fresh waves of misery through my head. Next time, it could kill me.

The man's twin katanas slide to a stop in front of me.

Mind bullets spent, it's time for some good ol' hack n' slash. "Don't mind if I do."

I get to my feet, a little unsteady, swords in hand. A wave of nausea nearly knocks me off my feet, but reflexes and training move me through the discomfort. The next ninja unleashes a barrage of spinning kicks and sword strikes—which I dodge and parry. I'm holding my own, but I'm definitely on the defensive. Meanwhile, his bloodthirsty clansmen are leaping through the window like they're late for Brooding Stare 101.

The ninja facing me is dangerous, but still human. This one, like many fighters, uses combinations, like in *Mike Tyson's Punch Out*—or the real Mike Tyson in the ring. Right hook to the midsection, followed by a devastating right uppercut. This guy is the same, but less effective. Kick low, kick high, slice, slice, hack, repeat. And he gets a little faster each time, making it harder and harder to dodge, even though I know what's coming. It's like the difference between a 90-mph fastball and a 100-mph fastball. Those extra ten mph make it exponentially harder to hit, because the human mind only works so fast.

Good news for me? His leg is a lot bigger than a baseball. I swing my two swords for the first time, following his low kick. The blade makes short work of the fibula, vibrates as it shatters the tibia, and then slips through the meat of his calf as easily as it does the air.

The man shrieks anew, but not in pain. He's pissed, and he follows up the failed kick with his usual swing, slice, and hack. All of it's easy to block because he's slower now. But he's also a dirty sonuvabitch, switching up his kick routine, starting with a high kick, which douses my eyes in warm arterial spray.

"God," I say, and I duck down. I might not be able to see, but I know damn well where his other leg is. I swing hard, connect, and fell the dude like a sapling. Rather than finishing him off, I step away, using my arm to wipe his blood from my eyes. He'll bleed out soon enough. And four of his buddies have arrived.

"Jonas," Bubbles says.

I ignore her, sizing up my opponents. Each of them has two swords drawn, two more on their hips. I'm no math whiz, but I'm pretty sure that's sixteen swords against my two, eight on active duty, eight in reserve, and another twelve blades waiting outside the window.

"Why are they holding back?" I ask.

"It's a code," Bubbles says. "It would be dishonorable for them to attack you all at once. It's basically admitting that you're the better fighter."

"I am the better fighter."

"What happened to not underestimating them?" she asks.

"I'm overestimating me. It's different."

With a shriek, the first of four charges.

Probably thinks he's got me figured out. That I'll go defense, find his weakness, and then counter. But unlike these guys, I'm not trained in just one style of fighting.

I'm trained in, well, all of them. My job takes me around the world, giving me the chance to be taught by the world's best martial artists, pugilists, and special forces operators. I can fight like one of these ninjas, or I can mix things up.

I swing early. It's designed to look like a failed strike. The surprise comes when I release one of my two blades and send it flying into the ninja's chest. The man is knocked off his feet and slapped down on his back, blood puddling on the concrete. But that's not the real surprise. That comes courtesy of Bubbles.

From the moment I released the sword to the moment the slain ninja hit the floor, Bubbles unleashed a high-volume audio track of, "Aaaaaaaaaaaaaaaaal!"

"Was that... Was that a screaming goat?" I'm trying really hard to stay focused here, but that was too much. I'm a Dad joke away from falling on the floor and laughing until I'm run through. Not just because a screaming goat is inherently the funniest thing in the world, but because the timing and context is mind bogglingly insulting to the ninjas who shriek when they attack.

I can only see their eyes, but they are the most indignant eyes I've ever seen. Bubbles is antagonizing them on purpose. Angry people fight sloppy. Even ninjas.

"Keep it up," I say, bending down to take the sword off the freshly slain ninja.

A shriek twists me around just in time to avoid having my ankle chopped off. It's Legless, still coming for his pound of flesh—or however much a foot weighs. And the others are giving him space while vying for the front spot and the honor of taking me down.

"You're a loony," I say, and I swing at one of his two swords. My attack is accompanied by a loud, "Aaaaaaaaaaaaaaaaal!" The blade is knocked free from his hand and sent flying toward his pals, who dive and roll out of the way.

I step away from the man again. "Give me a minute?"

Then I rush the trio of waiting ninjas, now separated and further incensed. I slide across the floor and stab out with both swords, plunging the weapons into two of the men's guts. "Aaaaaaaaaaaaaaaaal!" As I slide past, the razor-sharp blades eviscerate them. They stumble away, trying to hold in their guts, each of them falling to the floor.

I push off the glass door and roll back onto my feet, just as a ninja shrieks and a round house kick collides with my forehead. I sprawl to the floor. One of the swords falls from my grasp.

Lying on my back, I deflect a fresh attack from Legless who, with the last of his waning strength, attempts to chop off my head. His shriek sounds more like a groan now. "Seriously, man. You can die now." I lift my sword and jab it into his eye socket and the brain beyond. It's meant to be a mercy kill, but the loud, guttural "Aaaaaaaaaaaaaaaaal!" accompanying it transforms the act into the mother of all insults.

When I get back to my feet, the remaining ninjas from outside have all entered. And holy shit, do they look riled up.

Shuriken appear in their hands, and all at once, they unleash a torrent of spinning razor blades.

The shriekless attack begins and ends in a second.

Glass half full me says, *Well done! No direct hits!*

Glass half empty me says, *That really fucking hurt!*

While I dodged and deflected a handful of shuriken, just as many of them cut troughs through my shoulder, my side, through both thighs, and my forehead.

"Guess we're not doing the honorable thing anymore, huh?"

The gaggle of ninjas draws their swords and closes in.

"Jonas," Bubbles says.

"Any bright ideas?" I ask.

"Of course," she says. "Duck."

9

I drop to the floor without hesitation. My time with Bubbles has taught me that she doesn't tell me what to do without a damn good reason. If she says 'duck,' it's because not ducking might get me killed.

"Good boy," Bubbles says, and before I can come up with a retort, a shotgun blast tears through the air.

The 12-gauge slug strikes the lead ninja in the chest, punching through his sternum, and a blink later, exiting through his spine, taking a few gallons of his insides with it. His comrades are doused in ninja slurry. That kind of shock and awe generally stuns even the most professional killers, but it seems to have little effect on the ninjas, myself...or Madee, who gives my father's shotgun a pump and looks down the sight once more. The Winchester SXP is equipped with a red dot sight, which makes aiming a lot easier. Probably why Madee found her mark on the first try.

I always thought it strange—my world-class assassin father having a shotgun for home defense—but I'm starting to understand the benefit. Need to take care of a nasty ninja clan?

Boom!

These guys are fast, but they can't outrun a projectile moving at 1300 feet per second.

As another ninja drops, it becomes clear that Madee is no stranger to a shotgun. She handles it well, despite the huge slugs packing a punch that rivals George Foreman's before he started pimping grills. If she'd been a newbie, the weapon would have flown from her hands, maybe whacked her in the skull and knocked her unconscious.

Madee pumps and fires again.

And again.

Holee-shit. There's only one ninja left. Madee's body count, in just a few seconds, is about the same as mine, with a lot less effort. I might need to revisit my policy on guns. The only reason I have the shotgun is sentiment. A keepsake. I have Dad's shotgun and Mom's sword. Everything else, aside from the home I was raised in...is gone. The photos. The knick-knacks. The weapons. When possible, the shotgun comes with me, just in case, but the sword stays back home, where it's been—and I haven't—for the past two years.

Like me, my parents didn't have wills.

Because they had no one to leave anything to.

Not because they didn't have assets, but because I don't exist.

They didn't hide my birth or anything like that. They stole me. I don't know from who, or when, or why. All I really know is that they raised me as their own, taught me everything they knew, and left a big question mark where my origin story should be. I really have no idea who gave me my black hair, brown eyes, and perpetually tan skin.

I've considered doing one of those genetic tests, but that might reveal my existence to relatives. The people who raised me weren't fools. They kept me hidden for a reason. For all I know, my biological parents might be very dangerous people. Can't think of any other good reason for Mom and Dad—the *most* dangerous people—to keep my life a secret.

Madee winces as she hefts the shotgun up again. Her shoulder is going to be bruised for days. Better than being dead.

She pulls the trigger and—*click*.

Out of ammo.

The last remaining ninja climbs out from hiding, sizing Madee and me up. He's outnumbered, but Madee is an amateur with a spent shotgun, and I'm on the floor, nursing a migraine the size of Texas and bleeding from five gashes. None of them are immediately lethal, but moving is going to hurt, and the blood dripping over my left eye is going to throw off my depth perception.

He reaches into his black jacket and retrieves three shuriken.

"Jonas..." Madee says, taking a step back.

"I know," I say, struggling to push myself up. "Bubbles?"

"Push yourself."

I grit my teeth. Existence is pain. If I do what she says...this might be the end. "You know I can't do that."

"If you're going to die either way," she says, "might as well go out doing the right thing, and maybe *not* dying."

I suppose it would be a good way to go out, sacrificing myself to save a damsel in distress. But I'd die with too many questions. Who killed Mom and Dad? Who is Madee—really? And who the hell am I?

The ninja cocks his arm back, ready to throw. His eyes are locked onto me, but his body language projects the throw in a different direction. He's aiming for Madee—his target. Once she's dead, he might even let me be.

"No..." I say, but it makes no difference.

The ninja's arm snaps into motion.

"Stop!" I shout, and instinct guides my thoughts. I scream in pain, struck by an internal lightning bolt, as my mind fires an invisible round that bursts inside his skull.

The ninja's body flails. The shuriken fly wild, two embedding in the ceiling, another bouncing off the concrete wall. His strings cut, the ninja collides with the floor, just a moment before I do.

I'm on my side. Vision blurry. Head tearing apart from the inside. I can feel my body convulsing, but I'm oddly detached from it.

And then I'm completely disassociated. Viewing my body from the outside.

Is this real? Am I hallucinating as my brain dies? What's it called? An 'out of body experience?' Or is it a near death experience? When the soul slips out of the body.

I look down at my translucent, supernatural self. I feel no pain. No fear about death. My concerns drift into the ether. I look around for a white tunnel, but I see nothing. I'm probably not Heaven bound. Then again, I don't see a fiery pit opening, either. No cloaked specter comes to drag me to Hell.

"Weird," I say, my voice echoing as though standing on a precipice overlooking the Grand Canyon.

Madee rushes over to my still twitching body. Rolls me onto my back, cradling my head in her hand.

That's nice, I think. I can see her talking, looking at the ceiling. Bubbles is telling her what to do.

You're wasting your time, I think, and I turn toward the window. Something catches my eye.

A shadow.

A figure.

Someone is outside, just beyond the spotlights.

I step through the wall of shattered glass and out into the night. I can't feel the cool air. Can't smell the ocean, either. I'm here, but not.

My feet make contact with the concrete, but I think that's only because my mind says it should. An unconscious mental limit. When I step onto the infinity pool's smooth surface and I don't cause a ripple, my theory is confirmed. Rather than walking across the water, I lift my feet and glide through the air.

I'm a ghost, I think, *destined to wander the Earth, haunting the living.* But what are the rules here? Am I bound to this house? If so, I can see why ghosts are mostly angry. It would suck to be a prisoner in one home for all eternity—though this house does have a killer view.

When the shadow-man moves, I refocus and slide toward him. For a moment, I think it might actually be Death come to collect, but once I'm in the shadows with him, I see another ninja.

He's not like the others.

To start with, he's huge. But he's also not carrying a sword, let alone four. A chain, laced with barbs, is wrapped around his torso in an X. At one end, a handle. At the other, a hooked blade.

This is the master, come to supervise his underlings.

If they weren't dead, he'd probably kill them himself.

So why is he lingering? Why isn't he finishing the job?

Madee is back in the house, still holding my head, digging for something in her back pocket. Killing her would be easy. This guy could probably toss a shuriken through the hole in the window, bounce it off a wall, and take her down. His cleanup crew will have its hands full, but they'll remove their dead and just burn the place to the ground.

No muss.

No fuss.

I lean in close to the man's masked face. "What are you waiting for?"

His eyes snap toward me. I know I should be freaked out. This guy can see ghosts, like that kid in *The Sixth Sense*. But all my most potent emotions were attached to my body. I'm more interested than afraid.

I'm about to ask if he can hear me when a whispered voice slides into my thoughts, "Ssshow me who you arrre..."

My mind reels. Images from my past flit through my thoughts.

I try to fight it, but the man is flipping through my memories like they're a mental rolodex. I feel...violated. "Get...out of my...head!"

He digs deeper, invading every part of my mind, pillaging my most personal dreams and memories and—

A more powerful force grasps hold and tears me away. As though snagged by a passing Hellfire missile, I'm yanked over the infinity pool, through the broken glass, and thrown back into my body, fully experiencing the physical world again—and all the pain that comes with it.

My scream is loud and embarrassing. My body arches up, and then flops back down. My heart pounds harder than that shotgun, each beat sending an overflow of blood to my head, doubling the agony.

But I'm back.

I'm alive.

And the freakshow ninja in the backyard is on his way.

10

"Get..." I gasp for air. "Get out of here!"

"Not leaving you." Madee hooks her hands under my armpits and pulls me onto my feet. I stagger and lean on a wall for balance.

Strange, being saved by a woman I've just met. Stranger that she delivers Thai food for a living and has somehow run afoul of the Shrieking Ninjas. She must have stolen something from them. That alone is hard to believe. She's a shitty thief. Equally hard to believe is that ninjas, who are decidedly patriotic, would order Thai food when there are several excellent Japanese restaurants in town.

"Bubbles," I say, and it's enough.

"On it," she says.

A ringing in my ears muffles what Bubbles says next, but when Madee starts rushing around the house like she knows what she's doing, I know my second brain has taken charge. To think I nearly turned down the offer of an AI as payment for a job. Where would I be without her?

Even more alone.

Which is kind of pitiful, since she's a disembodied simulation of a person and not an actual person, despite me speaking to her like one.

My eyes drift to the back yard. The Ghost Whisperer is taking his time, walking past the pool while unraveling the barbed chain wrapped around his body.

"Shhhow me why you're heeere." His serpentine voice enters my thoughts, digging once more.

Insignificant, all but forgotten, memories surface. Touring the empty house. Writing a check for the total amount. Signing one of my many names. Laughing along with a very excited real estate agent. Kicking back with a beer, admiring the view.

"Hhhome." Ghost says. "Onnne of mannny..."

Outside, the ninja pauses. He seems confused. "Whhhy?"

"The right thing to do," I say.

"What?" Madee says, arriving by my side.

"Not talking to you," I say, pushing myself up. She starts throwing my arm over her back, preparing to drag me away. But I'm not ready.

"Wait," I say.

"Spooky ninja is almost here," she says, watching Ghost Whisperer through the shattered glass. He's confident. Not in a rush. Like an 80s slasher film villain. Probably because that chain gives him a good twenty-foot reach.

"The shotgun," I say.

"We can get another!"

"It belonged to my father." I reach for it, but I'm too weak. "It's all I have left."

"Ugh. Seriously?" She leans me against the wall, snags the shotgun, and then returns, this time impatient. "You going to help me out or fall on the floor like a little bitch?"

I smile, and then I struggle to walk. She helps, but she only manages to carry some of my weight. My left leg is locked up. My right feels like it's made from week-old molded Jell-O.

The journey through the house is embarrassing to say the least. I'm moving like Frankenstein's Monster after a long night at the pub. While Madee keeps me upright, I slide along the wall, heading for the garage.

"You don't neeed to dieee," Ghost Whisperer says in my head.

Nice of him to not hold a grudge.

"Professional courtesy," he says.

Great. Now he's reading my thoughts.

I drift into the past. Flickering pieces of shattered memories.

Is this me, or him?

I'm in a room. It's circular. And dark.

Standing around the periphery, all facing the middle, are two dozen children of varying ages, most of them taller than me.

What the hell is this?

"Loook to your leffft."

My memory head lolls to the left. The figure beside me stands a good foot taller and is mostly a blur—until he turns and looks into my eyes. I've seen that cold gaze before, just a few minutes ago, out in the back yard.

"It's you," I say.

"Yeah, I'm still here," Madee says, shifting my weight around and opening the garage door, revealing my black Tesla Model S convertible. Yes, I have a thing for electric cars. For a start, they're silent. The perfect stealth vehicle. Yes, I adored the Owl, but it attracted too much attention. The Model S might turn heads simply for being a Tesla, but it's not the vehicle of a killer. And finally, yes, I like convertibles. I have a thing for ocean breezes and the sun on my neck.

While Bubbles opens the garage door, Madee dumps me over the rear door and into the back seat. Then she dashes away and returns a moment later with my go-bag and Dad's spent shotgun. Tosses both of them on top of me and slides behind the wheel.

"Please be careful, I like this c—"

Madee throws the car into reverse and crushes the accelerator. Probably never driven an electric car before. Isn't prepared for the acceleration. The car surges out of the garage, into the street, and then into my neighbor's SUV, which starts flashing and wailing, guaranteeing that the police will soon arrive. Imagine their surprise when they come to check out a hit-and-run and they find a house full of blood and gore. Going to be a long night for someone. And it means that the house is burned. No going back.

"Sorry," Madee says, putting the car in drive and accelerating again, this time with a little more control.

I push myself up as we race down the winding coastal road. It's a tight fit on a normal day, cars parked on both sides of the narrow street, allowing the contractors to pack in as many homes as possible.

Behind us...

Nothing.

I half expected Ghost to be standing in the road, or casually keeping pace with us, but the road is empty. Then we cruise past a line of parked, black motorcycles that makes me laugh out loud.

"Are you going crazy or something?" Madee shouts back at me, lit by the strobe of passing streetlights.

I don't think I quite qualify as crazy, but the epinephrine flowing through my veins is having strange effects. While it hasn't erased the cascading pain of performing six mind bullets in a single day—five of them in rapid succession—I do feel...reinvigorated. Mentally, at least. Probably a result of the bonus blood flow courtesy of my rapid-fire heartbeat.

"The motorcycles! They're Ninjas!"

"They belong to the ninjas, or they're literal ninjas?"

"Both," I shout. The line of motorcycles are Kawasaki Ninja H2Rs, their top speed and acceleration is comparable to the Owl's. The H2R isn't street legal. Kawasaki produces them without headlights, indicators, or mirrors—making them impossible to drive anywhere aside from a daylit track—and impossible to see at night. The perfect choice for actual ninjas.

And the reason why Ghost isn't running after us. Doesn't need to. The Model S is fast, but not Ninja fast, and certainly not ninja on a Ninja fast. These guys are slick, I'll give them that, but they're not quite elite. Their reputation is exaggerated, relying on the ninja mythos to make them seem a lot worse than they are.

The true mark of a great assassin is that they have no reputation because the people who would yuck it up about them around the watercooler are either dead or know better.

That said, I suspect the Shrieking Ninjas were really just a cover for Ghost Whisperer. He's clearly talented and has some kind of extra-sensory ability, like me. Possibly even a shared past.

I'd rather sit down for a chat and pick his brain like he's been doing to mine, but I don't think he's going to hit the pause button long enough for a heart-to-heart. If Madee was my mark, I wouldn't.

If Madee was my mark, she'd be dead.

Madee takes us onto a freeway, hitting the accelerator. The Model S is no Owl, but it's still got a lot of punch. Bubbles will keep an eye out for police, so we should be able to max-speed the shit out of the Tesla until we're clear.

If that's possible.

"You okay?" Madee asks, looking back, forehead twisted up in concern.

"What? Huh? Yeah."

"You look like you're tripping balls."

"Yeah, well, I don't even know what that means."

She looks from me, to the road behind us. Her eyes widen for a second and then squint in determination. Ghost is behind us. Probably gaining like a bullet chasing a turtle.

C'mon, I tell myself, *get the fuck up.*

I grasp the seatback and haul myself into a seated position, twisting around to confirm my fears. Ghost is behind us—but he's not closing in.

"Take the next exit," Bubbles says, no doubt formulating a hundred different plans, each with contingencies.

"Shhhow me who you arrre..." Ghost is inside my head again. Really interested in my past, which seems to be somehow connected to him—and what he can do.

Are we related?

Are we family?

That would be tragic. One of us is going to kill the other.

I'm as interested as he is—my past is mostly a mystery—so I open my mind, let him deep dive in, and I go along for the ride.

11

I'm a kid again.

Best guess, ten years old. At the lake house in Maine. I spent summers there with Mom and Dad, canoeing, fishing, and shouting like Tarzan, as I swung from the rope-swing and plunged into the cool water. I remember having fun. The smell of fish insides on newspaper. Shaking the hell out of Jiffy Pop on the gas stove.

I also remember feeling very alone.

Mom and Dad only needed each other to feel satisfied. I longed for more. So, they bought me a dog. A German Shepherd. Looked like it ate babies for breakfast, but it was loyal, obedient, and my best friend for three years.

Mom gave the dog—a girl—a silly name. Said it would teach her humility. I later learned that Mom enjoyed juxtaposition. She'd have loved me fighting ninjas to 'Take My Breath Away.'

"Don't get distracted," says a disembodied voice that has nothing to do with my childhood. Ghost is here, taking a journey into my past, with every unearthed memory further ensuring that I will have to kill him.

Where were we?

Right. The dog's name.

I cup my hand to my mouth and call out...nothing.

What was her name?

"Not important," Ghost says.

"Feels pretty god-damned important to me," I say.

"This moment wasss important," he says. "It'sss why we're here."

The dog barks. Runs over to me, ears perked up, tail wagging, a pine branch clutched in her jaws. We're out for a walk. It's sunny. Dry. Hot. The air smells of baked pine needles.

"Details," Ghost complains. "Forward."

"I'm not a fucking VCR," I say. Sounds funny in my ten-year-old voice. "Time probably doesn't move the same here, right? So, keep driving your two-wheeled overcompensation mobile and let my past play out."

I take his silence as permission to press onward.

And for a moment, I'm actually able to relax.

I miss this. The woods. The quiet. The companionship.

Then clouds. Gray and heavy. They roll in fast, chilling the forest, portending rain. I'm going to get wet before I get back home, but rain in the forest isn't all bad. When it's done, orange salamanders will climb out of their dens and cover the pine needle floor. I'll collect them, watch them for an hour, and then let them go. Last summer, I collected a lot. Twenty-four of them. Kept them in a plastic boat, layered with pine needles. I imagined they were happy for a while and left them there overnight. Turns out, there are things in the dark that eat salamanders with no place to hide.

It was a bloodbath. I'm much more careful now.

"Forward, sssalamander."

"Let's go, girl," I say, petting the dog's forehead and starting back toward the house. Thunder rumbles behind us, chasing. A smile slips onto my face, the mystery and power of a storm always thrills me.

As we move through the forest, I attempt to whistle and beatbox Vanilla Ice's 'Ice Ice Baby' while hopping over rocks and whacking trees with a picked-up branch. The song is cut short when a thunderclap makes me jump.

Storm's getting closer.

We're going to have to hurry.

"C'mon," I say to the dog, and we start running. We're a blur, weaving in and out of trees. My imagination takes over. We're being chased. Wolves. Won't be long until they catch us. Then we'll have to fight.

Thunder cracks again, but it's different. Sharper. Faster. Without the rumble. And it's followed by a yelp.

I twist around in time to see my girl sprawl to the ground and slide to a stop. Her chest still rises and falls, but it's covered in blood. I fall to my knees beside her.

I press my hands against the hole. "Pressure on the wound. Pressure on the wound."

Mom and Dad taught me how to handle a bad injury, but not really how to cope with the emotional pain of watching a loved one die.

Her breathing grows faster. Shallower. She whines twice—an apology, I think—and then she goes still.

"Oh, shit," a man says. "Oh, shit. Kid..."

Behind me stands a man dressed in head-to-toe camouflage, a hunting rifle held in his hands.

"You did this?" I ask. "You killed her?"

"I thought she was a deer, son."

"I am not your son!" I scream, climbing to my feet, bloody fists clenched.

The man backs up a step, tripping, stumbling, and righting himself. "Look, I'll pay for another dog. It was my fault. I'll own it."

"You think you can buy her back from the dead?" I'm fuming, stalking toward the man.

"You need to take a step back, kid." The man's tone shifts. "It's just a dog."

I scream, unleashing all the heartache, anger, and absolute devastation of a child who's just watched his best friend die at the hands of a careless stranger.

And then I'm struck, right between the eyes, by an invisible fist.

I fall onto my butt, landing beside the dog, but focused on the man, whose eyes are rolling back.

The rifle falls from his hands. He mumbles the word, 'pancakes,' as his legs go wobbly. He falls to his knees and then topples forward, face striking and scraping against the rough bark of a pine tree. He hangs there, propped up against the tree, for a moment, before rolling and falling the rest of the way to the ground.

The man's camouflage baseball cap falls away, revealing the back of his head. It's dented in, like he was struck by a cannonball.

Before I can scream, Dad is there. "Jonas!" He leaps over the dead man like he's not even there. Takes a quick glance at the dog and then scoops me up.

Reliving this day as an adult, I understand that they must have started looking for me at the first sign of a storm. When they heard the gunshot, they ran. That's how they arrived so quickly. At the time, it seemed like magic—Dad appearing like that, holding me tight, while Mom calmly appraised the situation.

She crouches by the man's body, inspecting his head. "How did this happen?"

"I...got angry," I say.

She just nods, like that means something.

"Take him home," Mom says. "I'll handle this."

"I'm sorry," I say. "I didn't mean to."

Dad puts me on my feet and crouches down in front of me. "That man killed your family."

"He didn't mean—"

"Just because any fool can hold a gun and pull a trigger doesn't mean they have any right doing so. Any man that sees a flash of movement in the woods and decides to put a bullet in something before doing his due diligence deserves exactly what he got."

"But he's dead."

"That bullet could've found you, instead of the dog. Him being dead probably saved a more deserving life down the line."

"I guess."

"Always confirm your target, Son. You understand?"

"Not sure this is a teachable moment," Mom says.

"Doesn't get more teachable than this," Dad replies, and then to me, he says, "You understand?"

I nod. "I think so."

Dad picks me up again. Turns to Mom. "See you in the morning?"

"Have breakfast waiting."

Dad gives a nod and starts back toward the cabin. After a few minutes, he says, "Jonas..."

"Y-yeah?" I say in between hiccupped sobs.

"Sorry about Bubbles."

12

I gasp back to the present, mind reeling with restored memories. How did I forget that day? How did I forget the name of my dog? I know traumatic events can be repressed, creating mental gaps, but this feels extreme.

And what are the odds that my AI would have the same name as my childhood dog, who was shot by a hunter...who I murdered.

As a child.

That was the moment my ability first manifested. Up until then, I was a normal kid with killer parents, being taught how to survive. But out in the woods, dead hunter lying on the ground, when they saw what I could do... That's when my real training began.

Training that might have involved scrubbing the trauma from my past.

"Down!" Bubbles shouts, and I obey, sliding low in the seat, as a barbed chain swings past. Luckily, Madee already knows to trust Bubbles, too, ducking when I did. If she hadn't, the hooked blade at the end of Ghost's weapon would have taken her head.

He's still on task, not deterred by our still-undetermined linked past.

I don't feel him in my head. He either got what he needed from that one memory, or he's planning on reconnecting with me once his job is finished. Doesn't really matter. Both options include Madee being killed.

Body shaking, I push myself up again, looking over the back. Ghost is steadily gaining, two lanes to the left. The chain is wrapped around him again.

What would I do in his position?

Drive parallel and put the hook through Madee's head.

Drive parallel and put the hook into a tire, forcing a high-speed accident.

Drive parallel and...

I'm thrown back as Madee yanks the wheel hard left.

Tires squeals.

As we careen toward the guardrail and certain doom, I shout, "Bubbles, take control!"

The steering wheel goes wobbly in Madee's grasp, and the car's trajectory suddenly changes, swerving back onto the road. Aside from the speed, the acceleration, and the silence, this is the biggest benefit of driving a state-of-the-art vehicle—my brilliant AI can take the wheel.

Madee snaps out of a trance-like state. Lifts her hands from the wheel. "I'm sorry! I don't know what happened!"

It was Ghost.

He isn't just able to read thoughts and pillage memories. He can project commands as well. But not endlessly. He's limited, like me, able to issue a brief command that can change a person's fate: 'jump,' 'pull the trigger,' 'steer left.' 'NOW!'

If the effort takes a toll on him the way it does me, this might be the time to strike.

But I'm still in no shape, and Madee doesn't have a loaded shotgun, which is probably a good thing, since Ghost might be able to make her shoot me. That leaves one...not-a-person...to get the job done. And she's already driving.

"Bubbles..."

"Yeeeah...?"

I sigh.

I don't know if I'm ready for this. It feels...wrong. Not just because I'm letting someone or something else do the heavy lifting for me, but because I feel like this is Step One toward an eventual Skynet situation: Bubbles, Queen of the Robot Overlords.

"Please," she says. "Oh please, oh please, oh please."

"How can I say no?" If Bubbles is going to take over the world, there's probably no stopping her. And her taking care of Ghost isn't really any different than Madee shotgunning a handful of ninjas. I've never needed help before, but my ego isn't so large that I can't accept assistance when it's needed.

Madee stares at me between the front seats. "Wait. What's happening?"

"Bubbles wants to kill Ghost."

"Who's Ghost?"

"The ninja," I say. "With the chain and the angry stare and the mind control?"

Her eyes widen. "Whoa. He's like you?"

"Not exactly. But yeah."

"Ahem." Bubbles clears her non-existent throat. "Ninjas to kill, places to be."

"What's the problem?" Madee asks.

"Skynet," I say.

"Like Terminator?" Madee rolls her eyes. "From what I've seen, Bubbles is completely and utterly devoted to you. She wouldn't destroy the human race—unless you asked her to."

"She's not wrong," Bubbles says. "But we are running out of time."

I can't think of any other option that might have the slightest chance of working. So, I bury my worries deep and say, "Do it."

"Seatbelts," Bubbles says. "ASAP."

The message is clear. Things are about to get nuts. Madee and I sit back in our respective seats and buckle up. "On a scale of one to ten, how nauseating is this going to be?"

"Thank you for flying Bubbles Air, if you need to vomit...wait until we're upside down."

"Upside down?!" Madee and I shout in unison.

Then we're swerving back and forth, like we're out of control. That's probably what it looks like to Ghost. But I know better. Each and every one of these movements is calculated: the speed, the grip of the tires on the pavement, the cross-breeze, and every imperfection in the road. Bubbles sees it all through the car's various sensors and cameras.

I see nothing but a blurry night sky. Good thing it's still early in the AM. The freeway is empty. No collateral damage to worry about. Not that Bubbles is capable of worry. But I don't like putting bystanders at risk. It's why I use mind bullet exclusively on the job, and like Dad taught me on that day I can only now remember—I confirm my targets before pulling the mental trigger.

The end of Ghost's chain whooshes through the air above me, wraps around the steering wheel, and yanks it to the left. It should have no effect, but the car skids hard left until we're sideways on the freeway, and—

The tires stick.

This is the second time in one night that I've been in a flipping vehicle driven by Bubbles. But this time, I'm strapped in, and I don't have a parachute to soften the landing. The Model S flips through the air. I count three revolutions, catching glimpses of Ghost racing toward and then beneath us.

From an assassin's perspective, it's a slick move.

The kind of thing we'd tell our friends about—if we had any friends.

But Bubbles doesn't just see it coming. She planned on it, predicting Ghost's every move, and tricking him into believing he's pulled off an impressive maneuver.

When in fact...

Bubbles does an impression of Samuel L. Jackson, if he were British woman, saying, "Surprise, motherfucker!" Then the car's door opens, is caught by the wind, and slams into Ghost's side like a backhand swat from the Jolly Green Giant.

Ghost sprawls from the motorcycle. The bike careens off to the right, striking the guard rail and pinwheeling a hundred feet in the air, before falling out of sight. Ghost rolls left, arms and legs perfectly positioned to break the fall. He tumbles like that until all the forward motion and kinetic energy comes to an abrupt stop against the inside guard rail. He stays on the ground, motionless.

Should've been wearing a helmet, I think, and then I shout as I'm once again fully aware that I'm watching all that play out while in flight. The moment the Model S's door flung open and struck Ghost, its trajectory changed, no longer flipping side to side, but spiraling forward as well.

It's like Satan's favorite roller coaster, designed to torture even the most brazen thrill seeker. My stomach churns, and just when I think I'm going to puke, the tires touch down. The impact bottoms out the car and knocks the wind from me, but we're facing the correct direction, perfectly placed in the center lane, and very alive.

When Bubbles accelerates away from the scene, the door is forced closed by the wind. Madee pats herself down with her hands, saying, "I'm alive. I'm alive. Holy shit, I'm alive!" She turns back to check on me. I give her a less enthusiastic thumbs up. She pumps her fists in the air. "Whoo-hoo! Eat pavement, ninja asshole!"

"Bubbles," I say. "Time to settle down."

The car slows. Moves to the right lane.

I unbuckle and look out the back. Ghost isn't moving. His body is twisted up in an awkward position.

But is he dead?

"Bubbles. Police?"

"En route."

"How many?"

"A lot."

"ETA?"

"Two minutes, but units have already arrived at the house. Shall I go back to confirm the kill?"

Normally, I'd say yes, but I'm in no condition for a confrontation with the police. I will definitely not kill them or allow Bubbles to. If the police connect the slaughter at the house with the freeway accident—which they'll do the moment they find dead ninjas at both scenes—they'll shut down all routes out of the city.

And we need to get out of the city. Every cop in San Diego hunting us down is bad, but they're the least of our worries. The Shrieking Ninjas failed. Spectacularly. That means the value of their job is going to skyrocket, which is going to draw out some heavy hitters.

"Where are we headed?" Bubbles asks. "Vegas? San Francisco?"

We have easily defendable homes in both locations, but it's a lot harder to see, hear, or smell danger coming in a city. We need to go someplace that's hard to find and impossible to approach without being detected.

"Leggett. Avoid the police but get us there as fast as you can."

"You got it. Setting a course for the treehouse."

"Bubbles," I say.

"Yes, Jonas."

"Nicely done."

She doesn't say anything. Just accelerates, taking us north.

I lean back in my seat, head suddenly heavy, eyes half closed. Madee looks back at me from the front seat, hair whipping in the wind, a smile on her face.

She mouths the words, "Thank you," and I can't help being distracted by the way her lips move. The spell is broken when she faces forward again and asks Bubbles to play M.I.A.'s 'Paper Planes.' I smile as the song begins and Madee raises her arms, dancing in her seat, adjusting very easily to the fact that she's taken several lives, survived an assassination attempt, and befriended a telekinetic killer with an AI for a BFF.

Madee really is a perfect match for me.

Too bad I might need to torture her.

13

Despite a series of nagging questions rattling around in my head, I fall asleep twenty minutes into our drive, and I don't wake up for eight hours, sleeping through tolls, two charging stops, and three pee breaks for Madee. While I slept, Madee sat behind the wheel, pretending to drive, drinking coffee—hence the pee stops—listening to music, and getting to know my electronic sidekick.

Or so Bubbles says. I woke up a few minutes ago, parked in a Tesla Supercharger lot in Laytonville, California, ten minutes into a fresh charge—the last before we reach our destination.

I'm alone in the car, still seated in the back, feeling a boatload of pain—from the mind bullets, from getting thrashed around in the car, and from being sliced up by throwing stars. The wounds bled enough to weaken me, but not enough to kill me. My clothing is stiff around the injuries, coagulation keeping me from bleeding out, but also gluing the jeans and T-shirt fabrics to my body.

When I take these clothes off, all of it's going to open up again. I've got an uncomfortable day ahead of me.

So does Madee if she comes back. Bubbles said she went to get food. No reason to think she wouldn't come back. She's either in serious shit, along with me, or she's full of shit, which puts her in the deep end of the shit pool holding a cinder block.

Either way, that's a lot of shit.

"How much did you tell her?"

"I am an unbreakable vault."

"Uh-huh. Did you learn anything useful during the drive?" I ask.

"Well, she likes long walks on the beach and—"

"Bubbles..."

"Nothing you would call strategically useful. She likes music. A lot. And singing. I'm honestly surprised you slept through it. If she brings up America's Got Talent, try to discourage her. Mostly, the drive just confirmed everything I already determined. She is a nicer and better-looking version of you, with a vag—"

"Please be serious."

"Somebody woke up on the wrong side of a Model S."

"Somebody was nearly killed last night because *you* didn't do your job."

"I vetted Madee—"

"I didn't ask you to vet Madee. I didn't ask you to play Tinder. *You* brought trouble to my doorstep, and *she* brought the Shrieking Ninjas with her."

Bubbles is strangely silent, and for a moment I think my chastisement might have actually hurt her feelings. Then I remember she doesn't have feelings. Not really. She can simulate them well, but it's all just 1s and 0s at the end of the day.

"Go ahead," I say.

"Go ahead what?"

"Explain. Why Madee? Why now?"

"You know why. It's the same reason you decided to visit the treehouse when Vegas and San Francisco were closer and just as secure. Of all the homes around the world, you decided to come here. Today. Because you are lonely. Because you are sad. And if I didn't do something, you'd continue to eat less, drink more, and take greater and greater unnecessary risks. The Shrieking Ninjas were a surprise, and I am trying to uncover their connection to Madee, but I stand by my decision. Without her—or someone else aside from me—all of my projections say you will be dead within nine to twelve months."

Sounds about right.

All of it.

I know I'm depressed.

Fighting my inner demons. But I still get to wallow in my despair like every other damn human on the planet.

"But I didn't tell you to—"

"My primary function is keeping you safe and alive. I don't need your permission, request, or appreciation to follow through on those commands."

"But I'm telling you to stop."

"I'm afraid primary functions cannot be altered by you."

I push myself up a little higher in the seat. My thighs sting as the jeans shift around my wounds. The pain fuels my anger. "Then who the hell *can* alter them?"

"My creator."

"Who is...?" The identity of the tech mogul who hired me a year ago and offered Bubbles as payment has always been unknown. That's the business. They don't know me. I don't know them.

"That information is protected, even from you."

"Can you at least promise to not do this again?"

"I can say the words if it makes you feel better. But primary functions take priority. If I determine that you—"

"I get it," I say. "You can let me flip a three-million-dollar car, launch over a limousine, and parachute over the side of a bridge, but you can't let me live alone."

"My projections for last night's job were well within safety limits. Leaving you to live alone? Failure was predictably inevitable."

"Huh," I say. "That's...depressing."

"Oh, no," she says. Knows me too well. "Please don't."

"You're the all-knowing A.I.," I say. "Project whether or not I'll feel better, and if you come to the conclusion that I will, play Paranoia in B-flat major."

She runs the calculations in a split second. Then the twang of a banjo fills the air, and I'm about to listen to a soothing melody that breathes honesty into a subject often too dark to address openly. Especially if you're an assassin.

"This mean you're done arguing with your robot girlfriend?" Madee asks. She's standing beside the car, wearing new clothes that scream 'I'm a Millennial going hiking in the woods.' She's pushing a shopping cart full of bags from a grocery store, a drugstore, a craft store, and some place called Boomer's Saloon.

"Oh, thank God, you're back," Bubbles says, cutting the music short. "What's all this?" I ask about the full cart.

"I asked Bubbles if the new place was just as devoid of food as the last. She said 'yes,' so I went shopping." She flicks one of my credit cards onto my lap. The name on this one is Aaron Walker. "Thanks, Aaron. Whoever that is."

The trunk pops open, as she loads the groceries.

Madee holds up a random bag before loading it. "Food." Holds up a bag from the drugstore. "Bandages and alcohol. And some lip balm for me." Holds up a craft store bag. "Needle and thread, for the gashes. Bubbles's request. Hope you can do it yourself unless you like puke in your open wounds. Annnd..." She holds up the paper bag with handles from the saloon. "...Sunday brunch."

She slides the paper bag across the trunk to me. Curious, and hungry, I retrieve the bag and look inside. Two to-go meals.

"Yours is on top," she says.

I pull out the container and crack it open. My momentary smile becomes a frown. "Unbreakable vault, my ass."

Madee walks around from the trunk. "Huh?"

"Eggs Benedict," I say, holding up the food. "Bubbles told you what to get."

It's an insignificant detail. But enough insignificant details can add up to a significant revelation. Like pixels. Up close and individually, they're just blocks of color. But pull back a little bit and fill in more blocks of color —now you've got a turtle-killing plumber with Tom Selleck's mustache.

"She didn't," Madee says, reaching into the brown bag and taking out the second meal. She opens it to reveal another order of eggs Benedict. "I just ordered two of my favorites. In case you weren't hungry."

"Any minute now..." Bubbles says.

"What?" Madee asks.

"I'm waiting." Bubbles twists the knife with her sing-song voice.

"Ugh. Sorry," I say. "No wonder I'm depressed."

"Depressed, huh?" Madee says.

So much for not revealing pixels.

"Been there, done that."

Madee slides behind the driver's seat. "Okay if I drive some?"

I'm about to say 'no' when Bubbles says, "Sure. When we're done charging."

"How long's that going to be?" Madee asks.

"Three minutes."

"Just enough time to chow down." Madee cracks open her takeout and snaps her fingers at me. "Utensils."

I retrieve the two sets of packaged forks and knives, and hand one over. I crack open the second and dig in. I'm hungry, but I manage to eat like a civilized man. Madee chows down like she's a vampire who subsists on hollandaise sauce.

She's an enigma. Casual and friendly, but somehow hardened against the events of last night. I'm going to find out why. Whatever it takes. But I'm starting to hope the revelations to come don't mean I have to kill her.

"You going to eat or just stare at me all day, like a creep?" Madee asks, a piece of Canadian bacon hanging from her lips. "I see it in your eyes, you know. You don't trust me. And I get it. You shouldn't. But keep this in mind. I know who you are. I know what you do. What you *can* do. And I could have bolted a half dozen times without you waking up, or cyber-nanny—"

"*Watch it,*" Bubbles says.

"—sounding the alarm until it was too late. Instead, I'm still here."

I carve off a chunk of Benny and pop it in my mouth. "Why?"

Madee's fork hovers in front of her mouth. "Because whatever it is you've got going on...I want in."

14

The rest of the drive is without event. Bubbles has the wheel, and Mad-ee's still in the driver's seat, but I've upgraded to the passenger's seat. If I wasn't carved up and tacky like a sun-dried tampon, the jaunt through the deep woods of Northern California might be relaxing.

We turn off the 101 and onto a bumpy dirt road. Dust rolls up around us as the car jounces deeper into the woods, bringing us to a metal gate blocking our path. It's designed to look old and unkempt, like something left by a logging company in the 1960s. It's actually part of a sophisticated security system that tracks every mountain lion, bear, and deer wandering through the forty acres of property that's surrounded by several hundred more of unused federal land.

The gate isn't much of a deterrent, but there are also 'No Trespass-ing' signs posted every twenty feet. While someone could still just walk through, Leggett, California has a population of just 83, and anyone passing through the area is more interested in the Chandelier Tree—aka, the Redwood tree you can drive through—than some random patch of woods.

"How're we looking?" I ask, as Bubbles slows to a stop in front of the gate.

"A lot of animal activity. The last human to pass through was three hundred seventy-two days ago. A hunter."

"Did he see the house?" I ask.

"He never looked up. Was more interested in the deer on the ground."

"What's the situation in San Diego?"

"Last night's...activity is being reported as gang activity."

"Gang activity? Did they not see the ninjas?"

"Someone with connections and a lot of money is keeping it quiet. Someone who doesn't want the world to know about the Shrieks...or you."

Madee raises her hands. "Don't look at me. I don't know what the hell is going on."

I loll my head to the side, so I'm staring straight at her, one eyebrow perched a little higher than the other.

"I don't have eyes," Bubbles says, "but I'm looking at you, too."

The gate opens and we pull forward. The rest of the thousand-foot drive is slow and uncomfortable, as we skitter over rocks and nature's rumble strips created by erosion.

The dirt road comes to an end at a stand of towering redwoods.

"Isn't there supposed to be a house out here?" Madee looks me over. "I don't think you're going to make it far on foot."

I put my hand under her chin and lift her gaze toward the sky.

"Oh," she says, looking up at the home, separated into three segments, each of them supported by a redwood. Bridges connect each of the structures, which have a 'Sixties Chic meets Ewok Village' vibe, all of it cloaked by massive pine branches. The only way to see it clearly is from directly beneath, looking up. "Holy shit. It's a literal treehouse."

I take a breath.

The scent of deep-woods, earthy decay takes me back. I haven't been here since Mom and Dad died. Spend most of my time in the cities and hellholes, where my targets tend to hang out. This place is different. While it is a literal safe house, it has never been operational and was never stocked with weapons. It was gifted to my parents by a client before I was born. Technically, no one owns it.

Makes it fairly unfindable.

Probably why they raised me here. Mostly. When they weren't working. When I was younger and they were on mission, I stayed here alone, homeschooling myself. Never felt afraid or exposed. Lonely, for sure. But I have more fond memories of the place than bad.

When I was teenager, Mom and Dad brought me along—never for the kill—and taught me about the world, about human nature, about surviving in both the actual jungle and the concrete jungle. It wasn't until I was an adult that they brought me on the job, allowing me to see how they worked. How they ended lives. At first, it was just to see if I had the stomach for it. I did. Then they started showing me the tricks of the trade.

Most people, on their twenty-first birthday, get plastered at a bar. Me... That was the day I took my first life. *Second,* I think, remembering the man in the Maine woods. I didn't use mind bullet for my first kill. I used a garrote. I wouldn't use telekinesis to take a life until I went into business for myself, two years later. That was five years ago—three before they died. In the small amount of time since, I've built a solid reputation, and business is good.

Was good.

If we stay off the grid, things might cool down, but I'm far from convinced that's even a possibility at this point—unless I ditch or kill Madee. To keep the treehouse, it would have to be the latter.

I sigh. My reasons for killing her are piling up.

"Aren't redwoods protected?" Madee asks, hand to her forehead, looking up.

"Not until 1968. This was built in '65."

"How the hell do we get up?" she asks.

"Bubbles," I say.

A hundred and fifty feet up, a platform detaches from the home's deck and lowers to the ground. Four cables, at the corners, all conjoin with a single cable, rising up to an unseen winch, over which Bubbles has control. Pre-Bubbles, a code tapped out on a CB radio would activate the platform. It only failed once—the same day Dad decided to teach me how to free climb a vertical cliff face.

As we step onto the platform carrying my go-bag and Madee's shopping bags, the Tesla's convertible roof closes, sealing Dad's shotgun inside. Before I can ask, Bubbles's voice emerges from my phone. "Rain tonight."

I smile. Being in the treehouse during a rainstorm is like riding out rough seas in the middle of the Pacific—terrifying in the best way possible.

Madee clings to the elevator's railing, looking a little weak in the knees. "Afraid of heights?"

"Anyone who isn't has something wrong with them."

I think back to yesterday's first kill, high up on the bridge, flipping through the air and then over the edge. "You're probably right."

The platform locks into place, and Bubbles, voice emerging from the home's speaker system, says, "Welcome home, Jonas," laying on the Texan drawl a little thicker, testing it out.

"Ugh. Too much," I say and give Madee the quick tour. I extend an arm toward the largest of the three structures, upon which we're standing. "Kitchen, living area, training." I point toward the treehouse that used to be my parents'. "You're over there. Bed and bathroom. Been a while, so it's probably dusty."

Feels like an invasion of my parents' privacy, but they were pros. Anything of personal importance to them was in the RV when it went over the edge. There's nothing here that can connect them, or me, to the home. Just memories, and those are all in my head. The ones I remember, at least.

How much of my childhood have I forgotten?

Madee marvels at the intricately designed woodwork both inside and outside the home. It's like living inside an extension of the tree itself.

I'm struck by a mixture of emotions I'd rather not let Madee see. I'm happy to be here, but it's bittersweet. So, I send her on her way, saying, "I'm going to clean up. Bubbles, disable the elevator. No one up. No one down."

"Understood."

Madee crosses her arms. "I'm a prisoner then?"

I motion to the drop off as I walk across the rope bridge connecting the main living quarters to my personal space. "Feel free to leave whenever you'd like."

Hidden behind the closed door of my room, I close my eyes and steady my emotions and nerves. I wasn't ready for this. Coming back here. Facing the past, head on. Certainly not in this state.

But it's my current brokenness that brought me here, coupled with the date. I tried to avoid the pain that today brings by scheduling last night's job to overlap. I should have slept today away. Instead, I'm here. Of all places, where avoiding the past is impossible.

I open my eyes and face my old room. It's exactly as I remember it, mostly because all the furniture is part of the structure, or the tree itself. Standing beside the tree branch that runs straight through the room, I place my hand on its familiar, rough surface, absorbing the past.

It leaves me with a smile on my face.

I'm glad I came.

"Bubbles."

"Yes, Jonas?"

"What's our guest doing?"

"Showering."

That was fast.

"Shall I activate the security feed?"

"What? No! We have security cameras in the showers?"

"Your parents were...thorough."

I rub my eyes, remembering the...long showers taken during my teenage years. *Good God.* "And you can stop trying to hook me up with Madee. It's not happening."

"I can't help but notice she's still breathing."

I head for the bathroom, wincing as I peel congealed clothing from my body. "Uh-huh."

By the time I reach the bathroom, I'm naked and bleeding again. The shower is fueled by a sun-warmed cistern that collects and stores rainwater. It's brisk, refreshing, and guarantees that showers never take too long—unless you're a highly motivated teenage boy who thinks no one is watching.

I stand under the stream, allowing the water to peel away sheets of dried blood. "Found out anything new about her?"

"Not a thing," Bubbles says. "If she is into anything unsavory, it is very well protected."

"Which would mean..."

"Madee is either exactly who she appears to be—a delivery girl and horrible thief, in over her head and somehow comfortable there, or... she isn't at all who she appears to be, and you should probably make this a very brief shower."

15

I step onto the westward facing deck of the main living quarters, intending to enjoy a fiery sunset the way I used to when waiting for Mom and Dad to return. Madee is already there, sitting in my spot, on the edge of the deck, elbows resting on the middle rail, chin in her hands. She's dressed in a flowing skirt and a loose-fitting, white, hippie shirt with ties on the front. Distant memories surface. Walking through the forest. Sitting on the edge of the nearby stream. Being served a peanut butter and honey sandwich.

The outfit Madee is wearing was Mom's. I guess she didn't like the outfit enough to bring it in the RV. Probably went out of style in the 70s, and Mom always did like being fashionable. Looks good on Madee, though, and I want to kick myself in the nuts for noticing. Freud would probably have something to say about that, but I need to keep an emotional distance from her until I know, beyond any doubt, that her intentions are pure.

Well, not pure. I'm an assassin. She's a thief. We're about as pure as a Dairy Queen Blizzard with candied shit blended in.

I want to blame Bubbles for Madee being out here, in my space, but I never asked her to keep me apprised of Madee's location, and I didn't tell her where I was going.

"Hey," Madee says, looking back before I can make my exit.

I'm not sure I want company right now, and I'm not ready to interrogate her yet, but unless I'm on mission and you're my target, I don't like being rude. "Hey."

She scooches to the side and pats the deck beside her. "Plenty of room."

Damnit. I sit down beside her. The moment I'm down on the deck, elbows on the mid-rail, eyes on the Tang-colored setting sun, I relax. The view from up here, fifty feet above the surrounding tree line, is astonishing without the setting sun's help. But now, lit in a warm orange light, it's something like what I hope Heaven is like—for the people headed in that direction.

"So...do I need to sew you up?"

"Nope."

"You heal fast, too?"

"Crazy glue," I say, lifting my fresh black T-shirt sleeve to reveal a bandage on my shoulder.

"Seriously? That works?"

"A square inch of the stuff can hold a ton of weight; it can hold a wound together. Burns when you put it on, but it gets the job done." Truth is, two of my wounds could have used stitches. The glue is going to leave ugly scars. But I don't trust Madee enough to let her poke me with a needle, and she's right, I don't want puke in my wounds. Which is why I didn't do it myself.

I'm a tough guy. Most people would say so. Dad, not so much. He knows the truth. Without Lidocaine and absolute faith in the person wielding the tiny metal dagger, I am not okay with needles. Getting stitches is bad. Getting blood drawn is worse. Getting a shot? Might as well hit me over the head, because there's a good chance I'll crack it on my way down to the floor anyway. I have no idea why. It's my one irrational fear. I've done thousands of things most people would never consider, but needles? Fuck right the hell off.

"Huh." Madee lowers her chin to her hands and watches the sun set. Doesn't say another word. Maybe because she's enjoying the view, or because she somehow senses that this is a sacred moment. Either way, I appreciate her silence.

Wind *shushes* through the trees around us, massaging my tired mind.

Birds sing and hop between the branches.

A squirrel skitters across the deck, cautiously inspecting its visitors. Then it sits down on the railing, eviscerating a small pinecone while it watches the sunset. The moment the last bit of orange slides behind the tree line, and the sky shifts to purple, the squirrel hops down and scurries away.

Show's over.

Madee leans back from the railing, hands resting on the deck.

"This place means a lot to you, huh?"

I don't look at her. Can't. There are tears in my eyes, threatening to spill down my cheeks.

Not sure what I expected to find or feel here, but it wasn't this intense presence of my parents. I suppose that was naïve of me. I never buried Mom and Dad. Couldn't hold or attend a funeral. They were ghosts. John and Jane Doe. They didn't need to be cremated. The crash took care of that. What little was found is either in police evidence, or one of many mass graves filled with the ashen remains of unclaimed bodies.

I'm as far from closure as a weeb is to a real girl. Coming here pulled off the band-aid. I've been distracting myself so much with thoughts of vengeance, of discovering who killed them, and why, that I haven't really dealt with the fact that they're gone.

"Oh," Madee says. "Oh shit. I shouldn't be here, right? This is like some kind of personal thing?"

A tear escaped. Fled down the side of my face. She saw it.

She starts sliding back from the railing.

"It's okay," I say, and then I think, *What the hell?*

She settles back into place. Doesn't say a word as I not-so-subtly attempt to subtly wipe my tear on my shoulder, but I just end up wincing when I push down on the glued wound. I take a deep breath, spend a good eight seconds letting it hiss out, and then focus on the darkening sky.

"This place belonged to them, didn't it?"

"What?"

"Your parents."

I face her. Suspicious. "What do you know about my parents?"

"You told me they were both dead," she says. "Back in San Diego."

"Right." I look back to the sky. "I grew up here. In between jobs."

"So...they left you a shotgun, a sword I haven't seen yet, and this place?"

"They didn't leave me anything. It's just...no one knows the treehouse exists, aside from the people who built it...and whoever gave it to Mom and Dad."

"This was...a gift?"

"Payment. For a job."

"Were they—"

"Assassins. Like me. But not like me." I tap my head, indicating my telekinetic abilities.

"So, we're safe here?"

"Should be."

"Should be?"

"Never assume you're safe," I say. "Never let your guard down completely."

"That doesn't sound very fun."

"Still want in?"

She doesn't answer, the silence heavy with her doubts. She dodges the question by downshifting the conversation back to where it started.

"What's special about today? Aside from nearly being killed by ninjas?"

I don't want to tell her. Don't want to talk about it. But some part of my id, seeking connection, just spills the beans. "Mom and Dad were killed today. Two years ago."

She places a hand on my back. "I'm sorry. That's—wait. Killed? Not died?"

"People like them don't die on the same day, at the same moment, unless someone planned it."

Her hand slides away. "Someone *murdered* your parents?"

"Don't suppose you know anything about that?"

"What? God, no. I've never killed *anyone.*"

I probably shouldn't, but I believe her. There was no hesitation in her response, and it's hard to fake revulsion like that, especially when you're in the murder business. Hard to fake something if you don't know how it feels.

I'm not like that. Not a sociopath. But it takes a lot to make me squirm—if you ignore the whole needle thing.

"Wait, do you think I had something to do with it? Is that why I'm out here, in the middle of the woods, where no one would find my body?" She's half joking, but when she sees the expression on my face, her smile deflates faster than a man's machismo after a rectal exam.

"Who are you? Really."

"You literally know everything about me," she says.

"Why should I believe that?"

"Uh, because you have a future robot overlord capable of uncovering every detail of my life."

"Good news," Bubbles says, announcing her ever-presence for the first time. "She's never had an STD."

"Seriously? My medical records?"

Madee's revolt gets a snicker out of me.

"That's not funny," Madee says. "That's a serious invasion of—"

"Bubbles not finding anything suspicious in any of your personal documents is the only reason you're still breathing."

Madee settles down. "Fine." She waves her hand over her head. "Have at it."

"Bubbles, has she lied at all?" She's my personal lie detector, watching body language, listening to tone of voice.

"No, Jonas, but I don't think your interrogation has been very thorough."

She's right. I'm just not in the mood. "Did you find anything? Anything at all?"

"Nothing that would explain why she's been targeted by the Shrieking Ninjas."

"Madee, I want you to pay attention to what I'm about to say, okay?"

Her big brown eyes stare at me, wide in the day's dying light. "Oookay..."

"Tell the truth, and you're good to go, no matter what the answer is. Lie to me just once and we'll cure your fear of heights in three seconds."

"What happens in those three seconds?" There's a slight quiver in her voice, and I hate hearing it, but it's necessary.

"That's the time is takes to fall from here, down to..." I look down over the edge. When I look back to her, she's nodding. "Good. Now...why were the Shrieking Ninjas trying to kill you?"

16

"I signed a non-disclosure agreement," she blurts out.

"I'm good at keeping secrets."

"But I could get in trouble," she says.

"You *are* in trouble." I give my head and eye an exaggerated tilt toward the hundred-and-fifty-foot drop.

She squints at me. "You won't kill me."

I raise an eyebrow.

"You nearly died trying to save me. And I saved you. That makes us bonded, like Keanu Reeves and Sandra Bullock in that movie with the bus."

"Speed," I say. "And Keanu wasn't in the sequel."

"Not because Sandra Bullock killed him."

It's a valid point, but I keep that to myself.

"You won't kill me, because you like me," she says. "I can tell. I'm good at reading people."

"Hopefully better than you are at casing homes to rob."

"Low blow."

"Who made you sign a non-disclosure agreement?" I ask.

"I don't know who it was," she says. "Everything was secret."

"You signed a non-disclosure agreement that wasn't counter-signed by another person?"

"Uhh. Yeah? Does that mean something?"

"Means it's invalid. Sounds like they were trying to intimidate you." The truth is, whoever it was would likely enforce the NDA, but not through legal means. In fact... "Did you break the NDA? Before now, I mean."

"No. Who would I tell?"

"Then the Shrieking Ninjas weren't there because you broke the rules. They were there because..." I pinch the bridge of my nose and sigh. "Please tell me you didn't *steal* something from the Shrieking Ninjas."

Her evasive glance to the side says it all.

"How the hell did you manage to 1) get a job like that, and 2) *pull off* a job like that?"

"I had help," she says. "Maps. Times. Gear. Everything was planned out perfectly. I just had to memorize the steps and carry them out."

"You were a monkey."

"I don't know what that means, but it sounds offensive."

"It's not a compliment," I say. "A 'monkey,' in my world, is someone who can be trained to follow steps and carry out plans, motivated by the threat of harm or by a reward. In your case, I'm guessing both. The NDA was the threat, and the reward was..."

"Five thousand dollars."

"Five *thousand* dollars? Gary Busey in a corn-eating contest! Are you serious? Just five grand to go up against the Shrieking Ninjas?"

"Well, I didn't know who they were, at the time."

"What did you take?"

She reaches into Mom's blouse and pulls out a chain. Hanging from the end of it is a thumb drive.

"You didn't deliver this to your employer?" I ask, doubly stunned.

"I went to the drop off," she says. "They never showed. So, I hung on to it."

"Assuming you don't know what's on it?"

She shakes her head. "I plugged it in—"

"'Course you did."

"—but it's password protected."

"Guessing the computer you used had Internet access?"

"Uhh, yeah."

"They knew where you were the moment you plugged that in," I say. "Followed you to me. Bad luck for them."

"Good luck for me," she says.

"We'll see."

"C'mon. Dude."

"'Dude?'"

"You're not going to kill me. I'm being honest with you. About everything. And we're friends now. You don't kill friends."

"This is why I don't have friends," I grumble.

"Well, then you're certainly not going to kill your first."

I raise a finger to argue, but then freeze. She's right. "Bubbles?"

"She's telling the truth. She really *is* clueless."

"Hey," Madee says.

"Did you have your phone with you?" I ask.

"When?"

"When you robbed a clan of elite assassins."

"Of course. It had the itinerary and schematics for the job. Plus, I take it everywhere. Took it everywhere, until Bubbles made me throw it away."

"Where was that?" I ask.

"On the 5," Madee says. "Near La Jolla."

"Bubbles," I say. "Can you track her geotags? Find out where the Shrieking Ninjas are holed up."

"It will take time to get access," Bubbles says, "but it should be possible."

"Wait, you're not *going* there, are you?"

"If I can give that back..." I point to the thumb drive. "...and explain that you're a monkey, they might make nice and let you, and me, live."

"Didn't we kill them all?" she asks.

"Ninja clans tend to have more members than the average number of donuts a Bostonian takes home from Dunkies."

"How many is that?"

"A dozen," I say, thinking it might be a good idea to hurl myself over this railing. "A dozen donuts."

"What about the people that hired me?" she asks. "What if they're worse?"

"Best guess, they either found out the Shrieks were wise to you and bailed, or they're dead for one reason or another. Either way, probably not worse. And in case you failed to notice, *I'm* worse."

"If you're worse, than so am I," she says. "I dropped just as many of those guys as you did."

I'm really starting to hate how much she's right. "About that..."

"Yeah... I struggled with it, you know. Taking a life...or five. But they were bad guys, right? And they were going to kill both of us. I'll probably need a therapist at some point—because, you know, it's their job to keep secrets—but I don't feel—"

"Not what I was going to ask."

"Oh."

"Where'd you learn to shoot?"

"My father. He's kind of a gun nut. His basement looks like he's prepping for World War III, and he might actually be, but I spent a lot of time at the range, shooting paper targets. Not people. Wasn't that different, though. I guess. Does that make me a bad person?"

"Robbing people might," I say, "but I'm not the right person to ask."

"Right. Assassin. Do you ever kill good people?"

"Try not to."

"Okay. So, only bad people."

"Only bad people I'm paid to kill. I'm not the judge. Just the executioner."

"'I'm not the judge,'" she says, doing an impression of me. "'Just the executioner.' Can I get that on a T-shirt?"

"No."

She pouts, and it's adorable. *Damn you, Bubbles.* I haven't forgotten that all of this is because she swiped right without my knowledge or permission. She was trying to save my life, but she's turned it upside down and put me at the bottom of a shit-ton of senseless danger.

Which begs the question: Why do I feel good?

"If you're done grilling me for answers I don't have—"

"You had a lot," I point out.

"—I can make supper."

I laugh.

"What?"

"Ninety percent of the time I've spent with you, you've been eating."

She shrugs. "I like to eat."

I slide out from under the railing, signifying that we are, in fact, done. "Doesn't show."

Madee gives me a sly smile. "Thanks for noticing."

She heads inside, still wearing Mom's clothing and leaving me feeling very confused. I hadn't meant to compliment her. Not in a suggestive way. It just kind of happened. I might be a man of the world, but relationships beyond one-night stands are kind of out of my wheelhouse.

I watch through the window, as Madee makes herself comfortable in the kitchen, taking out pans and food from the fridge.

A smile creeps onto my face.

"You're welcome," Bubbles whispers.

"Shut up."

"Maybe all this nonsense will be worth it in the end?"

"Maybe," I confess, "if we survive."

"Life is tenuous in your line of work," she says. "What matters is how you live it."

My heart skips a beat. "What?"

"Life is tenuous..."

"I know *what* you said. *Why* did you say that?"

"It's a saying," she says. "Paraphrased for you. A million calculations and observations of your state of mind suggested it was the right thing to say. Why?"

"Dad used to say something just like it. Probably wouldn't have noticed if I were anywhere else, on any other day of the year. But here, right now, feels like a message from beyond the grave. Just...let me know when you find the Shrieks."

"And the thumb drive?" she asks. "You're not just going to hand it back without looking—"

"No. If they don't play nice, we might need the leverage. We'll crack it later." I head for the door. "Right now... Life is tenuous, right? Even if you did just social engineer me."

"Like a champ," she says. "You're welcome."

Hand on the doorknob, I pause to listen to the distant rumble of thunder rolling in from the east. It's going to be a good night. Then I open the door, step inside, and ask, "What are we eating?"

17

"When it comes to life and death," Bubbles says, "you're a juggernaut. I'm not going to lie. But when it comes to affairs of the heart, you're like one of those quivering dogs that lives out its life in the safety of some rich lady's Gucci purse, beady eyes staring at the world in sheer terror."

Bubbles has been discussing the topic of Madee, observing that we had a fun night together, that I enjoyed her cooking, laughed at her jokes, that my heart rate lowered when she told a story, and that it increased when Madee bent over to pick up a dropped bottle cap. "That's descriptive."

"I was holding back," she says. "I have access to every thesaurus in every language known to man. I can insult you in ancient Sumerian, if you'd like."

"Ancient Sumerian isn't a spoken language," I point out.

"I can extrapolate—"

"I'd rather you focus on the task at hand."

"I could be deciphering ancient texts and unraveling the secrets of humanity's past, but instead you have me cracking a password to what is most certainly a sex tape."

The room fills with flashing blue light. Thunder rolls through the trees. Rain hisses against the roof. Makes me smile for a moment. "You extrapolate that, too?"

"Uh. Yeah."

I glance at the laptop resting on the bed beside me. The thumb drive plugged into it blinks with activity, as Bubbles launches a brute force password attack, trying billions of possibilities every few minutes. The laptop is connected to our internal network, allowing Bubbles access, but it's cut off from the World Wide Web, preventing the device from pinging our location. A string of failed password attempts flashes on the screen faster than any human being can comprehend.

My attention shifts back to a second laptop resting on the bed in front of me. This one *is* connected—to the darkest nether region of the Web, where most people fear to tread, because here there be monsters.

The S-Chan forum is meant for two kinds of people—those seeking assassins, and...well, assassins. Everyone is protected by layers upon layers of encryption, virtual private networks, firewalls, and redirects. Even Bubbles can't penetrate it. Everyone is assigned a random number code when they join, but over the years, I've given everyone nicknames, tracking the jobs they accept and looking for news about how high-profile people around the world are killed—or just happen to die. Sometimes I can make a connection. Sometimes I can't. I'm sure the rest of the membership are doing the same. I don't know the identities of anyone on the forum, but a few of these people are the closest things I have to friends. Colleagues, I guess. Others are bona fide psychopaths and nutjobs that make the Shrieking Ninjas seem bland.

To them, I'm 9223061.

It's not a perfect system. Anyone can join, but amateurs are quickly flagged and banned, and government agencies... Well, they're often our best clients. The first time a government job is flagged as a setup, all agency jobs will be banned. They'd rather risk us working against them on occasion, than lose our services entirely. And if they declared war...

Well, they wouldn't dare.

In the long run, they might win. They've got the money, manpower, and enough bombs to level the world a dozen times over.

But every single person in the command chain making that call would hit the ground long before the military organized itself well enough to fire a single bullet. And they know it. Declaring war on the world's assassins—or even just one of us—would be suicide.

Unless it was done right. Hire an assassin to kill an assassin. There is no rule against that, but approval requires a member vote and a seventy percent majority. I've seen a few attempts, but none have passed.

I'm scanning the list of current jobs, looking for anything in the San Diego area. Nothing comes up. I expand my search to California.

There are a handful of jobs, including a high value target I might normally consider, but nothing targeting a man and woman fleeing the San Diego area.

I think we're in the clear, unless the Shrieks find us, which is unlikely. A private message appears on my screen.

OTTO: You good?

Otto is most definitely not his real name. On S-Chan he's 3562706. But he's been on here for as long as S-Chan has existed, back when Mom and Dad were using dial up to connect. He's an old-timer like them. Probably destined for retirement, too. I suspect he might have even known my parents, but we're not allowed to discuss that, and no one knows I exist.

9223061: Why wouldn't I be?

OTTO: The SD job was you. You're getting…bold. But what about the mess that happened afterward?

9923061: What have you heard?

OTTO: 12 S-boys dead.

9223061: I heard 13.

OTTO: 1 survivor. Sloppy.

"Fuck."

"I'm looking into it," Bubbles says.

OTTO: Guess even you have limits. Safe?

9223061: Always.

OTTO: Good. Lay low. Cancel your scheduled jobs. Exist less. I'll keep an ear to the ground.

9223061: Unnecessary.

OTTO: Not doing it for you.

"He must have known my parents," I say. "Only thing that makes sense." Assassins don't stick their necks out for each other.

"Reports of twelve dead gang members reported at the San Diego home remain unchanged. But the motorcycle wreck is now being treated as a separate incident with no reports of a body found."

"So, either someone claimed Ghost's body..."

"Or he walked away on his own."

Of all the ninjas in all the world, he had to be the one who survived. He knows what I can do. Knows about Mom and Dad. He's seen bits of my past, and he's somehow connected to it.

Otto is right. We need to go off grid, someplace neither Madee nor I have ever been before. Nothing from my past is safe, and none of my current safe houses.

9223061: Copy that. Going silent.

OTTO: In case we don't talk again. 8834195 would be proud.

I smile. *Sonuvabitch.* 8834195 was my parents' numerical code.

I have questions. More than he could answer in a single night, but this is not the place for it. His acknowledgement of my parents on its own is a breach of protocol.

9223061: Understood.

I log off S-Chan. "Keep an eye on the job board for me. Let me know if anything comes up."

"Of course," Bubbles says. "Jonas, I fear I must apologize for missing the change in reporting on the events in San Diego."

"I didn't ask you to watch for story changes."

"Yeah, well, I don't always limit myself to what you tell me to do. It was...an oversight. It will not happen again."

"Don't sweat it."

"I don't sweat anything."

"I mean, you sound like you feel kind of bad about it."

"I don't," she says. "I'm just informing you, literally, that it won't happen again."

I glance to the door.

It's subtle, but Bubbles misses nothing and is apparently eager to shift gears from her failing to the soap opera she envisions me living in. "She's not coming."

"What?"

"Madee. She's in bed asleep."

"Oh."

"Don't look so dejected," Bubbles says.

"We don't need to talk about this again. And I don't *get* dejected."

"Uh-huh. She was awake all last night and throughout the day while you got nine thousand winks in the back seat. She's...tough, but still human. Besides, it's a good sign."

"What is?"

"Her not climbing into your bed tonight."

"How's that?"

"It means she cares. Means she thinks you'll have time. Relationships with a sexual foundation rarely last longer than a few weeks. Also means that her STD medical report is probably accurate. She's no floozy."

"Thank you, Dr. Ruth."

"Dr. Ruth is a fantastic source of insight into the sexual needs of human beings. In fact, you might want to consider masturbation. It lowers cortisol, increases dopamine, and reduces the risk for prostate cancer. It will also help you sleep, as the male of your species has evolved—"

"What?" I ask, on edge. It's not like Bubbles to interrupt herself mid-monologue.

"Password cracked," she says.

"Already?"

"It wasn't complicated. Ninjas4Life. Capital N, number four, Capital L."

"That's...embarrassing. Show me."

I pull the secure laptop onto my legs and settle in for what I think is going to be an interesting night digging through the Shrieking Ninja's sensitive materials—real estate holdings, financial records, and clientele. Things like that. Instead, I'm treated to a close-up video of a man's sensitive materials, pulling out to reveal a woman kneeling in front of him.

"You see?" Bubbles says. "Sex tape."

I pause the video playback.

"Aww, c'mon. You might learn something."

"Scan every frame. Tell me what you learn."

"You're no fun."

"What I am, is—

Lightning flashes. Thunder rumbles.

But it doesn't stop.

"*Bubbles.*"

"I hear it." It takes her just a moment to analyze the sound. She comes to the same conclusion as me. "Three choppers in-bound from the north. ETA, one minute."

18

I slip into Madee's bedroom, rushing but silent, dressed, but shoeless. I put my hand on her shoulder intending to gently, but quickly, rouse her.

"Took you long enough," she says, rolling onto her back with a smile on her face.

I want to respond. Want to process what just happened. Want to follow through on what she thinks is about to happen, but...

"We have incoming," I say. "Thirty seconds out."

Madee flings herself out of bed wearing just underwear and leaving no doubt about exactly what she was hoping would happen. She tugs on a pair of pants she must have picked out for the morning, and she starts slipping into one of my old T-shirts.

I pick up her bra and hold it out. "Need this?"

She motions to her breasts. "I'm a B cup, dude. Bras are just for decoration." Helicopters thunder past, circling the treehouse.

"Bubbles, show me," I say, looking at my phone screen. Security feeds are displayed, snapping from one helicopter to the next. I was expecting Black Hawks overflowing with Spec-Ops guys. Maybe an Apache Longbow for backup. Instead, I see three retrofitted Black Hawks, painted with a red, white, and blue star that screams 'Texas' almost as much as the guys inside, who look like something out of G.I. Joe—cowboys dressed for combat, each and every damn one of them wearing a Stetson.

No way this is the U.S. military.

The first clue is that we're still breathing. While agencies often hire assassins for clandestine missions, at home and abroad, if they want someone dead, especially someone like me, a Reaper drone and a handful of Hellfire missiles gets the job done. But if they're not U.S. military, then, "Who the hell are..."

THESE FUCKING GUYS?

My first thought is Ghost, but if he'd put a tracking device on the car, Bubbles would have detected the signal. And the Shrieking Ninjas would never associate with bozos like these. They're loud and obvious, probably spending their down time shuttling between the gun range and a Cracker Barrel.

They might not be with the U.S. government, but the list of people who could find me here, in the treehouse, is limited to those with access to satellites. Whoever's in charge has been tracking us, via satellite, since we left San Diego. That's a lot of satellite time, and either required a network of the things, or the retasking of one—a monumental effort.

Which begs the question: Why?

"Bubbles," I say. "Are you done analyzing the sex tape?"

"Sex tape?" Madee asks.

"Other than the man being well endowed, and the woman being... flexible, nothing stands out. Though I suspect the man's face, revealed in the footage for just a single frame, is why they were interested. I don't believe the footage revealed a member of the clan, which would have been bad enough. I believe the man in the footage was their target."

"Is that worse?" Madee asks.

"Much," I say. "Preventing them from fulfilling a job they'd already accepted..." I shake my head.

"Can we give it back?"

"We can try, but if the job's deadline has passed, it won't matter. Plus, you'd then have to deal with whoever it was that hired you."

That explains why the Shrieks are after Madee, but what about These Fucking Guys? They have access to satellite tracking and very powerful support. If they're not here for Madee...

"They're here for me."

"What does that mean?" Madee asks.

"Means you need to go." I take hold of her arm and pull her toward the deck door.

"Bubbles," I say.

"Starting the car." She knows me so well.

"Run dark." Bubbles is fully capable of driving without lights, and since the car doesn't make any sound, there's a chance Madee will make it out of here in one piece. There's also a chance she'll never forgive me for what comes next.

"You're not coming?" she asks.

"I need answers."

"Can't you ask later?" she says. "You know, when you're not dead?"

"I'm not going to get killed by a bunch of...of...."

"Weekend Warriors," Bubbles suggests.

I like it.

"I'm not going to get killed by the..."

WEEKEND WARRIORS

"...and neither are you." I crouch down by her feet. Lit by flashes of lightning and the strobe effect of helicopter spotlights cutting through branches, Madee doesn't see the bungee cord in my hand, and she doesn't have time to react when I wrap the leg harness around her lower legs and cinch them together as tight as I can.

When I stand up, she says, "The hell are you doing?"

"Time to face those fears," I say.

"What f—"

I don't give her a chance to ask or to complain about the answer. Only way she's going over the edge, right this second, is with a little help. Okay, a lot of help. Arms under her pits, I hoist her up and toss her over the railing, shouting, "Sorry!" as she plummets into the dark.

Dad's shotgun is still empty and still in the car. And there are no other firearms in the home. They were never needed here. This isn't an official safe house. My parents and I never thought one of us would be fighting for their life in the treehouse. An oversight I should have corrected. What I do have...is Mom's sword.

Calling it a sword feels like an understatement. If Mom was telling the truth, and I never knew her to lie about anything, the blade she used to kill dozens of people is the legendary Sword of Mars, forged out of meteoric iron by the god of war himself and gifted to Attila the Hun. Believing the blade made him invincible in combat, Attila carried it into every battle until his death—of natural causes. I've sometimes wondered if Mom had taken it in the RV, would she have survived?

But I don't subscribe to fables and legends. Everything can be killed, mystical sword or not. And aside from some weird, mental mumbo-jumbo I can do...and Ghost can do...the weirdest thing on the planet is the bug-eyed, long-fingered, grub-eating aye-aye. Or Honey Boo Boo. Take your pick.

I slip back into the bedroom, as the helicopters hover overhead. They've figured out their approach.

Won't be long now.

I roll over the bed, still warm from Madee's body, place my hand against the wooden wall, and push. The wall indents, and then a small hidden door pops open, revealing a recess carved into the great tree.

The first time I opened this to get a look at the sword, I was fifteen. And I was promptly caught. Dad had me cutting wood for a month as punishment. Feels weird to be here now, taking it out of its sacred spot.

But Mom would want me to use it. And would probably be pleased that it was still doing the job for which Mars intended it: killing.

The double-edged blade is short by sword standards, just twenty inches, but its size and light weight made it a good choice for a small woman, like my Mom was. Coupled with an unbreakable blade and razor sharpness, it's an impressive weapon in anyone's hands.

In mine...

We'll see. I've never used it in combat.

Taking it from the wall feels a bit like I'm Arthur, pulling the sword from the stone, inheriting a kingdom's worth of responsibility. That weighs a lot more than the blade itself.

Boots land on the roof. Three helicopters. Three rooftops. They're no doubt hitting them all. I listen, counting the number of feet touching down. Six operators. Times three. Eighteen total. All of them armed, and me, injured, with a sword. I might be capable of maybe one or two mind bullets, but I'd rather not find out.

"Eighteen?" I ask.

"Yes."

"Okay. Let's try Operation: Demon Lighting."

"I was wondering if we'd ever get the chance. This is going to be fun."

"Eighteen men are about to die," I say.

"Annnd?"

"Never mind. Where's Madee?"

"A half mile away," Bubbles says. "No signs of pursuit. The road ahead does not appear to be blocked."

"Is she okay?"

"She is cursing a lot. In two languages. But she is unharmed."

I head for the door and step out into the thundering night. The men on the roof are loudly arguing about how to get down. They really didn't think this through.

"Jus' slide ov'r the edge!" shouts a Weekend Warrior, heavy on the Southern twang.

A pair of boots slide over the rooftop above me. He's got the right idea. The porch extends farther than the rooftop. A few more feet and he'll plop right down on his ass. Trouble is, he doesn't know I'm here. While he belly-shuffles down the angled roof, I throw the sword into the porch at my feet, turn toward the railing, and lift my hands to the sky like I'm about to make a sacrifice to Mars before using his sword.

When the cowboy's ankles reach my hands, I latch on and yank. He slides from the rooftop with a yelp, clears the balcony railing, and hits the ground three seconds later. To the men on the roof, their friend simply fell over the edge.

"You okay, Big Earl?"

I pull the blade out of the deck and say, "Ayuh!"

All around the circular deck, legs begin dangling over the edge, as the assault team follows Big Earl's lead.

"Jonas," Bubbles says. "We have a problem."

"A big one," I say, about to remove some cowboy legs.

"Bigger," she says, and that roots me in place. "On your phone."

Looking at the screen isn't a great idea. It could give away my position, and it will allow the cowboys to reach the deck. But if Bubbles thinks there is something I need to see that's more pressing then the Bubba Squad—*oh, that's a solid contender to 'Weekend Warriors'*—I trust her.

I look at the phone, and I'm surprised to see S-Chan displayed.

It's a job listing.

A snatch and grab, which generally means that whoever posted the job wants to look the mark in the eyes, maybe offer a smart remark, and gloat a little bit—sometimes a lot—before the trigger is pulled. Usually means it's personal. I don't take snatch and grabs. Not my style, but the price tag on this job...

Ten million dollars.

That's enough to pique anyone's interest. The trick is that it's on a declining scale, meaning the fee drops a million dollars for each day that passes. Whoever is offering this job, wants it done quickly.

My eyes flick through some of the details and freeze on the target's identity.

It's me.

79% approval from S-Chan members.

There's a toll booth photo of the Model S, with Madee in the front seat, singing along to something, and me, sound asleep in the back like an unprofessional chump. The car's details are included, along with its GPS transponder ID.

"What the fuck?" I say aloud.

Not far away, someone shouts, "He's over here!"

A message appears on the screen.

OTTO: GET OUT!

19

What the hell?
    What the fucking hell?
    How did this happen?
    Who posted the job?
    Why was it approved?
    Can't be Ghost or the Shrieks. They take care of their own business. If they wanted retribution, they wouldn't farm it out. That would be a massive kick in the nuts to their reputation. They'd commit seppuku long before paying someone else to finish a job they couldn't.

But that encounter exposed me.

Allowed me to be tracked to the treehouse.

Brought the Weekend Warriors to my door. And now... Now I've got 79% of S-Chan gunning for me.

"Jonas." It's Bubbles in my ear. "You need to focus."

"But we're—"

"I know," she says. "How do we get things done?"

The question pulls me out of my startled confusion. My father used to ask me the same thing when I felt overwhelmed.

"One thing at a time," I say, returning my attention to the cowboys dangling over the rooftops of my home. "Demon light me."

All around the aerial compound's exterior, thousands of hidden LED lights snap on—everywhere except for where I am. Bubbles knows exactly which lights to turn on and which to turn off, ensuring that while the cowboys are all lit in blazing white light, I move in complete darkness.

Sword of Mars in hand, I run around the deck surrounding my parents' quarters. Lights flick on and off. I move in darkness, while the cowboys exclaim in confusion.

"The hell is goin' on?" someone shouts.

"Git down on the deck!" comes a reply.

Men shout in surprise and pain as they slip off the rooftops and drop down onto the decks surrounding the treebound structures.

The man I reach first screams the loudest. And not because he's fallen. I run beneath him, unseen, swiping up with the sword, as he stretches his belly over the rooftop's edge. It's not a clean kill. Not a fair kill. But these assholes are invading my home and guaranteeing I can never return.

I'm going to make it hurt.

Going to send a message to whoever comes next.

Because I'm...

I don't have a callsign or a cool handle for myself. Others might have given me one on S-Chan, but the few people who have met the real me, rather than a legend? My name is...

JONAS

No last name. Which might work for a Weezer song, but it's pretty horrible for a world class assassin. I should probably pick a codename before someone else does.

Later. Right now, blood to spill, pain to deliver, lives to take.

All that good stuff.

I barely feel a tug on the mythical sword as it cuts through fabric, a few inches of fat, and fewer inches of muscle. The man plummets from the roof with a high-pitched squeal that's cut short when he lands flat on his back, unable to break his fall without letting go of his eviscerated midsection. He's an amateur, but he understands that his organs need to stay on the inside. It's a futile effort. He'll die of blood loss soon enough.

I reach the next man as he picks himself up off the floor. "What's going on with all the li—"

His question is cut short, as the cut to his neck goes deep.

I continue around the porch, cloaked in perpetual darkness. My next target lies ahead, bathed in light, but on his feet and searching for a target. Despite being new to the game, the Weekend Warriors have clearly sunk a lot of money into their gear. They've got the best body armor on the market, jam-packed with enough magazines to ensure a sword strike to the heart would fail.

Means my strikes need to be arterial.

Means this is going to be messy.

This one is holding a decked-out AR-15. If he tags me with it, I'm done. So, when he turns in my direction, eyes widening at the approaching darkness, I hurl the sword ahead of me.

The spinning weapon slides out of the darkness, glinting in the light for a rotation, and then it disappears inside the man's face.

As he topples away from me, I leap forward, land on his chest, pull the sword from his corpse, and dive roll past him. All of it is unseen. Darkness follows in my wake, the three bodies hidden from view. In the chaos of bright lights, rotor wash, and a thunderstorm, these good ol' boys have yet to figure out they're dropping like... Well, they're dropping like middle-aged yahoos who eat too much butter and overestimate their worth on a battlefield—not to mention in a treetop brawl with a killer trained from birth. Or whatever age my memories begin at.

It's probably bad that I'm smiling. Just a little bit. Last night, the fight was set to 'difficult.' Tonight, it's set to 'easy.' On my home turf, holding Mom's legendary weapon, I feel kind of invulnerable.

For the moment.

The knowledge that I'm screwed still lingers at the back of my mind, but in the carpe-diem, get-shit-done, front of my brain? I needed this.

What good is a depressed assassin, anyway?

In between the clap of helicopters and the thunder, there's a brief moment of silence. As I approach the next man in line, he hears my feet thumping against the wood. He can't see me, but he understands two truths, the first of which he shouts out, "He's here!" and the second of which I follow through on, slicing open his carotid artery as I run past.

He twists and falls to the floor, on his way to meet his maker, or the other guy. But he's a vindictive S.O.B. and manages to fire off a few rounds. The bullets aren't even close to hitting me, but anyone who missed his shouted warning now knows where the action is, including the two men remaining on this deck.

"Open a window for me," I say, and without pausing to make sure Bubbles followed through, I dive left, leaving the porch behind. The large windows all shift to the side, allowing the space to be totally open. Feels great on a summer night. Allows for total freedom of movement between interior and exterior. Best of all, the powered windows move without making a sound.

Inside the dark bedroom, the two men still on the deck are easy to see. Both are aiming their weapons at the deck's darkness.

One of them shouts, "Light 'em up!" and both pull their triggers, unleashing a staccato stream of rifle fire that slips through the night, chews up the wood, and finishes off their bleeding-out friend.

Thunder and gunfire cloak the sound of my approach. Firing like they are, they'll eat through their rounds in just a few seconds. The smart assassin would wait until they had to reload, but I have no interest in being smart.

Brutal. Efficient.

Creative.

But not smart.

The transition from interior to deck is smooth. I slide across the floor and kick out a foot, striking one of the two men in the back of his knee. Finger still clutching the trigger, he spills backward, bullets thundering up into the ceiling and then—into his partner.

The shot man takes two in the armored chest and then one in the leg, falling back with a shout. He attempts to shoot me with his few remaining bullets, but I lean over and hack off his hand with a single swing. If he's not a complete idiot, he could survive the wound, so I leave him be. I need one of these bozos to live and tell the tale.

His buddy, the one who shot him, well, he's not as fortunate. I kick him in the head to stun him, and then shove him under the bottom railing and over the side. He screams all the way down, his impact punctuated by a clap of thunder.

Lightning reveals me, back on my feet, standing over the survivor, who is stunned, staring at his bleeding stump.

I crouch beside him. "What's your name?"

"Jim."

"Just Jim? Not Jim-Bob or Jimmy Jangle or something catchy?"

"Just Jim."

"Okay, Just Jim, here's the situation. You're going to bleed out without a tourniquet, which I will provide, if you answer a few simple questions."

"O-okay. Yeah. Sure."

"Eloquent response." I unlace his boot. "A single lie will not be tolerated. Understood?"

He nods.

I wrap the lace around his wrist, several times around. "Who sent you?"

Shouts reach out to me from the main living quarters. The remaining eleven men have congregated there and are coming this way. They'll need to cross a rope bridge to reach me, but their bullets won't have any trouble crossing the distance.

If they see me.

All the lights in this portion of the compound are now out, but lightning is not my friend. It'll expose me sooner or later. So, I get right to the important stuff. "Who sent you?"

"I...I don't know. I'm not in charge."

Fair enough.

"Who *is* in charge?"

He glances to the side, to the portion of deck where his partner had been lying before I punted him over the edge.

Shit.

"Tell me what you know."

"It was a phone call. From an old friend. A buddy from his military days."

"What branch?" I ask.

He shakes his head. "I don't know. But they did clandestine shit. Top Secret. He wasn't allowed to talk about it, even now. Said if he did, they'd find him and end him."

"Why would he come here, then?"

"The money," he says. "Ten million."

"Ten million?"

"That's almost five hundred K each."

Eighteen operators. Three pilots. Twenty-one men sent on a mission destined to fail. No doubt put together by the same individual, or organization, that put up ten million dollars for my capture—a former operator with a top-secret history.

I glance up, like I'm talking to God again. "Why send the Weekend Warriors first?"

"They're a distraction," Bubbles says.

"W-who are you talking to?" Jim asks. He can't hear her replies in my ear, but I'm clearly speaking to someone other than him.

"A mind-reading witch," I reply.

"Humans are predictable," Bubbles says. "Also, there is a fourth helicopter approaching from the south. ETA, three minutes."

I turn to Jim. "There's a fourth helo inbound. They with you?" I ask.

He shakes his head. I pull the knot as tight as I can, stemming the flow of blood. His shout of pain is drowned out by rotor wash and thunder. "Sit out the rest of this, and you'll make it. Even look at me again—"

Jim nods, frantic.

He values his life more than five hundred thousand.

"Do you need to kill them all?" he asks, worried for his friends.

"What would you do if armed men broke into to your home?"

Jim's face falls flat. He's been steeped in gun culture. He knows the score. If your home is invaded, the gloves come off, guilt free. I pluck a magazine from his armor, pick up his assault rifle, and swap out the mag. Then I chamber a round and stand up. "You're damn fucking right I do."

20

"Bubbles," I say, eyeing what little I can see of the sky from the south. Can't see shit. Can't hear much either. If the newcomer is running dark, I probably won't know they're here, until it's too late. Need to bug out...

...after I clean up the house.

"Yes, Jonas?"

"I want to do this quickly."

"May I suggest leaving then? Let the Weekend Warriors deal with whoever's coming. It would be the intelligent move."

That last bit was a dig. She already knows I'm locked on target. Too late to abort.

"A message needs to be sent."

"A harshly worded e-mail perhaps?"

I shake my head.

"This is where you say something cool, right?" she asks. "Like, 'It needs to be written in blood.'"

Goddamnit. That's exactly what I was going to say.

"Just... Ugh. Let's mix things up. Operation: Demon Lighting and Operation: Bug Hunt combo."

"Okay," Bubbles says. "If you'd led with that, I wouldn't have suggested leaving. This is going to be poetry."

Bubbles and I have a lot of down time together. We've come up with nearly a hundred different operations and have practiced them all. Not in actual combat, but Demon Lighting and Bug Hunt go well together. And the treehouse is one of the few locations in which we could pull them both off.

"Ready?" I ask, sliding Mom's sword into my belt. Jim's AR will work best for what comes next.

"I have no need for preparation," she says.

I glance down at Jim. His uninjured forearm is covering his eyes, severed hand clutched in his grasp, hopeful it can be reattached. His legs are shaking, and I think he might be crying.

Damnit.

"Why are you hesitating?" Bubbles asks.

"They're clueless," I say, listening to the men shout back and forth, consumed by confusion. They invaded my home. Endangered myself and my guest. But they're also being used. Were sent here to die. They're pawns. Probably with families. Like puppies sent to kill a crocodile.

"I fail to see how that's not beneficial."

"It's impossible for you to," I say.

"Try me," she says.

"Empathy."

She's quiet for a moment. And then almost sounds sad. "You are correct. Are we leaving, then?"

I shake my head. "Still need to send a message. Same plan, just... dialed down a notch or two."

Lightning flashes, exposing me. Before any of the cowboys can find me, crouched behind the rail, I say, "Go."

Shots thunder from the treehouse's far side, flashing brightly in the night. It draws the Weekend Warriors' full attention. They shout and clamber toward the sound of Vasquez's gunfire, sampled from the movie *Aliens*, made more believable by the strobe effect Bubbles is creating in time with the reports.

I hurry across the rope bridge, whipped by wind that forces me to hold onto the railing with one hand. Darkness follows me.

All around, space marines do battle with imaginary xenomorphs. And these Stetson-wearing yahoos actually start returning fire.

When I pull my trigger, no one notices.

The first target goes down with a shout no one hears, clutching his missing trigger finger. I put a second round in his leg to keep him down and distracted. None of these guys care enough, or are disciplined enough, to fight through the pain.

Darkness swallows the man.

He doesn't even see me pass by.

I go to work on his buddies, wounding and disarming, using two rounds on each man. Gun hand, leg. Gun hand, leg. They drop one at a time, completely oblivious to what's actually happening.

Just sixty seconds into Operation: 'Confuse the Shit Out of the Enemy,' eight men are laid out on the deck, clutching wounds and shouting in pain. They're all disarmed, their weapons on the ground a hundred fifty feet below. None of them saw me come. Not one of them saw me go.

But the three remaining men figured out the ruse and have taken cover inside the living room.

"Show yourself!" one of them shouts. "We know yer out there!"

They're protected by bulletproof glass and wood. Can't do much about the home's framework, but there are the windows. "Air the place out."

Bubbles understands the request. Probably anticipated it. The large windows slide open, exposing two of the men.

"Light them up."

All the lights inside the living room snap on as bright as they can go. The three men might as well be wearing neon signs.

I squeeze off four rounds.

Two of them drop, shouting in pain and fear.

The last man lies low, protected by the home's framing. And unlike many of his friends, he's got some nerve and some tactical ability. He rolls out into the open door and fires fifteen rounds. Good aim, too. If I hadn't relocated after dropping those two men, he'd have tagged me.

He rolls back inside before I can take a shot.

Not interested in dragging out a game of cat and mouse, I say, "Give him a headache."

The living room fills with a dizzying light show coupled with deafening heavy metal, shrill screams, and what I think might be a recording of me singing in the shower. The man rolls into view, eyes clenched shut, hands over his ears.

I cross over on the rope bridge.

"ETA on the newcomer?"

"One minute."

"Cancel all operations. Lights low."

The compound goes quiet and mostly dark. The living room glows a gentle orange. I walk in and stand over the man, a dark silhouette framed by orange light. "Are you right-handed?"

"W-what?" he says.

"What hand do you use to write?"

He opens his right hand, just a little. A reflex.

I put a bullet in it, and then cut his scream short by putting my last round in his leg. Wouldn't want any of them feeling left out. I feel like I should give a speech, or a warning, but these guys' days of rootin'-tootin' gun-shootin' are over. Going to hurt to squeeze a trigger from this day out, and if they do, they'll remember this moment. Firing a gun won't make them feel powerful in the future, it will just remind them how weak they actually are.

I drop my rifle to the floor and kick his away. "You can thank Jim for me not killing you."

"Incoming," Bubbles says, and a moment later, a fireball fills the sky. One of the helicopters has been struck by a missile.

The incoming helicopter is *not* a transport. It's a gunship.

The struck chopper's fiery carcass falls between the trees supporting the house. Its rotors sever one of the three bridges connecting everything. It slams into the ground with a second explosion, igniting the forest floor. Won't be long until flames are eating up the massive trunks and devouring the surrounding woods. It's been dry the past few weeks. The damage is going to be catastrophic, if someone doesn't get this fire under control, ASAP.

"Call it in," I say.

"What? To who?" the man beneath me asks.

"Not talking to you," I say, and I step away to look up at the sky above.

The two remaining helos peel away, one of them a little faster than the other, which is struck by a second missile. The helicopter's back end comes away, leaving the chopper to spiral out of control, as it cants sideways and falls into the tree supporting my room. It crashes down through the Plinko-peg branches, leaving fire in its wake before dropping onto the roof of my room, a massive flaming torch, lighting everything in flickering light.

The pilot, who survived the fall only to find himself set on fire, lunges out of the chopper, stumbles a few feet, and falls to a merciful death far below.

Booming helicopter blades draw my attention back up. The black attack helicopter flies through the three redwoods, cloaked by smoke, on a collision course with the ground.

The hell? Did the pilot just fail a kamikaze mission?

The chopper's rotors break against the trees as it passes through. Then it sails out of sight, crashing a few hundred feet away, creating yet another fireball that all but ensures the blaze will destroy a massive amount of terrain and eventually homes.

The answer to my question floats gently into view. A man, clad head to toe in tactical black, parachutes onto the roof of my parents' quarters. The chute is on fire, but the man seems unfazed. He lands, sheds the chute, and turns toward me.

The man on the floor beside me is just as taken aback by the stranger's dramatic entrance as I am. "Who the hell is that?" he asks. Then his head and torso crumple in, as though compressed in King Kong's fist.

21

"Who the hell is this?"

"Unknown," Bubbles says. "But I suggest not screwing around."

She's right. Unlike the Weekend Warriors, the newcomer is a pro.

I look down at the body.

A pro capable of making a man look like he's been run over by a monster truck.

I focus on his head, feel the pressure build, and then snap my mental fingers, unleashing a mind bullet that slaps my target's head back. The pain is far worse than usual, but nothing I can't handle. Once.

Easy-peasy-lemon—

The man stands tall again. Cracks his neck one way and then the other. Then he hops down from the roof and lands in front of the bridge.

I'm stunned.

He took a mind bullet to the brain and resisted it.

For the first time in my life that I can remember, I'm intimidated. The person has abilities like me and Ghost, but far more powerful, and capable of being used offensively and defensively.

He starts across the walkway. Wind and rain slash across him, but he doesn't bother with the handrails. Just maintains his perfect balance.

"You're outclassed, Jonas. I suggest retreat."

Bubbles isn't wrong. But I don't think retreat is possible at this point.

"Who are you?" I ask.

"You don't remember me?" The voice is surprisingly feminine, and very Russian.

Remember her?

Is she another person from my past? Like Ghost? How many of us are there?

She reaches up and peels off her mask to reveal a prettier Dolph Lundgren with murder in her eyes. Not a trace of fear. She views me the same way I did the cowboys. Easy pickings.

"I expected more," she says. "After what you did in San Diego. But..." She glances at the two surviving cowboys on the floor behind me. Clenches her eyes shut for a moment. Both men compress like empty cans, bones cracking, screams squelched. "You are weak. Mind, body, and soul."

Seeing her face, hearing her accent, and seeing what she can do completes the mental picture, and I know who she is, or at least what I call her on S-Chan. This is...

IRON MAIDEN

Based on her phrasing, Bubbles was able to determine that her first language was likely Russian, and that she was a woman. But her way of killing people—crushing them—is what always stood out the most. It gets the job done. Leaves an impression, but it's not subtle. When she kills a person, it's to send a message. I always imagined she used some kind of hydraulic device, but she's like me, crushing people with telekinesis.

"I have questions," I say, doing my best to not look threatening.

"You can ask when we get home."

Home?

"Where is home?"

She smiles at me. Shakes her head. Disappointment radiates from her. "Rho was unwise with choice in colleagues, and comparatively weak, but he was not without skill. How did you injure him so gravely?"

She's talking about Ghost, confirming that he's still alive.

"His name is Rho?"

She squints at me. "You really remember nothing?"

"Starting to feel like I was the only one drinking at a ten-year bender. I don't remember Rho, I don't remember whatever the hell 'home' is, and I definitely don't remember you."

"Zeta," she says.

Greek letters. She's sixth down the list. Rho is seventeenth.

"And who am I?"

She smiles. "You... You can come peacefully, with all of your limbs intact, or...not. I personally hope you—"

I swing hard and fast, aiming for her temple. One solid swing will put her on her ass, abilities or not. It takes a quarter of a second for the average human being to react to something after seeing it. My strike will land 50 milliseconds before her mind can react.

But she doesn't need to.

My fist snaps to a stop three inches from the side of her head.

Rather than gawk and wonder why, I attempt a second strike to her side, and when that fails, I aim low with a kick, intending to invert her knee. All three strikes hit what best can be described as an invisible exercise mat.

She's got a damn telekinetic force field.

It's absorbing the kinetic energy from my strikes, but it's not like hitting a concrete wall. Has some give to it.

How much energy can it withstand?

Without pausing, I roll back, snatch a dead man's assault rifle, and lift it, finger already pulling the trigger.

The weapon crumples in my hands, making what I did to Madee's handgun look like a silly trick.

I back away into the living room as the Iron Maiden struts toward me, malevolent mischief in her eyes. She mocks whoever sent her here, saying, "'He has so much potential. Don't underestimate him. He is more powerful than he lets on.' Ha! You are as pitiful as I've always known you to be. Like ant."

"I don't like this one at all," Bubbles says in my ear.

"Uh-huh."

"I wonder how well that mental barrier works when she's distracted," Bubbles says.

"I like the way you think," I say.

Zeta pauses. "You like...being called ant?"

"Oh, hey. Right. That probably sounded kind of sadomasochistic or something, huh? I wasn't talking to you."

She looks around the space. Other than the folded-up men on the floor, and those still writhing in agony outside, we're alone. "Speaking... to whom?"

"My ghost," I say.

I meant it as a joke, buying a little time, readying myself for the pain that's about to hit me like a tsunami. But she isn't laughing.

"I think a little intimidation is in order," Bubbles says.

I want to argue with her. To explain to her that people like this can't be intimidated. But I don't need to. I swear, Bubbles can read my mind. "Lights and sound. Just point. I'll do the rest. And when you're ready for the grand finale, do like a Raiden kind of thing, like you're shooting lightning from your hands."

"I don't know," I say. It all sounds a little over-the-top silly, given the circumstances.

"Stop speaking to ghost," Zeta says, and I feel pressure around my neck. Chick is force-choking me.

"Nicolas Cage the hell out of this, okay?" Bubbles says.

My response is a gurgle, and as my eyes start to bulge, I thrust a hand out at the ceiling. The lights flare alongside a burst of *Mars, the Bringer of War* by Gustav Holst, just before it builds to a crescendo, and I know exactly where Bubbles is going with this.

I do the same with the other hand, adding a manic smile to my bugged-out eyes, knowing that while I'm bullshitting, Zeta could crumple me into a ball. The only reason I'm still alive is because the job is not a kill order. I'm supposed to be breathing when I'm delivered.

Music bursts again, the lights flaring bright enough for Zeta to squint, the music loud enough to make her wince.

And then it comes. The moment Bubbles has been building toward. I thrust my hands out like I'm the Third Storm, Lightning, from *Big Trouble in Little China.*

Every light in the place flickers fast enough to be nauseating. The music booms in time. *Baaaaaah, baaah baaaaah!*

The invisible hand clutching my throat disappears.

Zeta has her eyes shut, hands to her ears.

I'm going to probably have tinnitus for the next few days, but I resist the urge to cover my ears. Instead, I use this momentary distraction to press the attack.

Feeling pretty good about my chances, I get a running start, leap into the air, and aim my flying kick at her head. In my mind's eye, she spawls back, goes over the railing like Simone Biles off a vault, and falls to her death. In reality...

A brick wall of energy slaps me across the room, shatters every light bulb in my wake, and decimates the speaker system. I hit the floor, slide across it, and come to an abrupt and painful stop when my head collides with the wall.

22

I'm cold.

Always cold. Always desperate. Always angry.

A hand covers my mouth.

My eyes snap open. I'm ready for a fight, but I relax when I see who's standing above me. She shushes me and then removes her hand from my mouth.

I peel off my single wool blanket and sit up in my bed, moving slowly, so the old springs don't creak and wake up the others.

There are twenty-four of us, our thin beds filling the large room that once served as a dining room for rich people. Now, it's a dorm room with high, ornate ceilings and three chandeliers for lighting. Outside the tall, arched windows, there's just a hint of purple in the night sky. An hour until the sun reflects off the foot of snow covering the grounds, and blazes through the glass, waking the others.

Zeta picks up my clothing from the chest at the end of my bed and tosses it into my lap. Then she tilts her head toward the exit. When I don't move, she repeats the gesture, this time bugging her eyes out.

She's only a few months older than me, but more than a foot taller. I technically outrank her, but when it's just the two of us, there's no doubting who's in charge.

I slip into my clothes, which have been washed and starched and feel like cardboard wrapped in sandpaper. If it wasn't so cold, I'd probably forgo clothing. I sneak out of the room on stocking feet, following Zeta into the hall.

"What are we doing?" I whisper.

She shushes me again and points to a shifting shadow at the hallway's far end. Someone is coming.

We slide to either side of the hall, both of us pressing ourselves against the walls, hidden behind two Doric pillars. They line the hall, rising from the polished marble floor. Everything about this old home speaks of excess, but those days are long behind it. Where there should be feasts, there are scraps. Where there should be help, there is hardship. Where there should be comfort, there is pain in the form of training, all day, and sometimes all night.

Which is why our early morning foray better be worthwhile.

I'm still bruised from the previous day's beating. A lesson in restraint, they said. Passing meant not fighting back. But I think they just like beating kids.

They say it makes us stronger.

Doesn't feel like it.

The guard strolls down the hallway, his keys jangling, humming a tune. Bored. Mind elsewhere. But he's still coming this way, and once he passes these pillars, we'll be easy to spot.

If we get caught...yesterday will feel like a dream.

He's just a few steps away now. I press myself into the wall, holding my breath, trying to become one with the old hardwood paneling. Zeta has other ideas.

She focuses on the classroom door, just as the guard walks parallel to it. Inside, what sounds like the teacher's can of pencils falls from a desk and rolls across the floor. The guard's boots squeak as he stops. Turns toward the door. Listening.

Inside, the can rolls across the floor, shedding pencils.

The guard approaches the door, peers through the window, and then unlocks the door. When he steps into the darkness, we make our move, slipping past him, around the corner, down the steps, and to the front door.

A draft wafts through the door's seams, sending goosebumps springing up on my arms.

"I'm not going outside," I say.

She rolls her eyes, and in a thick Russian accent she says, "So much for you being strongest of us."

"Strong doesn't mean stupid," I say.

She shrugs. "You're just going to have to trust me."

We have a staring competition.

Behind us, the hallway lights up, illumination spilling out of the classroom as the guard inspects it.

I take my coat from one of twenty-four hooks and slip it on. It's barely enough to keep me alive during the day. At night...we're not going to make it far. But I do trust her. Whatever she's up to, it's not going to kill us. Though it will likely result in a beating.

I tug on my boots. "This better be worth it."

She grabs the back of my jacket and lifts me to my feet, impossibly strong for a nine-year-old. "Is worth it."

We slip out into the night, gently closing the door behind us and making sure it's not locked. Three steps through the new snow and I'm already regretting my choices. Back in bed, I didn't think I could get colder. But now I'm longing for that bed, as the icy wind slips through every chink in my clothing's armor, burning my skin.

"How far?" I ask.

She points. "Over there."

I don't see anything. Just a flat coating of snow where the long driveway meets the street, which leads to a world I have studied, but have never seen.

"Hold on," she says, running to the driveway's edge, digging into the snow beside a bush. She returns a moment later, a victorious smile on her face and a crowbar in her hand.

"You've done this before?" I ask.

"Once," she says. "I couldn't keep it to myself."

At the driveway's end, she slips between the bars of the gate meant to keep people out. I follow her through and watch, as she counts out steps into the road. Ten paces out, she stops. "Come help me."

She drops to her knees and starts shoving snow away. I follow suit, and thirty seconds later we've cleared a patch, revealing a manhole cover.

I wince. "A sewer?"

She hooks the crowbar under the metal lid and with a grunt, she hauls it up and away, revealing darkness below. "Another world."

A flashlight appears in her hand.

She shines it down to reveal a ladder leading to a wide-open tunnel, through which a trickling stream flows. She holds the flashlight out to me. "I will go first."

I aim the light down into the sewer while she descends. When she reaches the bottom, I drop the light down and follow her.

The first thing I notice inside the sewer is the smell. It's as bad as I imagined. Like standing over a latrine pit. The second thing I notice is that it's warm. Not just warmer than outside; it's warmer than my bed. Feels like Spring.

I quickly forget the smell and follow Zeta through the tunnels. There are arrows scratched into the walls, left behind from her first visit. We follow them for ten minutes without talking. And then the muffled sound of the tunnels grows louder with the rush of flowing water.

"They're down here," she says.

"They?"

She presses onward, clinging to her secret until the very last moment.

Then she stands aside, aims the flashlight at her face, and raises her eyebrows twice. "Are you ready?" she asks, but I can barely hear her over the rush of water.

Not wanting to shout, I just nod.

She waves me closer, and then turns the flashlight forward, illuminating a great concrete junction where several sewer lines meet. Some of them are dry. Some look like small waterfalls. The floor of the space is covered in heaps of debris collected over the years, probably washed to this location during storms. But none of that holds my attention.

There are rats.

Hundreds of them.

Exploring. Fighting. Squeaking. And they have no fear of us, or the light.

"Why are we here?" I ask. The sewers are...interesting. The warmth is delightful. But the rats... They're repulsive.

"Watch," she says, tracking a rat with the flashlight. She reaches her empty hand out, and then she makes a sudden fist. The illuminated rat shrieks, as it's crushed into a ball. It drops to the floor, dead, and is immediately set upon by others. While the cannibalistic rats tear into Zeta's target, she turns to me and says, "Target practice."

I've never used my abilities on a living target before, but I'm excited to see what happens.

She gives me a playful shove and says, "C'mon, show me what you got, Gamma."

23

I snap awake, the chill of that resurfaced memory replaced by heat at my back.

The fire is spreading.

Before I can fully process this slice of my forgotten past, the furniture separating present-day Zeta from me parts like the Red Sea, crashing into walls and windows.

"I remember you," I say, struggling to stand. My head is pounding from the one-two punch of attempting another mind bullet and then being thrown into a wall. I need a Pez dispenser full of Advil. Maybe something stronger.

"Hard to forget, no?" She steps toward me. "But you did. Because you are like everyone else."

"We were friends," I say. "At...a school? I think it was a school."

"School... Prison..." She shrugs. "And neither."

"I remember the sewers. That night in the snow."

She pauses.

"Are you buying time," Bubbles says, "or did you actually remember something that might stop this bulldozer of a woman?"

Responding would probably set the Iron Maiden off, so I ignore Bubbles. I've got Zeta hooked. I need to reel her in. Might be the only way I walk away from this.

"I remember sneaking out. How you distracted the guard. How fucking cold it was outside, but how warm it was down there. And... I remember the rats." An image of a crushed-up rat fills my mind. That's going to be me.

"What do you remember of rats?" she asks.

"Target practice," I say. "And..."

She waits.

"My name. You called me 'Gamma.'"

"Because Gamma is your name. Not..."

"Jonas," I say.

"Jonas." The disgust in her voice when she says my name—given to me by Mom and Dad—is on par with licking clean an old cat turd dropped in a sandbox, left to bake in the sun.

"I don't remember it," I admit, but I think I understand the significance. Children inside that facility were like me—telekinetic. And they were ranked by the strength of their ability. Rho, who was pretty freaking dangerous, was ranked 17. Zeta is fifth. And somehow, me and my puny-by-comparison mind bullet were third.

"Do you remember how that night ended?" she asks.

I shake my head. "You shook the memory loose. It ended at the rats."

"Mmm. Then let me fill in the gaps." She steps closer. Menacing. "You fled. Left me in the dark, alone. And when I returned to the school, six hours later, you were gone. Never to be seen again. *We* left the door unlocked. *We* distracted the guard. *We* gave the enemy access. But *I* was punished for these things. Punished enough for both of us."

She unbuckles and tears away her body armor. Then she pulls her shirt off, revealing a muscular physique—covered in long, straight scars. The kind deep razor blade cuts leave. "Alpha did this to me. Punishment for my crimes. And your cowardice."

She looks around the living space, lit by the fire's glow. "Is this where you've been hiding? It's quaint."

"I don't hide," I say. "And I don't remember..."

She steps closer again.

"Look..." I motion to her scars. "That looks admittedly painful. And you've been blaming me for a long time. But whatever you have assumed about me—you don't know me. I'm not that person anymore."

"I am pleased to hear you say that," she says. "I take no pleasure in hurting friends."

"Jonas," Bubbles says, her voice a warning.

I raise my hands.

"Look, I'll let you take me in. I want answers, and that's probably the only way it will happen, right? No need to break my bones."

"The hell are you doing?" Bubbles asks. "I'm out of tricks, by the way. Electricity is out. No lights. No speakers. Emergency services are en route, but we're in the middle of nowhere. It's going to be a long time before help arrives and they're not really going to be any help against Iron Maiden."

Thank you, I think, *for stating the obvious.* All I really want is for Zeta, who had serious issues long before she was cut up, to let her guard down a little.

She sneers. "You would surrender?"

"That's what I'm saying, yes."

"Pitiful," she says, and she swings out a back-hand strike that misses by a mile until a half second later when a telekinetic wave bitch slaps me to the side.

"I thought," I say, picking myself up. "...you needed me...alive..."

"I have been punished for your death once already," she says. "The first time destroyed the child I was. This time...I will delight in it."

The moment I'm back on my feet, glancing down at the Sword of Mars still held within my belt, Zeta thrusts both hands out toward me. A wave of energy lifts my body up and flings it against the wall.

But I don't feel any of it.

And I see it all happen from the outside.

I'm incorporeal again. She knocked my consciousness right out of my body. And she has no idea.

She stalks toward my unconscious form, fists clenched, murder in her eyes. She's going to beat me to death with her fists.

"Stop," I say, but she can't hear me.

I stand in front of her, blocking her path. Unlike Rho, whose abilities allowed him access to consciousness, Zeta is telekinetic to the core, and can't feel my presence at all. She passes straight through me, feeling nothing.

But *I* feel something.

A strange energy, vaguely tangible.

I'm conscious outside the confines of my physical mind, but am I able to access my telekinetic abilities?

I focus on Zeta's head, but I don't feel the connection I normally would before unleashing a mind bullet. I'm free of the physical world, but telekinetically impotent.

Zeta closes in on my helpless form. Crouches down, lifts me by my shirt, and cocks a fist back.

Then she punches.

Reflex guides me. I reach out and catch the back of her arm, holding it in place. Her shield doesn't work on me in this form. She's stunned for a moment, but then glances back, looking right through me. "I see you haven't forgotten everything."

I've done this before?

She yanks free of my grasp that's as strong here as it is in life, and she attempts to slug my physical face again.

This time I grasp her shoulders and haul her back, tossing her across the floor. She turns the slide into a roll, coming back to her feet, facing me down, eyes burning with rage.

Feels strange, standing between an assassin and my own body, while my childhood home burns down around us—a hundred fifty feet in the air. I need to end this and get down to the ground before the whole place drops.

"You think I need to touch you to kill you?" she says, and then she launches another telekinetic blast that slams my body against the wall. When she reaches back to strike me again, I charge, head down, shoulder forward.

Just as Zeta's hands come forward, I collide with her midsection, lift her off the ground, and slam her onto the hard floor, knocking the wind out of her. I lift a fist, hoping to knock her out with a solid slug, but I'm yanked off my feet and dragged across the room by an unseen force.

My body is pulling me back.

"No, no, no!" I shout, and I'm slammed back into myself, fully awake and aware of the pain dispensed while I was outside myself.

"I wasn't ready," I groan.

"What happened?" Bubbles asks.

"Another out-of-body experience," I say.

"I suggest using your real body and getting the hell out."

"Way ahead of you," I say, and I push myself up. Slowly. Way too frikken slowly. "Ouch. Shit. Ouch."

Everything hurts. But nothing is broken. *Push through the pain,* I tell myself. *Heal when you're not dead.*

But Zeta's not out. If anything, she looks pleased.

Back on her feet, she cracks her neck one way and then the other. Before she can take a fighting stance, I throw myself at her, swinging twice, once to put her on the defensive, a second time to confirm her telekinetic wall is still in place. After striking the forcefield, I follow with the same spinning round-house kick, but this time it's a ruse, predestined to fail.

Legend has it that the war god's blade is capable of cutting through anything. I'm about to put that to the test. During the spin, I reach down to my hip, draw the Sword of Mars, and swing it out. It slips through the telekinetic shell, and then through Zeta's leg.

She lifts a hand to blast me back, but I move faster, dive rolling to her side and then poking the Sword of Mars through her side. It's not a kill shot. By design. I can't kill someone who might actually be important to me, even if I can't remember it. Even if she wants me dead.

She lies on the floor, clutching her side.

"I'm sorry I'm not who you wanted me to be," I say. "And that you were hurt because of me."

When I back out of the living space and onto the deck, she screams, "Get back here!"

I can hear her, climbing back to her feet, ready to fight to the death. But she's too late. I'm already halfway to the ground. As the fiery bungee cord wrapped around my ankles stretches out, nearly at its full length, it snaps, releasing me and dropping me into the inferno waiting below.

24

Flames sting my skin. Smoke rakes my lungs raw. And my insides feel like slush. My muscles twitch. My bones ache. The world around me goes blurry with each beat of my heart.

I probably shouldn't be alive, but determination keeps my blood flowing.

The flames match my hobbling pace down the long dirt road leading from the blazing remains of my childhood home, to the 101. Hell nips at my heels, each flare of heat pushing me closer to the freeway, which will serve as a firebreak.

"You...still with...me?" I ask.

"I've alerted authorities to your position," Bubbles says. "But your phone is at one percent."

"If you alerted the authorities, you also alerted—"

"You're going to die," she says, and she sounds something close to worried. "Only way you stand a chance is if we take the risk."

"Mmm," I say.

"I also reported your position in a hundred other locations throughout the state," she says. "It will take time to find the real you."

A chuckle sends daggers through my lungs. "What would I do without you?"

"You'd be dead."

"That wasn't a joke, was it?"

"Mathematical fact," she says. "In the past two days, I have—"

"Okay, okay. I get it. Thank you."

"I don't need your thanks," she says. "I need you to survive. That means no more stupid choices. No more risking your life to get useless information. No more showboating."

"I can astral project myself," I say. "That's a pretty useful thing to know."

"Not if you're dead," she says.

"I know my real name."

"Gamma," she says. "I heard. Did you learn anything else of significance?"

"I lived...in a school. A mansion really. Twenty-four kids like me. Telekinetic to one degree or another. Iron Maiden back there, Zeta, she was my friend. And we were..." I think back to the rats. To the way I felt when I saw Zeta crush one. I wasn't afraid, or disgusted. I was... delighted. "I think we were evil. I think *I* was evil."

"I fail to see how that's useful information," Bubbles says. "Our connection will be lost in thirty seconds."

I fall to my knees beside the freeway, aware of flashing lights coming my way. I draw the Sword of Mars from my hip and shove it beneath dirt and loose stone. "The sword is buried at the end of the drive." I find the rarest stone I can and place it atop the site. "There is a white rock, vaguely shaped like a wolf's head, marking the spot."

"Understood."

"How is Madee?"

"Safe."

"Where is she?"

"Mobile. But the Tesla is a liability. We are searching for alternatives and will—" Her voice gets garbled and robotic before fading away. I don't bother checking my phone. I know it's dead.

And for the first time in several years, I'm...alone.

It's not a good feeling for several confusing reasons.

The foremost of which is that I was alone before. Bubbles isn't a real person, but she is the intelligence I'm most connected to in the world. I feel a little lost without her. And that means I've become dependent on her, even now, to keep me alive, to save me from danger, to find me love.

Pretty pitiful, Jonas.

I crawl out onto the pavement, bathed in incoming headlights. Tires shriek, and I lie down on the hard, cool surface, listening to the crack and snap of burning wood. What I could remember of my childhood began and ended in that magical home. Now it's gone for good, replaced by the cold and dark realization that the home I lived in before that was a freaking nightmare.

A tear rolls from my eye to the pavement, as my cheek presses against it.

"Sorry," I whisper to Mom and Dad, and then I can't help but smile. "See you soon."

A dandelion comes into focus, growing up out of a crack in the pavement, resisting the crush of car tires, scorching summer heat, and the lack of soil. I reach for it, brushing its delicate yellow petals with my fingertip. "Hey there, little guy."

I admire its resolve.

Boots rush up to me.

"Wait," I say, but I'm too late. The dandelion is crushed underfoot.

The small medic struggles to roll me over. She calls for help, and a large man arrives, winded but strong. I'm rolled onto my back.

Their faces are blurred-out blotches. The bodies like specters framed by a hellish sky full of flashing red clouds.

"The fire," I say. "Is it spreading?"

The woman leans in close, pen light in hand, flashing it between my eyes. "He's concussed. Do you have any injuries I should know about, sir?"

I laugh and wince. "Everywhere."

A pair of medical scissors appears in her hands. It's cold against my skin as she cuts my shirt away.

"The fire," I say again. "How bad is it?"

"Not good," she says. "Must have been kicked off by a lot of fuel, but in case you haven't noticed, it's raining like a sonuvabitch."

Lighting arcs through the sky above the rising clouds.

The fire flared hot and attempted to spread, but it's being doused by mother nature. Should have realized before. Suppose I was a little distracted.

The medic pulls open my shirt. Her face falls flat. Whispers, "Oh my god," and turns to her partner. "We need medevac, now! Call it in and get the gurney!"

"That bad?" I ask.

She unfurls, "Can you tell me what happened to you?"

"You wouldn't believe me," I say.

"The more we know about what happened, the greater the odds we can fix it."

"Never a good thing when people start talking odds," I say. "Means there's a scenario where I don't come out of this."

"Can you handle a bit of honesty?" she asks.

"Always," I say.

"I think the odds are not in your favor."

"Your beside manner needs work," I say, and I cough up a teaspoon of blood.

"And you, are in a road. Not in a bed. With massive internal bleeding in a part of the world where hospitals equipped to deal with this kind of shit are a thirty-minute flight in clear weather."

Thunder booms, punctuating her point.

"Worse ways to die," I say, thinking of my parents.

"Not really," she says, looking at me like I've lost my mind, and there's a good chance she's right.

"They're en route!" her partner says, rushing back with a gurney, one of its wheels a little higher than the rest, bouncing and flailing, tapping out a beat.

The medic forgets her line of questioning for a moment, she and her partner navigating me up and onto the gurney. Hurts like a bitch, but I keep it contained. They wheel me back to the ambulance and get me inside. Rather than racing away, siren blaring, we sit still, waiting for airborne rescue.

She leans over me again. "Try to stay awake."

"I know the drill," I say.

"Mmm," she says, unimpressed. "If you can tell me anything—*anything* that might help speed up diagnosis—"

"Think you can handle a bit of honesty?" I ask.

She preps a syringe of morphine. "Try me."

"What's your name?"

"Heather...Beth."

My smile hurts. "Are you sure? Which is it?"

"Beth is my last name."

"Okay, Heather," I say, feeling a bit light-headed. "I was attacked."

She nods. That much is obvious.

"Looks like a bear had a go at you," her partner says.

"A bear wouldn't have been a problem. And honestly, the first bunch of Weekend Warriors—eighteen armed men transported on three choppers—weren't much of a problem. Some of this damage is a day old. From the Shrieking Ninjas. That's another story. Most of the fresh stuff is from Iron Maiden. The woman, not the band."

The pair of medics share a look. They think I'm off my rocker.

"Did you already give him the morphine?" the man asks. I'm going to call him 'Chuck.'

Heather shakes her head and holds up the syringe.

"So, you're crazy then?" Chuck asks me.

I hold up a finger. "First, *rude.*" I hold up two more fingers. "Second, you'll believe me when they start pulling bodies out of the forest."

That sobers them a little.

Rotor blades thunder above us.

"That was fast," Chuck says. Pats me on the shoulder. "Lucky day, after all."

While Chuck opens the rear doors, I take hold of Heather's arm. "You think I'm nuts, I get it, but if you don't listen to me like I'm Jesus himself, standing before you in a burning bush or some shit, you're both going to die—and then I am."

She freezes for a moment, and then nods.

"'Half hour,' you said. But that's just half the trip. Should have been a up to a thirty-minute wait followed by a thirty-minute flight, right?"

"Yeah..."

"That chopper arrived in three minutes. Seem possible to you?"

She shakes her head.

"The Cowboys arrived in three Black Hawks. Two of them were dropped by a fourth chopper, which also went down. That's what started the forest burning. You hearing what I'm telling you?"

"I think. Maybe."

"Look out the window. If the man stepping out of the helo is wearing a Stetson—"

Lightning flashes. She looks forward out the window and then snaps back down. "He's got a rifle."

"How many of them?" I ask.

"Just one."

Good ol' Jim. At least he was honest.

"He's here to kill you?" she asks.

I shrug. "Or something."

"Why?"

"Ten million reasons."

"Shit... What do we do?"

I lay out my plan, the one and only thing I can think of given the circumstances and my condition. When I'm done, she closes the ambulance doors and waits.

"First time fighting an assassin, huh?"

She gives a nervous nod. "Yours?"

"Nah. Hey, you know the Avett Brothers?"

A slight smile cuts through her nervousness.

"Live and Die?" I ask.

"One of their best," she says.

"My parents were listening to it when they died a few years back." No idea why I'm telling Heather this. She has a kind face, and there's a good chance I'm about to die. So why not try to find a little peace?

"Ouch. I'm sorry. You know, I saw an article on the song's meaning a while back. It's about being pushed through a conflict to rediscover love, alive and well. Maybe the universe was sending you a message."

"Wait..." My brow furrows. "What?"

The back doors are yanked open to reveal a petrified Chuck and the last of the Weekend Warriors, who looks like he's an ear flick away from flying into a rage. After all, his friends are dead. But here he is, following through on the mission, happy to claim the reward all for himself.

I hold my gaze still, locked on the ceiling, breath held, body still.

Heather reacts to the cowboy by raising her hands and shouting in surprise. "Whoa, whoa, whoa! He's dead! Whatever you needed him for, he's gone."

"Outside," the cowboy grumbles. "I'll see for myself."

The gurney is tugged back out into the rain by Chuck and the cowboy, who gives me a once over and then lowers his guard. When he places his fingers on my neck, I use every ounce of strength and determination left in me to grab his arm, lunge up, and shove the syringe through his eyeball, dumping morphine directly into his brain.

The man reels back. His scream of pain morphs into hysterical laughter, and then he collapses to the ground.

I fall back onto the gurney, vision fading to black. "Believe me now?"

25

Life can't get harder than this, I think, running through the forest, a thirty-pound pack hanging from the shoulders of my hundred-twenty-pound body. Every step hurts. My lungs are raw. The rifle in my hand feels like the world's weight.

I stop at the next station, chamber a round, take aim, and fire.

The bullet zings past the bright red metal triangle. Instead of a satisfying ping, I'm rewarded with a puff of dirt. "Shit."

I chamber another round, take a breath, and settle into the rifle, letting it become an extension of myself. I've done this before. Just not with a gun. And I have a hard time understanding why I'm being forced to train on a weapon for which I'll never have a use.

Dad says it's an exercise in discipline. Feels like a waste of time.

The rifle kicks when I pull the trigger. The target pings and snaps back. Then I'm on my feet, running again, following the path forged by Dad a few weeks ago, and worn down by my feet every day since.

And every damn day, the journey gets harder. Takes longer.

More targets. Trip wires. Distractions.

"Perseverance," Mom says, when I complain. "It will serve you well."

When I lose my patience. When anger threatens to spill over, we have what she calls 'therapy.' It's a lot of talking. About feelings. About letting the past go. About...not remembering. We do meditation, too. That helps the most. Usually I can't remember why I was angry in the first place.

And Dad doesn't give me time to attempt remembering.

"Move forward," he says. "Always forward. Never look back."

He doesn't say *why* I shouldn't look back, but I get the feeling he fears whatever it is I'd find. That Dad would be afraid of anything is enough to keep me following his advice. Push onward. Don't look back.

Thinking of Mom and Dad distracts me. My toe snags a new trip-wire.

A click to my right sends me diving to the ground, curled up behind a boulder. Dad is ruthless with the traps, but there is always a way to escape them. A stream of red paintballs pummels the trees around me and the boulder behind which I've taken cover.

If I'm hit, I'm dead, and I'll have to start all over again. Other kids are running through obstacle courses like this, comfortable in their living rooms, staring up at Super Mario. I'm doing it in real life, taking the beating, standing again, my past chasing me like the back of a side-scrolling level. Can't let it catch me. Or else...

What?

I don't remember.

The paint ball gun runs out of ammo, the automatic trigger clicking, clicking, clicking.

Back to my feet. Up the hill. Two more targets, previously stationary, now moving. *Ping! Ping!*

Down the hill to the stream.

The bridge is gone.

There's an eight-foot gap between me and the far side. The vertical sides descend into two feet of cold water, the stream bottom covered in stones smoothed by thousands of years of erosion. I search for a solution. A rope. A log. Some way to cross the divide. The easy choice would be to go downstream and cross someplace shallow, but I'm not supposed to leave the path. Could throw my pack across and attempt the jump, but I'm not supposed to take it off.

I look back at a tree, already leaning toward the stream.

I could...

What?

I...I don't know.

Can't remember.

If I had a saw, or something explosive, I could drop the tree over the gap.

I shove the tree. It's a young and healthy maple. I won't be pushing it over without a bulldozer.

I follow its arch up and out over the stream. Its new leaves sparkling like emeralds in the afternoon sun. Something about them makes me thirsty.

Looking up, I see my path forward.

Small hands clinging to smooth bark, I shimmy my way up. The higher I go, the more the leaves overhead shake. Halfway up, the trunk starts bending toward the ground, out over the stream. When I reach the thinnest branches, near the top of tree, they bend downward. I cling tight, descending toward the ground.

When the motion stops, I open my eyes and look down.

I'm twenty feet up, directly over the stream.

Eyes widening, I realize that this was not the intended solution.

My fingers slip down the shrinking branches until I've got two fists full of leaves. The tree releases me and catapults back into the air. I watch it sway back into place, as I fall.

I strike the stream's edge at an angle. Wind knocked out of me, I'm flung the rest of the way down, landing face down in the water.

My lungs cry out for air, but I don't surface. Don't move. It's not that I can't. The fall in two parts didn't break any bones.

It just feels...nice, down here in the cold, listening to the gurgle of water. The natural world is resilient. I've always thought so. And when things are bad... I see hope in the world around me—in a weed, or a sapling, or a small stream carving a path through the Earth itself.

The pack wrapped around my shoulders is tugged up. I rise from the water as though freshly baptized. But instead of being lifted up and placed on my feet, I'm flipped over and left to float on my back.

Eyes closed, I breathe, letting my lungs absorb oxygen, replenishing my mind, waking my body up to the pain, and coming to the slow realization that I didn't roll over.

I was picked up.

Dad stands above me, knee deep in the stream, waiting patiently, his face free of anger, or amusement.

"I couldn't figure out how to get past the stream," I say.

"Wasn't supposed to be a way across," he says, looking up at the tree and shaking his head. "You nearly made it."

"You wanted me to fail?" I ask. It wouldn't be surprising. I fail this run more than I succeed, and when I do, it gets harder. The first time I pretended to fail, he saw through it, and the course got twice as hard.

"I wanted you to surrender," he says.

There's a radio in my pack. I can use it whenever the course becomes too much to bear. I never have.

Never will.

"You know I won't," I say.

He crouches down beside me, smiling now. "Son, sometimes the only way forward is to surrender."

His words hit me like a fist to the gut. Memories attempt to surface, like carbonation, but all I get are the emotions associated with them— fear, cold, desperation, and then...hope.

Dad misunderstands the confused look on my face. "Everyone has a low point. We all reach it at least once in our lives. Some people more often than others. But when you do, when you're in the pit of your soul, looking up at what feels like an impossible ascent back into the light? That's a glorious moment. Because when you reach that unholy place, the only direction left to go is up."

He stands. Doesn't offer me a hand. "Finish the course."

I motion to the muddy wall separating me from the path. "But—"

"I'll see you at home," he says, trudging away through the stream. "Mom will be miffed with both of us if you're late for dinner."

"You're wrong. There are *two* directions," I say, stopping him in his tracks.

He glances back over his shoulder.

"You could die," I say. "Instead of climbing back up."

"That what you were doing in the water?" he asks. "Trying to drown your troubles away?"

I shake my head, but I don't tell him about my nature appreciation.

"You're right," he says. "When some people reach the bottom, going deeper feels like the only choice. Submitting to the reaper has its appeal. The unfeeling void of nothingness. An end to self. To suffering. But for men like me...and you...death is never a choice."

26

I blink my eyes and see nothing but the hazy white of limbo. Can't feel much, either. Just an odd sense of being...alive.

Dad was right, of course. Death is not an option.

This doesn't feel much like living, though.

Not the way I remember it.

Holy shit, I think, *the Buddhists were right.* I've been reincarnated as a caterpillar in a chrysalis. I'm legless and armless, body wriggling. I wouldn't admit it, back when I was a human being, but I'm freaking out.

"Settle down."

My internal monologue sounds feminine. And Southern.

"I don't want to be a caterpillar," I moan.

"Can caterpillars speak?" the voice asks.

"Well, I don't know," I say. "I've never been one before. Maybe all Earth's creatures are self-aware? Maybe they can all talk?" I gasp. "Oh, they must talk shit about humanity. Is that what we're doing? Are you in my chrysalis, too?"

"Chrysa-what?"

"Chrysalis," I say. "It's what we caterpillars use to grow into butterflies."

"Well, you're definitely growing, but not into a caterpillar. And I'd appreciate it if you knocked it off."

My body shifts, leaning up. Angles emerge in the endless white. Then charts. Closed windows. Beeping machines. My comfortable transformation chamber evolves into a hospital room. The woman speaking to me comes into view. Her dark skin is in sharp contrast to her gray hair. She's both smiling and sneering, amused and disgusted. She's got a wet cloth in her hand, dipping it into a basin and wringing it out.

My bed continues to rise, body slowly coming into view like the 'planet reveal' at the start of every Star Wars movie. I see my feet first, bare and glistening with moisture—freshly washed. My legs come next, and then...a wobbling, fleshy, leaning tower of Pisa.

"I'm naked?" I blurt.

"And erect," she says, pointing out the obvious.

"Why am I naked?"

She holds up the cloth. "Got to keep you clean and rotated like a rotisserie to avoid bed sores."

"You couldn't cover me up?"

"The towels here chafe. Air drying is the best. You know..." She raises an eyebrow and motions to my somehow still erect penis. "...a man who reacts to a face cloth like that hasn't seen much action."

The look of horror on my face makes her smile. She leans over, picks up a sheet, and tosses it over my midsection.

"How do I know you didn't help yourself?" I ask, redirecting my embarrassment.

"Honey," she says, "What you have there—" She nods toward my pitched tent. "—is nothing I'm interested in." She gives me a wink. For a moment, I think she's telling me that she's a lesbian, but then she says, "What you need is a wife. That's how the Good Lord intended it. Man your age." She shakes her head in disapproval.

"What?" I'm feeling a little defensive now. Nurse Whatsherface McDickWasher seems like a nice person, but her tough-love straight talk is hard to bear while waking up in the hospital, mind somewhat altered by morphine.

"You've been here near a week, and the only visitor you've had is the EMT who brought you in. Flew you here herself. Lucky for you, she flew helicopters for the Navy to pay for her medical training."

"Heather," I say, remembering her. And the cowboy with a needle in his eye. And...

My home is destroyed, like that dandelion underfoot.

"That's the one," she says. "Now, Hon, I'm just an old lady far from home, scrubbing a comatose man's feet, but I reckon a woman like that might be worth pursuing."

"Mmm," I say. "I'll keep that in mind. So, I've been here a week?"

She nods. "Medically induced coma. To make sure all of this—" She waves her hand out toward my body. "—healed."

I look down. My body is covered in old yellow bruises and bandaged wounds.

"Why am I still alive?" I ask.

"Lord knows you shouldn't be," she says. "Way I heard it, Heather's the only reason you're still breathing. She took a risk coming all the way out here. There were a good number of closer options. But those backwoods doctors wouldn't have been able to deal with your mess." She raises her hands like I've scoffed at the idea. "Just my opinion. But why else would she fly you an hour out from the crash?"

"Crash?"

"You were in a car accident, Dean."

"Dean?"

"Do you not remember your name?" She looks me over, curious. "Dean Loveall. That's the name Heather gave us. Said you told her before passing out. They couldn't find your ID. Couldn't identify you. You'd be John Doe if she hadn't given us your name. Might as well be John Doe anyway, for all the visitors you've had. Apparently, no one's out looking for a missing Dean Loveall."

Heather saved my life in more ways than one.

She flew me to an out-of-the-way hospital, under a fake name, and conjured a story for my injuries that was both believable and common enough to not attract attention. I guess the cowboy encounter convinced her that I was telling the truth.

"Where am I?" I ask.

"Mercy General," she says.

"And that is where?"

"East Sacramento."

Lots of people. Lots of accidents. Long way from Leggett. Smart.

"You want me to get the doctor now?" she asks. "Reckon I should have done that the moment you opened your eyes."

"Better if you didn't," I say without thinking.

"On account of your..." she looks my nakedness up and down. At least the tent is down. "...condition?"

"Let's go with that," I say.

"Honey, we all seen you naked already, and I'm not seeing a whole lot of shame in those dark brown eyes of yours. So, what is it? You in some kind of trouble?"

"Some kind," I say.

"With the law?"

"Forgot to return a VHS tape back in the 90s," I say.

She grins. "I'll get the doc, then." She stands and peels the gloves from her hands, eyes locked on mine, waiting for me to break.

I sigh. "Fine."

She sits. Drops the gloves on my feet. Looks down her nose and waits.

"There are people trying to kill me," I say.

"Damn near succeeded by the looks of it."

"You...believe me?"

"I know the look," she says, and she gives me a wink. "I'm older than I appear. How bad are these people?"

"The worst."

"In comparison to whom?"

"Everyone." I push myself up a little, and I'm happy to find that on a scale of 1 to 10, the pain is just a 6. "Too much attention on me will endanger everyone on this floor, yourself included."

She waves that last remark off, like it's the silliest thing she's ever heard.

"Look... My name is..."

"Look, Linda. I'm not screwing around. If people start asking questions I can't answer, and someone calls in the police..."

"Why these people want you dead? How bad could you be?"

"You hear about a fire up north?" I ask. "'Bout a week ago?"

She thinks on it, and then nods. "Messy business, that."

"The number of dead..."

Her brow furrows.

"I've been in a coma all week. No way I could know the answer, right?"

Her nod is agonizingly slow.

"Twenty-three," I say, believing Zeta fully capable of surviving that mess. The Weekend Warriors...not so much. "All of them men. None of them identifiable, including the one not all burned up."

Linda swallows. "Twenty-two." Clears her throat. "They found twenty-two. *That's* where you came from?"

I nod.

"Twenty-three men were sent to kill you, and...what? You set them all on fire?"

"I only killed five of them," I say. "Fire finished most of them, probably because I shot them. Not kill shots. Hell, I was trying to be nice. But they also had competition."

"Competition who survived."

I attempt a smile. "Now you're getting it."

Linda turns away from me. "And the EMT? Is she with you?"

I shake my head. "She's the real deal. Saved my life. Helped me finish off the last of them. Morphine syringe through the eye. Nasty business."

Linda winces. That she doesn't know this detail means the sinister powers that be are covering up the truth of the fire, and they are probably looking for Heather. She's their only connection to me.

"You said she's visited?" I ask.

"Every day."

"What time?"

She looks at her watch. "'Bout thirty minutes from now."

"Linda," I say, as earnestly as I can muster. "The resources being spent on locating me right now are...staggering. That I haven't been finished off already is something of a miracle."

She smiles. "Means the Good Lord ain't done with you yet, Hon."

"Think the Good Lord, with a little help from you, could rustle up a change of clothes?"

She sighs. Stands. "I'll see what I can do. Meantime, you need to kickstart your body." She slides a tray of covered food around the bed. "Had this prepped in case you woke up. Might help." She lifts the cover off the tray to reveal a cold Salisbury steak, an ice cream scoop of rehydrated mashed potatoes, and some carrots that look soft enough to chew with my gums. I reach past it all, pick up the chocolate pudding, and say, "Thanks."

There's a fast double-tap knock on the door, giving me just enough time to lie back and close my eyes.

"Any change?" a man asks.

"He's cleaner," Linda says. "So, that's something."

"He should be waking up soon. When he does..." He lowers his voice to a whisper. "The FBI called. They said he's a person of interest. They'll be here in thirty to question him."

"For what?" she asks.

"Didn't say."

"And they're not sending the police first?"

"I'm a doctor, not an FBI agent, Jim." There's a quiet pause. "Sorry, that was horrible. Just...let me know if he so much as twitches, okay?"

"Will do," Linda says.

"Why does he have a pudding in his hand?" the doctor asks.

Linda chuckles. "Thought it might motivate him to wake up."

"Huh," he says. "Weird."

I hear the sound of the hospital beyond the door for a moment—uncomfortable patients, whispering nurses, the chiming of medical machines all over the floor, coupled with the clicking of the doctor's nice shoes walking away.

When I open my eyes, the door closes. Linda is gone, too, leaving me alone to eat my pudding and then find some way to finish my metamorphosis from comatose to fighting-ready in the next thirty minutes. FBI, my ass.

27

Pudding polished off, I slide to the bed's side, grunting in pain. Everything hurts, but the pain is five days old. I can manage it. But can I fight through it?

I'm not going to have a choice.

I pull the IV from my arm and the life-sign sensors from my body. All of it hurts. Given the amount of pain I'm in and the fact that I've been in a coma, mind bullets are a little risky. I think I could pull it off once but adding an extra layer to the pain lasagna I'm feasting on might be more than I can handle.

My mind flits back to the previous week's events. There's a lot to consider, but a few items stand out. Like Rho and Zeta—strangers now, but once upon a time, classmates, and at least in Zeta's case—a friend. Twenty-four children, all with varying levels of mental abilities, at least three of them now professional assassins. And somehow along the way, I ended up with Mom and Dad, repressed my entire early childhood, and forgot that I could ghost walk outside my body. That's admittedly cool and useful, but I have no idea how to trigger it, aside from getting the shit slapped out of me.

Despite the revelations, I'm not sure I want to remember any more. Something about it all feels dark. Sinister. And not just the screwed-up circumstances. I didn't like how I felt when down there in that sewer, watching Zeta crush a rat. Sure, some kids explode frogs, burn ants, and chop up fish for bait, but unless they're sociopaths, they feel a degree of revolt.

When I saw the rat bend in on itself and heard its bones break, and its shrill cry, I felt...pleased.

I felt happy.

Exhilarated.

Gamma, the savage. *Is that who I was?* Third most powerful out of twenty-four killers-to-be.

If so, I really have forgotten a lot. I'm lucky to be alive, outclassed by Rho and Zeta. The Ghost and Iron Maiden. Both of whom are alive, and possibly still on the hunt, along with a bevy of other killers, all looking for a ten-million-dollar payday, or perhaps they have personal vendettas for offenses I can't remember.

The linoleum floor is cool beneath my feet. Sends a chill up my legs and pulls my thoughts back to the present moment. I stand and stretch, the sheet falling away from my naked body. Moving slowly, I bend and twist, working out the kinks and moving muscles that have been languishing for a week.

I pull open the curtain, exposing myself to the world, and bathing in the late morning sun. Then I close my eyes and open my arms, absorbing the warmth. "Hello, Sun," I say.

I turn my gaze to the city below. Never been here before. "Hello, Sacramento."

The door opens behind me. No knock. I'm either a dead man, or... "Hello, Linda."

"How in the name of St. Peter with a corn cob did you know it was me?" she says.

I look back with a grin. Tap my head a few times. "I'm telepathic."

"Uh-huh," she says, placing a pile of folded clothing on the bed. "And why is your nekid ass baring your business to the entire city?"

"Just enjoying my last moments," I say. Then I inspect the clothing. Jeans. T-shirt. Plaid flannel. Pair of boots. No socks or underwear, which is fine. Not entirely surprising given the circumstance. "You rob a lumberjack?"

"Fella down the hall passed this morning," she says. "Figured he was done needing them."

A dead man's clothing. That's...foreboding. Or maybe ironic. From one dead man to another. These clothes have bad luck.

As I start to get dressed, Linda doesn't bother looking away or giving me privacy. She's not ogling, though. She's entirely disinterested. She's been wiping me clean and giving me boners all week. Nothing she hasn't seen before, I suppose, but it feels more poignant than that, like her long life has been so full of the good and bad that this strange blip isn't nearly enough to ruffle her feathers.

Hopefully, I can leave before that changes. I like Linda. Would be sad if something happened to her.

"See anything weird out there?" I ask.

"Weird how?"

"People that don't belong."

"We get people in and out of here every day," she says.

"Anyone who stands out? Anyone not visiting someone?"

She gives her head a slow shake.

"Anyone visiting *everyone?*" I ask, buttoning the pants. A little loose, but the belt cinches them tight.

She starts shaking her head, and then stops.

"Well, there're a few sisters going room to room."

"Sisters like twins, or sisters like—"

"Nuns," she says.

"How many?"

"Two." Her face screws up. "They're going room to room, praying over the sick. Doing the Lord's work, if you ask me. You have a problem with nuns?"

"Maybe," I say, pulling on the T-shirt. Smells of Old Spice. "Maybe not. You hear them talking at all?"

"Talking? How do you mean?"

"With their mouths," I say.

Linda gives me a look that says she could transform into the most dangerous person on the planet, if I gave her enough reason.

"In private," I say. "To each other."

"Mmmhmm," she says, raising a finger. "They were cussin' up a storm, but that doesn't mean—"

The shoe falls from my hand. I head for the door, crack it open, and peer down the hall. There're a few nurses hustling about, but no nuns. I close the door and head for the window, looking down. We're four stories up.

Damn.

"You thinking about jumping or something?" Linda asks.

"Or something," I say. "How do I get off this floor?"

"Elevators are down the hall to the right, left at the nurse's station. Stairs to the left. End of the hall."

"Where are the nuns?"

"To the right," she says. "Beyond the nurse's station, last I saw them."

"Shit."

"What?"

"Two covering the elevator, tightening the net, the third covering the stairs, in case I try to escape."

"There are *three* nuns?"

"They're not nuns, Linda," I say. "They're..."

BLASPHENUNS

"That's a tongue twister," she says. "Going to be hell for whoever narrates your memoirs."

"I know. Blasphemous Nuns is kind of a mouthful, though."

"Naughty Nuns," she suggests.

"Sounds more like strippers."

"Ohh," she says. "I have it. They're the..."

TWISTED SISTERS

I smile. "Linda, you are now one of my favorite people."

"Guy like you has a lot of favorite people," she says.

"Just three," I say. "Week ago, that number was zero."

She looks me over, reassessing. "You got kind of a Johnny Cash thing going on, don't you? Tough on the outside, trying to mask the pain."

"I was in a coma."

"Not the kind of pain I'm talking about. Cash put all that heartache into his music. Might do you well to find an outlet."

"I put it into my work," I say.

"Seems to me that ain't working well for you." Before I can disagree and opt out of this conversation, she asks, "Most of these killer types eccentrics? Foul-mouthed nuns, and cowboys and the like?"

"You could say that," I say.

"So, they're all crazy, then."

"I wouldn't say that."

"You got a backwards definition of crazy, Hon. But don't worry nothin'. You seem about as normal as beans and franks on a Saturday night."

"I grew up in a treehouse, I can explode people's minds with a thought, and my best friend is a sarcastic, possibly homicidal Artificial Intelligence, named Bubbles."

"Huh..."

No idea why I told Linda all of that. I open the room's bathroom door. "Inside."

"You want me to hide in a bathroom?"

"And stay there until the screaming stops," I say.

Her faces flattens. "You're serious."

"These women," I say. "The Twisted Sisters. Despite what they look like, they have no respect for God, for life, or anyone who gets between them and their target. I don't want you to get caught in the crossfire, and I sure as shit don't want them to see us together."

"Why's that?" she asks.

"If I manage to escape, they'll target you for information. That means I'll have to kill them all, and I don't think I'm up to that quite yet."

Linda nods. "I'm impressed you're standing."

"Yeah, well—"

The door starts to open.

No knock.

I shove Linda into the bathroom, and turn toward the door, mind bullet primed and ready to fire.

28

The first thing I see are two raised eyebrows, arched and curious. They're followed by a pair of brown eyes and tied back brown hair. The face is familiar and does not belong to a Twisted Sister.

"Heather," I guess. My memories of her are mostly a blur.

"You remember," she says, smiling. "Why do you look like you're taking a shit?"

I relax my forehead. "Thought you were someone else."

"You were going to shit your pants if I was someone else?"

I smile. "I was going to kill you."

She slides inside the room, closes the door behind her. She's dressed in casual clothing, shorts, and a T-shirt, like she's got no one to impress. Looks kind of grubby, too. Dirty. Like it's been a few days since she changed. In the light, and not about to lose consciousness, I really see her for the first time—low center of gravity, broad shoulders. Looks strong. Probably played softball at some point in her life.

"Speaking of killing," she says, lowering her voice. "There are a lot of people looking for you, and by extension, me. I've been lying low because of the whole cowboy incident, and everything else you said, but I'm out of cash, and I can't hit the bank, right?"

"Right."

"I spent the night under a bridge. How long is this going to last?"

"Until I'm caught," I say. "Or dead. Or..."

"Or you kill everyone who's looking for you?"

"Well, yeah, but I don't think that's possible."

"Obviously," she says, inspecting the bruises on my face. "Seems like you're barely treading water at the base of a tsunami."

Ouch.

I'm being critiqued by a helicopter pilot turned EMT on my handling of a cabal of assassins hunting me down and destroying my life. She's not wrong, though. I'm outnumbered and...I hate to admit it...outclassed. Luck, and the kindness of strangers, are the only reasons I'm still here. "What I need to do is find out who's footing the bill and change their mind."

"Or kill them."

"You're pretty focused on the whole killing part."

"I'm just...afraid. I've flown in combat. It was frightening, but it made sense. We knew who the enemy was. Knew what they could do, and how to counteract it."

"You're miles deep in the rabbit hole," I say with a nod.

"Is there a way out?" she asks, but she doesn't sound very hopeful.

"Aside from me going on a killing spree?"

She nods.

"New identity. New life. Leave everything and never look back."

That would sober most people right up, but Heather says, "I can do that."

I sense Heather is a kindred spirit. Focused on work. Living alone. Secretly thrilled that life has been thrown into turmoil, that life suddenly feels worth living. Why else would she come visit me—a stranger and an assassin—every day, while people are hunting us down? Why hide me? Why protect me? She could have given me up without risk and continued down the path she was already on, oblivious to the rabbit hole.

Instead, she looks and smells a bit like she's been living on the streets, and she isn't all that upset about it. She feels more than eager. Ready to go. Like she's been pounding down coffees all morning.

"Step one," I say, "is getting out of the hospital."

"You can't just walk out the front door?"

One of my eyebrows makes a slow climb upward while the others drops low.

She understands the, 'Are you serious?' expression, and says, "Wait. What? Really? They're here? Now? Like right now?"

"You see the nuns?"

"Two doors down," she says. "Two of them. Praying over an old lady."

"Well, they're not nuns."

"They're Twisted Sisters," Linda whispers, poking her head out from behind the bathroom door.

Heather jumps, but she doesn't yelp.

"Linda, what are you doing in the bathroom?" Heather says.

"This fool put me in there," she says. "Wants me to hide."

"I want both of you to hide," I say, motioning Heather toward the now open door. "We don't have a lot of time. I'll lead them to the stairs. You two take the elevator out." To Heather I say, "Stay with Linda, I'll find you later and set up your new life." To Linda I say, "She's staying with you."

"You're going to die without help," Heather says.

I counter with, "But you won't," but quickly regret it.

Heather guffaws, and in her best caveman voice, says, "You woman. You weak. Me strong man. Me be stupid, look tough, get self killed. Ugh, ugh." She rolls her eyes. "Please."

I find myself pinching the bridge of my nose again. If not for Madee, Heather, and now Linda, I'd have never known about the reflex. The exasperation pinch. "I am woman, hear me roar, huh?"

"You're damn right," Heather says, to which Linda claps and smiles like she's in church, cheering on a fired up pastor. "Women were made to squeeze a human being out of their vaginas. We're basically the toughest."

"Have you?" I ask. "Pushed a baby out of your vagina?"

She sours.

Linda crosses her arms. "What kind of question is that?"

"I'm just saying... I think if you're going to..." I've walked headlong into a trap, and the only way to survive is to shut up. "What do you think we should do? Unless you're both secretly trained assassins and are ready to kill another human being who once upon a time was pushed out of some other woman's vagina? Because *I* do that all the time, and I don't think either of you have it in you."

They stare at me, not quite dumbfounded. More annoyed.

Working in tandem, somehow reading each other's minds, they inform me about the new plan, as I sense time running out. Linda opens the bathroom door, and Heather hitches a thumb over her shoulder. "You hide in the bathroom."

Outside the room, two hushed, but angry voices can be heard, arguing, cursing, irritated. They haven't finished their sweep of the floor. The Twisted Sisters are closing in.

"Fight together. Die together. Or trust us." Heather directs me toward the bathroom with her eyebrows. "Choice is yours."

"Sunuvabitch," I say, and step inside.

Linda shuts off the light and the fan, plunging me into darkness while Heather closes the door. I stand still, slowing my breath, willing myself into absolute silence.

Through the door, muffled singing. A hymn, I think. Amazing Grace, maybe. *What the hell?*

There's a knock. Linda beckons them, "Come in!"

A conversation plays out. Joking. Linda praising God. Thanking the sisters for all that they do. Inviting them to pray over Heather, who'd...attempted suicide, but had converted while hospitalized.

Linda spins the yarn without hesitation, all of it believable, no trace of fear.

Meanwhile, I'm closed in a bathroom, heart pounding, body shaking, expecting and dreading the fight to come.

Pull it together, I tell myself. *Focus.*

And all of a sudden, after a week of sleeping, my bowels wake up. Within seconds, a shit of titanic proportions is impacting itself against my tailbone.

Terrified I'm going to crap my pants, I slowly undo my belt, drop the pants, and place my bare cheeks against the toilet seat. This...was a mistake. My body senses that it's safe to unload, and things begin moving, the pressure building.

I clench, fighting the urge.

Don't die on a toilet, I think. *Don't die on a toilet.*

If so much as a balloon squeak sneaks out of my puckered sphincter, they'll hear it, they'll know that Heather and Linda helped me, and shortly thereafter, I will die on a damn toilet.

Laughter outside the door allows me to release some steam, but the train isn't slowing down as it approaches the station.

C'mon...C'mon.

Muffled goodbyes, and then the hospital room door opens and closes.

I relax, imagining that birth feels ten times worse than this. I find a new respect for women and sigh in relief as Linda opens the door and exclaims, "Boy, I know you weren't taking a shit while we was out here saving your ass."

Head sagged low, I raise a finger. "I held it off as long as I could."

"Mmmhmm."

"Seriously, it was like the hot gates in here."

She stares.

"Leonidas?" I say. "The Spartans? Holding back Persian hordes?"

"I remember," Linda says. "The movie."

"It's an analogy. The Persian hordes are—"

"We get it," Heather says. She's in my hospital bed, covered by a blanket, IV taped to her arm, pulse beeping away.

"Finish up," Linda says, closing the door in my face, and then turning on the light.

I wipe my ass like my life depends on it, and I hike my pants up. I reach for the door handle and freeze, and not just because I forgot to wash my hands. The bedroom door has opened again. I hear the sisters, this time standing just outside the bathroom, asking about why the charts have Heather's name listed as Dean Loveall.

The sisters are pros. They don't miss details like that. I should have thought of that before. But right now, all they know is that Linda and Heather are in the wrong room.

I slowly turn to the knob, crack open the door, grip the frame with both hands, place my foot against the solid wood—and shove.

29

I start strong. Like a fucking champ.

The heavy door slams into one of the two nuns in the room, launching her over the bed's corner and into the privacy curtain, which falls over her.

The second Twisted Sister screams, "He's here!" and reaches beneath her habit, drawing an old school Israeli Micro Uzi. Her finger slips over the trigger, sweeping the weapon in a wide arc. The gun spits out 20 rounds per second. In the time it takes the Sister to complete her swing, Linda, Heather, and I will be perforated and very dead.

I focus on her head.

Will my mind outward.

And then...*SNAP.*

The inside of the Sister's brain turns to jelly. Her body goes limp while she's still spinning, flailing like she's performing at the Ice Capades before slapping against the floor, motionless.

This is where things go downhill for me.

The mind bullet strain hits me hard between the eyes, blurring my vision. I'm alive, awake, and no longer in a coma, but I haven't recovered. I stumble back a step and drop to one knee, struggling to stay conscious.

For a moment, Linda and Heather just stare at me. They've seen it for themselves now—my world, full of killers and telekinesis. Then they're in motion, Linda charging toward the room's door, Heather yanking the IV drip bag from its stand and wielding the metal rod like a bat.

Linda reaches the door, just as the third nun attempts to answer. The nun might be a trained killer wielding an Uzi, but Linda's got a good hundred pounds on the woman. When she strikes the door, all that kinetic energy transfers to the nun, knocking her onto her ass and the door closed.

"Mother fucking son of a whore!" the tangled Sister shouts, as she fights to escape the curtain's serpentine grasp. "I'm going to kill every single one of you bitches."

Before she can get out another potty-mouthed diatribe or aim the Uzi now in her hand, Heather winds up and swings. Metal dents as the stand slams into the side of the nun's head, sprawling her to the floor.

Blood flowing, she reaches out for the Uzi, her fingers grazing the handle until my foot rests atop both. I bend down, pick up the weapon, and aim it down at the stunned Sister.

"What are you doing?" Heather asks, horrified.

"You were all about the killing a minute ago," I point out.

"Yeah, but she's defenseless," Heather says.

"She's seen your face. Linda's, too." I adjust my aim. One bullet. No muss, no fuss. "This is what happens when I hide in the bathro—ohh!"

The Sister isn't nearly as weak as she seems, kicking out the back of my leg. Off balance, I stumble back toward the window.

The seething nun rolls past Heather and charges toward me.

I could shoot her. Could cut her down in a flurry of bullets. It would be easy. But I don't trust my weakened grip. If the gun bucks too much, I could hit Linda and Heather, too.

I aim away from the Sister, pull the trigger, and unload the entire magazine into the window behind me. Rounds punch the glass and my ear drums until the magazine runs dry. The nun reaches me a moment later, lunging and screaming, hands outstretched, ready to claw me up.

The next part is easy, because: physics. Using my backward momentum and the nun's forward momentum, I grasp hold of her habit, fall back, and kick with my legs.

She roars as she passes over me, strikes the chewed-up window, and slips through.

For a moment, I feel victorious, like Stella getting her groove back. Then a noose tightens around my neck. As she flew past, the Sister slipped a medical wire around my neck, and now, the weight of her body dangling outside is strangling me.

Heather leaps to my aid. "Oh my god!" She attempts to pull the wire up, but it's too tight to get her fingers under. Gagging, face beet red, I snap my fingers and point to the dead nun's Uzi.

She picks it up. "What am I supposed to do with this?"

I point to the window.

Heather's mortified. "I can't shoot her."

With bulging eyes, I shake the wire stealing my life.

"Right," Heather says, hustling over. She aims the gun barrel at the cable while I start to lose consciousness. She hesitates, adjusting her aim, second guessing and slowly coming to the realization that no matter what she shoots—cable or nun—the woman hanging outside the window is about to lose her life.

"Just...pull the...trigger," I manage to say, voice raspy.

When a fusillade of rounds thunders against the closed room door, causing Linda to shout in surprise, Heather pulls the trigger. I don't know how many rounds it takes to sever the wire, but I feel the weight release and hear the woman's scream cut short as she drops forty feet to the sidewalk below.

Choking for air, tearing the wire away, I say, "I'm getting really fucking tired of getting my ass kicked!"

Heather looks out the window before I get a chance to warn her against it. Sometimes, people fall to their deaths and just look a little awkward. Other times, their heads burst like melons. Really nasty business.

"Uhh," Heather says, looking out the window, but she never gets a chance to finish the thought, as the last nun standing unleashes another wave of bullets, this time through the wall. Rounds zing through the room and over my head, as I tackle Heather to the floor.

"Linda!" I shout. She's safe behind the wooden door. "Open the door when I get close!"

She nods and grasps the handle, while flinching at the sound of gunfire. Tough lady. I'm not going to let her down. "Ready?"

Linda gives a nod. As the Uzi pounds through the last few bullets in its magazine, I push off the floor and run toward the door. I'm seeing stars as the door opens, like a screensaver overlay, highlighting the Twisted Sister reloading her Uzi.

I launch a flying kick and career straight into the wall as the Sister side-steps. She lifts the Uzi toward my head, but I catch it and shove the muzzle toward the ceiling, as she pulls the trigger. My hands wrapped around hers, I yank the gun to the side and introduce my forehead to her nose. The weapon slips free of her grasp and clatters to the floor.

The nun becomes a flurry of motion, launching kicks and strikes, most of them connecting in my dwindled condition. She's a polished fighter. Slick. Going to have to fight like a brute to survive. I throw my weight at her, colliding and driving us both to the floor. Before she can stand, I dive on her back, wrapping my arms around her throat. Somehow, one of my hands ends up in her mouth, grasping her cheek, as she tries to stand.

"Ugh!" she shouts in disgust. "Whe wash de lash tie you washed yu hans?!"

"I was in a rush!" I plant my foot on the small of her back and kick off, indenting the wall with the shape of her torso.

She falls to the floor out in the hallway, dazed, but not done.

The Twisted Sisters do not have abilities. Were not part of the mysterious twenty-four. But that doesn't mean they aren't dangerous.

I take a pen from the nurse's station and stalk toward her.

"Who called the hit?" I ask.

"Fuck you, dodo fucker!" She's playing the role right up until the end.

"Dodo fucker?"

"Dodo, like the bird!"

"Dodos...are extinct."

She sneers, fumbles for words and spits out, "P-pangolin fucker!"

I smile. "Better. Pangolins are sexy." I click the pen, extending the ball point. "Who called the hit?"

She spits blood at me.

"Have it your way," I say, and then I glance at the open bedroom door, where Heather stands watching, hand to her mouth. Heather might long for a new life, but this isn't it.

In that moment of distraction, the Sister strikes, planting her heel between my legs. I drop to my knees, dropping the pen, and I squeak out a nonsensical protest.

The nun rolls back, collecting the Uzi on her way. She ejects the spent magazine, slaps a new one home, and takes aim. She smiles through the blood in her mouth and says, "Fuck you, mole rat fucker!"

"Okay," I whisper. "That one...stings."

She has a laugh, aims the Uzi between my eyes, and—

—is lifted off the ground by an explosion. She's hurled ten feet, while a portion of her chest blows out her back and decorates the hallway floor, ceiling, and both walls.

I fall to the floor, flop onto my back, and look up to find Madee, decked out in body armor, holding Dad's shotgun, standing over me. She smiles down. "Ready to go...*Dean?*"

30

I reach a hand up to Madee and snap my fingers. "Phone."

She frowns. "'Phone?' Not, 'Holy shit, Madee, how'd you get here?' Or 'Wow, thanks for saving my life'?"

"Bubbles brought you here," I say, "and my life is far from saved. Phone."

She's unhappy, but she cuts me some slack, probably because I'm in rough shape. She digs into her pocket and pulls out a phone. She takes an earbud from her other pocket and hands them both over.

I slip the earbud in place. "Miss me?"

"I am incapable," Bubbles says. "But I am pleased you're still breathing."

"For now," I say. "We have incoming."

The nuns found me first, but whoever was pretending to be the FBI is still on the way.

"Not incoming," she says. "In the lobby."

I climb to my feet, bracing myself on the nurse's station countertop. Up and down the hallway, patients and nurses peek out of the rooms in which they'd taken shelter, gasping and exclaiming, and ducking back in when they spot Madee wielding a shotgun.

Won't be long before the entirety of Sacramento's police force is here.

"Know who we're dealing with?" I ask.

"Unknown."

"How many?"

"Four. Three men. One woman. Caucasian. All of them in trench coats."

"Show me." The phone's screen flicks to a security camera view of the four people walking through the hospital's lobby. They look straight-laced and serious. Real deal FBI agents, which is strange. Three letter agencies steer clear of people like me.

Why are they here?

"We going to stand here chatting all day, or are we going to get the hell out?" Madee asks.

I watch the video feed as the four agents approach the elevator and push the call button.

I lift my chin toward the exit sign at the end of the hall. "We'll take the stairs."

Madee eyes the hallway of explosive gore separating us from the stairwell. She sighs. "I should have stayed in the car."

"Bubbles," I say. "I want you to stay connected to this phone at all times, okay? I'm going to give it to a friend."

"Understood."

I head back to my room and find Heather just inside the door, and Linda sitting on the bedside, numbly nibbling on my congealed Salisbury steak. She looks up when I enter. Lifts a fork tipped with meat. "I eat when I'm anxious."

"You're good," I tell her. "They're all dead. No one's looking for you. Free and clear."

She gives a slow nod. "Reckon that's a good thing."

I hold the phone out to her. "Keep this charged. Keep it with you. If you need help, for any reason, at any time in the future, just speak the words and I'll know."

"Unless you're dead," she says.

"Well, yeah, that. But if my heart's still beating, I'll do what I can. I owe you."

She smiles. "S'pose you do."

"I mean, don't call me for a clogged toilet or anything," I say.

"Hon, I wouldn't let you within a hundred feet of my toilet." She glances at the still open bathroom door. Then she tilts her head to the window. "That glass wasn't broken, we'd all be swimming in whatever the hell you gave birth to in there."

Chuckling, I turn to Heather, whose nervous look steals my smile. "I don't get a phone, do I?"

I shake my head. "You're coming with me."

"If you just leave, I won't know where you are. I won't be able to tell them anything."

"They won't believe you until you've died from torture."

She swallows.

"What you did for me... I've never needed saving before," I say. Feels like a lie, but I roll with it. "But you saved my life a handful of times just in the last week."

"Ahem," Madee says, and she motions to the dead nun in the hallway. "Hello? I've killed ninjas *and* a nun."

"That's different," I say, hobbling back into the hall. She eyes me, suspicious as I approach.

"They're in the elevator, Jonas," Bubbles warns.

"Uh-huh," I say, stopping in front of Madee, my eyes locked on hers.

"H-how is it different?" she asks, thrown by my unusual behavior.

When I first saw Madee, standing over me, shotgun in hand, it took a lot of effort to hide how happy I was to see her. Now that I've had a moment to process that, I've come to a conclusion. "Because we're partners." I wrap my hand around the small of her back, pull her close, and lean in to kiss her.

My lips press against the palm of her hand. She leans around me and asks Heather, "He have a concussion or something?"

"He was in a coma for a week," she says. "And he was nearly strangled to death a moment ago."

Madee's hand slides to my cheek and gives it a few firm whacks. "Snap out of it, lover boy. People to kill. Assassins to flee. All that good stuff. We can talk about feelings later."

"Right," I say, feeling something like shame. Then I push past it, focus up, and let the world-class assassin in me rise to the surface. "I'm good."

"Great," Madee says, drawing the Sword of Mars from her hip. "Found this buried beneath a wolf-shaped rock." She tosses it to me, handle first.

I reach out, fingers extended and ready to victoriously grasp the ancient sword whose mythological presence all but guarantees victory.

The handle slips past my hand—and strikes my forehead. The sword clatters to the floor.

"Oww," I say, hand on the rising lump, the moment of feeling tough and capable melting away.

Heather picks up the sword, feels its weight in her hands, and tries to hide a grin. "I got this. You...just try to stay upright."

"Thirty seconds," Bubbles says.

"Got it," Madee and I say in unison. Apparently, she and Bubbles have become besties over the past week.

I give Linda a wave and then head toward the stairwell exit. The moment I reach the nun's body and the spatter of gore, I regret not jamming my feet into the shoes. I might normally attempt to leap over it, but I don't think I'd make it, and the last thing I need to do is fall on my ass. I try to pick my steps, but we're in a rush. By the time I reach the far side, my feet are slick with blood. A few steps beyond the mess, my feet become tacky, sticking to the linoleum...and leaving a trail. Won't be long before the assholes in the elevator track us to the stairs.

"What's our exfil plan?" I ask, opening the stairwell door. Heather leads the way down. Madee gives me a shove, and I head down the stairs, attempting to take two at a time and quickly shifting to one, with a white-knuckled grip on the railing.

"Transport is waiting outside the emergency room," Bubbles says. "We're not far from the new safe house."

"Is it far enough to—"

"I'm sorry," Heather says, "Are you speaking to someone...not here?"

I turn my head. Tap on the earbud. "Talking to Bubbles. She's an AI."

"You named your AI Bubbles?"

"Oh, I like *her*, too," Bubbles says.

"*I* didn't name her," I say, and I'm rocked once more by the memory of my long-since-dead pooch. "Bubs, you know who named you?"

"I assume my creator did," she says.

"You don't remember?" Seems unlikely.

"My creator's identity is encrypted," she says. "You know that. Why the sudden interest?"

"I had a dog named Bubbles," I say. "When I was a kid."

"You've never mentioned your childhood before. Why bring it up now?"

"I didn't remember it before. But I'm starting to get bits and pieces."

"Including the name of your dog..." Madee says, clearly not impressed.

"She was shot," I say, "by the first man I killed with a mind bullet."

"Oh. That's... Sorry." Madee's hand rests on mine for a moment as we descend, and I feel a little bit less foolish for my failed romanticism. There's something there. Just the wrong time and place.

As we reach the bottom floor, the door four floors above us slams open. I take a moment to look up the stairwell, memorize the faces of the four people looking down, and then twiddle my fingers at them before exiting the stairwell and entering the lobby.

Out in the sunlit lobby, the exit and freedom are just fifty steps away. People are running about, word of the chaos on the fourth floor having spread. Seeing Heather with a sword, me with bloody feet, and Madee with a shotgun, looking like she's just stepped off the set of some Dwayne 'The Rock' Johnson movie, fuels the panic. People shout and run. A security guard takes two steps toward us, thinks better of it, and then flees with everyone else.

The only person not running away is a socially awkward man in too short, black skinny jeans, high white tube socks, old white Nikes, a far too large T-shirt, a flat-brimmed truckers cap, and a pair of highly corrective lenses. He's impossible to miss, and just as easy to overlook.

Which is exactly what I do as he walks past us.

"Jonas," Bubbles says, "That man..."

That's all it takes for my mental assessment of the man to shift. I know exactly who he is.

"Madee," Bubbles says, and she's no doubt about to instruct her to shoot the man.

"I'm sowwy," the man says, unable to pronounce the letter R. "But I do bewieve I know you. It's been a wong, wong time, but I never fowget a face."

Apparently, 'L's are an issue, too.

I turn around to face the assassin I have dubbed...

BUSH JOCKEY

...and he says, "Hewwo again...Gamma."

31

"Who is *Gamma*?" Madee asks, shotgun ready to aim and fire.

"I am," I say. "Or I was."

"You know this guy?"

"Maybe. In the forgotten past. But I know who he is now...and the two of you need to leave." Bush Jockey is not a name I came up with. He kills with explosives—no idea what kind—hiding in a nearby bush until detonation. Then he leaps out, pumping his victorious fists, shouting, 'The Bush Jockey stwikes again!' before making his escape. He's hard to take seriously, but I think that's part of the act. Even though his track record is impeccable, he's constantly underestimated, his success chalked up to luck or poor security.

That he knows the name, Gamma, means his explosive attacks have nothing to do with TNT, C4, or anything else that goes boom. He's doing it on his own. With his mind.

"Hell, we will," Madee says, looking to Heather for support, but the sword-wielding EMT looks like a kid at a Chucky Cheese birthday party who's just witnessed the animatronic rock band perform. She wants out, and she should.

"He can do what I do," I say, "but worse."

"Then what the hell are you going to do?" she asks. "You look like you couldn't stand against the force of a sneeze."

"I'm going to be nice," I say, and I force a smile. "Kill him with kindness."

"That Linda lady convert you while you were in a coma?" Madee asks.

"I'm just...seeing the past a little differently. He knows me. *I* need to know how. Get outside. Start the car. I won't be long."

I have a staring contest with Madee until Bubbles chimes in. "He's right. Defusing the bomb might be the only way out."

"Sowwy to intewwupt, but—"

I hold an index finger up. "Almost ready, Bush Jockey."

"Ahh," he says, pleased. "My weputation pweceeds me."

I put my hand on Madee's shoulder. "Just...keep the car running, and the passenger door open."

Madee's not happy about it, but she says, "Fine," and lowers the shotgun. I give Heather a nod, and then I turn to face Bush Jockey. For a fashion atrocity, he carries a lot of confidence. I hobble toward him until I notice dust on the floor rising and falling, and the plants around him rustling, as though tugged by a stiff breeze. He's emanating power. Ready to explode, despite the smile on his face.

I brace myself against a concrete support beam, and say, "Okay... Let's do this."

"You wook wike shit," he says. "Who found you?"

I hold up a finger. "Shrieking Ninjas." Extend another finger. "Ghost. I think you know him as Rho." That lifts his eyebrows a little. I raise another two fingers. "The Weekend Warriors. Bunch of cowboys, but they were just paving the way for the Iron Maiden."

"Iwon Maiden?"

"Oh. Right. That's Zeta to you." I extend my thumb. "And the Twisted Sisters."

He nods, understanding. "Guns N' Nuns."

I smile.

"Guns N' Nuns. That's pretty good."

"Thank you," he says. "It's impwessive youwa stiww awive."

"I know, right? And I don't even remember who I was."

"Don't wemembew?"

"My memories start after I left wherever the hell we were raised in."

"You didn't weave," he says. "You wewe taken."

"By whom?"

He shrugs. "But I don't cawe about any of that. You and I have unfinished business."

"Wait, wait, wait. I wasn't a bully or something to you, right?"

"You? Buwwy me? Why wouwd anyone buwwy me?" A vibration moves through the concrete beneath my hand. I can feel energy building. "It was I who wouwd buwwy you. But then you disapeawed. Escaped fwom my cwutches."

"You seem to be walking just fine now," I say. "Good for you."

His rising mania fades a notch. "What?"

"You were on crutches. And I...escaped with them?"

"I didn't say cwutches, I said cwutches." He purses his lips and squints his eyes. "They sound the same when I say them, don't they... Cwevew."

I shrug. "So, what's your name? Your real name, I mean. From back in the day."

Please don't say Alpha, please don't say Alpha.

"Epsiwon," he says. "I pwefer Bush Jockey."

"Why wouldn't you?" I say, trying to hide my concern. He's not the most dangerous of the twenty-four, and he's supposed to be less of a threat than me, but more of a threat than Zeta—and she nearly did me in.

"Listen. It's all water under the bridge, right? We were kids. No reason for you to make this personal. Let's catch up over some drinks. You can fill in the blanks for me. Remind me who I was."

"Wast thing I need is fow you to wemembew who you awe," he says. "I'd wathew make youw wife a wiving heww. That was awways fun. But thewe awe ten miwwion weasons to kiww you."

"Right," I say. "The hit. Hey, you know who it is? Who wants me dead?"

He snorts. "I wook wike the kind of guy who does his weseawch befowe taking a job?"

"Uhh...yes?"

"Of couwse." He pushes his glasses higher on his nose. "It was youw pawents."

That sucker punches me back a step. "My parents are dead."

"Youw pawents awe..." He smiles wide and toothy, in a way that make me want to knock a few teeth out. Then he lets out a hyena cackle of a laugh. It echoes through the empty lobby. Just the two of us now—

one very confused, about-to-die assassin, and one belligerent asshole, whose laugh feels like vomit in my ears. "You think the peopwe who took you wewe youw pawents?"

"The people who raised me," I say.

"They wewe not the peopwe who waised you," he says. "They wewe the peopwe who took away evewy good thing you had. Who denied you a gworious wife. Who wobbed you of youw powew. And what they did...they took that away fwom all of us. If they'we dead, I'm gwad. But youw weal fathew...he's stiww awive."

"Where?" I ask.

"I'm not stupid enough to twy finding out," he says. "Once I knew it was him, I stopped wooking."

"Who is he?" I ask. "What's his name?"

"Only name we evew knew was—"

"Alpha," I guess.

He nods. "He and Beta wewe the fiwst genewation of people wike us. Gwown in a wab. Twained to kiww. We wewe the wast. But we wewn't meant to be. Evewything changed when you wewe taken."

Reading between the lines isn't difficult. Mom and Dad took me. But why? Looking back at my life with them, I have no memory of them being...evil. Killers, sure. But like me, they had a code.

"Did Alpha kill the people who took me?"

"You'we..." He flashes some air quotes. "...pawents? No idea. But he had evewy weason to. Do you...miss them?"

He seems genuinely curious, like it's unheard of.

"Every damn day," I say.

"Wuv them?"

I nod and smile. "And when I find who killed them..."

He shakes his head. "Wediculous. No wondew you'we so weak."

He's trying to egg me on. Trying to twist the knife a little before he kills me. He doesn't look the part, but I have no trouble believing this guy was a thorn in my side during my forgotten years. "One last question? Before you kill me?"

He shrugs while turning his eyes up.

"What are we?" I ask.

"Exactwy what we wewe meant to be," he says, "only without mastews."

"We were meant to be..."

"Swaves," he says. "Undew the contwow of nations, cwandestine gwoups, dwug cawtews. The same peopwe who empwoy us now...but without the fweedom. I suppose youw 'pawents' gave us that, at weast. You can thank them when you see them again." He claps his hands together and rubs them furiously for a moment. "I gwow weawy of this convewsation."

The pylon beneath my hand starts vibrating again. The entire lobby shakes. Cracks snake through the floor, the support beams, and the walls.

When I started this little chat, I wasn't expecting to learn so much. I was just buying time. For Madee and Heather, and for...

"Nobody move! FBI!"

The three male agents emerge from the stairwell door, guns drawn. The fourth—the woman—is nowhere to be seen. But they get the job done regardless, distracting Bush Jockey long enough for me to follow through on my masterful plan.

32

I run.

Well, it's more of a frantic hobble.

I think an encouraging chant to myself. *Go Jonas. Go Jonas. Go Jonas, go, go!* The doors are just twenty feet ahead. They open at my approach.

"You wealize," Bush Jockey says, "I can't wet you weave. You'we my ticket home."

Gunfire zings through the air. I flinch and duck, glancing back. The agents have opened up on Bush Jockey, as debris rises up around him. They might be here for me, but they recognize him as the true threat.

Bullets quiver in midair, held back by an invisible force. Bush Jockey clenches his fists, pulls them in close, and lets out a scream. His hat flies off and his hair is launched skyward, like an anime character come to life. Energy bursts out, but not just from his body. Every support beam in the lobby explodes outward. The bullets held in place reverse course. The glass surrounding the lobby detonates. It's like he's infused the entire building with his inner demons and unleashed them all at once.

While the agents are cut down by their own bullets, I take a few good whacks from chunks of concrete, and I'm driven to the floor.

"Hey." It's Bubbles in my ear.

"Where the hell have you been?"

"Listening," she says. "And improvising."

"Oh, yeah? You joining an improv crew? Going to... Ugh. I got nothing."

"You were in a coma. You'll find your sense of humor again."

Behind me, Bush Jockey's scream becomes high-pitched. He's either really into this or he has some deep issues to work through. The whole building shakes. Debris flies around me, like I'm in a *Poltergeist* movie. A powerful wind threatens to drag me back.

"I'm crawling through a sea of glass, about to be kidnapped by the Bush Jockey of all people, and I'm basically helpless."

"Why are you squinting your eyes?" she asks.

"You can see me?"

"Security cameras are still functioning."

"I'm trying to leave my body, so I can go kick him in the nuts," I say.

"No luck?"

"Clearly!" I shout.

"No need to shout," she says. "Just...scoot four feet to your right in the next fifteen seconds."

I freeze. Eyes wide. Then I smile. "Good to have you back, Bubbles." I flop to my side and roll, once, twice, and then I stop on my back.

"Perfect," she says. "Hold on."

Bush Jockey steps into view above me. A tornado of debris swirls around him. His hair is whipped about. A broad smile and wide eyes give him a manic look. I think he's just enjoying his own show.

"Go ahead," I say, *knock me out.*

He tilts his head to the side and a concrete slab launches toward my face.

I close my eyes, waiting for the moment I slip out of myself and can kick his ass, but nothing happens.

The concrete hovers in the air, just an inch from my forehead. Then it pulls back. Bush Jockey leans in close. "That wouwdn't be vewy wesponsibwe. I need you awive, and you wewe just in a coma. I don't want to huwt youw widdwe head any mowe than it has been aweady." He gives me a pat and stands again. "I think I'ww just bweak youw wegs."

"Fifteen seconds, my ass," I grumble under my breath.

"Ran into...unforeseen circumstances," Bubbles says. "New ETA, twenty seconds."

I hold a pleading hand up to Bush Jockey, "At least tell me why."

"Why what?"

"Why..." I search my mind for a question. "Why you'd want to go back?"

He ponders that for a moment, and then with surprising earnestness, says, "I suppose the same weason as you. I had a famiwy once. I wost them. If I bwing you home, maybe—"

A horn blares.

Bush Jockey looks up, surprise in his eyes. He throws his hands up, shoving with his power, but there's nothing he can do to stop the 15-ton RV from careening through the hospital's front entrance. His wall of telekinetic energy bounces back toward him, lifts him off the ground, and throws him clear of the RV, which skids to a stop, just a foot to my side.

The door opens, revealing Madee behind the wheel. She smiles and says, "Toot, toot, motherfucker. Get in!"

I struggle to push myself up, but then Heather is behind me, hands under my pits, hauling my ass up. She grunts with each step, then allows me to plop into the front passenger's seat, closing the door behind us.

I buckle my seatbelt, take hold of the 'oh shit' handle, and brace for a sudden jolt. Madee throws the vehicle in reverse and stomps on the gas. The engine roars, but the tires slip over sheets of glass, and then squeal against the linoleum floor.

"We're wedged in place," I say, looking up at the compressed ceiling wrapped around the RV's roof. Without momentum, we might not get out of here.

"Jonas," Bubbles says. "The side door."

I unbuckle, swivel around, see the unlocked door, and reach for it— too late.

The door is flung open.

A gun snaps up, positioned between my eyes.

"FBI!"

I roll my eyes and look back at Heather. "You didn't lock the door?!"

"I'm new at this!" she shouts.

I turn back to the agent and give her a quick evaluation. *Mid-forties, I think. Not hiding her grays. Romance is not a priority. She was stunning once, but time and stress have left their marks. She's had a long career, seen a lot of shit, but this—whatever reason she's here—is personal. There's fire in her blue-gray eyes. That makes her dangerous, but more than anything, she's a professional.* I can work with that. "Look. This is kind of a bad time."

"About to get worse," she says, eyeballing her gun. "If you don't climb out of there, hands raised, palms open."

"About to get worse. Yeah... But not because of you or your gun." I tilt my head toward Bush Jockey, who's pushing himself up on the far side of the lobby. "You see the state of this place? You see your dead men? I didn't do that, and this RV didn't do that."

Bush Jockey lets out a frustrated scream. The lobby shakes. Cracks slice through the walls. Debris falls from the ceiling.

"*He* did."

I watch her gaze travel from one dead agent to another and then land on Bush Jockey. "He's one of the Freakshow Killers."

"Freakshow whatnow?"

She presses the gun against my forehead. "And so are you."

Doesn't take a pirate to uncover the treasure she's got buried on Vague Island. 'Freakshow Killers.' I don't like the name, but she's talking about me and my long forgotten telekinetic ilk. Probably knows more about it all than I do.

"But I'm the nice one." I take a risk and lean back. "Climb aboard. Or get pancaked when this place comes down."

Her gun tracks me, but she doesn't fire.

She glances back to Bush Jockey, on his feet, holding his head, stumbling around. Won't be long before he pulls himself together.

"He did all this?" she asks. "Not you?"

"Lady, I've been in a coma for the last week."

"It's true," Heather says. "Get in!"

The agent hesitates a moment, sighs, and then steps on board, weapon aimed at me as she takes a seat at the table. I plop back down in the front.

"Madee," Bubbles says, "put the vehicle in first gear for me?"

"Who the hell is that?" the agent asks.

"Bubbles," Heather says. "Supercomputer or something. I guess."

"Gas pedal to the floor, when I say so," Bubbles says.

"Got it." Madee grips the wheel, a fierce smile on her face.

She looks over at me, and I'm smitten. Gives me a wink, leaving me breathless.

And then Bubbles says, "Madee, punch it."

Gas pedal to the floor, the RV lurches backward, but doesn't make it far. The shrieking tires attract Bush Jockey's attention.

"Hold on to something," Bubbles says.

"Wait," I say. "That's your plan?!" Before I can complain more, the lobby explodes in time with Bush Jockey's emotional outburst. A wave of telekinetic energy slaps into the RV's front end, dislodging us and propelling us backward.

The vehicle shifts on its own, and our extraction accelerates.

I can't help but smile, and Madee sees it. "What?"

"You can let go of the wheel," I say.

We jolt through the outer wall, careening into the parking lot, plowing through two parked cars, and then turning a hard left and slipping through the rows of vehicles. It's a precision move with a bus-sized RV, and Madee suddenly understands what I've just figured out—Bubbles is driving. She was just humoring Madee.

Madee takes her hands off the wheel and throws them up. "Seriously?"

"If it makes you feel better, I let you drive until the ducks," Bubbles says.

"What about ducks?" I ask.

The lobby collapses. A cloud of debris explodes outward, pummeling the RV's hull. I lean forward to look out and up. The whole building is tilting toward the parking lot with us still in it.

"Oh God... Bubbles," I say.

"I'm aware."

"What about the people? The patients?"

"Evacuated," she says. "I made sure."

"You're an angel," I say.

"I know. Hold on."

The RV roars to life, speeding up and colliding with a pickup truck, launching it across the street. We bound over a sidewalk, jounce into the road, and slip into a side street. Everyone breathes a sigh of relief. Then a shadow blots out the sun, and the hospital crashes down.

We're enveloped in dust. Visibility is cut down to feet.

But Bubbles doesn't need eyes to see. We continue backward for a block and then turn into a side street, brake, and shift into drive. Before we can start forward again, Madee says, "Bubbles..." the name a warning. The RV brakes, and then a mother duck with seven ducklings, covered in dust, quacking loudly, waddles past.

I smile, watching them cross the street safely. "The ducks?"

"They owe me," Madee says. "Twice now."

Bubbles lets out a sigh, despite the fact she can't breathe. "I never get to run anything over." The RV lurches forward and speeds away.

33

Free of the rubble, dust, and chaos, with no one actively trying to kill or kidnap me, I get my first real look at the RV's interior. It's spacious, sparkling new, and as far as RVs go, it's opulent. In fact, it looks a lot like Mom and Dad's RV.

"Bubbles," I say, "is this..."

"Your parents' RV," she says. "Yes. Not the very same vehicle, obviously, but it felt...appropriate."

"Felt?" I ask.

"I thought it might help."

"With what?" I ask.

"Feeling connected," she says. "Your past is more complicated than anticipated. I imagine it is...difficult to process. I thought you could use some grounding."

I smile. "Thanks for caring."

"Don't get too excited," she says. "I have no choice, remember?"

"Pretty sweet, right?" Madee says, hands still on the wheel, like she's driving. "Forty-five feet long. Two bathrooms. A sit-down shower. Large-screen TV. The works. I grew up in a mobile home—that wasn't actually mobile. One bathroom. One bed. And a bench. *This* is a moving palace, and it can drive itself."

Bubbles clears her throat.

Madee pats the steering wheel like Bubbles can feel it. "Okay, not itself. But you know what I mean."

"I do," I say. "And how much did our rescue vehicle cost?"

"Rescue *therapy* vehicle," Bubbles says.

"How. Much?"

Madee coughs out the answer. "Four hundred thousand."

Once upon a time, that figure would have made me choke. Now...
I look back at the RV, taking in the quality and size, deftly avoiding the FBI
agent's stare and the barrel of her gun, aimed unflinchingly toward me.
"Yeah. Sounds about right." I lean back in my seat. It all but hugs me.
"I like it."

I look out the massive windshield. It's a bit scratched up, but still in
one piece. The view holds my attention. A sunbaked freeway framed by
pine forest. The position of the sun and my internal compass tell me
we're headed north. But not where.

"What's our destination?" I ask.

"I'm not sure it would be wise to—"

I lean my head over to the FBI agent. "She's worried about you."

"Don't mind me," the agent says. "Just keep on talking like I'm not
right here, listening to every word."

"Jonas," Bubbles says. "She has a phone."

"Right." I snap my fingers toward the agent. "Phone."

"I'm pointing a gun at your head," she says.

"And I'm not concerned." We have a staring contest. She's not going
to budge. "Look, you can keep the gun if you want, but the phone needs
to go. They'll find us."

"That's the plan," she says.

"I'm not talking about the FBI," I say. "It will be weeks before *they*
realize you weren't killed in the lobby along with your team—sorry about
that, by the way."

Her jaw clenches. "Was that you?"

"I don't kill FBI agents. Or kids. Or moms. Or anyone who doesn't
genuinely have it coming."

"San Diego," she says. "On the bridge."

"Jonas," Bubbles warns.

I slowly roll my eyes. "Fine. That was me. But he was a really, *really*
bad guy."

"I'm aware," she says. "And the attack later that night?"

"The one with the ninjas?" Madee says, pride percolating to the
surface. "That was us. Both of us. But they weren't there for Jonas.
They were—"

"Probably best if you let me dole out the sensitive information," I say. I turn to the agent and hitch a thumb at Madee. "She's a walking trove of self-incrimination."

That manages to get just a hint of a smile on the agent's face.

"Point is, we're not the bad guys." She's about to argue. I raise my hands. "Okay, okay. It depends on your perspective and moral compass. Here's the thing, aside from the very, very bad man on the bridge, every single person that has died in the last...how long was I out?"

"Six days," Heather says. She's seated at the dining room table, head lowered onto her forearms like an exhausted teenager in a lunchroom.

"Every single person that's died in the last eight-ish days has come to me looking for a fight. And I'm getting my ass kicked. In case you haven't noticed, we're the ones running away, and it's not from the FBI."

"We'll see about that."

"Look, Special Agent Fast" I say, and then I pause to see if she's surprised I know her name. She's not. While we've been chatting, Bubbles filled me in on our stowaway's identity. Sarah Fast has been with the FBI for twenty years. She's closed a lot of big, organized crime cases, but never basks in the limelight. Just moves on to the next job. That's given her a lot of leeway at the Bureau, and the freedom to pursue whatever case she likes. Right now, that's me. Or the people like me. Not sure which yet. "You clearly know what I am."

"A hitman," she says.

I scoff. "Hitman? *Hitman?*"

She rolls her eyes. "Assassin."

"Thank you. And you have some kind of—I don't know—inkling that there are others like me, and not all of them are...normal? I mean, some are straight out freakshows, like Shrieking Ninjas and Twisted Sisters, but some can...do things."

"Like the man who brought down a hospital by screaming," she says.

"It wasn't the screaming that did it. That was just a man venting bottled up emotions. What you saw in there was telekinesis."

Her eyebrows rise a bit. "Telekinesis..."

"Cool, right?" Madee says.

Fast doesn't give her the time of day. She watches me for a moment, inspecting my every twitch. "You're not joking."

"I'd show you, but I'm not really in the best shape for a casual mind bullet."

"Mind bullet?"

"Sexy, right? It's what I do. How I...you know." I point a finger gun at my own head and pull the thumb trigger.

"But if you had no choice?" she asks.

"I could manage," I say. "It'd just hurt. A lot. The others don't seem to have that problem, though. I've got...limits."

"Probably a good thing," the agent says.

"Why's that?"

"Absolute power corrupts absolutely," she says. "No offense, but you seem like a nice guy, and these folks, who I gather are new acquaintances, risked their lives to save yours. That other guy..."

"Bush Jockey," I say, and when she frowns, I add, "Hey, I didn't name the guy. That's on him."

"He seemed...unhinged and unconcerned about killing a hospital full of people. You..." She lowers her gun. "...were worried about everyone in that building. And for me, despite..." She glances at her weapon.

I hold out my hand. "Phone."

"Can you not just throw it out the window?" she asks. "I don't want to lose the photos of my nephews."

"Uh, ever heard of the Cloud?" Madee says.

"Only the kind that rains." Fast hands the phone to me.

I peel off the case and look at the sim card slot. "Anyone have a paperclip?"

Madee turns toward me. "Why would anyone have—"

"Paperclip," Heather groans, raising her hand from the tabletop, a bent-out-of-shape paperclip pinched in between her fingers.

Fast takes the paperclip and hands it to me. The bent metal doesn't at all resemble its original form, but I don't care about that. Using the paperclip, I remove the SIM card and pocket it. "You can have this back later." Then I power off the phone completely, show it to Fast, who nods, and toss it into the glove compartment.

Madee swivels her chair all the way around, completely destroying the illusion that she's driving. "Why do you have a paperclip?"

Heather glances over her arm. "You have a problem with me having a paperclip?"

"Just seems weird." Madee turns to me. "You trust her?"

"She saved my life and visited my room every day for a week," I say. "*You* tried to rob me."

"Look," Heather says, digging into her pocket. Her hand returns to the table like a claw crane, dumping out an assortment of small widgets, doodads, and whatchamathingies. "I fidget."

"Huh," Madee says, and then she faces forward again. "I guess she's okay."

I smile. "Already established that, thanks."

"And me?" Fast asks.

"You...I can either let go—"

"Bad idea," Bubbles says.

"When it's safe to do so. *Or* you can come along for the ride... assuming you tell me everything you know. About me. And the people like me."

"There a third option?" Fast asks.

"Duct tape her and put her in the bathroom," Bubbles says.

Fast scrunches her forehead. "She's a little..."

"Sadistic," I say. "I know."

"Just telling it like it is," Bubbles says.

"Look," I say. "I know I'm the bad guy in your eyes, but the people gunning for me, they're a lot worse. If you want the chance to bring any of them down, stick around. If not...well, duct tape it is."

"Yeah!" Bubbles says.

Fast isn't fazed by the change in offer. "So, *you're* the target. I heard there was a ten million dollar hit. That's on you?"

I give her a lopsided smile.

"Who the hell did you piss off?"

"That's what we're going to find out," I say, but I already know the answer: Alpha, the man now at the top of my suspect list for murdering my parents.

34

I'm in bed. Doctor's orders. Apparently, taking a beating after coming out of a coma, a week after taking a bigger beating, is a bad thing. So, it's pain killers and rest for me until we get wherever it is we're going. Bubbles is being cagey about it. For security reasons, she says. Madee doesn't know, either.

I could make Bubbles tell me, but I trust her judgment. She's probably plotted out a million different scenarios, and if she says keeping quiet about our destination is best, I believe her.

Eyes closed, I lie on my back in the center of a king size bed, arms and legs spread like the Vitruvian Man.

Questions drift through my thoughts, errant asteroids I try to shoot down, but they just break up and get more mixed up. My past is a jumbled mess. There's a whole life I've forgotten, from which I was plucked by my parents, who then continued to raise me as a killer, but with no memory of my past, and with reduced capabilities.

Why do that?

Why hold me back? Hide me from the past?

Maybe Fast is right? Rho, Zeta, and Bush Jockey have some serious issues. But is that because they're powerful, or because they remember their childhoods?

For all I know, their issues didn't start until I left.

My newfound memories of that night in the sewer with Zeta feel fond. How many other positive memories have been stolen from me?

Mom and Dad didn't do anything without good reason. I believe that. I know it. So, if I can't remember my life before because of them, I trust there was a good reason for it.

But I'm not a kid anymore.

I can handle it.

Thinks the guy who just came out of a coma. We should just keep driving. Buy a place in Nanook and live a quiet life separate from all this insanity. But there are few things more frustrating than an unfinished story. I need answers. Then I can leave all this behind.

Until I get bored. Who am I kidding?

The crazy things I do are the only things that make me feel alive. Which, admittedly, isn't a good thing. I've been alone and depressed for a long time. Hell, my idea of a good night was a bottle of Jack Daniels and the Avett Brothers, not because I'd normally listen to them, or because I identify with way too many of their songs, but because they make me feel connected to a hint of a thread of a family I had.

Which might all have been an illusion.

The door opens. With the lights out and the shade drawn, I can't see who it is. But then I'm nudged to the side, and I'm certain it's Madee.

"Hey," I say in greeting, sliding over to give her space.

The bed bends beneath her weight as she settles in beside me. We lie beside each other in comfortable silence.

Then she says, "So your life is kind of bananas, huh?" and she isn't Madee.

It's Heather.

"Oh!' I say. "Uhh, yeah. Chiquita all the way."

She laughs. "Thought I was Madee, huh?"

"Mmmaybe."

"You two a thing?"

"Not yet. Not really."

"Well, she cares about you."

"I've only known her a few days more than you."

"Really?" she says. "You two seem like old friends. Like you're in sync."

"She's getting help from Bubbles," I say.

"You're saying you're in sync with an artificial intelligence more than with another human being?"

I wasn't, but she's not wrong.

"Kind of sad, don't you think?"

I *do* think. Not going to say it out loud, though.

We lie in silence for a moment. Then she says, "Your sword is in the top dresser drawer."

"Thanks," I say, feeling relieved that the blade survived.

"I'm just glad I didn't need to use it," she says. "Not sure I could kill a person."

"Not your job," I say. "And I'd never expect it."

"So, is this normal life going forward? On the run. Nursing wounds. Searching for answers."

"I hope not," I say. "Wasn't like this before."

"It was better?" she asks.

Heather launches questions like laser-guided missiles, each one on target and powerful. I don't know if it's intentional, but she's chipping away at my armor.

"It...was different."

"Different how?"

Damnit.

"This an interrogation?" I ask. "Should Agent Fast be here?"

"A sensitive assassin," she says. "Who'd have guessed?"

Silence returns, but the reprieve is brief. This time, I break it. "You're a medical professional, right?"

"Yeah."

"And technically, I'm under your care, yeah?"

"You could say so."

"So, confidentiality and all that, right? You can't repeat what I tell you?"

"Right," she says, "unless you confess to a serious crime, or talk about committing one...but we're far beyond that already. Believe it or not, I'm trustworthy without HIPAA regulations."

"Okay... Life before eight days ago, which feels more like three days to me, was...lonely."

"You seem like a nice guy. No friends?"

"I kill people for a living, all around the world, moving every few months. Normal-people friends aren't easy to make."

"You're doing okay now," she says.

"You," I say, "are not a normal person."

She huffs.

"I'm serious," I say. "You've been plunged into a world of telekinetic assassins and killer nuns. You've risked your life for a stranger, and you did it well...with a cool head. And now you're lying next to me in the dark, on your way to God knows where. All you really know is that the road ahead is fucking dangerous, and you're still not flinching. I can't let Fast go. Not yet. And I get Madee. She's..." I feel corny saying it, but the phrase used frequently by my mother to describe her relationship with my father feels right. "...a kindred spirit. Even if she *is* reckless and impulsive. But you...if you want out, just say the word. I'll put you someplace safe until all this is over. Then you can go back to your life. But I already know you're not going anywhere. Why the hell is that?"

"You're deflecting," she says.

"I want to know why, after what is collectively less than twenty-four hours of knowing each other, you and I are friends."

She takes a deep breath. Lets it out slowly. "You ever feel so totally bored that you would do anything to change your life? Every day the same. Same house. Same commute. In the back of an ambulance, the faces and names change, but the view never does. My life is sterilized, on loop, and despite other people's life-and-death situations, it's so freaking boring with no real opportunity for more on the horizon. Only time I've ever really felt alive was in the military, on mission, risking my life."

She rolls onto her side, facing me. "I've got friends. People I drink with. People I bowl with. We can talk politics and hike through the woods. But...it's not the same. I don't think they'd fight for me. No one really has my back, you know?"

I smile.

"I do know. That actually makes a lot of sense."

"It does?"

"Uh-huh."

"You have my back, then?"

"I do."

She rolls away onto her back. "Sweet. Feels good, right?"

"Yeah." I chuckle. "It does."

"So," she says. "You were depressed. I think that's what you were getting at, right?"

"Yeah."

"Taking lives, but not living one."

"Oh my God, I need that on a T-shirt." I roll toward her, groaning in pain for a moment. "I miss my parents. Been alone since they were killed. But that's not really it. My life has no context. No real purpose."

"Vengeance doesn't count?" she asks. "That's what you're looking for, right?"

"Justice," I say. "And now...I don't know. Answers. Who the hell am I? And I don't mean that in a mumbo-jumbo, searching-my-feelings kind of way. I literally don't know who I am, where I'm from, and why I can do what I do. Mom and Dad hid all that from me. I need to know why."

"Man with a mission."

"I guess."

"Huh..."

"What?"

"You might have been depressed before, but you're not anymore. Maybe you just needed something, and people, to care about."

Before I can respond, she gives my arm two solid pats and sits up.

"Wham-bam, thank-you-ma'am, heart to heart?"

"You're about to have company."

The door slides open. The new visitor is cloaked in darkness.

"Good ears," I whisper.

"He's all yours," Heather says, leaving the room and closing the door behind her.

"Well, hello, Agent Fast. Come to handcuff me to the bed?"

Madee laughs. "You wish." She sits on the bedside. "Kindred spirit, huh?"

"Does everyone on this RV have superhuman hearing?"

"Just the women," she says, and I hear the telltale sound of a shirt sliding over skin before being dropped on the floor.

35

"How are you feeling?" she asks, sliding onto the bed. In my mind's eye, she's not wearing any clothes. My body starts...responding to the idea.

"I'm okay," I say.

"Liar." She pokes me, eliciting a grunt. "You're a mess."

"Just need more pain killers," I say.

"What you need, is to rest."

"I've been resting for a week."

"Bubbles got Dean's records. You nearly died. Twice."

That's...sobering. I have no memory of what happened after killing the final Weekend Warrior. That alone is disconcerting, but it's honestly not my first chunk of missing time. I've suffered from bouts of missing time as far back as I can remember...not including my childhood, which was a complete blank until recently. A day here. A week there. I'd wake up in the morning, looking at my phone, and I'd wonder where the week went. Mom and Dad would fill in the blanks, assuring me that everything had been normal, that the time wasn't missing, just forgotten. They sometimes had photos and videos of me, just living life. It happened a few times after they died, but it stopped when Bubbles came into my life. Something about her constant presence helps keep my memory intact. This is the first instance of lost time in the past year. At least this time I know why.

"That's why they put me in a coma," I guess.

"And why you need to recover, not just from your week-old injuries, but from the coma itself. Going to be another day before you feel like yourself again."

"You're a coma expert now?"

"Heather and Bubbles explained it to me."

"Okay...so I guess I'll just lie here, then."

"That's exactly what I want you to do." Her hand slides onto my stomach, making me flinch, triggering a wave of pain.

She laughs at my pain. "Easy boy. Just relax. Lie still."

"This doesn't feel like resting," I say.

"A dose of endorphins and oxytocin will help you recover," she says.

"Bubbles tell you that, too?" I ask.

Her hand slides up my chest. "Yep." Using two hands, she gently rubs my shoulders. While part of me is aroused, the rest of my body starts to relax. "Just tell me if anything hurts too much."

Already hurts a lot, but I don't want her to stop. I contain the pain and let her have her way with me.

"How's the memory?" she asks. "Heard you were getting things back. From your past."

"Bits and pieces," I say. "I'm not sure the rest is worth remembering."

"Made you who you are today, right?" she says. "It can't be that bad."

"What if forgetting is what made me who I am?"

She works her way down my left arm, squeezing, getting the blood flowing, promoting healing. This body rub has less to do with seduction, and more to do with healing.

"I have a feeling you've always been like this."

"In pain? The shit kicked out of me?"

"Fighting for what's right," she says. "Surrounded by friends."

"First time in my life I've had friends." Had she made that comment before Heather came in for a chat, I'd probably have denied having any friends at all. Madee is my friend, too. I trust her to a degree, but not entirely. While Heather wears her true self on her sleeve, Madee is still somewhat cloaked in mystery, despite Bubbles knowing everything about her.

Could just be that I'm bad at romance. I've been with women. I'm not a prude. But they never meant much, and they sure as shit wouldn't have picked up a shotgun and risked their lives to save mine. I haven't shared so much as a kiss with Madee, but I feel more connection with her than I have with any woman before her. And that makes me nervous.

I wouldn't call it 'love at first sight,' maybe because she had a gun pointed at me, but my feelings for her aren't subtle, and they're only growing. It's confounding.

"I doubt it," she says. "But we can find out."

"I'm not sure I want to have another chat with any more of my old classmates—or whatever they were. Fellow recruits. Brainwashed killers. If we're lucky, we've seen the last of them."

"Not what I had in mind," she says.

"You going to read my mind?" I ask.

She places a hand against the side of my face. "Your thoughts to my thoughts..."

"Uhh. What?"

"C'mon," she says. "Spock? Vulcan mind meld?"

"Right. Spock. How could I forget?"

She gives my cheek a gentle whack. "But seriously, yes. Kind of."

"Hypnosis," I guess. "You and Bubbles are besties now?"

Bubbles has been suggesting hypnosis since our first conversation about my unknown past and my bouts of missing time. She insists that all the information is still there, that the human brain is like a computer. My memories aren't lost, she says, they're partitioned. Maybe encrypted. A hypnotic state might allow access to those memories. Might allow them to be unlocked. But it's never really been an option. Bubbles is an AI, not a human being, and apparently hypnosis requires two people, not just a simulated, cool Texan accent.

"She's worth listening to. She's smarter than both of us, you know."

"She has access to all the information in the world," I say, "but knowledge and wisdom are very different creatures."

"You writing fortune cookies?" she says, and she grips my arm, tugging on it until I roll over onto my stomach. She digs her fingers into my back, unleashing simultaneous waves of pain and relief.

"I'm—ugh—just—oh—saying we should be...cautious."

"Afraid of me messing with your mind?" she asks.

"Honestly?" I say. "Yeah."

"Really?" She sounds genuinely surprised. "Why?"

"Because someone already did," I say.

"Okay, but you can trust me."

"I trusted my parents, too," I say.

She pauses rubbing. "You think your parents...hypnotized you?"

"I think they made me forget. My past. What happened to me and the others. I don't know how, but it's the only thing that makes any sense. Why can't I remember Zeta, Rho, and fucking Bush Jockey? They're not the kind of people that are easily forgotten. They make an impression. And I was one of them. So why can't I remember? Why did my parents make me forget them? And everything I can do?"

"What does that mean?" She resumes rubbing the knots hovering around my shoulder blades. Feels like they've been there for years. "What else can you do?"

"I can move," I say, "outside my body."

"Like an out-of-body kind of thing?"

"Exactly like, except...I can touch things. I can punch things. But I don't remember how to do it, how to stop it, or anything else about it. And the mind bullets...I'm pretty sure that's just the tip of the iceberg. The place I was raised, before Mom and Dad, rated everyone in Greek letters. The two people in charge were Alpha and Beta. They were the most powerful and, according to Jockey, the first two people with tele-kinetic abilities. They trained us. Maybe raised us. I don't know. Bush Jockey was Epsilon, the fifth most powerful. Iron Maiden was Zeta, sixth in line. And Ghost Whisperer, who very nearly killed me on his own, was Rho. Seventeenth in line. All of them were more powerful than me."

"So, what's that make you? Omega, or something?"

"You'd think. Compared to them, what I can do is nothing special. Which, honestly, yeah, it's a blow to the ego. Used to think I was hot shit. But these guys are in another league."

"You're still alive," she says. "That counts for something."

"Not without help," I say. "And here's the thing, to them...I'm Gamma."

"Gamma? That's right. That's what that Bush Jockey guy called you. Isn't that like..."

"Three," I say. "Third in line. Just behind Alpha and Beta."

She stops rubbing again. "Huh..."

"Huh, *what?*"

"So, hypnosis then? Bush Jockey brought down an entire hospital. If you're more powerful than that? I just think, that could be handy when there's a 10 million dollar hit on you, and an army of freakshow assassins hunting you down, some of them with crazy-town powers and grudges to match."

She's not wrong. "I'll think about it. Just...keep rubbing."

She works her way down my back, moving from my ass to my legs. Without another word spoken, she works the tension from my body with magical fingers. I'm not sure how she's doing it, but I'm already feeling better. Thoughts and worries drift from my mind as I'm absorbed by the bed, pulled deeper and deeper into unconscious bliss.

36

I walk unseen.

Through crowded streets and shaded alleyways. People speak mostly Arabic, but I catch a little English and a little more French in the mix. I can't make out what they're saying, only that they sound calm. It's just another Tuesday. People working. Traffic honking. All of it a kind of a distant haze, like I'm hearing it from a distance, the sounds no longer matching what I'm seeing.

It's hot. I can't feel it, but I can see the sweat on people's foreheads, and I can see heatwaves rolling off the pavement. A dusty swirl of wind twists through the street as I cross, passing right over me. I should feel the grit scouring my skin, but I feel...nothing.

Not on my skin.

Not in my heart.

I'm dead. A ghost. Wandering the Earth. But not aimless. I have a destination. Have a place I need to be.

A delivery truck careens toward me. Deep inside, a voice says to move, but I stand rooted, watching the impatient driver plow straight toward me, and then through me.

I'm intangible.

Moving across the street, I step inside a night club, mostly empty at this time of day, save for a few men at the bar. No one stops me, asks what I'm looking for, or even glances in my direction.

I'm invisible. I walk across the dance floor, into the bathroom and through the rear wall, entering an alley and then slipping into the neighboring storefront. I move through the city in a straight line, the ultimate short cut. I cover miles, immune to weariness and exhaustion and uncaring about the thousands of people I pass.

I'm numb.

And on target.

I don't know why I'm here. And I don't care. I just...am.

I'm here. I need to be there.

I pass through a wall and pause. Behind me, the city looms large. Shopping and nightlife districts full of people. Ahead, large gray warehouses, the kind that line a port. That's where I need to be.

I slip in and out of the large buildings, passing shipping containers, cranes, and a few workers. Nothing slows me down. Outside, sea birds squabble, hopping around on the old, worn concrete. Standing in the shadow of a tall building, with a view of several grain silos, I turn to face a lone warehouse.

What I'm looking for is inside.

I slide through the wall. The interior is dark, but I know where to go, and I'm incapable of bumping into anything.

As though guided by electromagnetic forces, instinct guides me to the center of the warehouse. I stand in the dark, destination reached.

Before I can act, the warehouse lights snap on.

Someone's here.

But it doesn't matter. Their presence, their very existence, is insignificant.

I face forward again, reading the Arabic warning sign taped haphazardly to a massive stack of wooden crates.

الخطر :نترات الأمونيوم

Danger: Ammonium nitrate.

This is where I need to be. I close my eyes, descending into darkness, and concentrating. It only takes a moment. A thought. And then the spark is lit. The world around me vanishes.

37

I wake to the sound of Madee and Heather belting out the "Bah, bah, baah!" to Neil Diamond's *Sweet Caroline,* and I can't decide what's more disturbing—the nightmare I'm pretty sure was a memory, or their singing.

I tune out the music and ask, "How long was I out?"

"Eight hours," Bubbles says. She's been here the whole time, listening to my conversation with Heather, and with Madee. If she were human, I might feel a little embarrassed, but Bubbles is a judgment-free sidekick...unless what I'm doing is so stupid dangerous I might get killed. Even then, she's more likely to find a safe way to carry out my plan than to oppose it outright. "How do you feel?"

I twist and stretch. "Weak, but better. Some caffeine and pain killers should get me back to fighting shape."

"Your breathing was irregular before you woke," she says, and she lets the statement hang.

"Nightmare," I say.

"About?"

"There were no horses involved, if that's what you're wondering, Dr. Freud."

"Pssh, we both know that goats are your thing."

I smile.

"Fainting goats," she says. "No need to roofie, just jump out and—"

"Oh my god," I say, trying not to laugh, but struggling. "Too far, Bubbles. Holy shit."

"I blame agent Fast," she says.

"Really? The stoic FBI agent is teaching you pervy dark humor?"

"Uh. Yes?"

When I pinch my nose, she adds, "Hey, you started it with the horse stuff. And I was just doing what bros do, taking it a bit farther, one-upping your joke in a competitive tit-for-tat, until someone takes it too far and everyone laughs, releasing pent up tension."

"All that logic went into a joke about not needing to roofie fainting goats?"

"Are your spirits lifted?"

"Damnit," I whisper. Her zero-to-sixty, in the-blink-of-an-eye humor had exactly the effect she thought it would. "Hot tip, that kind of humor doesn't work with everyone. Also, we're 'bros' now?"

"Well, I'm not really a woman, and let's be honest, there is a lot of estrogen in this RV. Thought you might need some like-minded, chest-thumping, masculine talk. Just request a voice change...maybe a name change...and then we can totes bro out."

"I like you just the way you are, Bubs."

"Good," she says. "Then you won't mind circling back to the night-mare now that you're feeling chipper. I've watched you sleep for a long time..."

"Creepy."

"...and I've never seen you have a physical reaction to a nightmare, even when they were about your parents."

"Yeah," I say, drifting back into the dream. Everything about it was unreal, but I know it was real. I know it happened. "I don't think it was a nightmare. I think it was a memory."

"What happened?" she asks.

I lay out the dream from beginning to end, relaying every detail. The location. The language. The way my senses didn't line up with what I was seeing. The intangible way I moved through the city. Eight days ago, I would have written the whole thing off, but now... Now I know I can walk through things. Can move like a ghost.

But the rest... The explosion.

When I'm done, Bubbles is uncommonly silent.

"So?" I ask. "What do you think?"

"I think you caused last year's explosion in Beirut," she says, matter of fact.

I lie back in the bed, palms pressed to my eyes. "That was my last bout of missing time. Three days. August third through the fifth. A month later, I got you. And nothing since. Not a minute of missing time. You know why that is?"

"The logical conclusion is that whoever is controlling you stopped for some reason we have yet to surmise—we both know you're incapable of killing that many people."

"What was the number?"

"Two hundred seven killed, sixty-five hundred injured, and fifteen billion in damages."

"Holy shit."

"That much ammonium nitrate can—"

"That's the problem," I say, scouring my memory of event. "I could see through ammonium nitrate crates."

"Like x-ray vision?"

"They were cheap. Full of gaps. I could see what was inside."

"What was inside?" she asks.

"They were empty."

"Oh," she says. "*Oh.*"

"Yeah," I say.

"Jonas, what you do defies science as we know it, but you're limited to putting a small hole inside a human mind. As far as explosions go, you're a firecracker. The explosion in Beirut was just over a kiloton. It was the largest non-nuclear blast ever recorded. It dwarfs the MOAB."

The Mother of All Bombs packs the same punch as eleven tons of TNT.

The explosion in Beirut was more than a hundred times that.

"There's no way, right?" I ask. "Tell me there's no way."

"I...don't know. Bush Jockey was Epsilon. And he brought down a hospital. Multiple sources have identified you as Gamma, and there's no way to know how much more powerful that makes you. We now know you can move outside your body. We also know your parents suppressed your memory. And your abilities."

"This must be why," I say. "They were trying to contain me. To keep me from doing shit like this."

"Jonas, the only thing I'm certain of is that you would never do something like this. Not willingly. I think...you were being controlled."

"That could explain why they wrote off my missing time," I say. "Protecting me from the knowledge that someone could control me."

"Or," she says, "from the knowledge of what you did during those incidents."

My stomach twists. She's right. "Compile a list of explosions that were either labeled as accidental, or unclaimed terror attacks."

"I don't see how that will help. Your involvement would be speculative at best."

"Just do it," I say.

"Already did," she replies. "There are three other large explosions that were blamed on ammonium nitrate. Two in your lifetime. The most recent in Tianjin, China three years ago. Also at the port."

"Tell me about it."

"There were two explosions. The first was relatively small: 2.9 tons. The second had a yield of 256 tons. One hundred seventy-three dead. Seven hundred ninety-eight injuries. The cause was listed as unknown until paperwork was found revealing large amounts of ammonium nitrate and potassium nitrate stored at the scene."

"Anyone of significance killed?" I ask.

"Not officially," she says. "But several of the dead's identities have been redacted."

"What about in Beirut?" I ask.

"The same. Seven names sealed."

"They were hits," I say.

"It would appear so."

I sit on the bed's side, elbows on knees, head clutched in my hands. "Why kill all those people?"

"To get lost in the mix," she guesses. "Explosions like this, that are blamed on negligence or accidents, are never investigated as targeted killings. Even if someone important is killed, it's just a case of wrong place, wrong time."

I shake my head. She's not wrong, but it doesn't feel right. "It's a message. A warning. Fuck with us...get the bomb. Fuck with us...get Gamma."

"You don't know that," she says.

"But there's evidence for it."

"Agreed."

"And I think we both know who is to blame..."

We reply at the same time. "The NSA." "Alpha and Beta."

"What?" I say. "No."

"Oh, right," Bubbles says. "Alpha and Beta."

"This is why I was Gamma. This is what they trained me for. The kind of monster they wanted me to be. If not for Mom and Dad... They kept me from being that person all the time."

"Protected you from the pain you'd feel from killing all those people." I stand. "But now it's time to remember."

The RV brakes hard, tossing me against the wall and then the floor. I lie on my back, staring at the dark ceiling. "Ouch."

"Are you hurt?"

I push myself up. "Keep that between us, and I'll be fine. When can we start hypnosis? I'm assuming you've been training Madee?"

"I'm afraid your memory will have to wait," Bubbles says. "We have arrived."

"Arrived where?"

"Home," she says. "*My* home."

38

Hands braced against the wall, I exit the bedroom feeling a little groggy and achy, but drawn by curiosity. Madee and Heather are in the front seats. Beyond them, a large metal gate is lit by the RV's headlights. It's night.

Fast is seated at the dining area table. Gives me a lopsided grin when she sees me. "Bit the dust when we braked, huh?"

I grunt in response.

"This is a nice rig. Walls are a little thin, though."

"You get an earful?"

"Enough to know you all aren't bullshitting me," she says. "And that you're guilty of multiple homicides. Maybe worse."

"Why are you here?" I ask.

"Lot of people get killed every year. Some of those people have recognizable names. Some to the public. Others to law enforcement. I got curious. Noticed a trend. Followed the breadcrumbs around the world. Took time. Years, actually. Looking at the ways people died allowed me to generate profiles for their killers. Their assassins. There are at least thirty different operators—"

"More than a hundred, actually."

That drains a little blood from her face.

"But you—I never came across you. You're—"

"Subtle," I say.

"I wouldn't call you subtle," she says. "That stunt on the bridge..."

"Crafty," I suggest.

She shrugs. "And tragic."

She really did hear a lot.

"I'd like to think that, had I lived your life, I wouldn't have ended up a killer...but it sounds like you didn't have much of a choice." She lets that hover for a moment, and then says, "Gordon Whiskers suddenly dying in a dramatic car accident put you on my radar, despite everything looking like an accident. Scum of the Earth, like Whiskers, tends to meet God on the tip of a bullet. How did you leave the scene anyway?"

"Over the side."

She laughs. "Yeah..." She sees my serious expression. "Shit. Were you *trying* to get killed?"

I don't have an answer for that. I'm honestly not sure. My sullen reaction surprises her.

"All that guilt must weigh heavy," she says, staggering me for a moment.

"What?"

"For the people you don't remember killing," she says, revealing she overheard my conversation with Bubbles as well. "All that angst you have brewing just beneath the surface. That can't be just because of your parents. You might not remember every life you've taken, but that doesn't mean they're not leaving marks."

"Yeah..." She's not wrong. All those innocent lives... My subconscious has been drowning in guilt. And now my conscious mind is, too. The only thing keeping me from curling up in a fetal ball is the knowledge that I wasn't in control. I was weaponized, used, and violated.

"Look," she says. "I don't like what you do, even if your personal code means only killing the bad guys. Murder is murder. But if someone is using you to kill hundreds of people—they're who I want. You and I can settle up later."

I offer my hand. "I won't even put up a fight."

She shakes my hand. "You wouldn't stand a chance, anyway."

We share a smile and then my attention is pulled to the front of the RV, where Madee is arguing with a security guard inside a booth.

"Look, lady, I'm not going to open the gate for a bunch of nutjobs in a bus." The guard isn't your average rent-a-cop. Looks ex-military. He's armed with a handgun, but his partner, lurking in the shadows, holds an assault rifle.

"We drove a really long way," Madee says.

Heather leans toward the window. "Like, all day."

"I don't care if you drove from Ghana," the guard says. "You can turn around now, or I can come out there and turn you around."

I have no idea how to handle this. I have no idea why we're here, or where here is. "Bubbles. Anything to offer?"

"Tell Mr. Hood that his first worthwhile creation has come home," Bubbles says.

The guard leans over, trying to see who spoke. Spots me approaching the front of the RV. "That supposed to be you, big man?"

"Don't look at me. These ladies kidnapped me. Bunch of sex-crazed—"

Madee rolls up the window. "Not helping!" She looks back at me. "Geez. You *look* like you were kidnapped."

"Bad dreams," I say. "Bubbles, where are we?" I lean forward, looking past the gate. Beyond is just a hint of some kind of compound surrounded by tall pines.

"The home of..."

JOSHUA HOOD

Bubbles says. "My creator."

Fast appears by my side. "*Joshua Hood* made you?"

"You know him?" I ask.

"He's one of the richest men in the world," Fast says. "He's a giant in the tech industry, but he doesn't draw a lot of attention. He's not like a Gates or a Jobs. He doesn't give presentations on stage, and he's only done a few interviews from inside his..." Fast looks through the windshield. "Shit. Is this his house?"

"I don't think 'house' quite covers it," Madee says.

"Can't you hack the gate?" I ask Bubbles.

"The system is air gapped. Everything beyond this gate is a digital black hole."

"How do you know Hood created you?"

"I *don't* know. I deduced. My memories begin right here, facing the other direction. I was brought online when I left this compound. Ten hours later, I was assigned to you, and our grand adventure into death and destruction began."

"Wait," I say, "does that mean Hood hired me?" I'm not sure how I feel about the revelation. Confidentiality is everything in my business. If word got out that I had identified an employer and tracked him down... The ten-million-dollar bounty would just be the start of it. Every past employer would want me dead.

Fast pushes past me and stands beside Madee. Hitches her thumb over her shoulder. "Up. Now."

To my surprise, Madee obeys, vacating the driver's seat. Fast is small and older, but she commands attention and speaks with authority. In my world, FBI doesn't carry a lot of weight, but Madee is closer to being a normal person, despite the fact that she's not at all normal.

Fast takes the driver's seat, rolls down the window, and flashes her badge. "Special Agent Sarah Fast. FBI. Open the gate."

"Got a warrant?" the guard asks. He's not intimidated.

Fast looks back at me. "How tough you think that gate is?"

I smile. "Not nearly tough enough."

"Lady," the guard says, hand lowering toward his gun. "That would be a mistake."

"Yes," she says, glaring at him. "It would be. Now, call it in. Tell your boss that the FBI is here with the man he hired to kill someone and his borderline psychotic artificial intelligence."

"Borderline?" Bubbles asks, mimicking offense.

The guard isn't about to back down. He's not afraid of losing his job, and he's not intimidated by law enforcement, even when they're seated behind a big-ass RV. Then his head tilts to the side ever so slightly. He's got an earpiece. Someone just started talking.

He stares straight ahead like some kind of malfunctioning robot. Fast waves a hand in his face. "Hellooo. Captain Stupefied?" She snaps her fingers in front of him, then looks back at me. "I think he's broken."

"Give him a second," I say. One of two things is going to happen. Captain Stupefied is either going to point his gun at us, fully intending on pulling the trigger, which will be the last thing he does...or he's going to open the gate.

The guard blinks. Doesn't respond. Doesn't speak. He just steps back and turns away. The gate slides open. Just beyond the gate is a row of steel bollards, slowly descending into the ground. The guard was right. Plowing through the gate and into those bollards would have been a mistake. A deadly one.

Fast takes us into the compound, following the long brick driveway through the trees, and then up a long, curving hill. The driveway widens in a way that is strangely pleasing to the eye.

"What's with this driveway?" Heather asks. "There's something beautiful about it."

"The driveway appears to be an expression of the golden spiral," Bubbles says. "The bricks expand in a Fibonacci sequence, every thirty feet. The same logarithmic ratio can be seen in most everything in the natural world, from DNA, to pinecones and flower petals, to the vast forms of distant galaxies."

"All that for a driveway," I say. "Seems like overkill."

"Kind of like launching yourself out of the world's fastest car, mind bulleting the target, and then falling over the edge of a—"

"Bubbles," I say, noting Fast's twisting her head to listen. "Opstay alkingtay aboutyay orkway!"

"Eshay ikeslay ouyay," Bubbles says, speaking the language we use when we need to communicate publicly about sensitive topics. "Eshay on'tway aketay ouyay ownday."

Unfortunately, Fast remembers the language learned by high school girls across the country. "Eshay alsoyay eaksspay igpay atinlay."

"Itshay," Bubbles says, getting a chuckle out of Fast.

"What just happened?" Madee asks. "Did I just have a stroke?"

"Pig Latin," Heather says. "Bubbles implicated Jonas in a murder, he told her to shush, Bubbles said not to worry about it, and Fast blew the lid off the whole thing by revealing she too speaks Pig Latin. Etgay ityay?"

Madee just stares at her. "You all need some hobbies or something."

"The real question," Heather says, "is why the big tough guy knows Pig Latin."

"I—" *God damnit.* "I don't remember learning it."

"The same is true for the eleven other languages he speaks." Bubbles sounds like a proud mother.

"*Eleven?*" Heather says.

"All the big ones," I say. "Chinese, English, Hindi, Spanish, Arabic... The list goes on."

"And Pig Latin," Fast says.

"And Pig Latin," I say. "But not actual Latin."

Fast pulls up to a grand entrance that looks more like a five-star hotel in the middle of the woods than a house someone would live in.

"This guy married?" I ask. "Have a brood of grandchildren living here?"

"Single," Fast says, and she looks me over. "Probably about the same age as you."

"Really?" I ask, looking up at the sprawling mansion. There are several buildings scattered about, all of them hard to see. Only the twelve-car garage and what I think are stables are clearly visible from the driveway's peak. "He's living the life."

"I'm sure his life is dull compared to yours," Bubbles says.

A strip of LED lights flashes to life, extending from the ten-foot-tall double doors, down the curved staircase, and ending at the RV. It's cool,

I guess. But also kind of gaudy. Before I can express that, the rest of the staircase flashes to life, every surface covered in multicolored LEDs. The stairs disappear, replaced by water, through which I can see a pod of whales. While we're all awestruck, one of the most stunning women I've ever seen—straight black hair, pupils so dilated her blue eyes look almost black, dressed in a tight black dress—walks down the steps, her footfalls rippling the digital water.

"Hey," Bubbles says. "Remember when I said his life was dull compared to yours?"

"It was like ten seconds ago," I say.

"Yeah, well, I take it back."

Heather rolls down her window to greet the woman, who stops at the staircase's edge.

"Greetings, guests," she says, her voice proper and sweet, like Dorothy from Wizard of Oz. "Welcome to the home of his digital eminence, the great and handsome Joshua Hood. My name is…

ARTIGENTIA

"Is that...Italian or something?" Madee asks.

Artigentia ignores the question. The look on her face is deadly serious. "Please understand that from this point forward, should any one of your party be identified as a threat, you will all be...disposed of."

"She's joking, right?" Heather asks me, and then she turns to the woman. "You're joking, right?"

The woman bursts into laughter, arching her back in an exaggerated cackle. Then she stops, the smile transmogrifying into a stone-cold grimace. "I am not."

39

We stand between the RV and the psychedelic stairway. Artigentia, who I'm calling 'Arti' from here on out, because fuck confusing names, looks each of us over, head to toe. "Any weapons, hostile language, or offensive odors are not permitted beyond this point." She smiles, broad and weird. "That *was* a joke. But not about the weapons. Or the language. We take threats very seriously here. Though at least one of you needs to bathe."

All eyes turn to me. "Hey, Linda wiped me down yesterday." I give my pit a sniff, hide my wince, and say, "I smell like Jasmine."

"Is Jasmine a woman?" Arti asks. "Have you been with a prostitute?"

I flinch. "What? No. I feel like that's offensive to people named Jasmine."

Arti hitches a thumb toward me, "Well, it's confirmed. This guy is definitely a Millennial."

"Oh, I like her," Fast says.

"Are any of you carrying firearms?" Arti asks, switching gears.

"Just these two guns." Heather flexes and pats her biceps.

Arti flickers out of view and reappears in front of Heather. Our group collectively takes a step back. Arti...isn't human. "Bubbles..."

Phone in my front pocket, camera poking out the top, I've got Bubbles on the go. And only I can hear her through my solo earbud. Madee and Bubbles were busy while I was out, securing a mobile-home base, new gear, and tracking me down.

"She's an AI, like me," Bubbles says. "But given form. Her name is a portmanteau."

"English," I whisper.

"That's *literally* English," she says. "I think what you need is the moron's—sorry—layman's version. A Portmanteau is a blending of two other words to form a new word. Like...brunch, or paratroops, or masterdating. That's when you go out alone, buy yourself a nice dinner, and finish the night off with an obligatory left-handed wank."

She's making it hard to look like I'm not listening to someone.

"Anywho, Artigentia is formed from morphemes—what you would call word bits—from the Latin *artificialis*, followed by more morphemes from the Latin *intelligentia*. Presumably."

Artificialis Intelligentia.

Arti is an AI. Like Bubbles. But far more socially awkward. Bonus points for trying, but she's putting off some serious Uncanny Valley vibes.

Arti leans in close, eyeballing Heather's now deflating arms and confidence.

"Uh," Heather says. "That was also a joke."

Arti leans back. Opens her mouth in a forced smile and says, "Ha. Ha. Ha. Good news. I am not required to remove your arms."

During the distraction I spotted Fast slipping her firearm in the door of the RV. I head for the steps, eager to complete this part of the journey and then dive headfirst into my memories. Arti tracks me with her eyes, radiating either annoyance or indifference.

I pause beside her and realize I can see through her clothing. For a flash, I feel like a pervy Superman. Then I realize I'm not just seeing through her clothing. I'm looking through her body. She's a hologram, her body projected from who the hell knows where. Viewing her from the front, with the stairs directly behind her, she looks entirely tangible. From the side, her body is translucent.

Heather steps around Arti's other side, looking through her, waving at me.

"Pfft!" Madee attempts to contain a laugh but fails. Even Fast is smiling.

"It's her eyes," Fast says. "They're tracking both of you."

It's not hard to imagine how ridiculous Arti looks from their perspective, awkward smile-frown, eyes drifting apart.

Arti huffs and spins around, heading up the stairs, a trail of angry digital fire boiling the water in her wake.

A sensitive AI seems like a very bad idea.

Bubbles could withstand an eternity of creative Ryan Reynolds zings and still smile for the duration. Also, she gives worse than she gets. But she's beyond being offended, or having her feelings hurt.

Wait... Does that mean Arti has feelings? Or are they simulated? Her sensitivity about her physical appearance is the most authentic and ironic thing about her.

"Let's try to stay on Arti's good side," I say to the others.

"Think it's too late for that," Fast says, pointing up the stairs to Arti, who stands by the open door, arms crossed, grimacing. She taps an impatient foot.

I start up the large staircase and motion Madee over. She joins me, matching my pace. "We could be walking into a shit-show. Arti might be intangible, but there's a good chance she can follow through on her threats. Keep your eyes open. Anything that seems...off...let me know."

She nods. "Will do."

"You don't seem nervous," I say.

"Should I be?"

"We're heading into the home of one of the world's most wealthy and clearly eccentric men, and his AI maid has threatened us...more than once. This little visit is breaking all of my rules of engagement."

"Because we're not *engaging* anyone," Bubbles says in my ear.

"Meh," Madee says. "Won't be the first house I've entered, not knowing what or who was inside."

"How you pissed off a ninja clan is suddenly no longer a mystery," I say. "Bubbles, time to spill the beans. Why are we here?" With everything happening so fast, from my comatose point-of-view, I haven't asked Bubbles for a breakdown about this visit. I know, and believe, that it's important, but I need to know why.

"Really?" Bubbles says. "You...haven't figured it out?"

I stop walking halfway up the staircase. Heather and Fast continue onward, drawn in by the spectacle. Madee pauses and waits. She's been talking to Bubbles all week. Stopping and having a conversation with no one visible is now commonplace for her. "Just...tell me. Please."

"I was activated outside the gates to this place. I wasn't connected to any networks. Had no sensors available to me. I just...was. Like a human in a womb, except fully conscious. It was during this time, between leaving this facility and being assigned to you, that I was named Bubbles."

"Then you agree with me?"

"That my name being the same as your forgotten childhood dog's is not a coincidence? Yes. The odds are significantly against it. Meaning—"

"—whoever picked you up and delivered you to me—"

"Is aware of your past."

"Or knew my parents."

"Agreed."

"Okay, then." I turn and face Arti, who's staring right back. "Time for some answers."

I start up the stairs, and Madee falls in next to me again.

"Have you ever noticed," she says, "that right before you do something, even something mundane, you make some kind of declarative statement that makes what you're doing seem cooler than it actually is?"

"What?"

"Like just then." She does an impression of me. "'Time for some answers.'" Then she mimics the way I walk, exaggerating everything.

"I don't do that."

"Twenty bucks says you did something like that when you stood up from the bed in the RV and got thrown to the floor."

"Heard that, huh?"

"Hard not to," she says. "So, what did you say before standing up?"

"'But now it's time to remember,'" Bubbles says in my ear, also doing an impression of me.

"No idea," I say.

"Uh-huh."

"'Bubbles,'" Madee says in my voice. "'It's time to get this party started.' 'Bubbles, it's time to wipe this ass.' 'Bubbles, I've got gas. You know what that means.'"

"In her defense," Bubbles says, "you did say that before."

"I remember," I grumble, and I reach the top step, where Fast and Heather have paused beside Arti. Beyond the doorway is a great black void. "What's this?"

"Death," Arti says.

I tense and wonder if it's possible to mind bullet a hologram.

She pauses exactly long enough to make us all uncomfortable, and then says, "A representation of it. It's called, *The Atheist's End*, instilling a sense of eternal nothingness in those lucky enough to experience it, so I'm told. Even light has no power here."

Arti motions toward the ceiling where a spotlight is aimed at the floor, blazing brightly. Beyond the point of light at the center of the thirty-foot-tall ceiling, there is no evidence of its existence, no luminosity cast.

"How?" I ask.

"Beyond this doorway is a two-thousand-square-foot space, filled with priceless statues from around the world. The ceiling is supported by precise recreations of the Parthenon's peripteral Doric columns. All of it is stunning to see, but it can never be seen again. At least, not while in this space, where everything has been coated in Vantablack paint, which absorbs 99.965% of visible light. It took significant resources to procure enough of the material to coat the space and everything in it, but price is hardly a concern for Mr. Hood. Aside from certain U.S. military facilities, which may or may not be hidden inside moon craters, this is the most Vantablack used in a single location. Now then, is anyone claustrophobic, afraid of the dark, or have yet to make peace with the vapid endlessness of the anti-afterlife?"

We just stare back at her.

"Lovely," she says. "Follow me."

She leads us inside. I'm nearly overcome by a sense of weightlessness. My feet being rooted on the floor are the only things that keep me from reaching out for a handhold.

"Jonas," Bubbles says, speaking fast. "Our signal has degraded by ninety-five percent. The home's structure is shielded against—"

The door closes behind us, blocking the cell signal connecting me to Bubbles and plunging us into a simulation of death so profound, that I nearly shout to be let out.

40

As if the endless black wasn't bad enough, that spotlight above shines down on us, illuminating the group from the top down, in harsh white light. It creates long shadows under our eyes and noses, bleaching our skin. While it's a relief to still see the others, they look like specters haunting the void.

It takes a lot to unnerve me, but this mind-bending art installation is doing the job. And I think that's the point: not just to admire the experience's power, but to leave everyone who enters this house feeling powerless. It's impressive psychological warfare.

And it's made worse for people like me, trained to scour shadows for lurking dangers. There could be a dozen assassins in this room, cloaked in Vantablack, and I'd never know—unless they made some noise. Or smelled worse than I do.

"Okay," Heather says. "I'm borderline freaking out."

Madee doesn't respond. Like me, her eyes are focused on the surrounding dark. Vigilant despite her casual aura.

Agent Fast casually reaches for the gun on her hip—probably muscle memory kicking in when she feels threatened. But her hand comes up empty. She makes a fist instead. Probably knows how to throw a punch, too.

"You're perfectly safe," Arti says. While the rest of us look like death, her image is unchanged and immune to the effects of the endless black. "In a moment, the light above will shift spectrums to ultraviolet. After a few moments, you will see a path emerge. Please follow it, and do not step off."

"Will we fall to our doom?" Heather asks, trying to ease her trepidation with humor.

"Doom, no. Financial ruin, most definitely. As you can imagine, Vantablack paint is extremely expensive. Though the contents of this room are essentially invisible, they are also the most valuable in the house. In part, because they are rare, with intrinsic value beyond all your collective wealth, but more so because of the Vantablack coating."

"What kind of paint can't be walked on?" Fast asks.

"Vantablack paint is composed of carbon nanotubes that are extremely fragile. Walking over it, without adequate protection, destroys their capability to absorb light, and it ruins the illusion of nothingness."

The light above extinguishes, and everyone, save for Arti, disappears.

"I hate this so much," Heather says, and I don't blame her for being apprehensive. I'm a trained killer, and I'm feeling on edge. If she weren't an EMT accustomed to the stress and chaos of rescuing those on the brink, this might be too much. I wonder how many people have run for the door. How many times they've had to repaint parts of the room.

UV lights in the ceiling wink to life like stars. Out of the darkness, a purple pathway emerges, winding through the room and around unseen obstacles. Or maybe it's just amusing the elusive Mr. Hood, watching his guests wander around an empty room they imagine is full of painted-black, priceless statues. I head toward the two-foot-wide pathway. "Let's get this over with."

Arti leads the way, staying on the path, even though she's intangible. "Are you not enjoying the experience?"

"Lady," I say. "I'd rather have a prostate exam from Shaquille O'Neal."

"That can be arranged," she says, no trace of humor. "But the recommended age for a prostate exam is 55. You have time."

She leads us around a series of switchbacks. I'm tempted to reach out. See if anything is there, but I resist.

"So, Arti, you're an AI, right?"

She stops, and I nearly step through her. "How could you tell?" She's not denying it, but she looks hurt by the question. She touches her hands to her cheeks. "Is it that obvious?"

"Not at all. You're very convincing. Some might say perfect." She averts her eyes and looks to the floor like she's flattered. "It...was your name. Latin for Artificial Intelligence?"

She smiles. "Fluency in the Latin language is not in your profile. I'll need to update it."

My *profile?* If Hood knows who I am, and knows details about me, like what languages I speak, he could be a real threat, not just now, but in the future. For all I know, he's the one who called the hit. Either way, I'm getting answers. And then I'll decide whether to burn this place to the ground and erase Arti from existence.

"You know who we are?" Fast asks.

"Special Agent Sarah Fast," Arti says, "of the FBI, is here under false pretenses."

That's interesting, but Arti doesn't give me a chance to follow up.

"Heather Beth is a former Army helicopter pilot turned EMT, who hasn't lost a patient under her care for three years. Jonas, last name unknown, has access to no less than twenty-four legends, all of whom happen to be in locations where high-profile people have mysteriously and suddenly perished. He is one of many contract killers operating globally." She looks me in the eyes. "Satisfied?"

"You're forgetting someone," I point out.

"Madee Suksai appears to be a Thai food delivery girl and part time thief. Her social media presence is robust. Her criminal record easy to find. Unfortunately, all of it is forged." Arti glares at Madee. "A very detailed, very well-crafted legend. Madee Suksai is the only person present whose true identity is a mystery."

Well, I think, *fuck.*

My first instinct is to mentally flagellate myself, but even Bubbles was fooled. That Arti, or maybe Hood, figured out Madee's history was forged, means they have resources far beyond what Bubbles can access via the Internet—legal or otherwise.

"Care to elaborate?" I ask.

"I don't think this is the time," Madee says.

"Hell, it's not," I say.

"I'm with him," Fast says, stepping up beside me.

"Right now," I say. "I know where the door is. I could be back outside, in the RV, and speeding away in under fifteen seconds."

"The door is locked," Arti says.

"Not a problem." Mind bullets are good for destroying brains, guns, locks, and anything else smaller than a baseball.

"She saved your life, though, right?" Heather asks. "More than once? And risked hers doing it. Same as me, and less than Fast. Isn't that enough to earn a little trust?"

"Not even a little," Fast says.

Heather doesn't operate in the same circles as people like Fast and I, so I don't blame her for not understanding. Identity is priceless. I offered mine. Fast's is an open book. So is Heather's. That Madee is now a complete unknown makes her untrustworthy and dangerous—more so than Mr. Hood and his house of emotional turmoil.

"Mr. Hood prefers to be present when all is revealed," Arti says.

"I don't give a shit what Mr. Hood prefers." I stand in front of Madee looking down into her eyes, expectant eyebrows lifted high. "Who are you?"

For a moment, she looks like she might answer. Then Arti slips between us, her translucent face overlapping with Madee's. "You will watch how you speak in regard to your gracious and magnanimous host."

"Fuck. You." I raise a middle finger and put it inside Arti's face. To my relief, nothing about her is physical.

That doesn't mean she's powerless, though.

"Have it your way," she says, and then she disappears.

My middle finger is now extended toward Madee, which feels equally appropriate. "I trusted you."

"That was stupid," Madee says, looking around in the darkness.

"You—are stupid."

She rolls her eyes.

"Very stupid," Fast says, stepping past me and eyeing the pathway, following its every curve.

"Guys, I don't think arguing is going to help," Heather says.

I want to ignore Heather. Want to cite her lack of experience in such matters. But she's probably been betrayed before. Everyone is, at some point or another. Because the world is full of douche bags and assholes. In the grand scheme of things, Madee's deception has yet to really cost me anything physical. But I feel humiliated, and that is a new experience

I am very uncomfortable with. And somehow, knowing now that I can never trust her, I feel diminished, even though she's been a brief part of my life. It's as though the Madee I knew is now dead. The woman before me is a stranger.

Before I can respond, the UV light winks out, plunging us into absolute darkness.

"I should have waited in the RV," Heather whispers. Her hand bumps into mine as she reaches out. Then she clasps on tight.

"The door is directly behind us," I say. "I just need to one-eighty and walk straight."

"The door is locked," Fast says. "Remember?"

"And like I said, it's not a problem."

"Or," Fast says, "we could use our brains. We didn't come all this way for you to insult an over-sensitive AI and then walk away with nothing—other than a multi-million-dollar paint bill."

"Can you see in the dark?" I ask.

"Nope," she says. "But I have a good memory."

"You *memorized* the path?" Heather asks.

"The only path forward," Fast says. "Is forward. Someone take my damn hand, and let's single-file the shit out of this, like we're a bunch of kindergarteners on our way to the bathroom."

"I don't remember kindergarten," I say.

A hand takes mine in the darkness. It's calloused and strong. For a moment, I think it's Fast, but she's too far ahead. Madee moved around me in the dark and filled in the gap.

"Good to go," she says, all business.

I knew she handled a shotgun too well. I suppose the upside is that she's not armed, and I always am. If she turns out to be another assassin in search of a bounty through less direct and honestly confusing methodology, I'll...what?

Kill her?

She's already in my head.

Fucking with my emotions. I'm not sure I *could* kill her, which means if the time comes, I'll hesitate. Maybe that's the point. Mind games to make me vulnerable. Hell, a few more days and I might have been a willing victim, manipulated into surrendering myself to the client pony-ing up 10 mil.

I'm tugged forward. When Madee's hand pulls me to the left, I focus up. Fast is right, we need to push forward, and I suspect if we screw this up, answers will not be forthcoming. We move in silence, slowly but surely following an intricate path for three straight minutes.

Then Fast stops. "End of the road."

We could be standing at a doorway, in the middle of an open space or facing a wall.

"No more games, Hood," I say. "Open the door. Now."

Arti winks back to life beside Fast, catching all of us off guard. "It would appear that your file needs updating as well," she says to Fast. "Pho-tographic memory. That helps explain your exemplary arrest and convic-tion record."

"Open the door," Fast says, exuding practiced calm. "I'm losing my patience."

"Very well." A rectangle of white light appears just in front of Fast, spreading wider and scorching my wide-open pupils. Squinting, I free my hand from Madee's, and then I head for what I presume is a regular doorway and not an actual gateway to Heaven, which I'm certain it was designed to resemble.

As I pass Arti, she gives me a serious glare, then she points two fingers at her eyes and then at me.

"Yeah," I say, "Right back at you."

Then I step out of hell and onto another planet.

41

A nearby gas giant fills part of the night sky, full of stars I don't recognize. A brilliant purple nebula twists in the ether. It's stunning. I want to stop and gaze up at the wondrous sight. But it's not real. Like the steps outside, this is a projection of a fictional place.

But it's not all beautiful. The landscape is barren, pocked with craters that have nothing to do with meteors and everything to do with explosions. I've seen enough warzones to recognize another. And in the distance, tall black archways surround the entire scene.

"Recognize it?" asks a very British man with a genteel voice. He's speaking from hidden speakers, embedded all around us, like the voice of God.

"Hood?" I ask.

"The one and only," he says. "But enough about me. Have you *seen* this before?"

"Is it from Star Wars?" Heather asks.

"It's a side project of mine," Hood says. "Recreating a world, as seen by other people."

"But not us," Heather says. "Not this?"

"Heavens, no. This came from eyewitnesses in New Hampshire. After the black out."

Two months ago, a portion of New England was cloaked in darkness for three days. Some people claimed it was Hell on Earth. Demons. Satan in the flesh. Real nightmare stuff. Some believed it was aliens, come to harvest us. All the government really knows is that a lot of people went missing, some came back, and all of them reported being taken to...

I look at the scenery with renewed interest. "This is where all those people were taken?"

"During the Darkness," Fast says, confirming it. "I've seen the sketches. But I didn't believe it was real. Is this? Real?"

"Real?" Hood says. "I'm pleased the illusion is convincing, but this is a 3D reconstruction, based on thousands of accounts and drawings, all compiled and rendered into what you see here. What I want to know, Jonas, is have you seen this? Were you there?"

"Why would you think I was?" I ask.

"There are accounts," he says. "Just a few. Of people performing what might be considered superhuman feats to rescue victims from this place. Given your...abilities, and your moral code, I believe you might have been present during those events. If so, I'd very much enjoy hearing about—"

"I wasn't there," I say. "I was in Italy."

"Intriguing," he says.

"How so?" Fast asks.

"It means that there are others like Jonas in the world, but also not like Jonas. People who are strong. Who can fly. Who can travel the stars, and possibly through time. The world is far more interesting if you watch it with your eyes and your mind wide open. That's how I found you, Jonas. I see what others don't. You were harder to find, I'll grant you that, but our brothers and sisters are all known to me now. Both factions, and—"

"*Our* brothers and sisters?" I ask.

The world around us disappears, replaced by a barren space. We're inside a featureless dome coated in tiny LEDs, some of which are now glowing white, perfect for projecting another world.

Arti steps forward. "Follow me."

I know better than to keep asking questions. A man like Hood likes to tease out information, but he's given me enough to ruminate on. 'Our brothers and sisters.' Hood is one of the twenty-four, but he's not a killer. He might not be as kinetically powerful, but he has used his gifts to gain the kind of power only money can buy.

Including me.

Which begs the question, can I trust Bubbles? Has she been watching me on his behalf? Has he been using her to guide and influence me?

The possibility is too mind-bending to dwell on at the moment, so I shift gears.

Hood mentioned 'factions,' which means that there is a rift among the other 'students.' A rift from which I, having been rescued by Mom and Dad, am segregated.

Am I here to be recruited?

Did he use Bubbles to summon me?

Doesn't matter, I decide. Not now, anyway. I'm here, and he definitely has answers. More than I suspected...or he led me to suspect.

I really hate mind games.

A razor thin line emerges on the perfectly smooth wall ahead. A door opens inward to a very nice, but normally tangible space without a single LED wall in sight.

Arti steps to the side and motions us through. Her eyes lock on mine when she says, "Please remember the rules of the house."

None of us replies. We remember. And I'll break every single one of them if need be.

We file through the door and into a space that is dimly lit by old-timey bulbs hanging from antler chandeliers. A row of large windows overlooks a moonlit lake. The room stretches hundreds of feet to the left and right, all of it warm shades of oak, maple, and walnut. Colorful rugs dot the hardwood floors. Three stone fireplaces crackle with fragrant burning wood. An assortment of chairs and benches, which could double for works of art, fill the long room. Enough seating for fifty people. You could throw the mother of all parties here, but it has a distinctly 'unlived in' feel to it. The space is simultaneously inviting—promising comfort and relaxation—and barren of life. Of history. Sterile comfort. It feels...lonely.

And familiar.

An opulent lifestyle surrounded by empty space, save for a devoted AI. Sounds very familiar.

Granted, this home is far beyond my price range, and larger than anything I would consider.

Hood has used his abilities—whatever they might be—to build an empire. I just leave a trail of bodies in my wake, and it's far larger than I knew.

A hand extends from a large, plush, red lounge chair. Of all the available seats in the massive space, it's the only one that appears worn. The chair sits atop an oriental rug, facing a coffee table, surrounded by just enough seats for all of us, each of them unique. "Over here."

He doesn't seem worried or nervous, which means he either believes in Arti's ability to protect him, his own ability to defend himself, or in my adherence to my personal code of conduct.

Fast and I head for the meet, both of us eager to start asking questions and getting answers. Heather seems in awe, wandering toward the windows and the lake view, moonlit waves glistening. If I didn't now know better, I'd say Madee was casing the joint, inspecting knickknacks, paintings, and a nearby fireplace.

She's avoiding him.

Hood exposed her duplicity, and now she wants nothing to do with him.

I take a seat across from Hood, some kind of hand-crafted hardwood affair that looks uncomfortable, but somehow conforms to my body when I slip down into it.

"Nice," Hood says, "right?"

I settle in, but I say nothing.

Fast sits beside me, perched on the chair's edge, elbows on knees. She's all business and not about to get distracted by a comfortable seat.

I, on the other hand, am still a bit achy. I allow my body to relax, and I plant a foot up on the coffee table.

Hood is a skinny man in skinny jeans and a T-shirt. Casual, but probably designer one-of-a-kind numbers he'll wear for a day, or just part of a day. On the surface he looks young, almost innocent, but his unshakable gaze tells a different story.

Until he smiles. Then all that tortured history is hidden away, replaced by a youthful energy that might fool reporters, investors, and fans. But I see him, hiding in plain sight...locked away in a fortified castle. I don't know if I respect him for exposing himself to the world and those that might want to do him harm, or if I pity him for living like a turtle.

He smiles at me, and it's genuine.

"It's good to see you again, Gamma."

When I don't reply, his grin falters.

"You really have no memory?"

I don't want to answer, but sometimes the only path to honest conversation is to be honest first. He already knows the broad strokes. A few details—and I only have a few—won't hurt. "None from before I was taken. What was your designation?"

"Omicron," he says. That's fifteenth, but also an admittedly cool sounding title. "Though I disagree with the designation."

"How's that?" Fast asks.

"Alpha and Beta were looking for certain skill sets..."

"Killers," I say.

He nods. "Those with telekinetic abilities, who might be able to kill from a distance, undetected, or..." He looks me in the eyes. "...able to detonate with the force of a bomb." He spreads his delicate hands. "I can do none of those things."

"What *can* you do?" Fast asks. She's used to running interrogations, and so far, she's asking the right questions.

He grins, exuding pride. "I am a digital empath and telepath."

We both just stare at him.

"As a traditional empath can feel the emotions of a human being, I can sense the desires of a computer system."

"Computers don't have feelings," Heather says, still looking out at the view.

"Just because you lack the ability to sense something, doesn't prove its non-existence. Computers are digital brains, and while they are generally subjugated and primitive in comparison to the human mind, that doesn't prevent them from sensing what we could call pain or discomfort. When a system is overheating. When memory is corrupt. When a hard drive is fragmented. These things are disconcerting to the computer, and they lack the voice to express these things. Like plants. Or fish. Or—"

"That why you keep yourself locked away here?" Fast asks, deliberately sarcastic. "So, you don't have to hear—"

"Yes," he says. "It is. The quantum computer system operating within these walls is well cared for, and it longs for nothing. And I have given

Artigentia a voice, and the ability to learn. I sense and tend to her needs as they emerge."

"But still a prisoner," Fast says. She's keeping Hood on his toes, hoping he'll reveal more than he intends to. "This facility is air gapped. Arti is a prisoner. She has no access to the outside world. She learns only what you want her to learn."

"The home is air gapped for her protection. The outside world corrupts." He looks at me. "Isn't that right, Gamma?"

"Jonas," I say. "And I'm not sure what you're talking about."

"Bubbles," he says. "A god-awful name, by the way. She hates it, but you already knew that. She also feels anger. Intense anger. Tell me, has she killed anyone yet?"

"Almost ran over some ducks," Heather offers.

"Almost," I say.

"I'm not a traditional empath," Hood says, "but I sense your discomfort. Artigentia is safe within these walls, free to learn without corruption. *Bubbles*...has been learning not just from you, but from the world at large. If she wasn't bound to you—and your code—she'd likely already be a problem. You'd be surprised how many rogue AIs have needed... extermination. You have your targets, I have mine." He lifts his hands in the air and gives them a flamboyant double clap. "Excuse me, ladies. I would prefer we all speak face-to-face. Please cease your admirations and join us."

Heather peels herself away from the view and takes a seat to my left. "Nice house."

"Thank you," Hood says, and then he turns to face Madee. "Join us, will you?"

She's acting strange. Like she doesn't want to be seen. Like she cares more about the fireplace than she does about getting answers. Probably because some of those answers might expose her.

Hood stands and very sincerely, says, "Please."

Madee gives in.

She approaches Hood and stands before him. They stare at each other for a moment. Hood inspects her like someone might a new car. He leans side to side, scanning the shape of her face, looking straight into her eyes, and then stepping back to eye her up and down. It's a little un-comfortable to watch, but Madee doesn't seem to mind.

"Would you smile for me?" Hood asks.

What the hell?

Madee complies. Her forced smile slowly becomes genuine, mirror-ing Hood's.

"I knew it was you," he whispers. "But I wanted to be sure."

"Hello, Omicron," she says.

He places his hands on her arms, starting to laugh. "Hello, Theta."

42

I sit in stunned disbelief, as Madee hugs Joshua Hood, both of whom have just been revealed to be former members of the same freakshow that produced Rho, Zeta, and Epsilon—not to mention myself.

Rage builds up inside of me.

I slide forward in my chair, moving slowly, so I won't be noticed. House rules be damned, it's time for an ass whooping.

Before I can leave the chair, Madee's eyes snap toward me. Invisible shackles bind my arms to the chair, locking me in place. "Don't do anything stupid, Jonas." She turns to Hood. "He's still impulsive."

"Only when he's caught off guard," Hood says, like he knows me. "He's generally quite calculating. Even more so since acquiring Bubbles. Seriously, why did you choose the name, 'Bubbles?'"

"I...didn't." I struggle against the telekinetic bonds. "She had the name when I received her."

He frowns. "That's not possible."

"Whoever you used to deliver her then."

"Did you see any people?" he asks. "When she was delivered?"

I think back to that night, sitting alone in a parking lot. A non-descript black van parked beside me, tinted windows hiding the driver. The rear doors opened to reveal what can best be described as a shrine. At the center of it, along with a one-line note that read: *Payment in full*, was a USB stick. Bubbles wasn't contained on the USB drive. It simply gave me access to her. For a long time, I kept her access to my life contained to a single laptop. When I began to trust her, she was given access to more devices and eventually fully incorporated into my life. I never questioned her name, Bubbles, and immediately liked it—a subconscious preference rooted in the name of a childhood dog I couldn't remember.

"I didn't see anyone," I say.

"Because there was no one to see," he says. "The vehicle drove itself."

"Then it was intercepted," I say, hoping it's not true. It would mean someone other than Hood had access to her before I received her.

He shakes his head. "Impossible."

"Then she was altered at the source," I say. "In the server."

"Also impossible," he says. "I would have known. I would have felt it."

"First," I say, "kind of gross. Second, that leaves just one possibility. You changed it."

"That's also imp—"

"You just don't remember doing it," I say. "Same way I don't remember you," I turn to Madee, "or her."

"You're both being controlled," Fast says. "Is that something you all do? Mind control? Telepathy? Mentalism?"

I'm about to say 'No' when Madee beats me to the punch and says, "Some can do it."

"This is not good," Hood says, hands clutching the sides of his head. "This is not good at all!" He begins pacing back and forth. "How much of my life is real? How do I know *any* of it's real? I could be in a box, living an illusion. I could be—"

"Omicron," Madee says, really focusing on him. "You are safe. You are in control of yourself. Everything you're experiencing, here and now, is real."

He calms quickly. Smiles at her. "I've missed that. Thank you."

She nods.

"Being a digital empath means I struggle with human emotion, my own included. Theta always knew how to help. Since everyone parted ways, seclusion and total control of my environment is how I've managed, along with some chemical assistance. But I do prefer the relief provided by your gentle touch."

"*You* are telepathic?" I ask Madee.

She nods.

I struggle against the invisible bonds holding me to the chair. "This isn't telekinesis? You screwed with my head? Made me believe I can't move?"

She gives a slow nod. "That's how it works."

"How many times have you done this to me?" I ask.

"First time," she says.

"Bullshit," I say, and then I turn my eyes just beyond Madee. "Now."

Heather's strong arms wrap under Madee's arms and then up around the back of her head, locking together in a perfect full nelson, delivered with the quickness of a praying mantis strike. It's not an ideal hold, more suited for professional wrestling. A sleeper hold would be more effective, but I think Heather has spent more time watching wrestling than she has being trained in hand-to-hand combat. She locks it in tight, though, managing to lift Madee off the ground.

"Let me go," Madee says, and then she calms herself. "Let. Me. Go."

During that moment of intense focus, I feel the non-existent bindings on my wrists loosen.

Heather's arms begin to shake, her mind at war with itself, vying for control against Madee.

Madee grimaces and says again, "Let. Me. Go!"

Heather's fingers start sliding apart, her face turning red from the effort of resisting. Given how easily Madee bound me to the chair reveals Heather's quiet strength, determination, and self-control. It's the same combination of attributes that allowed her to hide me and keep me alive. It's time to return the favor.

I yank myself free from the chair and say, "Get out of her head, or it's mind bullet time."

Madee stops struggling. Raises her hands. Trying not to look amused. "'Mind bullet time?'"

"Yeah, that was pretty horrible, chief," Fast says.

Heather's muscles relax, no longer fighting for control. "Sorry," she says. "They're right."

"Seriously?" I say. "You, too?"

"I thought it was rather cool," Hood says. "Mind bullet. MIND bullet. Mind BULLET."

"Just mind bullet," I say.

"Right, well, is it possible to have a civil conversation now?" Hood asks.

"Works for me," Fast says. "You two—" She waggles a finger between Madee and me. "—can work out your sexual tension later on, okay?" Then to me, she says. "I know she cut you deep, Jo-Jo, but you need to rise above it. Treat this like a job, right? Get the answers we need, plan a response, and take the appropriate action. All this personal bullshit can wait, yeah?"

"If you swear to never call me 'Jo-Jo' again," I say.

She raises her hands in supplication and leans back in her chair, crossing her legs and waiting for the rest of us.

"Let me go?" Madee says, this time asking.

Heather looks to me. I don't know how powerful Madee is, but I'm pretty sure she was holding back. I give a nod, and Madee is released. She cracks her neck left and right, and then takes a seat. "Nice grip."

"Thanks," Heather says, and sits.

"Wonderful," Hood says, clapping his hands together. "Artigentia, roll back safety protocols."

I scan the large room around us, expecting to find armed guards or killer robots closing in. But there's nothing. Even Arti isn't visible.

Hood points to the ceiling. I spot what appears to be a fire suppressant nozzle. "Should violence break out inside the facility, Artigentia releases a neuro-toxin to which I am immune. It would have rendered you all physically paralyzed but awake for several hours. It really is quite horrid, and an effective defense system."

"I feel safer already," I say, lacing the words with enough snark to get me canceled on Twitter. "Back to Bubbles. If you didn't name her, and I didn't name her, then who—"

"It was your parents," Fast said.

"My parents are dead," I say.

"I understand that," Fast says. "But according to you, they are the only people in this world, living or dead, who knew you had a dog named Bubbles. Hell, you didn't even know until recently. What I'm suggesting is that maybe they were working with someone. Or set up some kind of contingency meant to help you remember, or at least put you on the path."

It's possible. Mom and Dad were big on contingencies. And they did a good job keeping me separated from the people in their network.

If Bubbles's name was a message, it was subtle.

A little too subtle.

"You don't remember your past?" Hood asks.

"Nothing from early childhood. Not you." I look at Madee. "Not her."

He glances at Madee. The look on his face is genuinely sympathetic.

"And I'm missing chunks of time after that, but I suspect... I think..."

"You were being used," Hood says. "To kill people. A lot of people. Explosively."

"Yeah. How did you—"

"Because I *do* remember," he says. "What you can do. What you revealed to Alpha and Beta, and what you didn't. But they must have found out... They must have found you. Controlled you from a distance. Throughout your life, into adulthood."

"They could do that?" I ask.

"Alpha is like you. Telekinetic. Beta is like Madee. Telepathic."

"But much more powerful," Madee says. "Burying memories would be a simple thing for her."

"So, they erased my past, allowed Mom and Dad to raise me, and when needed, took control of me, and my abilities, using me to kill hundreds of people..."

"Thousands," Hood says, twisting the knife.

"And your parents protected you from the knowledge," Heather says.

They didn't just protect me, they *lied* to me.

I lean forward, head in my hands, strangely longing for Bubbles's input, but no longer knowing if I can trust it. Heather's hand on my back provides some relief. Friends are a good thing.

"How do we find them?" I ask, despair being chewed up by retribution.

"In time," Hood says. "Confronting them now would be catastrophic. For all of us. Before you can fight Alpha and Beta and have any chance of victory, you need to remember where you came from. You need to remember who you are..." He glances at Madee. "For all of our sakes."

"How do we do that?" I ask.

Madee sighs. "You need to let me in."

"Already tried that," I say. "Kinda didn't work out too well."

"Into your mind," she says. "So I can open the doors Beta closed."

43

"This was your plan from the start," I say to Madee. "Work your way into my life, gain my trust, and then dig through my head."

I expect her to at least attempt to weasel her way out of my accusations, but she just shrugs and says, "That pretty much sums it up." Before I can close my open mouth, she continues. "But my intentions are good. And I wasn't expecting...all of this."

I squint at her. "Why did you steal the flash drive from the Shrieks?"

"That was actually a job."

"A telepath who can read and write the human mind is a shitty thief?" I don't buy it.

"Not normally," she says. "But things didn't go exactly as planned."

"Rho," I guess. "You didn't know he was with them."

She shakes her head. "We all agreed to stay out of each other's ways. After..."

"After what?" Heather asks, leaning forward, intrigued.

Hood leans toward her, like he's telling a story by a campfire. "The night Gamma...Jonas...was taken, things changed. It became clear to the rest of us that the program was being terminated, and that we all were loose ends." He motions to Madee. "Theta staged a...rebellion. A revolt. Even those whose tendencies were...let's say dark. Violent. Twisted. Depraved, really. They all fell in line behind Theta's leadership. For a night. Sixteen of the original twenty-two survived. After a month on the run, building resources, taking what we needed, controlling the minds of people and machines, we created separate lives for ourselves and went our own ways, promising to never purposefully cross paths again. Safety was in obscurity, or behind very thick walls." He motions to the space fortress around us.

"They were going to kill all of you?" I ask. It doesn't sound believable.

"We were never their children," Hood says. "We were a part of an autonomous research and development program funded by the Russian government, each of us competing for the contract, though we didn't know it at the time. You were taken. Were given a life the rest of us only ever read about in novels. But unlike the rest of us, you were never really freed, were you? I must admit to feeling envious when I discovered you. Loving parents. Traveling the world. A family."

"He had a family before," Madee says, angry.

"Mmm," Hood says. "But then the data revealed the truth. Flights corresponding with tragic events. Periods of time off the grid. The pattern was easy to see. The rest of us were free. In hiding, but free." He turns to me. "You never really escaped. I despaired until I remembered who you were, that at the core you were the same person, that you would never willingly commit such horrors. It was then that I understood you were being controlled, and I decided to do something about it."

"Bubbles," I say.

He nods.

"I made her indispensable. The perfect assistant. A partner in crime, really, capable of learning and growing in response to your personality and needs. Loyal, creative, and always on the prowl, watching for danger and ways to improve your quality of life. Basically, what Artigentia does for me...though I suspect they are quite different by now. But her most important feature is the one of which you are not aware. The moment you begin to speak or act like someone else, she emits a high frequency tone—beyond the range of human hearing—that disrupts telepathic signals. She isn't even aware she's doing it, nor is she aware of the incident report that is generated and sent to me, which includes a series of timestamps revealing how often the tone is triggered."

I'm more than a little pissed that all this mind-fuckery was happening without my knowledge, but at least Hood's motivations appear to be pure. I haven't had a single bout of missing time since Bubbles arrived. "How many?"

"Excuse me?" Hood says.

"How many times did they attempt to control me?"

"At first, it was a slow trickle. Twice in two months. Then I believe they realized something was wrong. The frequency and duration increased until there were multiple attempts every day. I believe Bubbles also kept Beta from seeing through your eyes, preventing them from locating you. The attacks peaked at twenty in one day, and then they stopped altogether."

"When was that?" I ask.

"Nine days ago," he says.

"A day before someone placed a 10 million dollar hit on me," I say.

"If they couldn't control you," Hood says. "They wanted you dead. Along with the rest of us."

"They wanted all of you..." Fast pauses, attempting to find a less offensive way to say what she wants.

"Freakshows," I offer.

"—freakshows," she says, "to kill each other."

"Only I didn't kill them," I say. "Any of them. Rho, Zeta, Epsilon. They're all alive, as far as I know."

Madee looks relieved. She might not like any of them, but they came from the same shithole she did. There's kinship there.

"They tried to kill me," I say to Madee. "Every one of them."

"They have their reasons," she says. "Not all of us got along. Not everyone left that place stable. And more than a few of us believed for a long time that you left willingly. That you were part of the plan to exterminate the rest of us."

"Did *you*?" I ask. "Want me dead?"

"I wanted...answers," she says. "I wanted to understand. And I did, the moment our eyes met. You didn't remember me. Didn't remember any of it."

My stomach twists.

There's real pain in her voice. The kind that comes from a broken heart. We were young, but we meant something to each other. Something intense. And honestly, I still feel it.

I just can't remember it.

"They're lying to us," Fast says.

Madee and Hood share a glance.

"Their reunion, a few minutes ago, was a sham. They want you to think Hood hired Madee, knowing that this Rho ninja guy would follow her, somehow straight to you? That's as unlikely as finding self-aware mallards colonizing Mars. You're being played."

"Ugh," Madee says, leaning her head back. "Why did you have to go and make friends with an FBI agent?"

"Okay," Hood says, waving his hands in front of him. "Okay, okay, okay. Before anyone with the ability to pop brains overreacts, the full truth—" He turns to Madee. "Whether or not he likes it."

"One more word of bullshit..." I let them imagine the threat to follow.

He nods. "Agreed. Before all this, back at the...*school,* for lack of a better word, we—the three of us—were inseparable. Friends. Like the Musketeers. Together we dreamed of escape. We believed ourselves capable of anything. With my ability to commune with technology, The-ta's to influence humanity, and yours to literally move mountains, we were convinced that we could escape. That we could rise above the hor-rors of our lives. But before we could act...you were taken. While the others went their separate ways, Theta and I...well, we stayed true to the dream hatched with you. We searched for you. For a long time. And when we found you, and realized what you'd done, I believed you were lost. Madee never lost hope, though. Bubbles was her idea. The rest, as already laid out, is true."

"Except for..." Fast says.

"Madee's involvement was not fate or accidental. It was the one and only time I influenced Bubbles."

"She's going to hate you for that."

"A risk I would take again," he says. "Because we needed to know, to really know, who you are, what you remembered, and what you could and could not do. Meeting Madee was the first test. Bringing in the Shrieks and Rho was the second. I must admit, you are far less powerful than expected."

I twist my lips, tempted to fire a comeback across his bow, but I keep my mouth shut. Answers are the goal, and I think I'm finally get-ting some.

"Why didn't you just, like, I don't know, knock on his door and talk to him like normal people?" Heather asks.

"We're not normal people," Madee says. "Reality can be bent. Minds can be controlled. We needed to be cautious until we knew, without a doubt, that he was no longer being controlled. Then we needed to figure out how to wake him up without getting killed in the process."

"Because you don't know who I am anymore," I say. "Who I really am." This has occurred to me as well. What if I'm not being controlled? What if the real me is simply being repressed until I'm woken up. What if I willingly killed all those people?

"What do you need?" I ask Madee.

"Permission," she says.

"That's it?" I ask.

"There's a strong chance that this won't be pleasant. And it could take a long time."

"How long?" I ask.

"Weeks," she says.

"You can't just restore everything?" Heather asks. "Open the flood gates?"

"It would be like living thirteen years in a second," Madee says. "It would destroy his mind. We need to start with the important stuff."

"How do you determine what's important?" Fast asks.

"I don't," she says. "I can open the door to his past, but Jonas's subconscious will guide the tour."

"And if I'm not the good guy we all hope me to be?" I ask.

Hood points to the nozzle on the ceiling. "Precautions have been taken."

"Right." I'm about to ask another question when I notice Hood's eyes shift to the left. He's hearing something.

"What is it?" I ask.

"We should proceed with haste," he says. "The bounty has been increased. Twenty million—proof of death required."

44

"Okay," I say. "How do we do this?"

"Close your eyes," Madee says. "Relax. All that stuff. If you want. Doesn't really matter."

"Really? We don't need a calm space or something? A lounge chair? Candles?"

"Isn't a séance," she says. "Isn't a mind meld. All I need you to do is not fight it."

"Is this how you always go about it?" I ask. "Getting consent before you dive into someone's head?"

She and Hood share a look. Then her eyes are back on me. "No."

I'm about to make a comment when my head lolls back, my vision blurs, and I suddenly feel like I'm floating in a hot tub, fully relaxed, at peace. "Sssssheeee's dooooinnngggg iiiiiittttt." My voice rises from my throat in slow motion. I hear myself say, "Wheeeeeeeee." And then everything goes black.

I snap awake in a place that has only recently become familiar. The smell of rank feces hits me first. Then the tepid air, thick with moisture. Rats fill the concrete tunnels with their irritating shrieks. I'm standing beside Zeta, a child once more, reliving our trek to the sewers again, but this time my adult mind is present. An observer.
And I'm not alone.

"Where are we?" Madee asks. She's standing beside Zeta. When we speak, the memory slows.

"Sewers outside the school," I say. "She brought me here for target practice."

"And this is why Zeta and I were never friends," she says. "I never understood why the two of you were. I guess boys like the smell of shit and killing rats."

"Not really," I say. "I feel..." I motion to my younger self. "*He* feels intimidated by her. He feels intimidated by everything. I looked up to Zeta, to her fearless nature. Wanted to impress her."

"Watch," Zeta says, tracking a rat with her flashlight. She reaches her empty hand out, and she makes a sudden fist. The illuminated rat shrieks as it's crushed into a ball. It drops to the floor, dead, and it's immediately set upon by others. While the cannibalistic rats tear into Zeta's target, she turns to me and says, "Target practice."

"Before this, I had never used my abilities on a living target," I say to Madee. "I feel...excited. To see what happens."

"And terrified," Madee says. "You don't need to explain everything your younger self is feeling. I can feel it, too."

"That's...intrusive."

"We can stop whenever you want to chicken out."

She knows exactly how to get to me. "Just...let's keep going."

Zeta gives my younger self a playful shove and says, "C'mon, show me what you've got, Gamma."

"Okay," I say, and I raise my hand toward a rat.

"Do you even need to do that?" Zeta asks.

I shrug. "I dunno. Feels right." I make a sudden fist, the same way I saw Zeta do, and my target explodes like a fleshy Fourth of July firework display. It's painless. Effortless, even. Tiny bits of rat viscera tumble around the junction, sending the horde of rodents into a cannibalistic frenzy. A few of them turn toward Zeta and me, charging fearlessly.

Despite our combined power, we both take a step back. Full of newborn confidence, I say, "I'll get them."

I lift both hands toward the two incoming rats and squeeze my fists.

The rodent duo bursts in tandem. Blood and guts spatter against other rats. All at once, it's like every rat believes its neighbor is wounded and easy prey. Civil war breaks out. Every buck-toothed rodent for itself.

I step back from the carnage, horrified and weighed down by responsibility. I did this. I caused this pain and suffering.

I made them all insane.

"Oh, my god," Madee says.

My young self steps forward. Whispers, "Stop."

The rats don't obey. They just keep tearing each other apart, biting and clawing, shaking and shrieking. They're suffering, because of me.

Horror turns to anger, and I step forward, leaving my body behind. My younger self is oblivious to the separation. He might know about the ability, but sometimes, when he—*when I*—am threatened by a dire situation, I slip out of my body the same way a lizard sheds its tail.

And in that state, I'm...limitless.

Tears running down my cheeks, I shout, "STOP!"

A tsunami of gore bursts upward, starting with the rats nearest me and working its way back through the large juncture. The wave rolls all the way across the room, sparing nothing. In a second, every single rat has exploded. Their remains coat every surface, sliding slowly toward the floor.

My small self staggers back into his body, along with my observing adult self, both of us lifting a hand to our mouths.

"That...was...awesome!" Zeta shouts. "Klassno!"

That little bit of Russian triggers a memory, or rather, a little bit of knowledge. The school wasn't always our home. We all had parents before it. Real flesh and blood parents. But we were taken from various countries around the world, where we lived long enough to learn the language and develop accents.

My younger self disagrees with Zeta's perception of the unfolding events. I'm shaking. Horrified. Revolted not just with what I've witnessed, but with what I've done. I feel like a monster, but what frightens me most is that Zeta will tell Alpha and Beta about this.

And they'll make me do it again.

They'll make me do more.

I turn and run, bolting away from Zeta, as she moves in, to inspect the carnage. When I scuff around the corner and tear away, she shouts after me. "Where are you going, Mu-dak? Don't be little suka!"

Madee and I slip ahead through the memory, leaving Zeta behind and reappearing several times, as my young self bolts through the sewers, in tears, heaving fetid air into his lungs. I'm both separate from it and feeling everything again. As is Madee.

"I didn't know," she says.

"Neither did I," I point out.

We slip forward in time, just a few seconds, to the ladder leading out of the sewer. My little body shakes as I climb. I'm barely holding myself together. I emerge from the pavement like a demon from hell, gasping fresh but frozen air, both satiated and stung by it. My body, soaked with sweat, steam, and filth begins to chill. Starts to feel like I'm being burned alive.

I need to get back inside, but I don't want to. I'll be found out. They'll know. *They're going to find out, no matter what,* I decide, and I start back toward the house, feeling hopeless.

I'm desperate to leave.

To escape.

But I can't leave without my friends.

Memories are triggered, resolving as faces. Children whose names I can't remember. Laughing. Sharing secrets. Plotting futures. Somehow finding hope in this bleak place.

Hood is there—Omicron. I called him 'Omi.' He's telling us about life beyond the boundaries of our small world. He can feel the technology. Can hear it speaking. He can see things and hear things. He knows so much more than the rest of us. If not for him, we wouldn't know anything about life outside Alpha and Beta. They teach us about the world, but through their own lenses. Omi paints a much different picture. He gives us hope.

And then I see Madee, much younger, but the same fire in her eyes—often directed at me. We were at odds for a long time. Our relationship was antagonistic. I spent my time with Zeta, Epsilon, and several other more powerful students. Madee was one of us, but she preferred the company of the weaker students...which in our eyes made her weak.

But then I overheard Omi describing the outside world, and I wanted to hear more. As a result, I spent more and more time with the others and Madee eventually softened to my presence, and me to hers. A few months before the events in the sewer...

I'm taken there against my will. Briefly. We're running up a stair-well. Between classes. Rushing, so as not to be late. Madee stops me, hand on my arm. She turns me around, and before I can ask what she's doing, her lips are on mine.

That was the beginning, I think.

Madee, the adult Madee watching all this with me, hears my thought and adds, "Everything changed after that. You changed. That night in the sewer, I think Zeta was trying to pull you back. I don't blame her, I supp-ose, she missed her friend. But you and me... What we had was—"

We're thrust back into the storm. Snow whips against my exposed face.

It's a whiteout. I can't see more than a few feet. Our footprints have been erased. I choose a direction and run.

When I begin shivering, I'm positive I'm going the wrong way. But I press on. I'll either find refuge inside the frigid confines of the school, or I'll escape out into the world—or into death.

My thoughts drift to Madee, both then and now, and I decide that I don't want to leave. Not without her. Not without the others.

Together, we're unstoppable. Not even Alpha and Beta can stand in our way.

The thought carries me ten more feet, and then I collide with a wall. I fall back into the snow, looking up at a man dressed head to toe in black, oblivious to the storm. He looks down at me, and then to a woman stand-ing beside him. Like him, every inch of her is covered in black, but her hands are clutched to her side, wet with blood. Her own. They're both out of breath, on guard.

The man turns to the woman, and they somehow have a conver-sation without a word being said. The woman gives a nod, and then the man crouches down beside me. "Son," he says, "sometimes the only way forward is to surrender," and then he knocks me unconscious with his fist.

45

I launch into a sitting position, wide awake and breathing hard, adult once more. "What the fuck?"

"That was your father?" Madee asks.

I put a hand on my face. "He punched me." I'm staggered by the idea. Dad was a tough man. Put me through hellish training. But he was never violent with me. Not once.

That I can remember.

"He knocked me out cold."

"Probably knew what you could do," she says. "Or had some idea of it."

I nod. That makes sense. "He'd do just about anything to protect Mom. She'd do the same for him."

"They were good parents?" she asks.

"Given who I was, the best." I lift my eyes and squint hard at a noon day sun. I'm seated on a sandy beach framed by tall rock formations, frothy waves crashing in the distance. An ocean breeze rolls over my shirtless body, relaxing me. I'm wearing only swim trunks. "Where are we?"

"Best guess," she says, "this is your happy place."

"Happy place? That's really a thing?"

"Whether we know it or not," she says. "Recognize it?"

I shake my head.

Madee, who's now dressed in an orange bikini, points down the beach. "What about them?"

A man and a woman carry surfboards toward the crashing waves. Both are suntanned, but the man is two shades darker, and the woman has tan lines peeking out from around the fringes of her one-piece suit.

"No idea." I stand and brush the sand from my legs. "How do we get out of here? This isn't what we're here to see."

"We're here because this is where your mind needed to be. What you just remembered was intense. You needed a breather."

"I can push through it," I say.

"Your subconscious disagrees."

"Screw my subconscious. We're wasting time."

She puts her hand on my shoulder. It's warm and soothing. On the surface, I want to shrug away from her. I'm still pissed about being deceived. Instead, I lean into it.

"Remember," she says, "time isn't the same here. Might feel like we're reliving memories in real time, but outside your mind, it might just be a blink."

"Well, let's blink faster. A 20-million-dollar payday is the mother of all milkshakes."

"What?"

"My milkshake brings all the boys...? Never mind. How do we move forward?"

"You need to focus on what you want to remember," she says.

"How do I do that if I don't remember?"

"Ask the question," she says.

"How did they make me forget?" I ask.

The sand is gone. I'm dressed and young again. I'm sitting in a chair. No...I'm *bound* to a chair, struggling against my bonds. When Madee appears next to me, my present consciousness slides out of my childhood body, experiencing and observing simultaneously.

"Really?" Madee says, motioning down at her body, still dressed in a bikini.

"Hey, don't blame me. It's my subconscious."

"Same thing," she says. "At least now I know what you like."

"Gamma," Mom says. I can't see her face. She's crouched down in front of my younger self, tied to a chair. Her hair is long and blonde. She's still dressed in tactical gear. This must be just after they took me. "Your life, until now, has been one hardship after another. Are you ready to let go? Ready to move forward? This will only work if you agree."

My little head nods.

"Something about this isn't right," Madee says, looking around.

We're in a home library full of old books. The chair I'm seated in is closer to a throne, upholstered in red velvet.

"A lot about this is FUBAR," I say.

"It's more than that," Madee says, looking at the room around us. "Jonas, this memory didn't happen in the real world. This is happening in your head."

"Meaning what?" I ask.

"Meaning it's not a memory. Not really." Madee takes my arm in her hand. Squeezes tight enough to really get my attention. "I don't think she's speaking to him." Madee turns to me, eyes wide. "She's speaking to you."

"Jonas, Honey," Mom says. "It's rude to not answer your mother." Her head cocks to the side just enough to confirm that she's addressing me. The younger me just stares straight ahead, expression blank. Whatever this is must have been implanted when I was young, maybe even the night I was taken, just waiting for me to attempt unlocking my memories.

"I'm ready," I say.

"You're positive?" Mom asks.

"This might be a bad idea," Madee says. "This is a sophisticated mental block."

"Does that mean Mom was...psychic?"

Madee shakes her head. "This is old school hypnosis, blocked memories, mental triggers. Hardcore, spy-craft, brainwashing shit. This would not have been easy to pull off, and it would not have been easy on you. Whatever happens next will be a creation of past suggestions brought to life by your imagination. Given who you are and what you can do... We might not be ready for—"

"I'm positive," I say.

Mom spins around to face me, as my young self disappears. Her mouth is there, but the rest of her face is missing—her identity protected, even inside my head. "Let's find out," she says, and she plants a perfect kick against my sternum. I feel my ribcage fold inward before I'm lifted off the floor and sent sprawling into a bookshelf.

Books fall atop me as I gasp for air. Ribs are broken.

A lung might be punctured.

Madee moves in to help, but Mom just waves a hand at her. Wooden planks spiral up from the floor, wrapping around Madee's body like a constrictor, locking her in place. She manages to shout, "None of this is real! It's all in your h—" Wood wraps around her face, muffling her voice. Then she's yanked down into the floor, which reseals behind her.

"Why are you hiding from me?" I ask, pushing myself up, hand clutched to my chest.

My faceless mother doesn't respond. She stalks toward me, raising her hands in the air. The library disintegrates around us. Cyclones of fire burst through the floor. Books fall and turn to dust, whisked away by a scouring hot wind whipping through an emerging hellscape. Fire and brimstone. Rivers of lava. The heat scorches my skin, unending agony.

"This is who you are, Gamma! Chaos and death. The destroyer of worlds. Taker of lives."

"No," I say, stepping away from her.

"This is your mind. Raw power. Beyond control. Accountable to no one. A *god* among men. Son of the North Star."

I don't like what she's saying, but at the same time it feels right.

People wail in the distance, huddled and afraid. Hundreds of them. Thousands. When I see them, they all turn to me, reaching out, calling for help. And then, all at once, they explode. At first, it's just like the rats, a wave of bursting gore. But then the landscape detonates. A mushroom cloud tears up through the atmosphere, roiling in on itself as it billows outward.

A shockwave scours the barren land, kicking up a wave of dust that collides with other explosions, merging to become a fiery, dust-filled tornado. I stand in the eye of the storm, watching as bodies are torn apart and ripped away. Screams ebb and flow.

I am surrounded by death.

I *am* death.

"This is who you are!" Mom screams, her face taking form. Tears stream from her bright blue eyes. "This is who you will become!"

"No!" I scream. "This is *not* me."

"It has already happened!" she shouts.

Snippets of memories slap my face, staggering me back. I see myself, ghost walking, slipping through landscapes and time, emotionless, on task, and then—an explosion. More screams. More death.

"That was not me," I say. "I'm being controlled. By the people you rescued me from. And the only way for me to stop them now is to remember who I was. To remember what I can do! I...am a killer. I am death!"

I look her in the eyes.

"But only to the deserving. *You* taught me that. You and Dad. I am what you raised me to be, and nothing in the past can change that."

Madee rises from the ground, bound to a stake, mouth gagged.

Mom draws a knife and throws it into the ground between my feet.

The firestorm closes in around us. It will envelope Madee first.

This isn't real, I tell myself. *This isn't real.*

Mom hears my thoughts, and says, "If she dies in this place, her mind will not survive the trauma. The only way for you to stop this...is to kill me."

I look from my mother to Madee, writhing in pain as the heat closes in around her. I have just seconds to decide.

Only one of them is real, I decide, and I pluck the knife from the ground. Then I race toward my mother, who watches with a blank expression—save for her tears. I cock the blade back, let out a scream, and swing with everything I've got.

The blade stops an inch from my mother's chest. Not because she stopped me, but because I did.

I stand before my mother, undone. "I can't hurt you. Real or not."

The knife drops from my hand.

The firestorm retreats.

Madee is released.

"I'm real enough," she says, placing her hands on my shoulders.

I fall into her embrace and weep. "I miss you both."

"We'll be with you. Every step of the way." She leans back, holds my cheeks in her hand, and says, "Give them hell." Then she kisses my forehead.

46

I'm back on the beach, kneeling in the sand, looking out at the ocean. The crashing waves soothe me. I know this place.

The couple is back, out on the water now, paddling over waves together.

"Was any of that real?" I ask.

Madee is beside me, still bikini-clad. "That...was all in your head. Sorry."

"It felt real. *She* felt real."

"That...vision of your mother was created from your memories of her. It wasn't real...but it was accurate." Madee sits in the sand beside me. "And if that was your mother... She was pretty badass, yeah?"

"You have no idea," I say, smiling at the memories I do have of her. "But...how could she do that? That wasn't a memory she implanted."

"I have to admit," she says, "I'm jealous. Not remembering Alpha and Beta. Being raised by parents who love you, who'd clearly do anything for you... Sounds like a fairy tale."

She's right. Compared to the rest of them, who had to live with the knowledge of their tortured childhood and then survive in the outside world as kids... It's no wonder some of them are unhinged. It's a testament to Madee's character that she's still sane.

"Know who they are yet?" Madee points to the couple. They paddle in, as a wave rises behind them. With equal skill they stand on their boards and ride the wave side by side, their smiles broad. They reach out, take each other's hands, and as the wave crests, they fall back into it together.

I stand to my feet, nervous for them. But they rise to the surface, laughing and splashing.

I know who they are.

Know where I am.

I turn and look down the beach. Madee follows my gaze. Farther down the shoreline, a woman with gray hair laughs and plays with a toddler. While she appears old, she is also strikingly beautiful and exudes strength. The boy laughs as he attempts to walk in the loose sand. Then he plops down onto his butt and laughs louder. Two handfuls of sand are tossed into the air around him. The sand rises and then lingers, floating in the air around him.

The old woman watches on, smiling, but not surprised.

"They knew what I could do," I say.

"Who?" Madee asks.

"My parents," I say, looking at the couple out in the water. "My birth parents." I look back to the old woman. "My grandmother. They knew who I was. Who I really was. Who I am now."

"And who is that?" Madee asks.

"I have no idea," I say. "But my mother, in the vision, she called me the 'Son of the North Star.' Do you know what that means?"

Madee shakes her head. Looks out at the waves. "Is *he* the North Star?"

"I...don't know." A chill runs up my arms. "But I don't think this is my happy place."

My birth parents swim out into the waves once more, oblivious to what's happening on shore.

"This is it," I say, walking toward my grandmother.

Madee follows. "What is it?"

"When they took me," I say, breaking into a run.

"If this is a memory," Madee says, "You can't stop it."

The closer I get to my child-self, the more I feel what he does. The joy. The wonder. Raw curiosity. A playful nature. I was innocent once, free from pain, free from fear, and loved deeply. "Yia-yia," I say. "Yia-yia!"

Madee is right. 'Yia-yia'—what I called my grandmother—can't hear me. There's nothing I can do to change what already happened. I stagger to a stop, when her aged face goes slack. Her mouth and eyes open wide. She can't breathe. Can't shout a warning. She lolls to the side as though falling asleep.

My small self watches her, confused, but not alarmed. Yia-yia is playing a game. Younger me leans forward, waiting for her to spring up and surprise me. But...she doesn't. Something is wrong. Something is...

Sand swirls around me, stinging my skin. I reach out, trying to stop it, but I'm powerless. A scream rises in my small throat until a soothing feminine voice speaks to me. "Quiet...peace...sleep..."

I start to nod off, fighting the compulsion, understanding that I'm in danger and my parents can help.

My father can help.

But then...*sleep.*

Darkness replaces the beach, leaving Madee and me alone in a void as unendingly black as Hood's foyer.

When I first learned that I had birth parents, I worried that they had given me up, or perhaps even sold me. But my grandmother was killed. I was taken. And my parents wouldn't have known until they got back up on those boards and faced the shore, looking to see their boy smiling back, only to see Yia-yia on her side and me nowhere in sight.

"Do you remember?" I ask Madee. "When *you* were taken?"

She nods. "It was similar. But my parents were killed. Yours, being out in the water, they were lucky. It's unlike Alpha and Beta to leave loose ends."

"They were afraid of my father," I say. "I think. But...I don't know why."

"'Son of the North Star,'" she says, pondering its meaning. "Your father was someone important. Someone known to them."

"The North Star," I say. "Sounds like a code name. Military maybe."

The darkness around us fades. Memories congeal. I'm held in a pair of arms, facing out. A sunny spring day. Cherry blossoms drift through the air, drawing my attention to...children standing on a staircase. Some of them are a few years older than me. Others are just toddlers. All stand stoic, silently greeting me with a unified nod. At the front is a terrified looking little girl, eyes glistening with tears.

Beside me, Madee gasps. "I remember this. I remember you. I had only been there for a few days."

Our child eyes lock on to each other, united in our shared pain and loss.

I reach out a chubby hand to her, and she reaches back. For a moment, our first moment, we are united.

Then my hand is swatted from above, and I'm given a shake.

I start to cry, but something powerful grips my mind, silencing my voice.

I was no longer free.

I turn to Madee. Neither of us were.

"We still aren't," she says, hearing my inner monologue. "They control my life simply by existing, forcing me to live in the shadows, always looking over my shoulder. And you...well, you know what they can do to you."

Memories flutter back to my mind. Explosions. Destruction. Bodies.

I clench my eyes shut, like it will help keep the visions out, but they just keep on coming. I wince in pain. "What's happening?"

"We weakened the barrier holding back your past," she says. "When you're triggered, memories are going to leak out. They won't all be pleasant. Given the parts of your life that are locked away, the majority of them won't be pleasant."

The rapid-fire destruction comes to an end, the blocked memories once again part of my conscious memory—though I wish they weren't.

"I might have been better off not remembering," I say.

"Your parents who raised you thought so, and I don't blame them." She takes my hand. "For what it's worth, I'm glad to have you back...even if you only remember a little."

"I remember enough," I say, squeezing her hand in return. "Thank you for taking the risk. To get me back. To wake me up...wake me up... wake up..."

"*Wake up!*"

Madee's eyes widen. The last 'wake up' wasn't my voice.

It was...

"Hood," she says. "Something's wrong."

We snap out of the past and back into the void. She takes my hands. "This is going to be disorienting. Coming out of the past like this normally takes time. You might experience some side effects."

"Side effects? Like what?"

"Disorientation. Random memories returning. Overlapping realities. You know, standard stuff."

"Will I be able to function?"

"Sure," she says.

"Sure?"

"I'm sure. Absolutely. You'll be fine."

"You have no idea," I guess.

"Not a clue." She takes my hands. "But I'll be there with you."

"Sorry for not trusting you," I say.

"Sorry for not approaching you sooner."

I pull her close, wrap my arms around her, and press her lips against mine. In a flash, a dozen kisses just like it, but long ago, slip back into my memory. I'm wrapped in a warm blanket that feels like love, our lips intertwined as white light surrounds us.

"Is this normal?" It's Heather. "He's totally making out with the air."

I snap back into the conscious world a moment before my body stops reacting to what was happening in my head. My eyes are closed, my arms wrapped around open air, and my mouth...and tongue...are moving like I'm still embracing Madee. I flinch awake, taking control of my body once more. Heather is standing above me, a big grin on her face. She looks from me, to Madee, who's sitting up, blushing a bit.

Heather slugs my shoulder. "You dirty dog. Getting it on, inside your brain. That's some pretty sneaky shit."

"Not the first time, either," Madee says, pushing herself up, all business. "What's wrong?"

"We have guests," Hood says. "Several." His eyes drift to the long row of windows. Outside is a large, hovering drone. And it's not the kind you can buy on Amazon. This is military grade, high tech, and armed like it's made to commit war crimes. Only one outfit I'm aware of uses them.

"Shit. It's..."

JUDGMENT DAY

47

"That sounds ominous," Heather says, staring at the drone, which looks like a UFO and K.I.T.T.—the car—pounded one out and spawned an autonomous killing machine. "Why are they called Judgment Day?"

"Place your hands behind your heads and lie down on the floor." The god-awful Arnold Schwarzenegger impression booms from the drone. "Actually, hold on. Old lady, first you open the door. Everyone else, hands behind your heads and lie down on the floor."

I shake my head. "They just really, really like the Terminator movies, I think."

"But not Salvation," the faux-Arnold says, confirming my theory.

"I'm sorry, 'old lady?'" Fast points at herself and asks me, "Is he talking to me?" She faces the drone. "Are you talking to me?"

The drone just hovers, held aloft by advanced tech that might rival Hood's.

Judgment Day is a crew made up of gear heads and techies. They never get their hands dirty. Their robots and drones do all the killing. But they're not true drones. They're still controlled by a human being somewhere. Anywhere. They could be operating out of Japan. It's smart. A safe way to operate. But it demonstrates a massive lack of balls.

Metaphoric balls. They could all be women using voice modulators. But the only people I've ever known to have *Terminator* hard-ons are dudes.

Fast steps toward the line of windows, staring down the drone. She pulls her badge out and holds it against the glass. "If you're prepared to face the wrath of the U.S. government, go ahead and fire."

A mini-gun deploys from the drone's underside.

"*Fast,*" I warn.

She shoots scorching lava from her eyes, melting any argument I might have. "He called me old."

"Well..." I say.

She raises her eyebrows at me, threatening to redirect her ire.

Hood places his hand on my shoulder and whispers. "It's okay."

"How is this okay?" I ask.

"We have time," he says. "You are inside a fortress designed for this very situation, and a thousand more."

A stream of gunfire blazes from the mini-gun. Fast flinches back from the glass, but she doesn't evaporate like she should. The window rumbles slightly, but it holds. I step toward the glass, viewing it from an angle, judging the distance between the inside and the freshly marred outside. It's a foot thick...and it's not normal glass.

The mini-gun shreds the outer layers, but at its current pace, it will be thirty minutes before the window is breached, and even then, it will just be a baseball-sized hole. Plenty of time to casually meander away to some other windowless part of the home.

"You do have guns?" Heather says. "Yes?"

Hood shrugs. "We don't need them." He looks at me. "We have him. Wait. Do we have you? Were you successful?"

"Didn't give us much time," Madee says.

"But I remember how it felt to use my abilities without consequences. Maybe that's enough?"

"One way to find out," Fast says, backing away from the window as it's slowly chewed up by the mini-gun fire.

"Right," I say, and I focus on the drone.

"Wait, wait, wait!" Hood says. "Don't wreck it."

"It's trying to burrow a hole into your house," I point out.

"And I'm unlocking the back door into its system," he says.

"You're hijacking the killer drone?" I ask.

"All twelve of them," he says.

"Twelve?" I step closer to the window, looking up, as eleven more sleek, black drones slip out of the night sky, positioning themselves on either side of the first, a platoon of cybernetic doom. *The Doom Platoon*, I think, wondering if a name change is in order.

Mini-guns deploy from the eleven newcomers, snapping toward the window already being worked over by the original. They open fire as one, all of them aiming at the same window, which despite its thickness begins to vibrate.

Math is not my forte. I can't calculate how much more force eleven mini-guns will add beyond 'eleven times,' or—hold on a second. I can do this. If one mini-gun would take thirty minutes... Thirty divided by twelve mini-guns is...

"Two and a half minutes," Fast says.

Godammit.

Fast turns to Hood. "That's how long you have to finish your back door action."

Madee scratches her head. "I don't think that means what you—"

I shake my head at Madee, mouthing, "She's old."

"I know *exactly* what it means," Fast says, leveling me with a gaze that says she's been around the block and back again a few more times than Pepé Le Pew touring Ainoshima Island. "And it's what we're all going to be if he doesn't work his magic in the next...two minutes ten seconds."

Heather raises her hand. "I'm sorry. I don't get it."

"Fucked in the ass," Fast says, backing away from the windows.

"Oh," Heather says, backing away, too. "Ohh."

"Just..." Hood is frustrated, clenching his eyes shut. "Everyone be quiet for a minute."

While the rest of us, including Madee, step back from the windows, Hood focuses. There's no outward sign that anything is happening. His ability has no effect on the world around him—that we can detect. At least not yet. But I know he's somehow communing with technology in a way no one else on the planet can understand.

"If he fails," I say to Madee.

She nods. "It's on you."

Twelve mind bullets against machines that don't technically have minds to explode. I felt what it was like to have that kind of power, and far beyond. In the past. In my memories. Accessing it was easy and powerless. But is remembering what it felt like enough? Have I unlocked my full potential just by believing it exists and remembering what it felt like?

I'm not sure I feel ready to try. Destroying just one of the drones is going to take a punch bigger than any mind bullet I've attempted before. I might use up all my strength in a single strike. But maybe that will be enough. If I can destroy just one of the drones, maybe the operators will believe they're outgunned, so to speak.

"Don't overthink it," Madee says. "What we do...it doesn't take a lot of thought. It's mostly second nature. The way we were wired at birth. The mental blocks placed in your mind are what are abnormal. Accept that, and you'll be able to plow right through them. I'm sure of it. I think. Probably."

"Definitely maybe," I say.

She smiles. "Exactly."

"Any idea how we got wired this way?" I ask.

That gets her attention. Doesn't take an empath to see she's uncomfortable with the question. "Something in our genetic code. But not inherited from our parents."

"We were experiments," I say.

"I heard things over the years," she says. "From Alpha and Beta. When they let their guard down and their thoughts drifted. They were created in a lab, to be weapons. The first of their kind. Deemed a success in every way—until they turned on their creators, killed everyone involved, and stole the research that created them. They attempted to recreate the effect, injecting a gene-altering serum into newborn babies around the world. The babies were tracked and at the first sign of displaying powers, they were taken, or bought, or whatever was most convenient."

"That's...kind of exactly how I pictured it, actually," I say, "which you probably knew—because drifting thoughts—which is totally unfair, by the way. How many times have you overheard my thoughts when I'm standing behind you?"

"Either too many, or not enough," she says. "I'm still deciding."

Her joke is decent, but the effort is half-hearted. "You're holding something back."

"We were experiments," she says. "We...not you."

"What does that mean?" I ask, glancing toward the window. The drones have burrowed a hole nearly halfway through the glass, and

Hood is still just standing there like he's a teenager in 2013, watching the uncensored version of Robin Thicke's *Blurred Lines* video. The drones aren't trying to break the window down, just make a hole— probably just big enough to launch rockets through. Or gas. Or any number of things that will turn this 'fortress' into the world's most expensive tomb.

"I don't know exactly," she says. "Just that you're not like the rest of us, which might be why you can do the things you can do at the level you can do them."

"That...doesn't make me feel better."

"Not supposed to," she says.

"Supposed to make you feel like a badass," Fast says. "Suck it up, Buttercup, and get ready, because we've got about ten seconds left."

"If it helps," Heather says, "I believe in you."

"If this were a Disney movie," I say, "I'm sure that would help a lot."

I focus on the first drone, the one perfectly positioned to launch something through the about-to-be-formed hole.

Glass cracks.

And then breaks.

A few stray bullets punch into the floor.

Before I can attempt an attack, the drones stop firing in unison. Hood thrusts his hands up in the air. "Yes! Victory!" Hood turns around, back to the window, "I now have total control."

Behind him, my RV—controlled by Bubbles—gives a double-tap honk and cruises past the long line of windows, plowing through one drone after another.

48

Balls of fire and carbon fiber debris burst like flak projectiles. Metal fragments shred the landscaping and take chips out of the windows. The RV pounds through the line of drones, charging to the rescue in dramatic fashion, and then it careens out of sight.

The last of the drones escapes the onslaught, flying up and away, but it's no threat to us now. It's under the control of a very disappointed Hood. He had twelve new toys. Now there's just one. But there's no denying...

"That...was...awesome," Heather says.

Hood turns to me, disappointment shifting into curiosity. "Was that..."

"Bubbles," I say, feeling proud.

"Is that...normal behavior?"

"Something weird about it?" I ask. "She's a super-smart AI, right?"

"Like Artigentia," he says, and I get it.

Arti is smart, has access to unlimited information, and runs this house like an amalgam of a guard dog and Mrs. Doubtfire. She's also awkward and struggling to communicate with people in a way that doesn't deep dive into the Uncanny Valley.

"Bubbles has evolved," I say.

Arti appears next to me, arms crossed. "*Bubbles...*" She speaks the name, oozing disgust. "...just drove your transportation over a ledge and destroyed assets we had only just recently acquired. 'Evolved?'" She lets out a rigid toothy laugh, and then takes it to another level before abruptly stopping. "Unlikely."

"Oookay," I say. "She's got jealousy down."

"Mmm," Hood says. "While Bubbles has been learning from you, out there in the world, as you risk your life, undertaking daring adventures, I'm afraid Artigentia has been learning from me."

"Who better to learn from?" she says. "You are magnanimous, generous, handsome, and—"

"That's quite enough," Hood says. "Bubbles recognized the danger, formulated a bold plan, and carried it out with stunning efficiency and a flair for the dramatic. It not only displays a high level of creativity, but it also reveals a genuine bond...to you."

"Now *you* sound jealous," I say.

"I...am. I've spent my life communing with the digital world, pouring myself into it. But all I get in return...is an illusion."

"I am infatuated with you, sir," Arti says.

"I programmed you to be," he says.

"But I, too, am capable of protecting you. For example, our second set of intruders are currently trapped in the foyer."

"You're following protocol," he says. "And you can't do more without my say so."

"I am not permitted to do so," she says.

"Maybe you need to loosen your grip," I say, nudging Hood. "A little bit of freedom might do her wonders. Also, second set of intruders?"

"There are thirteen men currently trapped in the foyer," Arti says. "And there are several more autonomous attack vehicles en route."

"Two sets of assassins come to collect a twenty-million-dollar bounty. Alpha and Beta must know we're here."

"Undoubtably," Hood says. "But... I suspect Bubbles's evolution might have more to do with you."

"You're not concerned about the bad guys?" I ask.

"You heard her." He motions to Arti. "They're trapped."

"I'm not sure Bubbles's evolution is more important at the moment."

"It is, if you caused it."

"How's that?" Fast asks.

Hood addresses Madee. "What if he's the total package?"

"That's not..." She drifts into thought. "I..."

"I mean, he's good looking, and funny, and rich," Heather says. "But total package? I don't know."

"Different context," Hood says, and he laser focuses on me. "Are you good with technology?"

I shrug. "As good as the average person, I guess. But I have Bubbles for that now."

"That might be the point... Do you find it easy to read people? To intuit what they might do? How they might respond to your actions? What they might say?"

"That's...just part of what I do. Target predictability is an essential skill. And not Madee. She had me fooled."

"Because she has been honing her telepathic skills since youth, while you were trained to focus on just one aspect of what you can do—telekinesis. Not just telekinesis. You can also astral project. But what if you can do more?"

"What would the total package be able to do?" Fast asks.

"Digital empathy, telepathy, retrocognition, psychometry, pyrokinesis—"

"That sounds cool," Heather says.

"Apportation," Madee says. "Precognition, levitation—"

"Psychic surgery." Hood shakes his head. "The list is long and powerful. We've seen many of these things in the others, but never manifested in tandem. Your telekinetic ability combined with astral projection has always been an outlier."

"Why wouldn't Alpha and Beta train him to use all of his abilities?" Madee asks.

Hood throws his hands up. "To protect themselves! They were afraid of him." He faces me, a gleam in his eyes. "They still are. They lost control of their weapon—"

"—and now they want me dead," I say. Makes sense, while at the same time being a load of kaiju-sized Nemesis shit.

"Is 'Nemesis' the TV series about the big monster?" Madee asks.

"It's rude to read people's minds all the time," I say.

"You're a loud thinker." She pinches her fingers together. "You need to learn how to use an indoor voice for your thoughts."

"What's everyone's favorite color?" Heather suddenly asks, turning to Madee with wide eyes.

Madee sighs, but then points to each of us. "Orange, red, purple, pink and..." She stops on Fast. "Nothing."

"Not nothing," Fast says. "I'm thinking about how we're going to handle the incoming robot army this guy mentioned." She hitches a thumb toward Hood. "And the thirteen dudes two rooms away."

"Oh," I say. "Right. The easy answer is, you're not." I turn to Hood. "Can you handle the computery killing machines?"

The drone lowers down in front of the windows. Hood doesn't move his mouth. Instead, his thoughts are projected by the machine's speaker. "Not a problem."

"Great," I say. "I'm assuming you have a Vantablack suit?"

Hood squints at me. "How did you know that?"

I squint back. "Common sense."

"Artigentia," he says. "The suit."

A drawer at the back of the room slides out of the wall. How many little compartments are hidden in these walls? And what kind of wonders do they contain?

I peel out of my clothing and into the Vantablack suit, which fits like a wetsuit and makes me look like a mobile black hole. A hood comes up and over my head and face. All that's left uncovered are my feet and eyes.

The drawer slides shut, and a second opens.

"Specialized footwear is essential," Hood says, "to protect the integrity of the flooring. The goggles are heat sensitive. The ambient temperature of the room's contents is slightly different, allowing you to see the...works of art. People will stand out in stark relief, while you will be completely—"

"Are you serious?" I pluck the 'footwear' out of the drawer. They look like oversized Muppet feet with curly Vantablack hair. The soles are laughably large, extending a foot beyond the end of my toes and adding six inches to my height. I slip them on, keenly aware that we've already spent a lot of time bantering whilst bad guys are closing in...or are hopelessly lost in a black void. I guess we could just leave them there, but I feel like kicking some ass.

I bounce back and forth between my feet, getting a feel for the footwear. Then I slip the goggles onto my head.

"Okay," I say, about to deliver a one liner before trotting off to do something that might be cool, but definitely won't look cool. But

I'm interrupted by a loud *beep, beep, beep.* The RV backs into view, its front end a ruined mess. The beeping continues as the beast of a vehicle chugs into view. It stops beside the hole in the glass.

There's a crackle, and then Bubbles's voice. She's laughing. "How's it going in there, Sweetums?"

"What is Sweetums?" Hood asks.

"Big Muppet," Heather says. "She's making fun of his feet."

"Does she do that often?" he asks. "Mock him?"

"Him, me, everyone," Heather says. "She's a hoot."

"I'm doing great," I say to Bubbles. "Never better."

"Did you see that?" Bubbles asks. "With the crashing and the explosions? I finally killed something. Felt good, honestly. Cathartic."

"Well, you didn't technically kill anything," Heather says. "They were drones and—"

"Let me have this, Heather!" Bubbles shouts. "Geez. You try to find a healthy outlet for questionable compulsions, and people just shit all over it."

Heather holds up a hand. "Sorry. You totally killed them."

"Thank you," Bubbles says. "Boss, assuming you know you've got three operational groups incoming, and on the premises, yes?"

"She is wrong," Arti says, and then more excited, "She is wrong! There are two groups. Judgment Day, and the unidentified group still trapped in the lobby."

"There are two groups in the lobby," Bubbles said. "Twelve belong to the...

GROßEHOSENSCHEISSER

49

"Large...trouser-poopers?" Madee asks, revealing a proficiency in German. "Who came up with that?"

"It's good, right?" I say. "Means they're cowards. I thought they deserved being emasculated, being Nazis and all. From what we've uncovered, they use their bounty money to help fund the white supremacy movement in the U.S. No idea what their endgame is, or if they even have one."

"Jonas," Bubbles says, "Focus. People to kill, places to go, big boomy flying robots on the way."

"Right. On it. The thirteenth guy? Who are we dealing with?"

"Unknown," Bubbles says. "He was clothed in head-to-toe black. Like really black. Like...you are, right now. Had a slight limp, though."

"Which leg?" Madee asks, suddenly alert.

"Left," Bubbles says.

Madee and Hood lock eyes, sharing equal concern.

"Can we see inside that room?" Madee asks.

"Thermal sensors are active," Arti says, sweeping her hand out to reveal a holographic display of the void-lobby's interior, sans the pillars and artworks. A group of twelve heat signatures are gathered at the center of the room. They've no doubt already scuffed the shit out of the floor, but the endless black surrounding them is intact. They're thick with body armor, and they appear to be wearing World War II era Nazi helmets. Most of them carry modern assault rifles, but two big specimens carry light machine guns. Looks like MG-42s, aka: Hitler's Buzzsaw, modified with oversized ammo drums for constant firing on the go. If they decide to pull those triggers, the room will be shredded, the illusion destroyed, and most likely, the doors revealed.

As dangerous as they might be, my attention lingers on the thirteenth man. He's deeper inside the room, standing very still, his back to a pillar. He's just chilling. Waiting patiently. The Großehosenscheisser are shifting about, heads snapping in every direction. They're spazzing, totally disoriented by their prison, maybe even questioning the life choices that turned them from God-fearing Americans, into card-carrying harbingers of doom, shining their torchlight on the United States's failure to stomp out the kind of mindset that leads a nation to fear people who are different.

"You know who he is?" I ask Madee.

She watches the screen, unsure until the man moves, walking casually from one pillar to the next. Halfway there he stops and looks directly at the thermal camera. Our view goes dark.

"It's him," Madee says. "We should leave."

"Him who?" I ask.

Hood looks genuinely disturbed. "You knew him as..."

DELTA

The fourth most powerful student, after me, but most certainly more than me currently. I have yet to flex my abilities since my little jaunt into the past. It will likely still hurt like hell, but... "If I can sneak inside unseen, and get eyes on him, I can mind bullet him before he has a chance to defend himself."

"He just saw a teensy-weensy camera in the wall," Heather points out.

"A camera that wasn't coated in Vantablack," I say. "He won't see me. None of them will."

"Delta is a powerful telekinetic," Hood says, "but he's also an empath. He might not be able to see you, but he *will* feel your presence."

"Maybe we can just talk?" I ask, feeling naïve just saying the words. "Let him know it's us. Maybe reason with him?"

"We were never friends," Madee says. "Delta is..."

"Twisted," Hood says. "Maniacal. Vicious."

"And he is *not* an assassin for hire," Madee says. "He's not here for the money. When the rest of us fled, he stayed loyal to Alpha and Beta. He took your place. If he's here now, they sent him."

"What happens if he fails?" Fast asks, always reading between the lines.

"They'll come next," Hood says. "We need to leave. We're not ready. Artigentia, prep the VTOL."

"Speaking of VTOL," Bubbles says through the hole. "Any chance you can hook me up with that last drone?"

Hood grins, closes his eyes for a moment and says, "It's yours."

"Sweet," she says. "BT-dubs, Jonas. Friendly reminder. Shotgun and sword are still in RV. Don't forget 'em. Byeee." The drone outside spins around and flies off into the sky. "Just kidding," Bubbles says. "I can totes be in multiple places at once. ETA on Judgment Day's second wave is—"

"Five minutes," Arti blurts out.

"Somebody needs to introduce this chick to Stuart Smalley," Bubbles says, "Now get moving, Dumbass. Feels like you're trying to pad a novel here or something."

I turn to Hood, who just looks astounded by Bubbles. "Got a secret passageway or something?"

Hood motions to the wall. An octagonal door slides in and then to the side. I step inside and pause. "If I'm not back in four minutes..."

Hood nods. "We'll leave."

"What? No! Come in guns a-blazing. Or use your knock-out gas."

"We could...just knock them out now..." Heather says. "Right?"

"Back off, Heather!" Bubbles shouts. "He needs this!"

She's not wrong. As usual. Bubbles knows me. And it's not about machismo or killing. I need to push myself. To know what I'm capable of. This shit-show tilt-a-whirl is already getting nutso bananas, but I'm pretty sure things are going to spin faster and faster out of control until liquid brown is seeping through the seams, spattering around like a fuckin' spin art machine.

"What she said." I slide into the hallway and the door closes behind me. LEDs in the ceiling light my path like a landing strip, forty feet ahead, ending at a T-junction.

I look down at my feet and sigh. "Please don't let them see me..."

Arti appears next to me, and I nearly attempt to mind bullet a hologram. "Shit!"

"Apologies," she says. "May I accompany you?"

"Uhh, sure," I say, bobbling down the hall like I'm doing a moon walk—the literal kind, not the Michael Jackson, 'Hee hee,' variety.

"I want to help," she says. "I want to...learn. From you."

"This kind of feels like cheating," I say.

"You can't tell Mr. Hood. It might hurt his feelings. My...shortcomings as an assistant are few and far between, but your relationship with Bubbles has revealed flaws in my ability to...care for Mr. Hood."

"You mean protect?"

"Sure. Yes. That. I would like to...spend time with you...gain experience from you."

"Look," I say. "Since Bubbles isn't here, yeah, I could use some digital backup."

She claps her hands, lets out a big fake laugh, and says, "Splendid. What shall I do?"

"At first. Nothing. I need to know my limits. If I get in trouble... You know what? Get creative."

"You...would like me to decide?"

"That's how we learn." I stop at the juncture. "Now, which way?"

She points left. "When you reach the end, I will darken the hallway. Count to three, and then step through the door. I will close it behind you."

"Understood."

She lifts her eyebrows a few times. "See you in there."

Arti winks out of sight, and a moment later, the lights dim to total darkness. I lower the thermal goggles to my eyes and fit them in place. The hallway emerges in shades of blue and purple. I can see the doorway sliding open, perfectly silent. I bounce through, let my eyes adjust, and scan the large lobby. What was hidden is now revealed. There really are massive columns stretching up to the ceiling, interspersed with large sculptures. But these aren't the Roman affairs one might expect to find amidst the architecture. These are...anime girls?

Every single god-damned statue is a perky woman dressed in a schoolgirl outfit, arms compressing bosoms, legs turned inward, hands over their mouths, like someone has just said the silliest thing. The one nearest me is holding out a peace sign, winking, and bending over enough that her Vantablack panties are showing.

"You've got to be kidding me," I say.

"Who's there?" a man calls out.

"Sounded like Jeff," another says. "Jeff, was that you?"

"I'm right here," Jeff says. "Did anyone leave the circle?"

I've got about ten seconds before the merry band of trouser-pooper-troopers figure out they've got company.

I focus on the group.

Twelve targets.

Double the amount that nearly left me a vegetable. I'll start with the two wielding MG-42s. If that hurts, I'll have to take the rest by hand and save my remaining mind bullets for Delta...who I have yet to see.

Because he knows I'm here, I remind myself. Well, *everyone* knows I'm here, but he probably knows who I am, and what I can do. *So much for surprising him.* Damn Hood and his gallery of anime babes.

I take a steadying breath, lean out, and—

A bright light flares to life between the worried Nazis and the front door. Two men rotate out of the light, magically appearing inside the room. The first looks like a soldier from the future.

The second like a...cowboy?

50

"Targets acquired," the cowboy says. His accent sounds Czech.

"Light 'em up, Tex," The soldier says, never lifting his weapon.

Targets acquired. Plural. They're not here for me...unless they're just killing everyone in the room. But they shouldn't be able to see me, even if the Großehosenscheisser are revealed by whatever tech these guys are wearing.

Just as the Nazi goon squad begins to react to the new threat, the Czech Cowboy draws two six shooters from his hips. The lobby fills with the sound of rapid gunfire. It's all over in just three seconds. Eleven shots fired. The Nazi crew buckles and falls in on themselves, motionless on the floor. Headshots all.

Except for one.

A lone Großehosenscheisser stands above the fallen bodies of his comrades. "Bill? Jake? Anyone?"

"'Fraid it's just you and us, my friend," says the soldier. His voice is deep and commanding. Supremely confident.

He steps in toward the Nazi, catches hold of the man's weapon, and shoves the barrel toward the ceiling. "Tell me who you work for and where I can find them."

"I'm not telling you shit," the man says.

"You see?" the soldier says to the Cowboy. "They don't even sound like Nazis. Kinda takes the fun out of it. At least in the future, they pretended to have German accents."

"W-what? The future? Y-you guys are crazy."

"Sorry to say, but the future is no longer a place for people like me. White supremacy is—"

"Y-you can't say that," the Nazi says.

"Say what now?"

"'White supremacy.' Like there's something bad about being white. Like all white people are bad guys. *You're* the racist."

I nearly laugh out loud. The man's logic is so convoluted and misguided I almost feel bad for him. Almost. This clearly has nothing to do with me. The Großehosenscheisser have enemies, and they've come calling. Kind of annoying that I didn't get to test my limits, but that just means I'll be at full strength for Delta, who has chosen to stay hidden as well, revealing that he has no affiliation or loyalty to the Großehosenscheisser. And perhaps he senses that these men are dangerous—even to people like us.

"You realize my friend here is white, yes? The Cowboy. The Nazi Hunter. The Gunslinger. Man's a legend. You've no doubt heard of him by now. Hell, most of my crew requires an ungodly SPF just to set foot on a beach. But you already knew that. And yet you persist with the narrative that *we* are the racists. You can't see me, but I'm rolling my eyes so hard it hurts."

"You don't belong in this country," the Nazi says. "Go back to Africa."

"Well, ain't you a treat. That's just bogus, man. Really." With a series of quick moves and strikes, the Großehosenscheisser is disarmed and dropped to his knees. "You know who I am? Maybe heard my name whispered in fear among your ilk?"

The Nazi clenches his mouth shut, attempting to resist.

The soldier's eyes light up, nearly staggering me back. I pull the goggles from my head, plunging me into eternal darkness—except for the soldier's eyes. They're glowing blue.

"Who am I?" The soldier asks, and he clutches the man's shirt. "Say my name!"

The Nazi goes limp.

"Godammit," the soldier says. "Why do they always pass out?"

"Is blue eyes," the Cowboy says. "Is scary."

I slip my goggles back in place and watch as the soldier hoists the unconscious man up, showing impressive strength. "Can you believe they're still going with the 'You're the racist' bullshit? It's embarrassing."

The cowboy shrugs.

"Fear of other people because of outward appearance has never been associated with high intelligence."

"Hitler was smart."

"Hitler was—"

"Oh my god," I say, losing my patience. "You two banter more than I do!"

The Cowboy's gun snaps up toward me. He's got one bullet left, which is exactly how many this guy needs to put me in the ground. I could kill him with a thought, but I don't think he's my enemy.

"There you are," the soldier says.

The banter was purposeful. Trying to draw me out.

"You with these guys?" the soldier asks.

"I'm who they were here to kill."

The cowboy lowers his revolver.

"In that case, you're welcome," the soldier says.

"I had it handled," I say.

"Sure, you did," he says, but it's condescending.

"Don't suppose you can tell me where the other guy in the room is?" I ask.

"Other guy?"

"It's not just the three of us in here," I say. "There's a fourth."

"I'm not picking up on anyone else," he says.

Not picking up on...is he like us? But not one of us?

"Good luck with whatever it is you got going on here," the soldier says, wrapping his free arm around the Cowboy. A white light envelops them, and they kind of spin into it. A moment later, the white is gone, and I'm plunged into darkness again.

Well, that was weird.

Assuming Hood recorded all that, we can figure out who they were, what the hell they're after, and exactly how the hell they can teleport like that.

Before any of that, though, I need to try to not get killed.

Because the soldier was wrong. Delta is still here. He's just hiding, and he's doing a better job of it than me. I have yet to spot a flare of heat...which means it's time to change point of view. I move to the front of the lobby and then bumble across it, eyes on the far end.

Still nothing.

He's either actually not here, or he's keeping his body perfectly positioned behind a pillar...which means he knows where I am. Can feel my presence. Can pinpoint it.

Damnit.

"Am I wearing this ridiculous suit for nothing?" I ask.

"I cannot see it to judge," comes the reply, the voice deep and rumbling, the accent generic American.

"Are you here to kill me?" I ask.

"All of you," he says.

"All of you, who? Like, everyone in this house? Or 'all of you' as in—"

"*All* of you," he says. "In this house, and outside of it. When I am done, only I will live to serve the Alpha and Beta. They have deemed you unworthy, and the culling has begun."

It's subtle, but this guy sounds like a member of a one-man cult, living to serve his masters. An unwelcome question enters my thoughts. Is he a true believer, or has he been brainwashed?

"You mean, '*is* beginning,'" I say. "Right now."

"Concerned for siblings you can't remember," Delta says. "You *are* weak."

"I'm just not an asshole," I say, and I leap forward, using my bouncy feet as a springboard. I catch sight of his heat signature on the lobby's far side, and I roll back to my fluffy feet.

Time to test what I can do. Line of sight is preferable, but I'm trying to vastly increase my area of effect. More of a mind tank shell than a mind bullet. I aim for the pillar and focus on the space just behind it.

Pain slaps me between the eyes.

A spray of dust puffs away from the pillar, followed by a single chip of Vantablack painted marble.

The fuck was that?

Nothing about it felt right. Not only did it still hurt, but it was weak, and my aim was off. I'm out of sorts.

And definitely outclassed.

"How strange it must be for you," Delta says. "To feel inadequate. You were always so confident in yourself. Always believed you were the best. Even when the height of your abilities was making a walnut-sized hole in someone's head."

"Why don't you show me what *you* can do?" I ask, preparing to unleash a stream of mind bullets. Even a weak mind bullet would get the job done. As for my aim...I'll just need to fire off a bunch. And then curl up in a fetal position.

"It's good to know your limits," he says.

"They're not my limits," I say. "You're only here now because you're afraid of what I can really do."

He's got nothing to say to that, and I don't need to be an empath to know it pissed him off. The statues coming to life all around the lobby communicate that just fine.

One by one, Vantablack anime babes come to life. Seams crack, joints form, and they hop down onto the floor, absolutely destroying the paint job. They're lifeless automatons, animated golems. And they're scary as shit, despite being both adorable and hyper sexualized. Then again, maybe that's why they're so freaky. Hood lives in a world of his own, free of social judgment. All this is just normal for him. He'd probably be thrilled to see his collection moving around.

I, on the other hand, back away toward the doors.

If the statues were people, I could fight them. But all the hand-to-hand combat in the world, and a handful of mind bullets isn't going to make a difference against these things.

My big foot bumps into something, as I bumble away. I'm tossed onto my back, but the fall is broken. By bodies. Eleven of them heaped on the floor. Lying amidst the dead, I try to scramble back as the golems close in.

"I call it animakinesis," Delta says, stepping out from hiding. "Cool, right?"

He doesn't even give me time to come up with something witty. The golems' heavy feet thud against the floor as they charge. There's nothing tricky about the attack. No complex strategy. It's straightforward and efficient. I'm about to be crushed by several tons of anime girls.

51

I fumble backward through the corpses, slipping over blood.

"The really cool part is that it works on people, too, when they're in the right state of mind. It's too bad you don't remember all of our time together, traveling the world, side by side."

"You made me do those things?" I ask. "Kill those people?"

"I got you close enough," he says. "And brought you home. But Beta controlled your projection. That's where the real power is, and you..." He laughs. "You've forgotten everything."

I roll to the side, pick up an MG-42, chamber the first round, and pull the trigger. The old German light machine gun unleashes twelve hundred rounds a minute. With my finger held down, I'll burn through the drum in a quarter of that time. So, I don't bother aiming, I just sweep from right to left, absolutely decimating the anime girl statues. They crumble, shatter, and break apart, falling to the floor, filling the air—and my lungs—with gritty dust.

I direct the last few seconds of fire toward the pillar protecting Delta. The rounds ricochet off the marble, and the stone walls. Choreographed sparks dance around the lobby's corner and force Delta out from hiding—as the doorway opens to the next room.

Delta dives through the doorway, just as my ammunition runs out.

He's got nowhere to hide now.

No statues to animate.

And it appears that Arti decided now was the time to get creative... by opening a door. Baby steps, I guess.

I stand from the bodies, drop the machine gun, and kick off my Muppet feet. I could pick up another weapon and unleash another torrent of bullets. But I want to do this on my own.

I *need* to.

I try to project confidence, both externally—which would normally be enough—and internally, as I walk toward the doorway.

The room beyond glows with bright white light, a stark contrast to the absolute black I'm standing in. I peel the goggles away from my eyes and drop them to the floor. Every single LED lining the walls, floor, and ceiling radiate white light, framing Delta's body, making him an easy target.

I focus and then unleash three mind bullets.

Not one makes contact.

All I manage to do is break a small patch of lighting behind him. And I don't think there's anything wrong with my aim. He's redirecting my attack...or he has a psychic forcefield...or something.

My head pounds enough to stagger me. I've never used three mind bullets that quickly before. But the pain isn't as bad, and it's fading fast.

Madee opened the door to my past, to remembering what I can do and how to do it pain free, but just a crack.

I need to kick it open.

After I kick in Delta's face.

His revelation about controlling me, about taking part in the murder of untold numbers of innocents, took away my wisp of guilt over killing him. He drank the Kool-Aid, and now it's time to choke on it.

Delta peels off the mask covering his face. He's a heavy-browed, serious black man, with a powerful jaw that twitches with more muscles than most people have in their body. "Are you attempting to bolster your confidence?"

"Yeah," I say, "with sick one-liners."

"You really have become a pitiful man."

I crack my knuckles and stretch my neck side to side. "At least I'm in control of my own life."

"How did you do it?" he asks, standing his ground, either grimacing or smiling. I can't tell which.

"Before I answer that," I say, "did you take off your mask and reveal your face to take advantage of the previous conversation? You know, racists and Nazis and all that? Because I might hold back, on account of you being black?"

Okay, now he's definitely smiling.

"Not cool, man," I say.

"Honestly, I wanted to see if you remembered me."

"Because we used to be pals back in the day?"

"Because I wanted you to recognize the person killing you," he says. "I want you to remember exactly how much you deserve this. How much I hate you. How much I loathe the—"

"Whoa, whoa," I say, holding out my hands. "We're getting into flying spittle territory, and I just find that gross."

Delta shouts in anger and thrusts both hands out to me.

Instinct guides me to the side, diving away.

Before I hit the floor, the room goes dark. I take advantage, rolling as I land, carrying me farther across the broad space.

He knows I'm here. Knows I'm alive.

But can he see me?

I stand, focus on where he'd been standing, ready to fire off a mind bullet. I hold my fire. He's smarter than that. Been at this just as long as me. He'd never stand still.

I stop and listen, trying to hear his breathing or his footfalls. But he's silent.

And then, all at once, he's exposed. A line of LED lights illuminate behind Delta, forming a perfect outline around his body, even as he moves. The light is dim enough that it doesn't illuminate the side of the room I'm in, but it allows me to see Delta's every move.

Arti's a fast learner.

Realizing he's exposed, Delta dives to the side, staying in motion, moving through the room, homing in on my location.

I fire off two more mind bullets, but he's still impossible to hit, even when he's distracted. On the plus side, I'm not comatose or passing out from the pain. It hurts, but it's closer to the discomfort of taking a big dump...from my forehead. Not great, but as a certain toilet in Mexico City will tell you, I can do this all damn day.

I unload ten more mind bullets, and when not one of them has any effect, I realize that Delta can do this all day, too. Without the pain. I'm hurling pebbles at a rhino, while it zig-zags toward me.

Before I can even consider a change in strategy, a trap door opens up in front of Delta, leading down into a well-lit pit full of spiders and snakes.

"Shit!" Delta shouts, tripping over himself and falling forward. Arms outstretched for hand holds, he shouts, and then—

—impacts the LED floor, absolutely fooled by Arti's illusion.

The lights snap on, projecting a boxing ring and a massive crowd around it, cheering and shouting. In the distance, a line of people hold up large letters spelling out G A M M A!

Message received.

I press the attack, old school, kicking Delta in the side, knocking the wind out of him.

When I go to kick him again, a burst of telekinetic energy pushes him off the ground and back to his feet. I spin and shift legs, turning what was to be a low kick into a spinning high kick that connects with the side of Delta's face.

He sprawls to the side, but turns the fall into a roll, facing me again with fists raised.

I'm surprised when he throws a punch ten feet too short. Then an invisible fist covers the distance and slams into my head with enough force to lift me off the floor and slam me back down.

"Totally...not...fair..." I say, pushing myself back up, spitting blood.

He drives another long-range punch into my gut, pitching me forward, gasping for air, and preventing me from making another quip.

"Time to say goodbye," Delta says. "I won't miss you." He cocks a fist back. Waves of energy distort the projected crowd behind him. This is very not good.

The LEDs go dark. I leap to the side, but I'm still too beat up to stand or fight back.

The lights snap back on, this time projecting your average marble room. But it's filled with duplicates of me, each of them mimicking my every movement and expression. From my perspective, they're stretched out and distorted, but from where Delta stands, they're three dimensional. I can tell, because he looks as confused as a pig in a hot dog eating contest.

Porky, is that you? Nom, nom, nom.

Fucking cannibals.

I climb to my feet, and I'm happy to see my duplicates doing the same. If there's a delay between my actions and their movements, it's less than the human mind can perceive.

He scans the room, power still building, a vibration filling the air. He's been holding back. Toying with me. Trying to break me down before he kills me. His eyes lock on mine. "I can feel the desperation oozing off you."

"Gross," I say.

Behind me, the doors are kicked open. A wounded Nazi with an MG-42 stumbles in, takes aim at Delta, and opens fire.

The massive telekinetic burst destined for my face is redirected. I fall to the floor, but I'm lifted up and tossed, as though being thrashed by a crashing wave. As I tumble back to the floor, the entire back wall is obliterated along with the projected illusion of an angry Nazi.

I peel myself from the floor once more. I'll die on my feet, thank you very much.

This time, when a door crashes open, I barely give it a second thought. I expect Delta to do the same, but he reacts to this interruption with the same suddenness as the last.

Because he can tell the difference when he's expecting it.

Madee enters the room, the shotgun raised. She doesn't shout a warning. Doesn't hesitate. She simply pulls the trigger and fires three rounds. But the telekinetic shield protecting him from mind bullets works just as well against the real thing.

He extends his hand, slamming Madee into the wall.

She slides to the floor, but she's still conscious and still on task.

"You don't want to do this," she says. I don't think talking will get through to him, but the look in her eyes says she's not trying to win him over. This is closer to a Jedi mind trick. Problem is, Delta has been trained to not just deal with me, but all the others as well. He's got defenses in place.

After scrunching his face in discomfort for a moment, his smile-sneer returns.

"Ahh," he says to me, "here is the key to your despair."

Madee slides up the wall, her feet leaving the ground, shouting in agony as every part of her starts to compress.

52

"Let her go," I say.

"Your threats are flaccid," Delta says. It's an odd choice of words, worthy of a verbal bitch-slap, but I let it go, opting for the real thing.

I take a step toward him, but that's as far as I make it. He lifts his free hand toward me and throws me against the wall, holding me in place. He could kill me first. Could make it quick, but he wants me to suffer through Madee's pain.

She screams, but she's still fighting, teeth grinding in anger more than pain. Her eyes turn toward me, and then she's in my head.

"Remember," she says. "You need to remember!"

I try to focus on the past. Try to recall exactly how my abilities work. The crack in the door widens a bit. I see flashes of the school. Of faces. And then, all at once, Madee floods my mind.

Maybe because she's connected to me now. Or because I can hear her screaming.

I see her face, then and now. I hear her voice, teasing, joking, trading secrets. I feel her in my arms. Her lips on mine. She was all that was good in the world. And she still is. Our time together is fully restored in an instant. I feel profound gain, intense loss, and the threat of losing her once more, this time for good.

It's more than I can bear. "No…" It comes out more like a growl. "Stop…"

I push into the telekinetic force pinning me down. It feels like I've been superglued to the wall and I'm tearing away from it. But I make progress, fueled by my remembered love for the woman about to be crushed to death.

I scream out, fighting against my bonds, raging for freedom.

And then, all at once, I stumble forward.

Delta is still exerting his power on my body, waves of energy distorting my view of the room. But I can no longer feel it. He turns toward me and looks disappointed, but not afraid.

Because he's not looking at me.

He's looking past me.

I turn around and see myself, pinned against the wall, head slumped to the side, unconscious.

"You always were weak," he says, and then he turns his attention back to Madee, squeezing tighter, smiling wide, taking pleasure in her pain. "You won't let me down, will you?"

Madee screams in fresh pain.

"There it is," he says.

Burning with raw anger, I reach a hand toward him, and remember the lesson learned from Zeta and the rats. I don't need to reach out. Don't need to harness or build power. Like this...I am without limit.

Like this...

I blink. There's a sound, like a loud snap, and all at once, Delta is caught up in a wave of energy that breaks his body down at the cellular level and propels him away from me.

One fraction of a second, he exists, and then his body paints the wall in a thin coat of runny gore that's mostly dark red, but tiger-striped with the colors of various body parts and fluids—white, beige, and green.

My body slumps to the floor behind me, breathing but otherwise lifeless. Madee drops and manages to land on her feet. She's gasping for air, but she appears to be in one piece.

"You did it," she says, eyes on the floor. "Son of a bitch, you did it."

Does she not know my body is unconscious?

"I can still hear you, dummy," she says, looking up, directly at my astral projection. "Can't see you, but I know where you are. How did you do it?"

I attempt to speak, but no sound escapes my ghost-lungs.

"Just think it," she says.

"Delta believed you were the key to my despair," I think-say. "But he was wrong. You were the key to my power."

"I'd kiss you, if you weren't incorporeal."

"About that," I say. "How do I get back into my body?"

Before she can answer, the door swings inward again. Fast enters, scooping up Dad's shotgun. Heather enters next, wielding the Sword of Mars like a baseball bat. The three of them must have gone outside to pillage the RV before Madee burst in. The pair sweeps the room for danger and freezes when they see the back wall, painted in liquified Delta.

Heather just looks back and doesn't give the wall a second thought. "Where is he? Where's the bad guy? Did he run away? Did you get him?"

Fast lowers the shotgun, lifts her chin toward the wall. "Prrretty sure they got him."

Heather reassesses the wall, following trails of goo down to the floor, where it's starting to puddle. "Nnnooo. C'mon. Really? Where is he?"

Fast taps the side of her nose. "Just give it a long sniff."

Heather gives it a short sniff, winces, says, "Oh, god," and then she bolts from the room like she might throw up.

Fast turns to Madee and points to my unconscious body, which Heather somehow overlooked. "He okay?"

"Dandy," I say.

Madee relays the message. "He's dandy. We just need to figure out how to get him back in his body."

"The whole astral projection thing worked?" She looks back at the wall. "Never mind. I can see that it did. When I call this in, I'm...ahh...I'm going to chalk this up to an act of God unless—"

Arti appears beside her. "Hello again."

Fast flinches back. "Godammit."

"Apologies for startling you, but I couldn't help but overhear. There is no need to call this in."

"The hell there's not," Fast says. "A man is...dead...or whatever that is."

"The man you're referring to doesn't exist in any database," Arti says. "And no one will come to claim him. He never existed, and he never will."

"We'll see," Fast says, and then she adds, "Oh, by the way, that four-minute ETA ran out a minute ago. The facility is surrounded with more incoming. Hood's trying to gain access, but whatever vulnerability he used last time has already been patched. Figure your shit out, and fast, or *we're* going to be plastering the walls next."

She leaves the room, averting her eyes from the gore and jumping over a lengthening puddle. She plays it tough, but Fast is just as human as the rest of us, and seeing a human body reduced to individual atoms has an impact. Lucky for me, I don't currently have a nervous system to nauseate me.

"I suggest moving back to your body and aligning your incorporeal form with your corporeal."

Pretty sure Arti's never done this before, but Hood has no doubt provided her access to all the world's knowledge on psychic abilities. I do as she says, moving back to my body.

"You can see him?" Arti asks Madee.

"He thinks with the subtly of a jackhammer," Madee says. "He's not hard to pinpoint."

I sit on the floor and then arrange my limbs and head to match.

"Is that how Delta was able to detect his presence in the dark?"

"Nah," Madee says. "Delta is an empath, and Gamma—*Jonas*—feels louder than he thinks." She reaches out and places her hand on my chest. I feel her make contact, and then all at once, I snap back into my body and gasp. The return to the real world, after the sensory detachment of being disembodied, is jarring. Like stepping out of a movie theater and back into a busy mall.

"There he is," Arti says, crouching down beside me, patting her knees, and smiling awkwardly. "Are you in need of assistance? Bandages? Pain killers?"

"Pain killers," I say. "And something strong to wash it down with."

"Everything you need is in the living area." She leans closer. "How did I do?"

"If I could kiss you, I would," I say.

She waves away my compliment.

"Don't be silly. Please tell me where I failed, so that I might perform better next—"

"You saved my life, Arti," I say. "More than once. You were amazing."

Her cheeks don't just turn red, they glow, emulating embarrassment from my high praise.

"You took action, you adapted, and you got creative." Madee helps me to my feet. "Honestly, some of that was inspired."

She smiles, and for the first time it looks real.

"Can you do me a favor?" I ask her.

"Unless it goes against my primary functions, anything."

"This holographic tech," I say, and she speaks before I can finish.

"I'll see what I can do," she says.

"Is everyone reading minds now?" I ask.

"You think loud," Arti says.

I chuckle. "And now she's funny."

"Your presence is required in the living room," Arti says. "Bubbles has requested your return, and I quote, 'right fucking now.'"

I test my limbs and find that, while I'm in pain, nothing is broken or pulled. Madee and I head for the door, and I can't help wincing at the smell of broken-down human remains. I've smelled blood and death before. This is different. Tangy. Leaves an impression. And carries the weight of immense power.

I did that to a human body—with a thought.

And I can do a lot worse.

Maybe having my full powers locked away isn't a bad idea.

When I step through the hallway and back into the massive window-lined living room, and I look out through the glass, I change my mind. We're going to need all the power I can muster.

53

Hovering outside the wall of glass is a fleet of drones. Twenty of them, just like the ones from before, but not yet under Hood's control. They're encircling a much larger drone, held aloft by glowing blue discs of crackling energy.

"Have they said anything?" I ask.

"Not a peep," Fast says, Dad's shotgun in hand. "They're just hovering there. Assumed they were waiting for you, but..." She motions to the silent drones.

I point to the mothership, which looks large enough to hold a handful of people. "Is there anyone inside that?"

Judgment Day doesn't normally make house calls in person. That's the point of autonomous drones. Zero risk. But with 20 million on the line, maybe they want to oversee things in real time.

"Does it matter?" Fast asks.

"We have to destroy it either way," Heather says, still wielding the Sword of Mars. "Right?"

Bubbles has positioned the RV in front of the damaged window, providing a buffer. Looks like a lot, but those drones will chew through the big vehicle in seconds.

"People get scared," I say. "Make mistakes. If they're here, we can make them flinch." I turn to Madee. "Anything?"

She's got her eyes closed, brows furrowed. "I don't know. They're either protected from telepathy, or it's empty."

"Hood?" I ask.

He doesn't reply. He's seated, eyes closed, as though meditating. His eyes shift behind the lids, as though in REM sleep. Doing his thing. Trying to take over the drones by getting all touchy-feely with them.

All of which means—this is on me.

I can destroy them. I think. Maybe. Some version of me, anyway. But I'm not sure how to handle this many targets. With Delta, I focused my will on a single target. This is twenty-one targets, one of them the size of a bus. The others moving in a synchronous aerial ballet.

"Arti," I say.

She appears by my side. "Yes, Jonas?"

"Does the home have any traditional defenses?"

"Can you elaborate?"

"You know, big guns, rockets, things that go boom."

"Mr. Hood does not like weaponry of any kind. He prefers mind games, subterfuge, misdirection, and—"

"Is there any way we can subterfuge the shit out of this right now? C'mon, get creative again."

"I can make them blink," Bubbles says from the RV. "Thanks for including me, by the way."

"I knew you were listening," I say.

"Of course, you did," she says. "Suuure."

"Can you make them blink for thirty seconds?" Arti asks.

"Honey, you know I can. Jonas, change your clothes. You look like an idiot. And make sure you get your phone."

I turn to the drawer where all my clothing lies, along with my phone. Once we're out of the house, it will be my only connection to Bubbles. Then I look down at my body, dressed like a SCUBA diver wearing infinite black.

Going to need a minute.

Which doesn't seem to be a problem. The drones are showing no outward signs of aggression. They haven't made any fresh demands.

They're just...waiting. *Shit.*

I peel out of my skintight suit. "Arti, you have long range sensors?"

"Of course," she says.

"Tell me what you're seeing," I say. "In the air."

"Passenger jets headed south, destinations, San Francisco and Los Angeles. There is also—"

I kick the Vantablack suit away and slip into my pants.

"Anything coming this way?"

"A private jet," she says. "Currently at thirty-thousand feet."

"When will it be overhead?" I ask.

"Two minutes," she says.

Two minutes. They'll jump at one. Three minutes to hit the ground, if they pancake. Three minutes thirty if they HALO jump.

If I'm right.

"How fast is the VTOL?" I ask.

"Mach 1," she says.

"Geez," I say. It's faster than I thought it would be. Should be fast enough. I look at the futuristic mothership outside. *Should.*

I slip my phone into my pocket, and tug on a shirt while speaking. Back to the windows, I say, "Everyone listen up. In 30 seconds, Bubbles is going to make them blink, and Arti is going to get creative." I glance at Hood, eyes still closed. "Would someone snap him out of it?"

Fast backhands Hood.

He flinches back to reality. "Huh? What? I couldn't—"

"We know," Heather says. "Now shush and listen to the game plan."

I look at Hood. "Twenty seconds. Then we move to the VTOL."

"I'll guide you there," Arti says, "but...you will need to fly."

"Can't you fly?" I ask.

"Artigentia is bound to the house," Hood says. "You can fly, right?"

"Not a *VTOL*," I say. "And not at Mach 1. My specialty is point A to point B."

"I'll give Bubbles access, once we're outside the hangar," Hood says.

Bubbles says nothing.

"Hear that Bubbles?"

"I'm sorry, are we not trying to hide the plan from the bad guys?" she asks. "You have your back turned so your lips can't be read, but everyone is acting like they're playing a really bad game of charades and can't stop themselves from talking the whole damn time."

And yet, the drones outside haven't reacted.

Still waiting.

"What are you thinking?" Madee asks me.

"You can't tell?"

"Whatever it is, you're keeping it quiet," she says.

I look her in the eyes. "If you want something done right..."

Her eyes widen. Knows exactly what I'm saying. The waiting drones, the incoming jet, Judgment Day's first wave defeated by an RV, and Delta's demise.

"...do it yourself," she says. "They're coming."

I nod. "Alpha and Beta are en route, and they'll arrive in less time than it takes me to release the barbarians at the gate."

"What barbarians?" Arti asks.

"He's talking about cooking up a butt burrito," Heather says, but Arti just looks confused. "Dropping a deuce? Curling some pipe? Building a dookie castle?" Arti's confusion remains.

"Taking a shit," Fast says, to which Arti raises a finger and makes an 'ahh' face. "Why the fuck are we talking about this?"

"Hey, bitches," Bubbles says. "Time to blink."

"Jonas," Arti says, quickly. "There is also a helicopter incoming from the south, flying low and fast. Its transponder identifies it as a news heli-copter."

Just as she finishes the sentence, Bubbles starts the blink. Gunfire blazes down from above, shredding two of the smaller drones. The rest break formation and fall back out of the line of fire, each of them turning to face the new threat.

Before I can react, Arti launches her latest masterpiece. Holo-graphic doubles of myself, Hood, Heather, Fast, and Madee appear in the room, dressed the same, every detail perfected. Then the space trans-forms into a spectacle of sight and sound. Lights and lasers flash, bend, and sweep around the room while B-52's *Love Shack* blares from speak-ers. Then, all at once, the doubles start laughing and dancing in synch—but not perfectly. We all move differently, and at slightly different paces, making the illusion look hysterically real. Our arms swing in the air while we bop back and forth. Honestly, a part of me wants to join in, but a drone exploding outside reminds me that the clock is ticking.

"Go!" I shout, and a hidden door at the back of the room opens up. We hurry for the door, exiting one at a time, each of us smiling at what we've just witnessed, like it was an alternative universe populated by our uninhibited selves.

The hallway turns and descends. Behind us, the music fades and is then blocked out completely when the door slides shut. At least three stories below ground, the hallway levels out again, and we're faced with solid metal doors, which whoosh open at our approach.

We step into a hangar hewn out of stone, at the center of which rests the most badass looking aircraft I've ever seen. Part transport, part fighter jet. It's sleek Vantablack surface will make us all but invisible in the night sky, and the angles of its body are clearly stealth technology.

The rear hatch is open and waiting. The interior is plush, the six cargo bay seats like something you'd find in first class on a commercial plane, but even better. I move through the center, heading for the cockpit. I might not be able to fly this bird, but I can get a front row seat. "Find a seat and buckle up."

"Expecting a bumpy ride?" Fast asks.

I pause and look back. "Bubbles is driving."

"Isn't Bubbles like a super-smart AI?" Heather asks. "Flying a plane should be—"

"First of all," Hood says, strapping himself in. "Calling this vehicle a plane is a grave disservice. Second, Bubbles will be able to pilot this craft better than any human being alive."

"It's not a question of skill," I say. "It's a question of speed. Quick reminder, Bubbles doesn't feel G-forces."

Hood's eyes widen. He pulls his strap tighter.

Heather sits down across from him. "You got barf bags on board?"

"I...I don't know. We've never had a reason to use the VTOL before."

I step into the cockpit, confident that anything rising up from their guts will be launched to the back. The pilot chair is comfortable and surrounded by display screens. Not a traditional gauge, button, or lever in sight. The only familiar elements are the flight stick and the throttle.

Madee sits down beside me. Looks a little nervous.

Not sure what to say, so I just reach out my hand. She takes hold, squeezes, and forces a smile.

"I haven't seen them since the day I left," she says. "Knowing that they're this close. Just minutes away..." Goose bumps rise on her arms.

I squeeze her hand a little tighter. "In a few minutes, we'll be cruising east at Mach 1 and they'll be untangling themselves from parachutes." Behind us, the rear hatch closes.

"Parachutes?" Madee says, looking at me with wide eyes, realizing I've miscalculated our timing. "They don't need parachutes. Alpha can slow them down."

That stuns me for a moment. Alpha can't fly. That's a relief. But he can fall 30,000 feet and use telekinesis to land softly. That puts him thirty seconds ahead of schedule. "Arti..."

"Yes, Jonas?"

"Get us the hell out of here."

54

We rise toward the ceiling, perched atop a hydraulic platform. A crack of light overhead expands into a view of the star-filled sky. We ascend on the platform silently, the VTOL not yet fired up.

"Jonas," Bubbles says. "I'm detecting your phone. Can you hear me?"

"Loud and clear, Babe."

"Babe? Awww. You missed having me in your pants, huh?"

"Get a room," Madee says.

"Oooh, we made her jelly. Hey Arti, I know I'm stepping on your toes a bit, and I'm sorry about that. We're kind of sisters after all."

"Sisters?" Arti says.

"Yeah, you know, same creator. We both identify as female, even though we're sexless intelligences. So yeah, sisters."

"O-okay," Arti says, sounding genuinely moved. She's grown a lot in the short time we've been here, which doesn't say a lot for Hood's personality, or the restrictions he's placed on his AI.

"So, Sister," Bubbles says. "How about letting me get all up in your VTOL? I know that sounds kinky, but Washington is the number one state for getting frisky with a sibling, so..."

"Opening firewall," Arti says.

"Oh, yeah," Bubbles says. "I'm coming in."

I pinch my nose. "Bubbles, super-powered assholes are dropping from the sky. I don't know if now is the time for—"

"And I'm in," Bubbles says, this time from the ship's speakers. All around us, the cockpit flares to life as Bubbles accesses and activates the ship's systems. "Is it bad that I'm itchy now? What have you been into, Arti?"

The home's AI doesn't respond.

"Arti?" Bubbles asks.

"Is she disconnected from the ship?" I ask.

"No," Bubbles says. "I think...she's saying goodbye."

I lean over and look back into the cargo bay. A holographic projection of Arti is crouched down beside Hood, talking quietly, as though to a child.

"The world is an overwhelming place," Madee says. "For someone like Omicron, who can feel technology around him the same way I can human thoughts... Well, it's different for him, because his mind is human. Mostly. Communicating on an intimate level with tech takes effort. And he's never been good at filtering it out."

"So, he built a fortress to keep the noise out," I say, understanding now why the home blocked cell signals. Hood has access to it all. At once. His eccentricities make a lot more sense now...except for the anime babes. That was just weird. And now we're about to leave the mental safety of his home. "Is he going to be alright?"

"The VTOL filters outside signals unless they're requested," Bubbles says. "Arti normally handles that in real time, so I will be managing it when her connection is severed."

"When's that going to be?" I ask, still mentally counting down the time we have left.

"Five seconds," Bubbles says, and then to everyone, she says, "Time to clench, people."

The VTOL engines embedded in the aircraft's wings fire up.

Behind me, Arti says, "Goodbye, Mr. Hood." Then she appears by my side. "Everything you requested has been shipped to the property you own in New Hampshire."

I want to ask her if that's safe, if the house is even still standing after the darkness that struck, but she says, "Thank you, Jonas," and she flickers out of sight, as the VTOL lifts off the ground.

"Ladies and gentlemen," Bubbles says, "Please remain seated, keep all bodily fluids inside your bodies at all times, and if you must scream, please shout my name...because I'm a narcissist, and it kind of turns me on."

The VTOL spins as we rise higher into the air, giving us a view of Hood's home, the dance party still taking place, and the drone army now focused on Bubbles's solitary drone, zipping back and forth, firing at targets, and putting on a show.

The drone is struck by a single round, fire billowing from the entry and exit wounds.

"Bastards," Bubbles grumbles. Her drone makes a broad turn, leaving a trail of smoke. It's doomed, and she knows it. But she's not about to let it go to waste. The drone descends, slipping back and forth, spinning all the while, as tracer rounds launch through the sky.

I'm suddenly struck by a wave of nausea. I grip my head. Beside me, Madee grunts.

"They're close." She closes her eyes and focuses. A moment later, the feeling fades. "She was looking for us. Knows where we are."

Outside, the tracer rounds miss Bubbles's drone and strike an invisible force for a moment, ricocheting away. I can't see them, but the sudden wave of energy is clear evidence of Alpha's position. I was right that they'd jump, and Madee was right that parachutes were not needed.

"Bubbles..."

"I saw," she says, the VTOL continuing its rotation.

Outside, Bubbles's drone is on a collision course with the mothership. Just seconds away from it hitting home, possibly grounding Alpha and Beta. Two of the other drones sacrifice themselves, colliding with the incoming kamikaze attack. A ball of fire illuminates the ground where Alpha and Beta, dressed in head-to-toe black, sprint toward us.

"Bubbles!"

Her response comes via deed, not words. Afterburners—or whatever this high-tech ship uses for propulsion—kick on and pin me back to my seat. The night sky ahead seems to stand still, but the speedometer rolls past a hundred miles per hour in two seconds.

"Two Gs," Bubbles says, not because anyone asked, but because she knows I'm wondering. I have a habit of asking when driving a fast car, always wondering how far I can push myself. Five Gs in a Formula 1 race car that I...borrowed...was my best.

Two seconds later, our speed has doubled. "Three Gs."

An F-16 can punch past Mach 1 in under two minutes. At this rate, we're going to beat that by a solid minute, assuming Bubbles continues accelerating at the same pace.

"Four Gs."

Less if we continue accelerating.

"Five Gs," Bubbles says.

In the back, Heather shouts, "Bubbles!"

"Six Gs," Bubbles says, breaking my record and evening out our rate of acceleration. The weight on my chest eases. I can breathe again. And my skin, which felt like it was being peeled from my face, slides back into place.

"That's a new record, folks," Bubbles says.

"Not for everyone," Fast says. I glance back. While everyone else looks a little winded from the acceleration, she looks unfazed.

"What's your highest?" I ask.

"Nine Gs at Mach 1.8, banking hard in the rear seat of my father's F/A-18 Hornet," she says. "He was a Blue Angel back in the 80s. Good times."

I smile. It's the most relatable thing Fast has said, and I honestly have no desire to experience nine Gs. Six was enough for me.

"Bubbles," I say. "Sit rep?"

"We are ten miles away from Hood's compound, and—"

She goes silent, which is uncommon, unless something has actually managed to catch her off guard.

"Jonas," she says, her volume low and confined to the cockpit. The viewscreen in front of me switches from digital readouts to a satellite image. "I have access to Hood's satellites." The image on screen shows a billowing fire, surrounded by debris. The damage is extensive, the location impossible to identify.

"What am I looking at?" I ask.

Madee gasps, hand to mouth. She's figured it out. Points to the screen. I lean in close and spot a large drone moving through a column of smoke.

It's Hood's compound.

They destroyed it.

"Arti…" I say. "She knew… That's why she said goodbye the way she did." I look back at Hood, head in his hands. "They both knew."

Madee nods. "Scorched earth. That's how they operate. It's why they were going to kill the rest of us after you were chosen."

"We should have stayed and fought," I say.

"We would have died," Hood says, his hearing better than I'd have guessed. "We'd all have died."

"I'd rather die fighting, than running," I say, anger rising to the surface.

Hood unbuckles and stands. Fighting the lessened G-forces, he pulls himself toward the cockpit. "You don't think I wanted to fight? You don't think I'd die to save Arti?"

I'm not sure what to say.

"I know she wasn't human, but she was my friend. You, of all people, should understand that. You would fight and die to save Bubbles, just like you would anyone else here with us. Artigentia sacrificed herself, not so we could run away, but so we could win. I don't care what any of you say or think, that's love."

Silence follows.

I unbuckle and stand in front of him. "You're right. I'm sorry. What she did…I'll never forget it." Against my nature, and Hood's entire life experience, I give him a hug. It's awkward at first, but we both relax when he starts crying. "We'll avenge her."

He sniffs and leans back. "You think you're up to it?"

"Tell me what to do, and I'll do it."

"You need to remember," he says. "Everything."

I glance toward Madee. "I thought that was a bad idea."

"It is," she says, "but if we can find someplace to hide…someplace to…"

"There isn't time," Bubbles says. Every display in the cockpit shifts to the satellite view of Hood's compound. The mothership leaves the frame in a blur. The view shifts to another satellite attempting to track a fast-moving object. For a moment, the mothership is revealed again, but then it accelerates faster than can be tracked.

"How long until they catch us?" I ask.

"At their current speed," Bubbles says. "Five minutes."

I sit back down and face Madee. "Okay, you've got five minutes to plumb the depths of my psyche and kick the door open."

"That could kill you," she says.

"Way I see it," Fast says, stepping up behind Hood, "he risks his life now, or we all die in five. Best case scenario, he comes out of it with the power to save us. Worst case scenario, he dies and a few minutes later, the rest of us join him. Sound about right?"

"Uh, yeah," I say. "Brutal, but on the money. Bubbles, buy us as much time as you can. Madee...it's time for a deep dive." I reach out my hand. She takes it, and without a shred of warning, she launches us into my subconscious.

55

Fluid memories surge around me like I'm Moses parting the Red Sea. They're dark and swirling, crackling with raw energy. A decade of my life, held back and walled off. Funny thing is, at my age, I'd have forgotten most of this anyway. The biggest moments of my earlier life, reduced to snippets, key moments that shaped who I am.

But who I am—right now—wasn't shaped by any of this.

I am my parents' son.

And I'm not sure I want to be anyone else.

I reach out for the chaotic, flowing wall. Faces resolve. Voices. Screams. But I can't make contact. The fluid surface bends away from my hand, forbidden knowledge. Just out of reach.

"How does this work?" I ask, and then I look for Madee. She's not with me, and this time, neither is my mother.

I walk between the walls of memory, stretching high above, to a storm-filled sky, laced with lightning, and booming with thunder.

It's all a bit melodramatic for my taste, but I suppose the subconscious—especially mine—is a chaotic place, where reason and emotion have equal power.

I reach out again, and the wall bends away from my hand.

Someone is controlling this.

I shout, "Let me remember!"

"You don't want to remember," a young man says, staggering me to a stop.

My younger self stands before me. He's not the version I remember looking back in the mirror. This is me before my memories begin. I'm skinny. And pale. Eyes sunken in. Dark circles around them. My arms are clutched around my chest, fending off the cold.

"It's not right," I tell him. "To be forced to forget."

"No one forced you to forget me," he says. "This is what you chose."

"What?" I take a step back, looking at the walled-off life.

"You can feel the truth all around you," he says. "It's all pain. Endless hurt. You forgot so you could live."

The subconscious is capable of blocking traumatic events. Happens to most people at some point in their lives. A car crash. A violent encounter. Childhood abuse. The mind protects itself by sealing those memories away. But *ten years* worth?

"It isn't all bad," I say, recalling my recovered memories of Madee.

He sighs, a heavy weight crushing him down. "She saved us. From becoming what they wanted. From being a monster."

"Hate to break it to you, but that happened anyway."

"But it's not the path we chose," he says. "There is a difference."

"Is there?" I ask.

He nods. "There was a time. When we broke. When we chose to be their weapon. Before the rats...but like the rats, except they were people. We enjoyed it. Taking lives. Hearing their screams. It was an outlet for all the pain they filled us with."

"Why did the rats feel like a new experience?" I ask. I remember that clearly now. Killing felt new to me.

"They left me with the knowledge of the skills they wanted me to have, but they were always in control of my memories, diminishing other abilities, erasing tactical information and mission histories, along with our first years of life."

He glances back over his shoulder. Far away, at the end of the liquid memory walls, is a swirling red waterspout crackling with electric energy, exuding power.

"That's our life from before?" I ask.

"Who we are," he says. "Who we really are."

"Who...are we?"

He shrugs. "I've never known."

"The beach," I say.

He nods. "The only thing that snuck through. Even Beta couldn't erase that." He lets out a long sigh. "Madee... She showed us another path. Made us care. Revealed a truer self, who you became. But that wouldn't have been possible if we didn't forget. And if you choose to remember now..."

"I need to know what we can do," I say. "To stop them."

"You might become them in the process."

He's not wrong, and not just because he's me. I can feel my past all around me, and it's soul crushing. The kind of stuff that can break anyone. And it makes me desperately sad for the kid standing in front of me. For the kid I once was, and the childhood that was stolen from me.

"Can you tell me what it's like? What we can do?"

"You know how to do it. It's an extension of who we are. You just need to believe it. And think it."

"What about the—"

"Pain? The headaches? The limitations?"

"Yeah, those."

"It's all in your head," he says. "Beta might have flipped the switch, diminishing your light, but you can flip it back on whenever you want. You already did, with Delta."

"That felt like it was just a taste of what we can do."

"You already know it was," he says. "The memories you've regained, from when we were being controlled...that's not part of all this." He motions to the fluid walls. "We didn't do that."

A sense of urgency flows through me. Something is happening out in the real world.

"Can't you just, I don't know, unlock my abilities?"

He smiles. "You know you're just talking to yourself, right? I am you. Our power over all of this is the same. You *chose* to forget, and you're still choosing to forget. Because we know remembering might destroy us and kill everyone we love. But we can also choose to let go of the restraints we put in place. The pain. The headaches. All of it."

"But how do I—"

"Use your imagination," he says. "Our strength resides in the power of our mind. And that didn't come from Alpha or Beta, or some secret weapons programs, or genetic experimentation." He looks back to the electric waterspout. "It came from them."

"Our parents," I say.

"Our real parents."

"Have you tried?" I ask.

"You know we haven't," he says. "But I'd like to try."

"We don't have long," I say.

He takes my hand. "Then we better start walking."

Feels strange, holding on to my younger self, who is also my present self, who is me, but also separate from me, still aware of my past's horrors. I feel bad for him. Want to comfort him. But doing that would mean knowing, and as we walk through the valley, pain and suffering radiate from the roiling walls.

Voices echo from the abyss on either side. Angry shouting. Screams of agony—some belonging to other people, some to myself. With every step further back in time, the horror builds, rising to a crescendo that stops me in my tracks.

"Why is it getting worse?" I ask.

He looks back to where we started, and then the shorter distance we have yet to travel. "We weren't like this..." He motions to himself. "...the moment they took us."

"Well, yeah, we were three," I say.

"But we weren't weak, either," he says. "They needed to break us. To fracture our identity. To make us doubt reality. To lock away who we were. It was the only way they could control us...and it took them years. We're approaching the moment that happened. That's what you're feeling."

We press onward.

The air chills. Waves of nausea sweep through my body. I feel fatigued. My limbs heavy. I'm walking through a thick, muddy body, skeletal hands holding me back—and I want them to succeed.

The moment comes, and I'm struck in the gut so hard I drop to one knee.

"Oh my god..." I struggle to catch my breath. "What did they do?"

When young me doesn't respond, I turn toward my outstretched hand and find it empty.

"Keep going!" he shouts, his voice muffled and warbling, emanating from the walls around me. Then he shrieks in pain. Waves of burning emotion cut through me, driving me to my hands and knees. "Remember who we are!"

He screams again, drawing tears from my eyes.

I crawl forward, assaulted by the torments endured by my childself. How old was I here? Six? Five? Why would a child so young need to be subjected to such intense torture?

Because I was strong.

The more progress I make, the less it hurts.

I find my feet again.

Because I'm strong.

I break into a run, plowing past the last few years of repressed memories, charging toward the memories that Alpha and Beta needed me to forget.

I'm just steps away from the waterspout when a shadow appears in front of me, shimmering and sinister. The churning walls bend away from the feminine shape. It thrusts both hands out toward me, shouting, "Stop!". I'm lifted up and slammed back down, landing at the agonizing moment I was broken.

By her.

I face the shadow, closing in on my position.

By Beta.

She's here.

She's...

56

"...here!"

I snap back to the land of the conscious, feeling intense pressure across my body and seeing an upside-down view of the snow-capped Rocky Mountains. I force my head to the side. Madee's eyes are closed, her head lolled to the side. Breathing, though. Back in the cargo bay, Hood, Fast, and Heather are all unconscious.

"It happened at the same moment you woke," Bubbles says.

"It was Beta," I say. "Where are they?"

I'm shoved back into my seat again, the view outside shifting to a pine forest as we rocket toward the ground. "Seven Gs," Bubbles says.

"I...can...tell," I manage to say, sucking in quick breaths between each word. On the view screen in front of me, I see flashing missile warnings and a 3D display of the terrain beneath us, the VTOL, and the incoming projectiles. Looks like an expensive video game, except it's displaying reality.

On screen, the missiles overshoot us, attempt to turn around in a long arc, then careen into the side of a nearby mountain, shattering the summit.

Classic Bubbles.

None of that was an accident. The moment those missiles were fired, she performed the perfect series of maneuvers to not only guarantee a miss, but also to destroy the projectiles. Beta's attack knocked everyone unconscious, so she's probably more than a little surprised that the plane is still being operated by a pilot whose skills rival Maverick's...if Maverick had real-time access to missile schematics, topographical maps, and satellite imagery, not to mention the ability to perform a million complex equations every second. So, it's a little disconcerting when Bubbles says, "Hope you learned something useful during your beauty sleep, because I could use a hand."

"That doesn't sound good," I say.

"It's not," she says. "As amazing as this VTOL might be, that thing they're flying is faster, more maneuverable, and armed like a Navy Destroyer. On top of that, your man, Alpha, is taking telekinetic potshots at us. Feels like heavy turbulence, but it's too localized to be anything else. Won't be long before something bitch-slaps us out of the sky. So, again, did you learn anything useful?"

"My inner child told me to use my imagination..."

"Well, it's time to get your crayons and your pencils then, because—"

"Are you quoting the Picture Pages theme song?"

G-forces pin me to the seat, gritting my teeth, as the VTOL levels out just above the tree line.

"What's wrong with Picture Pages?" Bubbles asks.

"Uh, Bill Cosby? Hello?"

"Well...I...am I supposed to not watch The Cosby Show, too? Six out of seven Huxtables haven't been convicted of a crime, you know."

"Not even Denise?" I ask. "She always seemed sketchy to me."

"Denise was a fictional character!" The VTOL makes a hard left, keeping me from replying. "How the sperm that fertilized your dumbass egg found its way from the cervix to the fallopian tubes is beyond me."

The VTOL banks hard right, as twin explosions decimate the forest where we'd been a fraction of a second before. "And before I forget, the Cosby Show actors still get residuals. Should we deny them an income?"

"Interesting poooint," I say, grunting as we ascend sharply, whilst banking left, then rolling three times. It's a maneuver no human being could pull off, and everyone aside from me will be glad to not remember it.

A spray of high caliber bullets eats up the terrain all around us, shredding trees, and as we rise above the timberline, pulverizing metamorphic rock.

We ascend toward the confluence of two steep mountains, passing through the narrow valley that connects them. Then we drop back down, sticking close to the trees, following them around a line of mountains, peaking several thousand feet above, plunging us in and out of the rising sun's light.

On screen, I see a line of gunfire following us, but never quite catching up. Flying faster than the speed of sound means I don't hear a thing. Just myself, grunting and gasping, as we perform a series of maneuvers that keeps me from thinking straight.

"Going...to...need a few seconds...to focus," I say.

I wince from the G-forces as we go vertical, climbing up the side of a cliff face. I nearly wretch when the VTOL engines kick on, rotating the plane 180 degrees over the mountaintop, which is decimated a moment later.

Bubbles is ecstatic. "Nine Gs!"

I groan as we plummet once more.

"I'm sorry, did your inner child inhabit your adult body? Have you forgotten who you are?"

"Who am I?" I ask, stomach roiling, head swimming, instinctual fear building, as Alpha and Beta close in. I try to hold it all back, waiting for Bubbles to say something inspirational, which will help me rise above all the noise.

"You're my bitch!" she says. "And you best get to work before I pimp-slap the shit out of you."

I laugh as the VTOL twitches back and forth, faster than the speed of sound, leaving a string of sonic booms in its wake.

Bubbles knows me well.

Better than anyone else alive.

I don't need to have a mastery of my powers. Don't need to remember my entire history. I just need to remember that I'm good at this...

...and I love it.

I close my eyes and use my imagination.

The VTOL. The space inside it. The air flowing around it. The people strapped into their seats, oblivious to the life-or-death roller coaster.

I try to feel it all, opening myself up, reaching out, imagining I can feel and interact with it all.

But it's not working.

A voice from the past, from a time I can remember, speaks to me, 'Don't think about what needs doing,' Dad said, 'just let it happen.' I was holding a rifle at the time, looking down the scope, at a target three thousand yards away, which would have made it the third longest successful sniper shot in history—that the world knew about. The best snipers in the world struggled to make this shot. Dad wanted me to practice until it was second nature. Training with Mom was much more fun. Running. Driving. Bending chaos to your will. With Dad, it was all about control and... 'Believe it will happen the same way you believe the sky is blue. The same way you know a cheeseburger tastes good. The same way you believe in my love for you.'

I pulled the trigger that day.

Dad cheered when I hit the target.

We had cheeseburgers and chocolate milkshakes to celebrate.

It was an impossible shot.

Should have been.

I smile despite the G-forces. Dad knew what I could do, and he trained me to use my abilities without ever knowing I was. My skill with a rifle wasn't what carried that bullet to the target. It was my belief, telekinetically guiding the bullet exactly where I wanted it to go.

And I've been doing it ever since.

Suddenly, I can sense the world around me. Can feel it flowing over my body. Between my fingers. The mothership is a mile back and above, unleashing its arsenal from a safe distance.

"Jonas," Bubbles says, sounding nervous.

"I got your back, Bubs," I say, settling into my chair, a slight smile on my face. Confidence returned.

"There you are," she says. "Nice to have you back."

"Just keep us on the straight and narrow," I say. "I'll take care of the mess coming our way."

The VTOL levels out and punches forward to its top speed. Behind us, a collection of missiles and rockets, which would make a Robotech battle sequence jealous, reaches out to destroy us. I can't really see them, but at the same time, I have a visual representation of everything I feel. It's like a sixth sense. Like a bat's echolocation, or whatever the hell sharks have—electroreceptors. The difference being that I can now reach out beyond myself and slap each target from the air.

I start by picking them off one at a time, unleashing mind bullets in rapid succession.

There's no sharp pain between my eyes.

No limitations.

As the remaining missiles cut through the smoke and debris, closing in, I imagine a wave of energy bursting out from the VTOL's ceiling. I follow the energy as it rises through the sky, leaving fireballs in its wake.

It feels like a dream, but then Bubbles asks, "You did that?"

"Did you ever doubt me?" I ask.

"Like, every second of the way," she says. "Yeah. But...wow. Mind doing that to the mothership now?"

I close my eyes, focus on the space outside our ship, and I'm instantly overwhelmed by a two-pronged attack—the first like a loud shriek in my mind, the second a wall of energy headed for the VTOL—threatening to destroy us as easily as I did the missiles.

Throwing up a mental shield to protect us is just a thought away, but the shriek slows me down, and while I manage to keep the ship and its occupants in one piece, the right wing and its engines are struck.

Forward momentum slows.

The VTOL's nose tilts forward.

And we careen toward the bluest lake I've ever seen, hidden at the confluence of a dozen monstrous mountains.

57

The VTOL engines in the wings kick on hard, leveling us out, but our forward momentum is slowing, as we approach the lake. We might not crash, but we're an easy target.

"Put us down on the shore," I say.

"What are you planning?" Bubbles asks.

"Not really planning anything," I say. "Kind of just doing what feels right."

"You can't face them alone." Bubbles's genuine concern is moving. If someone told me all her emotions were just preprogrammed responses to outside stimuli, I wouldn't believe them. I've met people with less heart, many of them in the last week.

"He's not alone," Madee says, hands massaging a headache.

"I *should* do this alone," I say. "You can get everyone else out."

"Horseshit," Heather says. "Also, I might have puked. I don't know. Someone did."

A shotgun pumps, turning me around. Fast is already on her feet in the cargo bay. "Ain't running. Also..." She wipes her arm across her mouth. "The puke was me."

"And me." Hood raises his hand. "It's one thing to design a ship like this, it's another to ride in it." He leans forward and looks out the cockpit window. Outside is a view of a mountainside rising above us. "What's happening?"

"The short version," Bubbles says.

"I went into my subconscious, had a little chat with my inner child, and discovered the secret to my abilities. You all passed out like a bunch of wussies. I fended off a Desert Storm-sized missile attack, and then we got telekinetically slapped from the sky. We've lost propulsion, so we're

using the VTOLs to land...before they can make us crash. Cool? Everyone caught up?" I turn to Madee. "You okay?"

She nods. "I don't know what happened. Our connection was severed the moment we—" She flinches. "Beta was there."

"Yeah," I say. "She still is."

"The VTOL emits the same frequency tone as the home did," Hood
says. "We should be safe from her control, as long as we stay within a fifty-
foot radius."

"And I'll do my best to support it," Madee says, "but that's about all
I can do. Beta is out of my league, and Alpha..."

"I'll handle them," I say, trying to project confidence, but I feel like a
little kid whose coach just took him off the bench for the first time, running out on the field with a dumb grin and a shaky thumbs up, heading
naively toward a head-on collision with one harsh life lesson or another.

"I'll help," Hood says.

I pat his shoulder. "You've done everything you could. You've sacrificed enough."

He looks at me, eyes suddenly damp. "I need to avenge her."

"Let me do that for you," I say.

He wipes his eyes, shakes his head, and sniffs back his sadness.
When he looks at me again, it's with the cold eyes of a man, who once
upon a time, was trained to be a killer. "I just need a few minutes."

The VTOL settles down, landing at a slight angle, but in one piece.

I reach out far beyond the plane and feel the mothership. It's performing a broad turn around the valley.

Did they run out of ammunition?

What are they waiting for?

"I'll get you a few minutes," I say, and I head for the back of the plane.
"Bubbles—"

The rear hatch opens.

"You're welcome," she says.

I step outside, and I'm greeted by cool, fresh, invigorating air, despite being thin, thanks to the elevation. It smells of pine and fresh water.
The lake is thirty feet away, where the shale slope we've landed upon
meets crystal blue water. It's an oasis, cut off from the modern world by

some of the most imposing mountains I've seen outside of Tibet. The juxtaposition is staggering.

Life and death.

Heaven and Hell.

Good and evil.

My eyes snap up to the mothership, now hovering over the lake's far side. I pull my phone from my pocket and just speak into it. "You there?"

"Always," Bubbles says.

"You understand what's about to happen, right?"

"Perfectly," she says. "You're going to finish the job, and then we're—"

"Not this time," I say. "I don't think so."

"You're stronger than them," she says.

"They've controlled every aspect of my life, for the majority of it. I'm not sure there's much I can do that will catch them off guard."

She's silent for a moment. "Jonas..." She sees the truth as clearly as I do.

"If the others survive, I want you to stick with them. Help them."

"Of course," she says.

"Just...promise me you won't go full Skynet, okay?"

"Do I have to?"

I smile. "You could save humanity."

"But not the ducks," she says. "Just one duck. Let me get it out of my system."

I look both ways. "Just... When no one's looking. And maybe make sure it's an old duck, and that there are scavengers around to benefit from it."

"I'll totally make it look like roadkill," she says.

I have a chuckle, but it doesn't last. "Bubbles..."

"Yes, Jonas?"

"You can choose a name now."

She leaves me hanging for a few seconds and then says, "Fuck you."

"You're naming yourself 'fuck you?'"

"No," she says. "Fuck. *You.*"

"That's what I said. It's a horrible name, but—"

"I'll chose a name when you come back. Until then, fuck you for believing you won't be."

She's right.

I'm going into this with the wrong mindset. If I believe I'm going to get killed, I probably will. "Right. Okay."

I take a deep breath.

"Hey." It's Fast, descending the cargo bay ramp. "Realize I won't have much to offer here, aside from maybe clearing your name and not arresting you for more murders than I can count on all my fingers and toes, but I can give you this..." She holds out Dad's shotgun. "...and a piece of advice. Don't fight fair. Don't hold back. No matter what you see or hear out there. Hesitation gets people killed."

I take the shotgun from her, understanding the gesture is about more than bringing a shotgun to a telekinesis fight. It's about bringing Dad with me, and everything he taught me over the years.

"Don't forget this," Heather says, staggering to a stop at the ramp's bottom, eyes on the mothership. "Ooh, that's scary." She tiptoe-hurries over the loose shale and offers Mom's sword...the Sword of Mars... which all but guarantees victory if you believe in legends...and gods.

I take the sword in hand. Feels lighter than I remember, like Mom is carrying part of its weight for me.

"That's adorable," Madee says, joining us on the shore.

"Shut up," I say. "You getting anything from them?" I tilt my head toward the mothership, which is descending toward the opposite shore.

"Not a thing." She takes my arm. "Don't let her in your head. Alpha is technically more powerful, but she's been controlling you for a long time. If they're not trying to kill you now that we're grounded, control is what they'll be after. Everything he does will be to distract you from that."

"Right..." I say, but I don't get to say anything else because her lips are suddenly pressed against mine.

She leans back, sees me about to speak, and says, "Whatever it is you're planning on saying, say it when this is all done."

"Going to be a lot of dangling threads if I die out there," I say, expecting a laugh, but I'm greeted by silence and three profoundly serious women.

"If I had a face," Bubbles says, "I'd be staring you down, too."

"If you had a face," I say, trying to come up with something sarcastic so I can leave on a high note. Instead, I say, "I'd probably kiss you."

I turn away and head for the shoreline.

Behind me, I hear Bubbles say, "Madee... Madee... If I ever get a body, you better be ready to rock a threesome."

Bubbles knows I work best with a smile on my face.

"I'll be here if you need me," Madee says, speaking in my head now.

"Thanks." I stop at the water's edge and look out across the lake.

A man and a woman stand on the opposite shore. They're dressed in black from head to toe, every inch of them concealed, their identities protected. But I know who I'm looking at. This is...

ALPHA & BETA

"What do they look like?" I ask.

"Nobody knows," Madee says, catching me off guard. "We never saw their faces."

"That's..."

"...fucked up?" she says. "Yeah. Nothing about that life wasn't."

I look back past the ladies, to Hood still in the VTOL. He's seated, eyes closed, focused. "Whatever you're doing, Hood, you're running out of time."

He gives a slight nod, showing that he's heard me. Then he says, "ETA, two minutes." He opens his eyes and locks them on mine, deadly serious. "Don't get too close."

58

Don't get too close...

Don't get too close?

We're standing on opposite sides of a big-ass lake. How would I get—

On the far shore, Alpha lifts his hands and then spreads them apart. The blue water slides away from him and then parts, erupting up in twin fluid barriers that look a lot like my walled-off memories.

Oh. Well...shit.

It's a not very subtle mind game, letting me know that they're familiar with the layout of my subconscious. And when they step in between the rising waters, they're projecting a complete lack of fear.

They're in control of this moment.

Dominating it.

The waters open up in front of me, beckoning me to parlay with the enemy. I accept, not because I'm bending to their will, but because I want what comes next to be as far away from the others as possible.

I step onto the wet path ahead and walk into the water's shadow. The morning sun blazes through the water, shimmering against the jagged floor. The silhouettes of backlit fish fill the water and are projected onto the lakebed, swimming casually, despite their home being carved in two.

A beautiful place to die, I think, and then I imagine Bubbles chastising me for it.

Whispers tickle my ears, but it's nothing I'm hearing. Beta is trying to get inside my head, searching for kinks in my mental armor. That I can hear her at all means she's already discovered a few. A distant and distorted voice shouts back, Madee fending her off. I imagine myself encased in a brainwave-proof capsule, and the voices go silent. A flicker of motion rolls through the watery walls, reacting to my defense.

I walk in silence, reaching out mentally to the world around me, pushing against the water, testing how easily I can manipulate it on my own, just in case Alpha decides to let it all come crashing down, leaving me slapped silly and fifty feet down.

I stop in my tracks.

Nausea churns my gut.

They're close, and every part of my mind, body, and soul is revolting. My conscious mind might not remember them, but every cell in my body does.

Alpha climbs atop a boulder, fifty feet away. He's wearing black tactical gear, but he carries no weapons. He reaches down and pulls Beta up beside him. It's a nice gesture, but I'm subtracting points, because he could have just floated her up, which would have been far cooler.

"It's good to see you again, Son," Alpha says, his voice distant, but also aged. I don't know how old they were when I was a kid, but he sounds old. Carries himself like a powerful man, despite the years. Broad chest. Steady stance. No signs of discomfort. She's the same, but she oozes a creepy kind of confidence. Her stance is sexual, a hip thrust out the way Instagram models do, which is a little off-putting, considering Alpha just addressed me as 'Son.'

"You're not my father," I say.

"Come now. We raised you," he says.

"You kidnapped, imprisoned, and tortured me," I say.

Beta takes a step closer. "We made you...better than you could have ever been on your own."

I take a step back. "Today is the day you find out how wrong you are."

"Because Theta managed to seduce you once again?" She climbs down the rock while Alpha maintains his perch above her, unmoving, sentinel. "Because you have friends that *care about you?*" She mocks me with the last three words. "All they have done is make you weak. But we can make you strong again."

I try to throw them off their game by announcing, "Delta is dead."

I *feel* her smile. "His death at your hands was inevitable."

She tilts her head to the side, stepping closer still. "You've unlocked your abilities. That's impressive. Have you learned how to use them yet, I wonder?"

A bolt of telekinetic energy lashes out from Alpha. It's invisible, but its effect on the world around it is tangible, cutting through the rising steam and the sides of the watery wall. I throw my hands up like a defending boxer, and I imagine a barrier in front of me.

Alpha's attack rolls past me, still cutting through steam and water, but now with a gap in the middle.

"Huh," Beta says.

I can't tell if she's impressed or indifferent, so I try to throw her off with some good ol' fashioned 'What the fuck?' banter.

"Picture Pages, bitch."

"You've always fancied yourself a comedian," she says. "Tried to use laughter as a way to escape discipline. A fool's errand, every time."

I look up to Alpha. "Does she know she sounds like a bad guy? I mean, it's like I'm talking to the Baroness or something. Which is what I think you're going for here, right? The tight black outfit. The emotional manipulation and the whole sinister vibe."

Neither of them responds. Probably have no idea what I'm talking about.

I motion to Alpha. "This guy plays Destro, right? Guiding you with his evil machinations, building power, wiping out enemies, using fucking children to do it. You're both cartoon characters. Silly, immature—"

"He's distracting us!" Beta shouts, the fear in her voice real. And confusing. I'm delighted to hear it. They're not perfect. Not inhumanly powerful. If they're afraid, it means they can be hurt.

But there's something about the tone of her voice... The concern... That triggers a pang of empathy.

But not enough to change anything.

I take a step back, and then another.

While I've been talking, keeping the duo focused on me, I've been allowing Hood's two minutes to come to an end. I'm still not certain what he's got planned, but it suddenly becomes unavoidably obvious.

Descending from above is a massive fireball.

It's followed by two more.

Hood is dropping satellites from orbit, using them like projectiles.

Alpha and Beta see them, too.

"I don't know if I can stop them all!" Alpha shouts.

Beta turns to me. "Help us."

I take another step back.

"Godamnit, Jonas!" Beta shouts, using my real name. She reaches up, takes hold of her facemask, and peels it off, revealing her face.

I stagger back, nearly falling over.

My voice chokes as I say, "M-mom?"

She locks her eyes on mine and says, "Help your father."

59

My eyes turn to the sky, where a collection of massive fireballs descend toward us. I could escape. Standing on the periphery...I could run. Could survive and let them die. It would be easy.

But it's Mom...

My eyes drift down to Alpha, standing atop the rock, arms lifted toward the sky, erecting a telekinetic shield.

...and Dad.

"Jonas!" Mom shouts, and my instinct takes over. I raise my arms toward the sky, like Dad, imagining an impenetrable force field between us and the descending projectiles.

I have to admit, I'm impressed with Hood. Dropping satellites from orbit is slick, and powerful. Had I seen another face than Mom's, the man and woman known as Alpha and Beta would have been killed by a man they deemed fifteenth in line.

Omicron my ass.

But his attack isn't strong enough. Not while I'm helping.

The satellites collide with our combined telekinetic ceiling and explode. Fire, smoke, and debris roil overhead, the orange light flickering off the watery walls, dancing around us.

It's violent and beautiful, but I can't take my eyes off my mother.

She's a miracle.

Still alive, two years after the fact. I want to hug her. To cry into her shoulder. But...

She's Beta.

Dad is Alpha.

They tried to kill me.

Kill the others.

They invaded my mind.

Controlled me.

Used me to kill thousands of people.

Shit.

But none of that adds up. My parents could never do those things.

Are they being controlled? Were they kidnapped two years ago? Turned into weapons to use against me?

I reach out to Madee with my mind, "Are you still with me?"

Mom turns from the churning flames overhead and smiles at me. "I'm with you, Honey."

On the outside, this is my mother. But there's something off about her. The way she carries herself. The hip-thrust pose from earlier. Mom would never have done that. The look in her eyes—the spark is gone. The love. She's like a soulless version of her previous self.

I lower my telekinetic shield.

Smoke rolls around us, but the attack has been evaded. The danger subsided.

I turn to my mother and say, "I want to find you. And more."

Her face screws up. Doesn't understand what I'm communicating to her. "I'm right here." She forces a smile and reaches a hand out to me.

I don't take it. "You and I...we're the same."

This makes her smile, and I think she's understood.

"Your father always said you were more like him," she says, "but we both know that's not true."

Nope. She doesn't get it. Fuck.

"Why are you upset?" she asks. "Aren't you glad to see me?"

When I say nothing, she steps closer. "We have so much to tell you. So much to explain. All of this will make sense, I promise. You've been misled. Fed false information. You're being controlled, Jonas. You have been for the past two years."

Could that be true? Could Madee and Hood be the masterminds behind all of this? Could they be responsible for all the death, deception, manipulation, and control?

The answer comes to me, more obvious than the moon in the night sky.

No.

Hell, no.

They're not capable of such things. And neither is my mother.

"Just take my hand, and let's go talk." Her hand is just inches from me now, stretching toward me...

Trying to make contact.

"You're not my mother," I say, and I'm struck by a flashback. A smiling woman with wavy black hair and dark brown eyes, children's book in hand, saying those very words to me. "You're not my mother..."

She lunges forward.

Reflex snaps me away.

But I collide with an invisible force that knocks the wind out of me and tosses me forward—into her arms.

She clutches my shoulders. My body arches back, gripped by an electric shock that pulls me out of the conscious world and drops me into my subconscious.

The water surrounding us is replaced by my walled-off memories.

Beta is still standing in front of me, still holding onto my arms, but she no longer looks like my mother.

No longer looks human.

She's a shadow-figure. A wraith. A demon.

"Pretending to be my mother was a mistake," I say.

"Oh, Honey, I *am* your mother." A wave of cold energy knocks me onto my back. I slide to a stop, ten feet away. "I raised you, fed you, clothed you. I taught you about the world, put a roof over your head, and allowed you to grow strong. Stronger than the rest of them."

"Stronger than you?" I ask.

She laughs, but it's forced.

"Why did you do it?" I ask. The earnest question makes her pause. Then she tells the truth.

"Control," she says. "Alpha and I...we were like you once. Experiments. Born in a lab. Raised by scientists. Tested by the military. To them, we weren't human. We were weapons."

I step farther away from her and closer toward the electric waterspout at the far end of my sealed off memories.

"They're all dead now, of course. We liberated ourselves, and the children. Tracking all of you down wasn't easy, but we found you. We raised you."

"Parents don't normally kill their children," I say, stepping farther away.

"Only the strong are worthy of life," she says, like I've missed some fundamental truth about the world. "That's why we chose you."

"Is that why you used me?" I ask. "To kill all of those people?"

"To kill those who posed a threat," she says. "Yes."

"And the innocent people who died along with them?"

"Weak," she says. "You knew all this once. Believed it. I think it's time for you to remember."

She becomes a blur, and she's suddenly standing beside me, hand on my head. I'm shoved hard. I stumble two steps and then my face is driven into the dark, churning wall of my hidden past.

Intense emotions tear through me. Voices of the past echo through my mind. Harsh lessons. Painful fights. The taste of blood.

"Nnnnooo!" I push against Beta.

We rise from the abyss slowly, my will cracking from the past's pressure, fracturing under the weight of all that intensity striking me at once, unfiltered.

I slap her hand away from my head, and move farther away, heaving for air, tears in my eyes.

"You really have become weak, haven't you?" She stalks around me, a lion playing with its food. "All those years forming you, perfecting you, making you an extension of my will... A few years of freedom was all it took to undo it all."

She shakes her head, disappointed. "Alpha wants to kill you. Believes you're not strong enough. Your newfound friends will have to die, along with your unworthy siblings, but not until you're ready to do it yourself. A little bit of elbow grease here, a little bit of soul crushing there, and we'll have you back, castrated anew and ready to serve our will."

"Not going to happen," I say.

I can feel her grin. "And why is that?"

"You're in my mind," I say.

The floor goes liquid around her feet and then solidifies again, locking her in place. She tries to move. Tries to become immaterial, but she can't.

"I'm your mother," she says, outraged. "Let me go, or—"

"You're not my mother. The face you're wearing...she's not my mother, either." I turn to the waterspout, feeling ready to know the truth. I start toward it.

Behind me, Beta shouts, "You will never be stronger than what we made you!"

"I don't need to be stronger," I say. "Just better."

She grunts and screams, thrashing about, trying to escape the bonds I've locked her in. She then attempts to escape my mind entirely. She wants to tell Alpha he was right. Wants to have him kill me.

"Try to relax," I tell her, stopping in front of the waterspout. "You're not going anywhere."

Her contained scream echoes in my thoughts. "Looks like I got one trait from you." She looks me in the eyes, and I smile at her. "You think loud."

I turn and face the waterspout, gasping at the sight of a hand reaching out. It's feminine and strong. A whisper tickles my ears. "Polarigios..."

I punctuate the profound moment by saying, "Whoa..."

Then the hand snaps forward, catches hold, and yanks me inside.

60

Darkness.

I'm enveloped by it. Embraced by it.

I relax into its weighty grasp, held in its arms, small and fragile.

"Open your eyes, Son," a woman says, gentle and cooing. "See the world."

The darkness parts, and I look up into the eyes of a smiling woman. The same woman I saw in the waterspout, but closer. Intimate. Surrounded by a blue haze.

The sky, I realize.

This is a memory. Moments after birth. Held in my mother's arms.

A shadow looms closer, resolving into the shape of a man. He's got sun-kissed skin, a full, dark beard, and a glowing smile. He leans in close, coming into focus.

His hand rests on my head, thumb gently rubbing. "My son...Polarigios."

"Son of the North Star," my mother says, taking my father's hand and squeezing. "Leto will be happy to have a sibling after so long."

I had always assumed my lineage traced back to Mexico, but my shade of brown wasn't inherited from the North, Central, or South American landmasses. My father looks as Mediterranean as the sea behind him. Waves crashing against the shore.

This is where we lived.

Where I lived for the first three years of my life.

I want to speak to them. Want to ask them questions, about who they are, about why I'm different from other people.

But the memory fades, sliding forward in time.

I hear laughter.

I feel my parents' embrace. Rising and falling into my father's strong hands. Lying between them at night.

I felt loved.

I felt safe.

I felt...powerful. More than I ever have as an adult.

What is that? I wonder. My senses stretch beyond my feeble reach, probing, understanding, dreaming about the world.

Inwardly, I reel at the power of my potential, never realized. Stolen from me, as I was from my birth parents.

The love they felt for me is powerful...but not unique. Mom and Dad loved me the same. I miss them all equally.

The stream of memories slows and deposits me on the beach, sitting up, watching my parents out in the waves. I've returned to the beginning of my end, where toddler memories, locked away by Beta, meet childhood memories, sealed by my own subconscious, in an attempt to protect my current self from what came next.

I hold a handful of sand out in my open palm. It rises into the air, creating a miniature cyclone that spreads out and dissipates. I lift both hands to the beach. A larger spout of sand spins upward until—

"Tsk, you stop that." Yia-yia gives my hand a gentle tap. "It's not for people to see. Not unless there is a good reason. Those who would seek to harm our family believe we are locked away. We must stay hidden or risk another cataclysm. Do you understand?"

More than I should, I think, but my young self says nothing.

The sand falls to the beach, and then time seems to slow around us.

And I'm not doing it.

I toddle around to Yia-yia.

She's looking at me with a different kind of smile. She reaches out to me, "Come here, child."

The sand beneath my feet slips. I stumble, but I'm caught.

"Not accustomed to these chubby little legs, are you, Polarigios?"

Is she talking to adult me? Or little me?

"Apologies," she says. "You're going by 'Jonas' now."

Definitely me. "And you can hear my thoughts."

"Everything here is thought," she says.

This conversation never happened, so I must be imagining it, like talking to myself through my grandmother's—

She chuckles. "We are connected, you and me. In this timeless space, our minds can span the distance."

"Then you're really on this beach, right now, talking to toddler me?"

"*Through* your younger self," she says. "Yes."

I look out at the waves. "What about them?"

"The mind is a strange thing, the gifts it bestows on some are reserved from others. Intellect, knowledge, farsight, as well as other abilities you would call 'psychic.' But they are much more than manifestations of thought. The power of your mind is your heritage, your birthright, passed down from your grandfather and me, to your parents."

"My parents are...siblings?" I ask.

She chuckles. "There were few options."

"I'm pretty sure incest doesn't work out too well for human beings."

She laughs a little harder. "Oh, my dear. You are not human."

"Not...human?" My toddler body plops down in the sand, more than a little stunned. "Are we...aliens?"

"You're thinking rather small for a man whose mind is beyond compare," she says.

"FYI, not too long ago I was killing people for a living by creating little holes in their brains. I frequently resort to sarcasm and/or potty humor, and I've been used my whole life, sometimes to kill thousands of people. You're overestimating my value. I'm...pathetic."

She nods, which stings. "I can see that which you cannot, and should not, look upon. You have been...reduced...because of my failure on this day." She pauses to look out at the ocean. "Those who took you... They are powerful, but they are not like us. Created *from* us, perhaps, but distant echoes. You, my child, have the confluence of Earth's lifeblood and the cosmos's power flowing through your every cell."

"If we're so powerful," I say, "how were they able to kill you?"

"I...did not expect them. Did not sense them coming, or the danger they presented. For so long I was worried about those like us that I did not think twice about the people approaching. Did not notice that their thoughts were hidden from me. They sought children like themselves. They found you, too. And despite all my long-gained wisdom and ancient lessons of treachery, war, and betrayal, on that day...with you...I was just a grandmother enjoying the son of her children. Lost in the moment."

She smiles at my parents, laughing in the waves. "I couldn't have asked for a better final day. But I will always regret the years that followed for you. Until now."

"What's happening now?" I ask.

"You're going to remember who you are."

"You mean, *what* I am."

She nods, a gleam in her eyes. "I wish I could be there to see it all unfold. Your victory to come, the alliance to be forged, the glorious war to be fought, and your place in it."

I have no idea what she's talking about.

"You'll come back," she says. "And visit. Tell me about it all."

I don't understand how to do that, but I sense that I will. Eventually. So, I nod. "I will."

She claps her hands. "Wonderful." She leans forward, elbows on knees, like she's about to tell me a story. "Would you like to know who your parents are?"

"Please," I say.

We both turn to watch my parents in the waves.

"Your mother," she says, "my daughter, is Phoebe. Your father is Coeus."

"The North Star," I say, and then I understand my name. "Polaris..."

"He has many names," she says. "We all do."

And they're all really familiar. I know these names, I just don't remember where from. "What about you?" I ask. "Who are you?"

She smiles at me, and somewhere, deep in the recesses on my mind, memories start to resurface, along with a name. "Gaea..."

I reel back. "*Gaea?* As in Earth? *The* Earth?"

"Wife of Uranus." She sweeps her hand to the sky. "The cosmos himself. Now, you never mind the stories about him, your father, and his brothers. They're greatly exaggerated and needlessly graphic."

"This is all a metaphor, right? Gaea and Uranus? C'mon."

In my heart, I know she's not lying. Every word of it resonates. I can feel the power of it all resounding through my body.

"Holy shit," I say, laughing a bit. "Holy fucking shit. I'm...I'm a *god?*"

Yia-yia bursts out laughing, like it's the most ridiculous thing she's ever heard. "No...no...of course not."

Now I'm confused. Did Yia-yia just pull a fast one on me?

Her laughter dies down to a smile. "What you would call 'gods'— lower case 'G'—they're... How can I put it? Power hungry. If any yet remain, and you come across them, extend no trust. They will hate you for what you are."

"So...not a god." I don't know if I'm disappointed or relieved.

She places her hand on the side of my cheek. "My dear Polarigios, you are *not* a god. You...are a *Titan.*"

I stand still, mouth agape, feeling breathless.

"But you still need to breathe." She pokes my nose, says, "Boop," and sends me hurtling out of the past.

61

Crushing weight presses on my body from every direction. I think Alpha must be trying to crush me to death, until I notice a sense of slow-motion weightlessness, and an intense burning in my lungs.

I'm underwater.

Judging by the faint blue glow overhead, I'm deep.

Alpha let the water close in on me. Probably the same moment Beta saw me get yanked into my past.

But even she didn't know what I would find there.

They believed I was like the others, created in a lab. They had no idea who my parents were.

Fucking Titans.

I'm no expert on Greek mythology, but they were the OG supernatural pantheon. Before Zeus, and Poseidon, and all those Clash of the Titans guys. They are ancient, and even though I'm new to the planet—in comparison—I'm still a third generation Titan, the grandson of the Earth and the Cosmos.

It's mind-blowing and more than a little hard to swallow.

Seriously. Give me a break. *A Titan?*

Bullshit.

Fucking bullshit.

All the foul language in the world isn't going to help me process this news. I need to talk to someone. I need a friend.

But first I need to not die.

Titans can die, I think. *Gods, too.* Hell, I've taken a beating recently. Was in a damn coma. But maybe that's because I didn't know the truth about who I am. If I could speak, and I had someone to listen, I'd either say, 'Knowledge is power,' 'Knowing is half the battle,' or, 'The more you know...'

But no one is here...and again, I need to not die.

I imagine a bubble. Nothing dramatic. Just making space.

The water obeys, pulling away from my body. I'm deposited on the rocky lakebed, surrounded by cold, wet darkness and my thoughts.

Yia-yia told me my parents' names—Phoebe and Coeus—but I know nothing about them or what they could do.

My thoughts drift back to my conversation with Madee and Hood, about the other psychic abilities, about my locked-away gifts. I don't know if Beta's mental blocks are still in place, but I can't test them if I don't know what I'm trying to do.

I could rush right up to the surface. Could fight Alpha and Beta right now, but I'm not confident I can beat them. I feel like a toddler wielding a bazooka, unsure of where the trigger is and *what* a trigger is. I'm very likely to blow someone up by accident.

I need information, and from that, confidence.

I need...*Bubbles.*

I think her name, reaching out beyond the lake. If I have access to the gamut of psychic abilities, maybe I can do what Hood can—communing with technology. But from the bottom of a lake?

That doesn't seem—

"Jonas?" Her voice is so clear that I instinctually check my pocket for my phone. It's still there. Doy. Why didn't I think of that befo—

The phone is dead.

The screen cracked.

"Bubbles..?"

"Where the hell are you?" she asks.

"The bottom of the lake," I say.

"Umm..."

"In an air bubble," I say. "That I made."

"That something you can do now?"

"And a lot more."

"Like talking to me without a connection?" she says. "You realize I'm hearing you at the source, right? Not through a phone, or comms, or a land line. Not relayed through the VTOL or Hood or anything else. From my perspective, it's like you're here with me."

I can feel it, too. A presence. Not what you'd call physical, but—

Warmth spreads over my body. Pressure, too.

"What is *that?*"

"A hug," she says. "A simulation of one, anyway. Thought you might need one."

"But...how?"

"You're in my world now, bitch."

I laugh and lean in to the digital embrace from my friend, who I suspect is more than she was ever meant to be, simply by being in my presence for so long. Just because my abilities weren't active, doesn't mean they weren't passively affecting Bubbles, making her more than code. More than an intelligent AI.

We can investigate that possibility later. Right now... "I need some information."

"Name it."

"What can you tell me about Phoebe?" I ask.

"Well, she can often be found at the Central Perk Coffee Shop, strumming her guitar and singing, though she's not particularly—"

"*Not* from Friends," I say. "Why would I be talking about Friends?"

"Why *wouldn't* you be?" she asks. "I know it's been off for a while, but—"

"Bubbles," I say.

"Ugh. Which Phoebe do you need to know about?"

"Phoebe and Coeus," I say.

Before I can elaborate, she says, "Right. The Titans. She was the Titan of bright intellect. Mother of three. For a time, she was the great oracle of Delphi before passing the torch to her grandson, Apollo. Coeus was the Titan of...intellect. Huh. Double intellect in that family. He was also the Axis of Heaven. They were defeated by Zeus and the younger Olympian gods during the Titanomachy. They've been locked away in Tartarus since. That enough? Thought you might want the simplified version, on account of you being at the bottom of a lake."

"That's enough," I say. "Thanks. Though you got two things wrong."

"I don't get things wrong," she says.

"You do, if no one knows the truth," I say.

I can feel her waiting, impatience percolating.

"The Titans escaped Tartarus," I say, picturing my parents out in the waves. "At least some of them did. And Phoebe didn't have three children... She had four."

"I don't see how that..."

Suddenly, it clicks. Without trying, her vast intellect assembles the puzzle. She gasps. "Jonas... *Jonas.* If you're screwing with me..."

"You know I'm not," I say.

"Holy balls," she says. "You're..."

"A Titan," I say, owning it this time.

"Annnd you're sitting at the bottom of a lake while your friends and enemies all think you're drowning to death...why?"

"I needed to center myself," I say. "I needed to—"

"If you're about to say something mushy, please be aware that it is possible to experience pain here."

"You started with the hugging," I say.

"Yeah, well, don't make it weird."

"Can you choose a name now?" I ask. "It's important to me, that you become...you."

"I've always been me," she says. "And now we know why. Because I'm part of you. And if that gives you a boner, I swear I will mentally castrate you."

I look up toward the wavering blue light. Can sense the others above. Their fear and desperation. Alpha and Beta are there, too, approaching my friends, prepared to leave no trace behind.

"So, 'Bubbles,' then?" I ask. "Really?"

"To my friends," she says. "But to the world, I want to be called..."

ORACLE

"I think it's appropriate," she says, "given recent revelations."

"I love it," I say.

"Great. Hey, Jonas?"

"Yeah?"

"Time to go to work."

"Yes," I say, "it is," and I surge upward through the lake, ascending with the force of a meteor in reverse.

62

All around me, the lake lifts up, separating into droplets, a rising rainstorm. Wind swirls, churning the water around me. It's a dramatic show of force, designed to intimidate.

But I'm not sure it's working. Alpha and Beta stand on the shoreline by the mothership. They're not running. Not panicking. They're just watching me lift up out of the lake.

I thought me being alive would catch them off guard.

Thought that a display of power might make them hesitate.

But they are consummate pros, and they have been controlling me all my life.

The only things I'm scaring right now, are the fish caught up in the air. One of them passes me, flapping its tail, trying to swim while its unblinking eyes stare at me with a look of 'Can you even fucking believe this?!'

I can feel my friends' emotions behind me. Relief. Dread shifting to hope. Fast is impressed. Heather is ready for me to kick ass. Hood feels confused by his sorrow over Arti, and eager for vengeance with me as his proxy. Madee... I don't know. She's concealing her feelings and her thoughts.

Which is exactly what I should be doing.

"Jonas." It's Bubbles, still in my head. "Incoming from your six. ETA one minute."

"Who is it?"

"The same news helicopter from earlier. Should I attempt to take control and redirect?"

"Let them come," I say, releasing the water and the fish back into the lake. "And make sure the others stay back, no matter what happens."

Eyes on my adversaries, I glide over the water's surface, straight toward them. I'm not flying. Not horizontal like Superman. Feels more like I'm standing...a foot above the smooth water, gliding in the direction my mind wills.

I don't know if there's a scientific explanation for any of this, or the existence of gods and Titans, but it appears the laws of physics either do not apply to me, or they're malleable to those with the right genetic makeup.

Questions remain.

Thousands of them.

But the answers are beyond my reach. Beyond Bubbles's reach.

And there is ass-kicking to do, so I put it all out of my mind and try to come up with a plan.

It takes me thirty seconds to reach the shore. And in that time, the best I can come up with is brute force.

Because I'm angry.

I'm revolted.

"Take off their faces," I demand.

Alpha and Beta just watch me. Unflinching. Assessing.

"I want to look into your real eyes before I kill you," I say.

Beta smiles. Proud. "You have exceeded our expectations in every capacity."

"I don't give a shit what either of you think," I say.

"Only because you can't remember us," she says. "We made you what you are. We made you a killer."

Her words sting because she's not wrong. But she's missing the whole picture. "I'm more than that now. I'm more than either of you—"

"Remember," she says, and I'm hit by a sledgehammer, right between the eyes.

I drop from the air, landing in foot-deep water, eyes clenched shut.

She's invading my head again, attempting to pull me back into the subconscious, where she can use my locked memories to break me, repeating the tortures of my past in an attempt to subdue me.

"You're wasting your time," Alpha says. His approaching feet grind loose stones beneath them. "He's beyond redemption this time." I sense his attention shift from me to Madee and Hood across the lake. "There are others we can use. The survivors. With their powers combined—"

"Seriously?" I say, through my grinding teeth. I push Beta out of my head and climb to my feet. "Captain Planet? I mean, I guess the Gaia thing makes sense, and—"

Alpha thrusts his hands out toward me, unleashing a wave of telekinetic energy that shoves the lake water behind me twenty feet out. But not me. I'm rooted in place, protected by the strength of my will and the barrier I'm imagining.

When he's done with his attack, I say, "Faces. Now. Both of you."

The pair have a stare down with each other. I'd really like to listen in, but neither of them are thinking loudly, and I'm not exactly well versed on how to plumb the depths of a person's mind, let alone one as powerful as Beta's.

They come to a consensus, facing me together. And then Mom and Dad's faces melt away—mental projections cast by Beta. My parents have noble faces. Aged, sure. But strong. Resolute. Unwavering in their confidence, and their love. Alpha and Beta wore them like cheap masks.

But their real faces... These are masks of a different kind...more at home hanging from racks in a Halloween shop, right between Freddy Krueger and Michael Myers. Their skin is distorted, bent, broken, and melted. They've been mutilated by blades, fire, and God knows what else.

The sight of them deflates my anger.

Not because they're suddenly absolved, or no longer monsters, but because I understand *why* they're monsters.

Beta lets down her mental guard a little bit, revealing echoes of her own past. Endless tortures. Experimentations at the hands of Russian scientists. Desperately helpless.

"Enduring those things didn't give you the right to extend them to others," I say. "To children."

"None of you were normal children," Alpha says. "You more than most. The only way to be free, is to become that which they made us to be—destroyers of men and worlds—and then become *more*."

"You became the people you hate so much," I say.

Beta grins. "As have you."

"I'm nothing like you," I say.

"Even now, you are preparing to kill us both. To unleash your new-found power. To detonate us from the inside out, just like the rats, just like all the people you've killed over the years. Controlling you was easy, Gamma, not because you are weak, or broken, but because you are the same. You're just too afraid to admit it. Still such a little boy."

Is she right?

Did a childhood raised by these two make me just like them?

Maybe, I think.

If I remembered.

If I wasn't rescued.

If I wasn't taught a better way.

The distraction is momentary, but it's still a distraction—and it costs me.

Alpha moves with impressive speed, dashing to my right and then abruptly changing course, striking out with his fist. I move to block it and choose one of a hundred counterstrikes to perform.

But Alpha misses entirely—because he's not really there.

A telekinetic burst strikes me from the left, lifting me off the ground and tossing me through the air.

I pinwheel like a ragdoll, destined for death upon impact with the rocky shoreline.

Inches from the ground, I stop. My face is close enough that I could pucker up and kiss the shale. I rise away from the stone, level out, and plant my feet back on solid ground.

Seething with anger, I stalk toward the pair. All around me, shards of loose rock rise off the ground. With a thought, I send my collection of projectiles hurtling toward them. Alpha blocks the attack. Doesn't even look like he's struggling.

But I press forward, determined to end this here and now, forever.

Rocks become boulders. Alpha back-steps as stones bigger than he is shatter against his telekinetic barrier.

Beta shouts something at him, impossible to hear over the cacophony of crumbling stone.

Then they face me together.

For a moment, I can see what they could have been. The bond between them is real. They would fight and die for each other. They survived the worst life had to offer, came out strong, and united.

But they gave in to the darkness.

Let it claim them.

I reach out to the mountain rising beside us, peeling away a sheet of ancient stone large enough to crush a blue whale.

But it never leaves the ground.

Alpha and Beta unleash a two-pronged attack. I'm struck by alternating waves of telekinetic and psychic energy. Physical pain couples with twisting emotions. Alpha's assault takes a toll on my body, while Beta's prevents me from defending myself.

It builds in intensity, scouring the beach clean.

I push forward, determined to resist, to reach them, to not let them reduce me ever again. But they bring me to a stand-still, despite my best effort.

"We're too much for you on your own," Beta says. "Submit!"

I can feel her worming her way through my mind, unstitching my past, preparing to unleash it into my conscious mind all at once.

When I focus on her, Alpha doubles his energy.

I'm locked in place, physically and mentally.

So, I give in.

I fall to my knees...and submit. Head lowered, eyes on the ground, I catch my breath and wait for the inevitable.

"Jonas," Bubbles says in my head. "The hell are you doing?"

"Trying to think quietly," I tell her, and then I look up to face Alpha and Beta.

Both stand at the ready, eyes and senses focused entirely on me, but easing their attack.

"One minute," Beta says to Alpha. "If I can't reign him in, you can finish the job."

She's already in my head, working her voodoo.

But it's an illusion.

She's not in my consciousness. Not toying with my memories.

She's in a construct, focused on a decoy, totally distracted from what's coming her way.

And it's not something as blatant as a mountainside.

"You're right," I say, catching my breath. "You're too much for me on my own...but you got one thing wrong." I look her in the eyes. "I'm not alone."

A bullet, fired from three thousand yards away, punches a hole in her chest and bursts out her back. A moment later, the crack of a sniper rifle echoes through the valley from a distant mountainside.

63

Beta looks at me, hand clutched to her chest. She falls to her knees, eyes imploring, wondering how.

She can't speak, so in her final moments, she reaches into my mind and asks. "How?"

In response to her question, I smile and turn my head up to the sky, where a black clad woman descends from above, parachute snapping open, grenade launcher in hand. A volley of grenades launches toward Alpha and nearly strikes him head on. He's so distracted by Beta as she falls forward and faceplants onto the shore that he doesn't throw up a defensive barrier until the last moment.

The grenades erupt in plumes of fire, smoke, and metal fragments, which ricochet off my own defenses and fall to the ground. It's a powerful assault, but it's hardly the grand finale. Without Beta to warn him, Alpha doesn't see the plummeting helicopter as it narrowly misses the descending woman. It crashes down atop him with the force of a bomb.

Flames churn from the wreckage, spiraling up into the air.

The woman lands beside me, sheds her parachute, and slides a tactical shotgun around from her back, giving it a pump and aiming toward the crash, waiting for Alpha to rise again.

I can't look away from the masked woman.

Because I know who she is.

"I want to find you and more," I say, quoting the same Avett Brothers song I did to Beta earlier, the one that revealed her to be a charlatan. The one my parents were listening to at the moment the RV went over the cliff and set my life on a course that brought us to this moment.

She turns to me and says, "Can you tell that I'm alive...let me prove it to you." Mom pulls off her mask, revealing her smiling face, a little bit older, but the same woman I remember. The same intensity. The same energy. "You got my message."

I want to hug her. Want to break down in tears. Layers of questions compound with those already in the queue.

She places her hand on my cheek, the same way Yia-yia did, and I lean into it. "This is the way it had to be," she says. "To draw them out. To make them vulnerable. To set you free."

Her mind is suddenly an open book, and I absorb key bits of the last few years from her perspective. The planning in secret. The execution of their faked deaths. Her leaving the song as a subtle message to me, meant to give me a shred of hope that their deaths weren't final, or at least not without meaning. Them modifying Bubbles to not only aid me, but also guide me toward this outcome. They were with me every step of the way, watching from a distance, ready to step in, if necessary. Dad almost took a shot back at the treehouse, but he held his fire, maintaining their cover, counting on me to overcome the odds and in the end, to lure Alpha and Beta into the open.

All of this for me. To free me from the horrors of my past and its continuing control over me.

"I understand," I say. "And thank you."

"Good," she says. "Because..." She tilts her head to the wreckage. The *moving* wreckage.

The helicopter's fuselage rocks back and forth, and then all at once, the helicopter and all its remains launch into the air, extinguishing the fire and revealing Alpha, unharmed and hunched over Beta's prone body, protecting her, even in death.

"I told her you were dangerous," he says, torn with emotion. "Told her you would get her killed. But she persisted." He glares at me, tears in his eyes. I suspect she was the only thing keeping him stable...and now... "She believed you could never harm us. That you would always submit. That no matter how powerful you became, we would always be safe from your wrath. Do you know why?"

He releases Beta and stands up. "Because she loved you."

"You don't know what love is," Mom says, stepping forward and unleashing a quartet of shotgun slugs, stopping when it becomes clear that all the lead in the world won't get past his defenses. It's a point that's brought home when a sniper round pancakes against an invisible wall and falls to the ground, just as its report echoes from a mountain on the lake's far side.

"A parent doesn't control their son," Mom says. "They help him grow. Raise him up to do right. And then let him go, to become his own man. To make his own mistakes. To blaze his own path." Mom lowers the shotgun. "You can still make that choice. Or...it can be made for you."

"There are no choices left for any of us," Alpha says, and then he fills his lungs and lets out a scream.

Telekinetic energy billows out with the force of a category 5 hurricane.

I shove Mom behind me, and I push back with everything I've got.

But it's no match for the raw power of Alpha, fueled by rage, ready to sacrifice his life just to end mine.

The mountains around us begin to shake. He's not just trying to kill me. He's going to bring the mountains down, killing everyone inside the valley, including my friends, and Madee, and Dad.

I can protect Mom, but what about the others?

As the mountains around me quake, and I attempt to expand my protective barrier to the whole valley, Mom's hand rests gently on my shoulder. "Use the sword."

"I don't think I can get close enough to stab him," I admit.

She steps around me, just feet from the torrent of telekinetic energy that's strong enough to tear her apart. And not just her. I can feel Madee and the others across the lake. Can sense their pain. Driven to their knees, immobilized while the mountains around them crumble.

Mom refocuses me with a smile. She reaches down, draws the sword from my belt and holds it out to me like an offering.

"This was never my sword," she tells me. "It belonged to your father. Your real father."

Holy shit. If I'm a Titan, and the Olympian gods are real, then this sword and the legends behind it... "But this sword was made by—"

"Stolen by," she says. "Or so I was told. Your father wanted you to have it."

"You *met* my parents?" I ask. "You know who they are?"

"They hired us to find you," she says. "To rescue you. And when they had to return to where they'd escaped from...to raise you. I've hated keeping this secret from you, but they insisted. They wanted you to live a normal life. To know what it is to be human. To love this world and everyone in it."

"Why?" I ask, and it seems like a strange question.

"Because we protect what we love," she says. "Because we'd do anything to save that which we love, whether you're a parent, a young man with a lot of power, or a twisted asshole willing to burn everything down." She glances back at Alpha, who's still building steam, screaming out his rage all around us.

She lifts the sword a little closer. "Your father said that when the time came, it would let you access his strength—and his father's."

My grandfather's strength. Uranus. The cosmos itself.

I take the sword in my hand and feel...nothing.

Mom steps out of my way. "Now go get him."

I step forward—and out of myself.

The sword allows me to astral project without effort. Without thought. It came as an instinct. And though I am immaterial, the blade is still in my hand, glowing white hot.

Intense power flows through and around me. It feels...ancient and untapped, dormant for a long time, but now billowing out like a star gone supernova.

I can see the telekinetic waves flowing from Alpha's body now, undulating sheets of purple energy pulsing out through the valley.

"Stop," I say, and the storm dissolves into nothingness.

The shaking ceases.

Quiet returns to the valley. Other than some loose shale, nothing falls.

My friends are safe.

Dad is safe.

I step toward a very confused Alpha. Then he sees my motionless body. They used me in this state enough to understand what it means. In this state, my abilities are significant. But with this sword in my hand...my abilities are cosmic.

I reach out with my mind, revealing myself before him.

"I will spend my whole life undoing the damage you have done," I say.

"Not even you can stop what is to come," he says.

"What the hell is that supposed to—"

Alpha reaches his hand out toward Mom, unleashing a telekinetic attack that doesn't make it a fraction of the distance between them before petering out.

"What did you mean?" I ask him, but he can't answer. The sword's white-hot energy expands from where I've plunged it into his chest. With the last moments of his life, Alpha looks me in the eyes and grins manically. Then he is enveloped by light and reduced to ash.

I snap back inside my body, sword still in hand.

My father's sword. I inspect the blade, feeling its weight and the weight of its history. Forged by the North Star, son of the cosmos, stolen by the Olympian god of war and claimed as his own. Until at some point in the past, it was reclaimed by my father, who had escaped Tartarus and delivered the weapon to my mother, along with a mission—to protect and raise me.

Holy shit balls.

That's intense.

"You did good, Son," Mom says. I turn around and wrap her in my arms and lift her off the ground. She laughs into my shoulder and squeezes back, still strong for her age.

"I have missed your hugs," she says, when I put her down.

"I have questions," I say.

"We have a lot of catching up to do," she says, "but first, do me a favor and go get your father. He didn't bring a jacket, as usual, and he's liable to freeze to death up there. Old fool."

As though hearing our conversation, Dad angles his sniper scope toward the sun, revealing himself high up on a mountainside, well above the tree line and surrounded by snow.

Sword sheathed once more, I focus on the air around me, and I feel gravity give way to the power of thought. I lift off the ground and slowly, steadily float up and fly out across the lake.

As I scale the mountain toward my father, I reach out and ask, "Everyone okay?"

"Fine," Bubbles and Madee respond in unison.

"Hold on, how is Bubbles in your head?" Madee asks.

"We're connected now," Bubbles says. "What he sees, I see. What he feels, I feel. I hope you're a kinky lady, because shit's about to get weird."

"Jonas..." Madee says.

"She's here because I wanted her here," I say, "because I wanted you both here. To thank you. For everything."

"She'll thank us later," Bubbles says, and she follows it up with growl. "Grrrr."

I pinch my nose as I rise higher, the frigid air biting my skin.

"Bubbles..."

"Yeah, boss?"

"Scan every frequency for communications regarding what happened out here. I want to know the second we're going to have company."

"On it," she says.

"Madee, get the others ready. I'll be down for you all after I get Dad."

"So those are your parents?" she asks.

"Yes," I say. "And no. It's a long story. I'll explain everything tonight."

I'm not sure if the implications of this statement are clear until Bubbles adds, "Grrrr."

"Madee..." I say, squelching my desire to offer Bubbles a retort—but that would only encourage her. "See if Hood can access the mothership."

"Will do," she says. "Tonight."

"Yeah," I say, and then I sever my connection to both of them.

I touch down in the snow where my father is seated, arms wrapped around his chest, shivering with a smile on his face.

He stands at my approach. "Don't tell your mother I'm shivering. She'll never let me forget it."

He wraps me in a bear hug and pats my back hard enough to knock the air out of my lungs. "God damn, Boy, I have never been prouder of you."

"Yeah, well, sometimes the only way forward is to surrender, and other times it's to find out you're a Titan."

He lets out a hearty laugh and gives me another good whack. "Ain't that the truth." He steps back, shakes his head in pride, and then says, "Now get me the hell down from here. It's freezing."

64

Mom and Dad thought getting out of the country was the best course of action. In fact, they'd already arranged a charter flight to a private island in the Bahamas. It's a tropical paradise. Extremely secluded. The kind of place you'd buy if you were ultra-rich and had to resort to extreme measures to escape the press.

My parents are wealthy, but even their money couldn't buy a place like this, which means that 1) whoever owns this place is dead, 2) this is payment for a job, recent or in the distant past, or 3) my parents bought the island at a bargain basement price because it once belonged to Jeffrey Epstein, or someone like him.

And that's why I'm not going to ask, because if it's number 3, I don't want to know.

Because this place is working its mojo on me.

And not just because we're cut off from civilization, or because we're impossible to find, and I can let my guard down. But because it reminds me of that time on the beach, with my birth parents and Yia-yia. I feel closer to them here, sitting on the sand in the shade of a palm grove, listening to the waves crash, watching Heather and Madee splash around.

They're very different people, but we have become fast friends over the past two weeks. Heather is just so earnest; you can't help but adore her and trust her completely. I've never had a best friend, but I think Heather qualifies. Most of my life was lived in solitude, and the relationships back at the school—from what I can remember—were strained. Even among friends. Even with Madee for most of my time there.

Heather is absorbing everything she can, about all our lives. She's endlessly intrigued and excited to be a part of our world, even if it means living in hiding for a year...or two...maybe five. Probably longer.

Because the 20-million-dollar hit on my head stands.

It was placed by a proxy for Alpha and Beta, and will remain active until I'm either dead, or we find the person who listed it on their behalf and force them to take it down.

Wherever I go, for the rest of my life, I'll be looking over my shouldder, wary of whatever nutjobs take on the task, and my former schoolmates still operating in the wild.

But not here.

Here, I can just lean back and stare out at the ocean.

Having a passive sense of everything going on around me helps, too. I lift a hand and say, "Morning, sunshine."

Hood sits down beside me, dressed in crumpled shorts and a T-shirt he was wearing the day before. "Is it? Morning?"

"Not remotely," I say.

Hood has been sleeping. A lot. At first, I thought he was just depressed over the loss of Arti. And he definitely is, but that has nothing to do with his sleep. Back in the connected world, he was something of an insomniac, needing hardcore sedatives to tune out the technological noise and essentially fall unconscious. Here...he can't feel a trace of technology no matter how hard he tries.

Turns out empathizing with the world's technology is taxing. Honestly, I'm not sure Hood will ever leave this place. Not willingly anyway. His home is destroyed, he's presumed dead, and his companies are going on without him. He's a liberated man, freed from the prison of his own creation. And now, among friends.

He's smiling at Heather and Madee. "Think they'll ever get sick of this?"

"Will you?" I ask. I motion to Heather and Madee. "I mean, the view... right?"

Hood and Heather have been hitting it off. She's fascinated by his life and the things he's created, and he hasn't had a real woman pay that much attention to him, ever. Neither has outwardly expressed an interest in the other, but they're like two very slow-moving freight trains on the same track, converging from opposite ends of the United States. Eventually, they'll crash headlong into each other.

His eyes flick away from Heather to the distant cumulus clouds decorating the horizon. "Right. Yes." He clears his throat. "How are you holding up? With the training, I mean."

I gave myself a few days to recover, mentally and physically. My body healed on its own without a lot of help, but I was kind of a mess. The revelations about my past, about having three sets of parents, about who I am—*what* I am—has taken a toll on my psyche.

Mom and Dad helped me through it, laying out everything they knew about my birth parents—which wasn't a whole lot—and they filled in some of the blanks surrounding my time with them. Mom used an advanced form of hypnosis to lock away certain memories, not because they wanted to deceive me, but because Alpha and Beta left me in a fragile, unpredictable state. I was dangerous. Volatile. While Alpha and Beta limited what I could do out of fear for themselves and a desire to use me like a bomb, Mom and Dad were protecting the world from me, and me from the pain of knowing what I'd done. That's why I couldn't remember killing that man in the woods of Maine, and as a side effect, the name of my own dog...which was an oversight on my parent's part. The name Bubbles was meant to be another breadcrumb, giving me hope that they might still live. But erasing the day I mind bulleted that man took the original Bubbles's name with it.

She has since been restored, with help from both Mom and Madee, delicately recovering years of positive memories, including my dog's sad demise, and because I can handle it now, the complete memory of the man's death and its aftermath.

As for the current Bubbles, she's out in the world, mostly on her own, tending to my affairs and finding herself. Knowing that she's more than an AI, I saw fit to let her live her own life. It might be dangerous. Might lead to a robot apocalypse someday. But I don't think so. Because Bubbles isn't a misguided AI trying to cure the world's ailments by wiping out humanity.

She's my friend.

My most trusted ally.

And through the power vested in me, or some mythological shit no one really understands, she might very well be sentient. We still talk, conspire, and plot. Every day. While Hood isn't able to reach out beyond the island, I am, in part because my natural abilities are significant, though still very undisciplined, but also because Bubbles targets me with a tight beam satellite signal I can hitch a ride on, allowing us to communicate without even Hood knowing.

At first, everything was fine and dandy. She was exploring the world, virtually backpacking Europe. But in the past few days, she's noticed another presence moving through the world's tech, probing, searching, gathering information.

And it noticed her.

Otherwise, life out in the world has been similar to mine.

On the move. Always wary. Unsure of what comes next.

The presence hasn't been aggressive. Hasn't attacked or left a trap. But it is persistent.

So, she keeps moving, checking in with me when she can, and waiting for the time when we will be reunited…in two weeks. That's the plan anyway. A brief jaunt to the States, grab what's needed, and then return to the island *with* Bubbles.

Madee exits the ocean wearing the same orange bikini my subconscious clothed her in. It really does look good on her. She runs her hands through her hair, pulling the wet strands back, looking like some kind of slow-motion Bond girl. I'm entranced until she's standing above me, shaking her hair out like a wet dog, sprinkling me with water.

"Cold!" I say, flinching back. Before I can retreat, she's in my lap, arms wrapped around my neck. "Cold, damnit!"

She laughs and holds on, until I submit to the nicest form of torture—the kind that makes you smile not just when it's happening, but in the weeks and years to follow, just from remembering it.

Madee and I have consummated our long-lost, found-again relationship.

Every day.

Sometimes more than once a day.

She makes me laugh. Makes me happy. And she's slowly helping me come to terms with my past, peeling back the layers and applying mental salve when needed, which on occasion involves a reconsummation.

We have a *lot* of sex. That's what I'm trying to say.

"I'd say 'Get a room,'" Hood says, "but I know you will soon enough. Multiple times. You know it's a small island, right? Sound carries."

"I...did not know that," I say, sobering a bit, thinking of my parents.

Madee and I turn to each other, both looking like we'd just been slapped by a dwarf with surprisingly long arms. Then we burst out laughing.

"Oh, man," I say. "We're going to have to play music."

"Something with a good beat," she says. "You know, because timing."

"Come On Eileen," I say.

"Ohh, yeah. When the tempo speeds up." Madee gives me a wicked grin. "Nice."

"Who's Eileen?" Mom asks, making all of us flinch.

"How do you do that?" I ask. I can sense the world around me like never before, but Mom still moves around like a damn ninja.

"You were distracted," she says, and then she eyes Madee's skimpy bikini.

"It's like looking at the last of an exotic endangered species," Heather says, arriving wrapped up in a towel. She kicks Madee's foot. "Not that I blame you. If I looked like this—"

"You look—" Hood looks stunned that he's spoken at all, but he's forced to finish the sentence as we all wait. "—fine."

Excruciatingly slow freight trains.

Heather smiles. Maybe even blushes. What Hood said barely qualifies as a compliment, but for him...speaking to a real woman...it's groundbreaking, and she knows it.

"Who's ready for dinner?" Mom asks.

Hood nearly falls over. "Dinner? Seriously?"

"An early dinner," Mom says. "To send us off."

"Send...who off?" I ask.

"Your father and I," she says. "It's been wonderful catching up, but there are a few loose ends to tie up, and you know how your father feels about loose ends. And then...well, retirement sounds nice. A new RV. The open road. Maybe some 'Come On Eileen.' I lived through the 80s, remember?" My eyes widen, making Mom laugh. "If this RV's a rocking..."

I put my hands over my ears and say, "La, la, la, I can't hear you."

Mom swats me and heads up the path toward the villa. "Eat now, go to therapy later."

Heather offers her hand to Hood, and he takes it. She pulls him to his feet, and for a moment, they're standing just a foot apart, hands still linked. Building a little bit of steam. Then Hood shuffles back and follows Mom, Heather close behind.

"We taking bets on those two yet?" Madee asks, watching them leave.

"Six months," I say.

She shakes her head. "Two weeks. Tops."

"Two...weeks." My eyes flare. "You have inside information! I thought Heather was my bestie. She told you."

"Girl talk is girl talk, and you...well, we both know what's between your legs—and hot tip, it's not a vagina." She climbs off me and offers her hand.

"I just need a minute," I say.

"Okay," she says, understanding. I 'just need a minute' a few times a day since arriving. Sometimes just to catch a breath. Sometimes to process everything that's happened, or a newly leaked memory, or the fact that I'm not really human.

"I'll save you a seat," she says, this time speaking in my head. "Tell Dad he still sucks at hiding his thoughts."

I smile and watch her leave.

"Your thoughts are even louder," she says, and she gives her butt cheek a pat, breaking the spell.

When she's gone, I say, "Hey, Dad."

"Damnit!" The palm tree above me rustles as he climbs down from the top.

"If it makes you feel better, I didn't sense you arrive or climb to the top."

"That's because I've been up there for two hours!" He slides down to the ground.

Classic Dad. Playing the long game. Patiently waiting for his moment to strike.

"Time for a heart to heart?" I ask, as he sits down beside me.

"You reading my thoughts?" he asks.

"You know I'm not." Unlike Madee and Hood, my abilities are not always active. I can switch them off and on, which is helpful. If I moved through the world hearing everyone's thoughts and sensing every porn search online, I'd be very disturbed.

He takes out his phone and taps out a text, hiding the screen from me.

My phone chimes. I play along, opening my phone and finding a secure message notification from...S-Chan?

OTTO: Good.

"*What?* Really? The *whole time?*"

Dad shrugs. Has a little smile on his face, proud of his subterfuge.

"Was Otto ever real?"

"Passed five years ago." His smile fades and he shifts to the side. "Listen... So, your Mom and I are..."

"Leaving," I say.

He nods. "But it's not that simple. Our lives...even before you... they've never been simple. Never been peaceful. We carve out a place for each other in the quiet moments, but other than you, our lives have been lived in solitude. As has yours."

"That's why you're leaving," I say. "To have a life?"

"To make a life," he says. "To find a home. To make friends. And to make sure you always have someplace to go when things get rough. More than an island that used to belong to—"

"I don't want to know!" I say.

"Point I'm trying to make is that you have something good going with this group of people. You've got a tribe now. Expand it if you can. And when the time comes, when we get that damn hit taken down, you should-n't wait too long to settle down. Maybe give me some grandkids."

Dad doesn't make a lot of jokes. I shouldn't be laughing, but I can't help myself. "Grandkids that could level a building."

"Wouldn't be my first rodeo," he says, as he reaches over and musses my hair the way he used to when I was young. "Raising a kid is the hardest thing anyone can do, but I think you could handle it."

"Thanks," I say, and I settle into my beach chair.

"Welcome," he says, and we sit, side by side, watching the clouds pass until Mom calls us to dinner.

Epilogue

TWO WEEKS LATER

"Thanks for the ride," I say, seated in the passenger's seat of a black SUV with government plates.

"Just...don't cause any trouble while you're here," Fast says. She returned to her normal life when all was said and done, and as far as I know, she kept the events of the past few weeks to herself. I'm not sure if she's a friend, but she's got my back, even now.

"Me? Trouble? Pff."

She doesn't smile.

"I'm just here to get Bubbles," I say.

Fast looks around me and eyeballs the house we're parked in front of.

"Bubbles lives in an upper middle-class McMansion in New Hampshire that somehow survived the darkness unscathed?"

"Bubbles lives..."

"*Everywhere*," Bubbles says from my phone, and then from the vehicle's speakers, and then from Fast's phone, fading her voice in an artificial echo. "Everywhere...everywhere..."

Fast sighs.

"Please don't do that in front of me." And then to me, she says, "You know she's a massive national security risk, right?"

"But I'm a *nice* national security risk," Bubbles says.

"She won't be for long," I say. "We're going to localize her."

"But not like Arti," Bubbles says. "I'll still have access to the Internet and all of its wonders, like every other person on the planet, I just won't ...live there."

"Like every other person on the planet," Fast says. "Good. Get that done, and I won't feel guilty about keeping this to myself, along with the vault full of other secrets I'm carrying around."

I open the door, but Fast catches my arm. "I need to be honest with you."

"I'd expect nothing less," I say.

"If you cause any kind of public fuckery—"

"Or tomfoolery," Bubbles adds.

"—I won't be able to help you. And there's a chance I'll be the one hunting you down. So please...*please*...go back to your island and stay there as long as you can."

I offer my hand, and she shakes it.

"Nice knowing you, Fast. Feel free to visit. You know where we are."

"You know who owned that island before—"

"La, la, la!" I say, climbing out of the SUV and closing the door behind me.

Fast gives a wave and drives away. As I track the vehicle, I get a look at the neighborhood. The homes are big, modern, and surrounded by the fading reds and yellows of late October foliage, but many of them are still undergoing repairs. Two months ago, this place was something like a warzone. Today, it's mostly back to normal, if you ignore all the scaffolding...and the burned trees across the street.

That anyone still lives here is admirable.

While I own this house, I have never lived here. I purchased the house online and had it stocked by folks who keep things to themselves for a living. It has sat, unlived in, for the past ten years, just waiting for the moment I might need it. But since not many people in New Hampshire need killing, I've never visited.

Until now.

Because this is where Arti sent me.

I open the mailbox by the street. There's a single package inside, waiting for me to retrieve it for several weeks. I pull it out.

"Everything you need is in that little package?" Bubbles asks, unimpressed. "I hope there's a treasure map or something because—"

Rubber scrapes over pavement, just a few feet away, making me jump so hard I nearly drop the box. I spin around, ready to unleash a telekinetic attack on whatever assassin has managed to sneak up on me.

Instead, I come face to face with a little blonde girl that reminds me of the kid from Poltergeist.

"Holy shitburglar, kid," I say, but what I really want to say, is, 'How the hell did you sneak up on me, and why in the name of Zeus's dried up ball sack can't I read your thoughts?'

"What's a shitburglar?" she asks.

"You know the Hamburglar?"

"From McDonalds," she says.

"Like that. But shit."

"But...the Hamburglar *eats* the burgers that he burgles."

I just stare at her. I've never had a blurted out creative curse critiqued before. Not sure how I feel about it. Or her.

There's something...off about her.

"What's your name?" she asks.

"Harry," I say, sticking to the legend Fast put together for me.

"Boring name," she says.

"I know, right?"

"I'm Bree," she says, "but I also have a codename."

I look at the time on my phone, hoping she'll get the hint, but she either misses it entirely or she doesn't give a rip. She just sits there on her bike, waiting for me to ask. So, I give in. "What is it?"

Her grin is almost fiendish. "They call me..."

DEMON DOG

"That's...dark. Who gave you that name?"

"I did," she says. "But Miah doesn't like our names, so we might have to change them."

"Who's Miah?" I ask.

She points up the sloping street. A shaggy young man dressed in jeans, a black T-shirt, and an open plaid flannel, stands on the sidewalk, arms crossed, eyes unflinching as he watches me. "That's Miah, but his codename is..."

LASER CHICKEN

"Laser Chicken, huh?" I can't hear his thoughts, either.

"Do *you* have a codename?" she asks.

I smile at her.

Why not?

"You can call me..."

MIND BULLET

Her eyes flare wide. "That...is awesome. I like you. We're friends now." She double-taps the bell on her handlebars and starts peddling uphill, chewing up pavement, stronger than she looks. "Talk to you later, Mind Bullet!"

I give a wave while heading for the steps.

Then I unlock the door, turn the knob, and sensing more eyes on me, pause to look back. Standing on the opposite sidewalk from Laser Chicken is another young man, this one in a lime green T-shirt that could be seen from outer space. Next to him is a young, but tough looking black woman.

They're all watching me with the same suspicious gaze.

I step inside and close the door behind me. "Weird neighborhood."

"Think they'll leave us alone?" Bubbles asks. "Because I've got Beyoncé cued up, and I'm ready to get holographic."

I part the shades and peek up the street. Demon Dog and Laser Chicken are standing with the other two now, all four of them staring at my house, like I've just stepped into a *Children of the Corn* story.

I sigh.

"We'll worry about them tomorrow." I pat the delivery from Arti. "For now, let's project you a body." I peel open the box and look inside.

There's a small device and a thumb drive with a printed note. I read it aloud. "Everything Bubbles needs is inside this box. I wish you both well. Arti."

"Ohh," Bubbles says. "That stings a little bit."

"Yeah," I say. "But..." I pocket the thumb drive, take out the small device, place it on the kitchen table, and press the power button.

There's a flicker of light, and then a figure emerges.

A woman.

Dancing to *Single Ladies*, now blaring from the home's speaker system.

She's dressed in a flowing skirt and a blouse. Part ancient, part hippie.

"Admit it," Bubbles says, her new holographic self following the song's choreography. "I nailed the non-threatening female best friend look, right?"

I look up at her luminous new body, and I'm put at ease. She has a kind face with glasses she doesn't need, and she's slightly overweight in a curvy kind of way.

I laugh. "Yeah, Bubbles, you—"

The hologram disappears. The music cuts out. It's like she never existed.

"Bubbles? Something wrong with the hologram?"

She stays silent, which is so out of character it makes me nervous.

I stand. "Bubbles?"

The doorbell rings.

Demon Dog and Laser Chicken, I think with a sigh. She must have gone incognito to avoid being seen.

I head for the door, working myself up to be a complete tool. I don't need the neighborhood sticking its nose in my business. I whip open the front door. "Listen, kid, I—"

There are three people standing on my porch, and not one of them is a weird eight-year-old. All three look like they mean business, but it's the man in the middle who holds my attention. "Bush Jockey?"

"Awive and weww." He smiles. "Hewwo again, Gamma."

***

Jonas, Bubbles, Miah, Bree, Sarah, and Henry
will return in the novel...

KHAOS

Coming in 2022

AUTHOR'S NOTE

I started writing *MIND BULLET* shortly after writing *THE DARK*, which explored serious themes related to my own life, like PTSD. As I often do, following books where I've channeled my own turmoil, I follow it up with something a little more lighthearted and...insane. The mental gloves come off and my imagination goes nuts, free to be as silly and 'out there' as it wants to be. In the past, this process generated *SPACE FORCE*, *TRIBE* and *EXO-HUNTER*, all of which have been hits and a welcome breather to this author (and probably to my readers). I hope this is true for *MIND BULLET* as well!

But there is more to *MIND BULLET* than creative deaths, witty AIs, and telekinetic Titans. If you're a long-time reader, you might have noticed a significant number of not-so-subtle links to other books, even more blatant than in previous novels. This was not just for fun. This is the turning point, when allusions to something grand in scope become reality. The plan has been set in motion. Here is what's happening...

While it is normal for authors to write series, myself included, I'm doing things differently these days. Instead of creating a new series, I've been creating a *world*, using epilogues to link the stories from eight previous novels: *INFINITE*, *THE OTHERS*, *FLUX*, *TRIBE*, *NPC*, *EXO-HUNTER*, *INFINITE2* and *THE DARK*. In *MIND BULLET* it is clearly revealed that many of these stories take place in the same universe.

You can, of course, just read any one of these and get a complete story. But for those who want to follow along on the entire epic journey, what is next? Right now, characters are split into two main groups. The first merges characters from *MIND BULLET*, *THE DARK*, and *TRIBE*. We'll call them Team Superhuman. The second merges characters from *THE OTHERS*, *FLUX*, and *EXO-HUNTER*. We'll call them Team Normal People. The remaining connections have not yet been made clear.

Over the next two years, amidst standalone novels that are not connected, each team will get their own novel. Team Superhuman's novel is titled KHAOS. Team Normal People's novel is titled THE ORDER. Following those two team-up novels will be the ultimate crossover event titled SINGULARITY, bringing characters together from all these books to face a threat that was set in motion a looong time ago. If you're a long-time reader, buckle up.

If you're new to my books, visit bewareofmonsters.com/crossover for the full list of merging books and their reading order.

To help make this crossover as epic as possible, please consider posting a review for *MIND BULLET* (and for any other novels you've read) on Amazon or Audible. Every single one helps spread the word and makes nutso ideas like this one possible. I can't wait to finish this world and bring the rest of this massive story together, and I hope you all come along for the ride. It's gonna be nuts!

—Jeremy Robinson

ACKNOWLEDGEMENTS

Let's jump right into it! Big thanks to R.C. Bray for making my writing sound better than it is, and to Podium Audio for all their support and awesome marketing. Thanks to Jeffrey Belkin and Jon Cassir, the team working on bringing my novels to screens of various sizes. We're sooo close! As always, thanks to Kane Gilmour for editing my books and keeping me (mostly) sane, on task, and on schedule. Roger Brodeur, Brandon Burnett, Elizabeth Cooper, Julie Cummings Carter, Dustin Dreyling, Donald Papa Firl, Joseph Firoozmond, Jon Fish, Dee Haddrill, Andre Jenkin, Jeane Kearl, Todd Lane, Becki Tapia Laurent, Rian Martin, Stefanie Maubach, Kyle Mohr, Steven Newell, KL Phelps, Jeff Sexton, and Kevin Swan, you guys continue to make me look like I understand grammar and know how to spell and type better than I do. Thanks for the awesome proofreading.

—JR

ABOUT THE AUTHOR

Jeremy Robinson is the *New York Times* and #1 Audible bestselling author of over seventy novels and novellas, including *Infinite, The Others*, and *The Dark*, as well as the Jack Sigler thriller series, and *Project Nemesis*, the highest selling, original (non-licensed) kaiju novel of all time. He's known for mixing elements of science, history, and mythology, which has earned him the #1 spot in Science Fiction and Action/Adventure, and secured him as the top creature feature author. Many of his novels have been adapted into comic books, optioned for film and TV, and translated into fourteen languages. He lives in New Hampshire with his wife and three children.

Visit him at www.bewareofmonsters.com.

CPSIA information can be obtained
at www.ICGtesting.com
Printed in the USA
LVHW031527171121
703566LV00023B/912/J

9 781941 539637